DANCE YOUR HEART OUT

a novel

Paul W. Best

To Katherine and James —

Many Thanks!

Paul Best

Dance Your Heart Out

ISBN-10: 0-980150108

ISBN-13: 978-098015010-0

Dedication

I dedicate this book to my family.

DANCE YOUR HEART OUT

1.

"Yep, it was always a real crowd tickler when Rumpulina dropped her britches," Jim Bob said. For emphasis he slurped a wad of brown snuff into a white styrofoam cup and placed it on the table in front of him. Then he picked the cup up again, rotated it exactly ninety degrees, and put it back down.

"Yup, a real crowd tickler," said Orville, who sat beside him. Orville took a drag off an unfiltered cigarette, inhaling so deeply I thought it might pop off his toenails. Then he broke out into a fit of coughing, real wheezy and raspy and dry, like he was trying to hock up the whole Sahara Desert or something.

They were sitting with me at a card table, Jim Bob to my right, Orville directly opposite me. Across the way, a tall, strikingly built blonde girl danced stark naked on what I figured was probably the dining room table. A rotating strobe light on the ceiling splashed red and blue and green off the lines of her body, flicking sparkles of color into the misty, smoke-filled air. In the background, a blaring stereo filled the air with C&W twang. A group of people around the table cheered and clapped and yelled and whistled as the blonde girl danced, twirling and twisting and spinning to the music in the iridescent glint of the strobe. Most of them were men, but I could see several women too. The women were all bare on top and covered by only the briefest of thong bikinis below. One of the women was clapping and yelling as loudly as any of the men.

"Place'd go wild when Rumpulina danced," Jim Bob said, munching on his chaw.

"Yup, go wild," said Orville. He coughed again a time or two.

There was another outburst of raucous cheering and clapping and shouting as the naked blonde girl on the table bent all the way over and waved back at the crowd between her legs. Her bare backside could have passed for the harvest moon. On the floor, a piercing wolf whistle shrilled the air. Somebody turned up the volume of the stereo even farther, until it almost rattled the windows. The topless girl in the thong bikini who had been clapping and yelling so loudly jumped up and down like a cheerleader. The applause in the room crescendoed like a flood.

"Not exactly all that solemn in here right now," I noted.

Jim Bob and Orville both looked at me for a moment, unblinkingly. Jim Bob munched on his chaw. Orville scratched under his chin. Coughed. Then they turned back toward the girl on the table as she continued her dance. She stuck out her behind to one of the men around the table, creating another uproar of applause and whistling. After a moment she spun away, twirling again in the splintering light of the strobe, the cheers and the clapping flowing over her like waves, as she cupped her hands under her breasts to show off their fullness, then ran her hands over the curve of her hips and down her thighs. Nature's plenty, I thought. Probably about five-eight. Early twenties. Had to be 38-24-38, at least.

"Rumpulina was better," I heard Jim Bob say.

"Yup, better," said Orville.

I tried to conjure up an image of that. Better? Maybe a cross between Supergirl and Xena, I thought. Jim Bob had talked about Rumpulina ever since the blonde girl had started to dance. The gist of it was that Rumpulina had this fantastic body, and she liked to show it off by dancing nude.

"So how'd she get that name? Rumpulina?" I asked.

Jim Bob slurped a wad of tobacco colored spit into the styrofoam cup again and put it back on the table in front of him. Then he picked it up again, rotated it ninety degrees and set it back down. Precisely. He worked his chaw over to the other side of his mouth, rolling it over with his tongue, then licked along his lower lip. He took a few more slow munches on the tobacco, then turned to look at me. Contemplatively.

"That Rumpulina gal, she had the best damn backside on the whole planet," he said. "That's how."

"Yup, whole planet," Orville said, nodding his head in confirmation.

I tried to seem appropriately impressed. "Wow! What a distinction!" I said. I thought about asking them if anybody had ever called Guinness, just to make sure the title went undisputed, but I decided to hold off.

They both stared at me again for a few moments. Jim Bob worked his chaw over to the other side of his mouth and back. Orville scratched under his chin again. Coughed. I looked for a glimmer of something in their eyes, but I couldn't find it. They just stared at me. Then they turned their attention back to the girl dancing on the table.

Jim Bob owned this house out in the country north of Dallas, I had learned earlier. Once it had been a farmhouse and Jim Bob had been a farmer, but he had given that up along the way, and the only use the house got now was when Jim Bob opened it up the fourth Friday of every month for the regularly scheduled meeting of the Dallas Swingers Club, also known as The Dallas Alternative Lifestyles. Jim Bob got an invitation each month because he supplied the location. Orville came along because he was Jim Bob's buddy.

Jim Bob looked to be about fifty, I figured. He wore a pair of faded blue jean coveralls with worn, ragged straps over the shoulders, a red and white plaid shirt with the colors long gone, scuffed brown boots, and a straw hat that had seen better days. A gray, unkempt beard straggled down from his jowls. His eyes were small and dark, his teeth yellowed. A generous beer belly bulged out against his coveralls. Orville wore a more or less similar getup, just as ragged and just as faded, but he was as lean and gaunt as Jim Bob was portly. His face was as lined as a dried prune, and his teeth were even more discolored than Jim Bob's. Compared to the rest of the crowd - most of whom were young and sleek and sexy - Jim Bob and Orville could have been the proverbial turds in the punchbowl. I had this funny feeling they wouldn't have been there, except for the house.

I watched Jim Bob's tiny little rodent eyes as they stayed fixed on the girl dancing naked on the table across the room. They were as unwavering as a pair of rivets. He had told me earlier that he hadn't missed a monthly party in five solid years now, ever since the Dallas Swingers had started their club and offered to rent the house. Nope, not a single one. I believed him.

"So how come she's not here now?" I asked. "This Rumpulina girl."

Jim Bob kind of squinted at me for a moment, then looked back at the girl on the table. "She got her ass killed down in Austin, that's how come," he said.

"Yup, she got her ass killed down in Austin," Orville said, nodding again.

That just naturally got me to thinking again, wondering about all the possibilities in this fabulous modern age. You just never know what medical science will come up with next.

"Did they try a transplant?" I asked.

Jim Bob and Orville just looked at me again. Jim Bob worked on that chaw a few more times. Orville scratched under his chin. Coughed again a time or two. I looked for a flicker of something in their eyes again, but the lights were off. Jim Bob slurped another wad of tobacco into his cup, put it down, picked it up again and rotated it exactly ninety degrees, then set it back down on the table before he spoke.

DANCE YOUR HEART OUT

"She's deader'n hell, that's what. They found her body out in the woods near some golf course down there. All butchered up and cut to ribbons," he said.

Orville nodded soberly. "Yup, all butchered up and cut to ribbons."

"My God," I said. "She really got killed? You weren't kidding. What happened? Did they find who did it?"

Jim Bob shook his head but didn't take his gaze one fraction of an inch away from the girl on the table, who still did her dance. Orville shook his head too.

"Nope. Been almost a year now. Ain't found a damn thing. Cops down in Austin cain't find they stupid damn ass with both hands in broad daylight," Jim Bob said.

"Yup, cain't find they stupid damn ass," said Orville.

"What do they think?" I asked.

Jim Bob leaned over again and slurped another wad of yellow-brown tobacco spit into the styrofoam cup, set it down, then picked it up again and rotated it ninety degrees before putting it back down. Precisely. That was significant, I suspected. It had to be. Probably part of the recipe or something. Or maybe the symmetry of the entire universe depended upon it. I wasn't sure.

"Oh, they been sayin' it's some crazy damn ritual deal or somethin', but they don' know crap about it, tell the truth. Whoever done it got clean away."

"They don't have any leads or anything?" I asked.

"Nothin'," said Jim Bob.

"Yup, nothin'," said Orville.

I was about to ask more, but I heard a voice call out, "Tape Time," and there was a sudden rustle of additional activity. As if on cue, people started grouping together in the center of the room. Most of them started getting down on the floor, and as they did, their clothes began to come off. They pulled off each other's shirts and pants and dresses and underwear like sharks in a feeding frenzy. Other people started gathering around on the periphery, watching and cheering and yelling and clapping. Video cameras popped up everywhere, all focused on the crowd gathering on the floor. Even the girl dancing naked on the table was forgotten for the moment. She hopped down from the table and made her way into the fracas on the floor. The cheerleader in the thong bikini hopped in too. A naked man pulled her down on top of him. The other two ladies in thong bikinis who had been watching the blonde girl dance also joined the action. Orgy city, full speed ahead.

"Not supposed to bring out the cameras 'cept for Tape Time," Jim Bob said. "That's the rules. That way you don' get photographed 'less you want to."

"Yup, 'less you want to," Orville said.

"What a relief," I said. "Sure don't want to invade anybody's privacy."

Jim Bob and Orville stared at me again. Jim Bob munched his chaw over to the other side of his mouth and back. Orville scratched under his chin. Coughed again. Then they looked back toward the action.

By now there were more than a dozen people down on the floor, I figured. Center stage. It was like watching a rattlesnake roundup with people. Bodies writhed and twisted and intertwined everywhere. Various body parts and hands and feet all floated together like a bunch of vegetables in a Campbell's can. People were doing everything imaginable to each other. Hardly an orifice went neglected. Some of the people standing around on the perimeter of the action bent down low or crouched down on their knees to get exactly the angles they wanted for their cameras. Some walked among the people on the floor, cameras pointed down, filming here, filming there. One little pot-bellied bald man seemed particularly eager. I watched as he got right up close to somebody's bent over bare behind - no more than a foot away from it - and filmed away. What impressed me most was the way he kept hitting the zoom button. Made me wonder if he was a Preparation H rep or something.

Across the way, a tall, lean, very trim, distinguished looking man with gray at his temples, wearing a red beret and horn-rimmed glasses, emerged from a hall leading into the back of the house. I hadn't seen him earlier. His eyes probed the room. He scanned the crowd on the floor, then the people filming on the perimeter, as if searching for something. Hieronymous Bosch, I figured, looking for his easel. Apparently he didn't find it. He turned and retreated back into the rear of the house.

After a few more minutes I excused myself, got up from the table and headed for the doorway across the room. Bathroom time, and it was down the hall. I glanced over my shoulder at the writhing humanity still going at it on the floor. The pace hadn't slackened. Jim Bob had also mentioned you had to show proof of a negative HIV test in the past year before you could participate in Tape Time. Thank God for safe sex.

The onlookers were going just as strong too, getting it all on camera. The little pot-bellied, bald Preparation H guy was still right in the thick of it too, I could see. He was crouched down behind somebody else now, only a foot or two away from somebody else's raw behind, filming away with the camcorder on his shoulder, still pounding the zoom button. I felt myself sigh.

I turned down the hall toward the bathroom. Halfway down the corridor I caught a glimpse into a side bedroom. A naked man, his hands tied behind his back with a pair of red underwear, knelt over the end of a bed. Standing behind him was a woman with blonde hair. As I watched, she spanked his bare behind with a stick. The slap of the impact was shuddering. I could hear him gasp. Then she smacked him again. This time he squealed. I could see blisters already starting to form on his buttocks.

My attention was drawn to the stick. It could probably have passed for a Louisville Slugger, and the domina swung it hard enough to humble Babe Ruth. The end of the stick appeared to be carved. Yes. The likeness of a human face. Maybe even part of a torso, sitting atop the end. Then there was another swing. Another impact. A cry of pain. I could see blood bulging beneath the skin of the man's backside.

The woman stood up straight and looked back over her shoulder at me, turning enough so that I could see her face. She wore a black garter belt, black hose, black pumps, and not another stitch. Nothing was hidden. I got a rush of images as her eyes met mine. Irises sparkling laser blue. Her lips wide and full, parted slightly over flawless teeth. The line of her jaw so sharp I thought you could probably cut yourself on it. Her neck long and slender. Her boobs standing out like a pair of 747 engines, only bigger and firmer. A waist like a ballerina's. Her bottom so firm and round and heart-shaped that I stared at it for a moment despite myself, almost expecting it to start throbbing or pulsating or something. Her legs long enough to reach to paradise. I was aware of swallowing. A tingling sensation arose in my groin.

"Yes?" she demanded.

I glanced at the naked man kneeling over the end of the bed. Little rivulets of blood had begun to work their way down his legs. I could see his muscles quivering from the pain of the impacts. I could also see flecks of red on the tip of the domina's baton. I dared to look back into her eyes.

"He's been a *very, very,* bad boy," she said reprovingly.

"Some people are just bad to the bone," I noted.

"Haven't you been a bad boy, Georgie?" she said to the kneeling man. "Haven't you! Haven't you!"

"Yes! Yes! Yes! I've been bad!" he gasped. "Bad!"

There was another awesome impact. More blood broke out on the surface of his flesh. He gasped again in pain.

"You're not sorry enough yet, are you, Georgie?" she said. "Are you!"

"Yes! I'm sorry! I'm sorry!"

"You still need to learn a lesson, don't you, Georgie?" the domina demanded. "Don't you!"

"Yes! Yes! Yes! I need to learn a lesson! I need to learn a lesson!"

"Don't you!"

"Yes! Yes!"

"I've got this funny feeling you're just the one to teach him," I said to her.

She glanced at me for just a moment. The corner of her mouth turned up in the slightest trace of a smile.

"Oh, he'll learn," she said. "He'll learn." She swung again. "Won't you, Georgie? Won't you!"

"I'll learn! I'll learn!" he squealed. She had called him Georgie, but the name didn't really seem to fit. I was already starting to think of him as Fire Cheeks.

I left before the next impact. The pit of my stomach felt vaguely queasy. I stepped into the bathroom at the end of the hall and shut the door behind me. After I had taken a leak, I walked back down the hall to the parlor. I didn't see a trace of Hieronymous, although this was the hallway down which he had gone. Other doors stood along the hall, all of them closed, probably leading to other bedrooms. Maybe he was in one of those. I had even heard there was party action out on the back porch too. I didn't feel like exploring. I didn't feel like looking into the bedroom with Fire Cheeks and the domina again, either. My stomach still wasn't quite right.

I rejoined Jim Bob and Orville at the card table in the parlor. Not much had changed. Tape Time was still in progress. I sipped at a beer, looked around. Yawned. More time passed. I asked again about the girl, Rumpulina, but Jim Bob and Orville were still absorbed in the festivities on the floor. Not much repartee.

Gradually the action wore down. Still more time passed. I had a few more beers. Just sat around. It was past midnight by now, and people had begun to split off. I figured the crowd was down to less than half its earlier size. I watched as people got dressed and left. With their clothes on, talking and mingling together, they looked like any other upscale yuppie gathering. It was easy to believe they might be just ordinary folks.

Then I saw Hieronymous leave. On his arm was the blonde girl who had danced naked on the table earlier. Not surprising, I thought. It figured she'd leave with someone. I looked for the domina too, but I didn't see her, and for some reason I still didn't feel like going back down the hall. I wasn't quite sure why. Maybe because I half expected to see Fire Cheeks' buttocks hanging on a hook outside the door. Made me wonder if we needed to call a meat inspector. I *do* hope he learns his lesson, I thought. Whatever it may be.

Then, as I watched, I saw the little Preparation H guy load up his video camera in its carrying case and head across the room to the door. I had already decided that would be my cue. I stood up and stretched. "It's been truly inspirational and edifying," I said to Jim Bob and Orville. "You fellas have a splendid evening."

Jim Bob dropped another wad into the styrofoam cup, put it down on the table, then picked it up again, rotated it exactly ninety degrees, and set it back down. Precisely. Orville scratched under his chin again. He took another full body drag on his unfiltered cigarette, then broke out into another fit of coughing, just as raspy and dry as always, like filing on sandpaper.

"I'd quit those cigarettes if I were you, Orville," I

said to him. "Sahara's a mighty big place."

Then, across the way, I saw the little pot-bellied bald man walk out the door into the night, carrying his video camera in its carrying bag, and after just a slight pause, I followed after him…

DANCE YOUR HEART OUT

2.

Trailing him was easy. I don't think it ever occurred to him somebody might be on *his* behind. In about fifteen minutes he pulled into the garage of a small frame house in Carrollton, northwest of Dallas proper. Down the street I turned off the engine of my Taurus and waited. After another fifteen minutes I felt satisfied he wasn't coming out. I started the car and drifted slowly by the front of the house. Then I headed back to my apartment and went to bed.

Next morning I got up and went to the Dallas Public Library. The Saturday morning literary crowd was on the meager side. I found back editions of the Dallas Morning News and started going through them. There wasn't much. I found only one brief reference to the death of the girl called Rumpulina. The library also kept back copies of the Austin American-Statesman. These contained only a little bit more. The death and subsequent investigation were reported in just a couple of issues. It was all basic stuff. Nothing that really told me much about it, and the reports faded out and ended in just a few editions. Rumpulina's story had died as surely as she had.

I drove back to my apartment and scratched my head. Finally I decided to call a friend from years past who just happened to be a homicide detective with the Austin Police. I still had his number on a piece of paper in my wallet, in fact. I felt a vague unrest in my belly as his phone rang.

"Hello," a voice answered.

"Sue?" I asked.

"Yes..."

"Sue, this is Walt Draeger. I haven't seen you in a long time. How've you been?"

"Walt? My God! Walter Draeger! I've been fine, Walt. We've all been just fine. How are you, for goodness sake? We haven't heard from you in ages and ages. Have you been okay?"

"Been fine, Sue."

"And how are Julie and …" Her voice cut short, embarrassed. "I mean … is Julie … is she … I mean …"

I rescued her. "Julie's fine, Sue. Doing fine. So is Bobby. They're both just fine."

I could hear the relief in her voice. "Oh, that's good. That's so good … I mean…"

I had faced this situation before. The best thing to do was to acknowledge it, I had learned. "I don't know if you heard it or not, Sue, but we're separated now. Split up about nine months ago. Bobby's with her. Don't know if you heard that or not."

"Well, yes … I … I mean, I *did* hear that, Walt …"

"Is Joe around?" I asked.

"No, he's not," she said. She seemed relieved again. Safer ground now. "He's in East Texas on an overnight fishing trip. He and Bob Richardson went down there yesterday. There's a bass fishing contest, I think. You know how Joe is about his fishing. I don't expect him back until late tonight."

"Think he'll be in the office next week?"

"I expect him to be, yes. All week."

"Tell him I'll call him on Monday or Tuesday then, okay?"

"I'll do that, Walt."

"Thanks, Sue."

Then, for some reason, I asked, "By the way, you think he'd know anything about a nineteen year-old girl they found dead by the Barton Creek Golf Course last summer? Girl named Jessica Nodman. He part of that by any chance?"

I fancied I could hear her breath catch short. I waited, listening. But all I could hear was silence, lying heavy on the line like a cloud, a shadow growing darker. I felt something in my gut start to tighten.

"Sue..?" I asked.

Silence again. Then she said, "Yes…"

I cleared my throat. "He a part of that? I don't mean to seem nosy. I was just wondering."

I could hear her swallow. I waited again.

"You'd have to ask *him* about that, Walt," she finally said.

More silence. I could almost feel her fingers gripping the phone on the other end of the line.

"Okay..," I said.

I heard her take a deep breath, then let it out slowly. "… I … I'm sure he'll tell you, Walt. You've known each other for a long time, after all. And you've worked together. I'm … I'm sure he'll talk to you about it. It's just that …" Her voice trailed off to a whisper, then disappeared.

I licked the sudden dryness off my lips. "So this is a bad one."

I couldn't actually see her, of course, but I could feel her nodding to herself. " … Yes … very bad …"

I could tell she wasn't going any farther with it. "Okay, Sue."

There were a few more cursory pleasantries, the sort of things you say when you're trying to get off the line. Her voice began to lighten up again. At one point she said, "Say hi to..," and then caught herself.

Julie and Bobby, I thought. Sure. "I'll do that, Sue."

Then we hung up, and I sat back and scratched my head again and wondered. She wasn't a nervous lady, and she'd been a cop's wife for almost twenty years. She'd heard of everything. But something bothered her.

There wasn't much to do, and I knew I wouldn't find out more until I talked with Joe on Monday, so I opened a beer and watched a basketball game on the tube. A few more beers and an ice hockey game and the afternoon was gone. Productivity. Finally I picked up the phone and made another call. I'd picked up the phone half a dozen times already during the afternoon but hadn't ever gone through with it. This time I did. I was aware of holding my breath while I dialed.

But all I got after four rings was the answering machine: Hi! Bobby and I are out of town for the weekend. Just leave your number and I'll get back to you on Monday. Bye!

I held the phone to my ear for a moment, then hung it up and sat there on the couch for awhile. It was almost night now, and with the TV off, the living room of my one bedroom apartment was dark. I could hear my breathing. Other sounds too. A neighbor coming in next door. A horn out on the street. The occasional creaking of timber. Finally I pushed myself to my feet and went out for a hamburger. After that I went to a little bar not far from where I lived. A romping, stomping Saturday night in Big D.

I sat at the bar, thinking and sipping at a beer. It wasn't very cold and didn't taste very good. Some smart entrepreneur ought to test the market for horse piss, I thought. Maybe Budweiser could get some extra use out of the Clydesdales.

I looked around. There were only a few other people in the place. Three or four folks sat in booths along the far wall, but I was the only one at the counter. I checked my watch. Half past eight. I yawned. What a fabulous Saturday night.

As I sat there, the front door opened across the way and a lady walked in. Light from outside silhouetted her for a moment in the frame. I paused, my can of beer halfway to my mouth. It was like watching an hourglass slide into the room. Nice shoulders. Small waist. Tight pants, probably leather, accentuating her hips and legs. High-heeled shoes. Then the door closed, and my eyes had to adjust to the darkness again. I couldn't make out much about her as she made her way toward me. She slipped onto a barstool a few spots down from me and motioned to the bartender, who poured a tap beer and set it in front of her.

The images began to come into focus as my eyes adapted. I could see more clearly what she was wearing: a red baseball cap; black sweater; red belt; black leather pants; red pumps. I was also struck by a flux of other impressions: the angle of her jaw, so sharp, so razor cut fine; the wide fullness of her mouth; how long and slender her neck was; the 747 engines straining out against her sweater. Her eyes were shadowed by the cap she wore, but I didn't even need to see them. I could picture them in my mind: the laser twins. She looked over toward me, and it felt like being speared. I thought she kind of smiled, just with the corner of her mouth.

"Small world, isn't it?" she said.

I nodded. "Little old spaceship earth. Gets tinier all the time."

She took a sip of her beer. "I didn't see you leave last night."

"Yeah, I snuck out early. Had to. My mama doesn't let me stay out late, even on weekends."

I could see the edge of her mouth turn up in the tiniest trace of a smile. She took another sip of her beer but didn't actually look away from me.

"Fire Cheeks finally learn his lesson?" I asked.

I could tell she was studying me for a moment. "Fire Cheeks?"

I shrugged. "What's in a name? I thought he had lots of talent."

She pushed her cap back slightly, and I could finally see her eyes, sparkling so blue against the white of her skin and the lush red fullness of her lips. All-American colors, sure enough. I shrugged again.

"I have a feeling he may need another lesson or two," she said.

I nodded knowingly. "Some people are just bad all the way through. What can you say? Probably their DNA or something. At least you're doing what you can."

She studied me again, her head cocked at an angle, her lips pursed.

"So how come they let you out of the convent tonight?" I asked. "Won't the other nuns be jealous?"

She took another sip of her beer, still studying me.

"You're a talker, aren't you?"

"Yeah, I have to admit. Been doing it ever since I was little. Started when I was six months old, my mama said. Still going at it."

She was still appraising me. "You're a bullshitter."

"Aw, now that hurts. I thought I had you fooled."

"I'll just bet you did."

The bartender came and set some peanuts or something on the bar for us. I think he asked us if we needed another round. I really didn't pay him any attention. I don't think I'd have paid him any attention if he'd been on fire. He was gone pretty quick. He may even have dematerialized, for all I know.

She kind of looked me up and down as we sat there. "You're certainly not little any more, are you?"

"Nope. Grew up along the way."

She took another sip of her beer. "So how big are you?"

"What's the reference to?"

She sort of smiled with the corner of her mouth again. "Sorry, but I'm not an anatomy freak. The reference was to your overall size. So how big are you? Let's see, I'd say … oh, about six-four. Maybe six-five. Something like that."

"Six-four would be about right."

"Two-thirty?"

"Little more."

"Football player?"

"Just high school. Messed up my knee. Colleges wouldn't touch me."

She kind of looked me up and down again. "So what did you play? Let's see if I can guess. I'm good at that. I'd say…defensive end, probably. Five A school. Probably All-State or something fancy like that until you got hurt. Right?"

"Not bad," I said, nodding. "Defensive end, sure enough. Houston Aldine. I made All-District when I was a senior. We won state that year. Got my knee banged up in the finals."

I could see her appraising me again. "Uh huh. I thought so. So what's your name, football player?"

"Walt," I said.

I could see a trace of that smile again, just at the edge of her mouth. "Walt ..," she said, testing it, rolling it off her tongue. " . . . That's a little surprising to me. You really don't look like a Walt to me. You look more like … a Lance … or a Todd …"

"So is that good or bad?"

She eyed me directly for a moment, and I held her gaze. The lasers had me.

"It's not bad," she said.

I swallowed. "And you? What's your name?"

"Stan."

I was the one to take a sip of beer this time. "Stan?"

"Stan," she nodded. "Short for Stannetta. I probably ought to explain. It just so happens my parents wanted a boy. They always called me Stan."

I let my gaze drop to the 747 engines revving over the bar. I didn't try to conceal it. Then I looked back into her eyes. Had to blink.

"They certainly didn't get a boy, now did they?" I said.

She laughed a little, like water bubbling over rocks, and wrinkled her nose for a moment. "Not quite. They never actually told me so, but I think they were disappointed."

"Disappointed with *you*? They certainly were picky, weren't they?"

She laughed a little again, and I dared to dance with the lasers. Her eyes locked on mine and held.

"So what's your last name, Walt?" she asked.

"Draeger. And you?"

"Hunter. Stannetta Hunter … so what do you do in life's great big world, Walter Draeger?"

I took another sip of beer. "Oh, these days, investigations, stuff like that."

"Hm. That's interesting."

"And you?" I asked. "Besides the convent, I mean."

She kind of laughed again. "I'm a legal assistant."

I nodded.

"So do you go to those parties often?" she asked. "I don't think I've seen you there before. I would have noticed you if you'd been there."

"First time last night. I'm new in town. Saw the club advertised in a swinger magazine. But I'm not much of a swinger type."

"Well, there's always time to learn," she said. Our eyes met again and held. The way she said that spoke more than just the words. I felt a tingling in my groin. "Mind if I move over?" she said.

"I'll sure try real hard not to be offended."

She sort of smiled again, just with the edge of her mouth, as she moved closer. She settled on the barstool next to me and pulled a package of cigarettes out of her purse.

"Mind if I smoke?" she said.

"Not at all."

There was a book of matches and a small ashtray on

the bar. I struck a light for her. She looked at me closely in the glow of the match as she leaned toward me. Her hand touched mine. The sensation in my loins intensified.

"Are there other things you like besides the bondage stuff?" I asked.

She didn't look away. "Sometimes. Very much. With the right person."

"What's it take to be the right person?"

She took a drag from her cigarette, cocked her head to the side slightly, and regarded me from the corner of her eye. Still didn't look away. I dared to keep dancing with the lasers.

"You have any special plans for the evening?" she asked.

"I may be making some right now."

"I tend to be pretty bold when I want something," she said. "That's the way I am. I hope you don't find that offensive."

"Not too terribly much." To put it mildly, I thought.

We still hadn't lost eye contact. She put her hand on mine again. I felt a tingle run up my arm.

"How do I know I can trust you?" she said. "The world is full of crazies."

She seemed to be studying me even more closely. I could feel the pressure of her hand on mine. What I saw in her eyes wasn't uncertainty.

"You can trust me," I said.

We just kept looking at each other for a few more moments. She seemed to come to a decision.

"I don't live far from here," she said.

"I'll bet I can follow if you drive real slow."

She smiled that half smile again, just with the corner of her mouth, and slid off the barstool. I followed her across the bar to the door. The tingling in my groin had become an I-beam as we stepped out into the parking lot. She got into a small pickup and I climbed into my Taurus.

Then I followed her as she swung out onto the street. For a moment I thought about Julie and Bobby, but their faces seemed far, far away. They were out of town for the weekend, and I didn't even know where they had gone. I tried to remember the lilt in Julie's voice as I had listened to the message on the answering machine, but I couldn't find the melody. I forced the images out of my mind. And followed Stan.

She led me to a ground floor apartment in a fairly typical, large, modern, big-city apartment complex. I closed the door behind us as we stepped inside. She turned to me, put her arms around my neck, and kissed me on the mouth. I kissed her in return and ran my hands down over her sides. She kissed me even harder and started unbuttoning my shirt, then ran her hands across my chest. I lifted her sweater off over her head and unsnapped her bra. The 747s looked ready for take off. She undid my belt. Slid my pants down as I did the same for her. In moments we were naked, our hands all over each other.

"You'll do nicely," she purred.

I touched her nipples and felt them harden. I could have stacked lunch trays on her breasts. I ran my hands down over her flanks and held her close to me, cupping her bottom. Tried once again to detect a heartbeat. Couldn't. Amazing. There had to be a pulse there somewhere. The I-beam was certainly throbbing. I could have stuck it in the blood pressure machine at Walgreens and gotten a reading, I'm sure.

"You're not all that bad yourself," I said.

She took my hand and led me to the bed in the next room. Her form in the darkness was a siren, moving shadow-like through the ether.

"I want to be on top," she said as she pulled back the cover and lay down.

Somehow I wasn't surprised.

I lay on my back on the cool crispness of the sheet,

and she slid down on top of me. Something in the back of my mind reminded me of the prudence of using condoms, but she was already beginning to move. I started to work together with her, slowly at first. She braced herself on her arms, up above me. The 747s were right above my face. I leaned up and kissed the starboard one, then the one to port. I heard her groan. The force of her thrusts grew stronger. I worked with her, keeping pace, doing nature's primordial dance.

Her first orgasm hit like a wave, cresting over both of us. I felt her tighten all over, then shudder as it passed through her flesh. She gasped. I ran my hand over the heart-shaped fullness of her bottom. I could feel the contractions of her muscles, pumping rhythmically. She groaned more deeply, then ground herself against me even harder. Faster too.

Her second orgasm was like an even bigger wave, almost tidal. She pumped more furiously, then tightened all over for what seemed an eternity. Finally it subsided. Then she started pumping again. I worked together with her, still keeping pace. I could feel the intensity of her thrusts increasing again. In all, she had several more orgasms. *Many* more. Counting them finally became meaningless. I held off, trying to make sure that she was satisfied. I stopped trying to match her thrusts. I lay beneath her, almost motionless, absorbing the impacts. Still she came and came and came again. I felt like the beach, taking hits from the ocean. Finally she shuddered one last time, trembled all over and collapsed against me. I felt all the force drain out of her frame. She lay on top of me, spent, her body a dead weight, breathing heavily like a runner. I rubbed her back and held her against me.

"Are you okay?" I asked after a minute or two.

"I'm finished," she said, still panting.

"I hope you don't mean you're dying."

"Maybe of pleasure."

She still lay on top of me, her breathing still not back to normal. "Satisfy yourself," she said. "You haven't come yet."

I was surprised she had realized that. "Maybe I did."

She raised up enough so she could look at me. "No, you didn't. I would have known. Satisfy yourself. I want you to do that. Please. It's important to me. Do it for me, if not for yourself."

I could see in her eyes she meant it. Well, I've always been one to make the big sacrifice. She laid her head back down on my chest, and I went to the task in workmanlike fashion. It didn't take long. In just a minute or so I found myself approaching the brink. Then I closed my eyes and held my breath and went right past it, over that remarkable edge. I clutched her tight. Then it was over for both of us. We lay together for several minutes, her weight on top of me. I stroked her back again.

Finally we got up and went into the bathroom and got into the shower. Soaping her all over turned out not to be all that bad an experience. I took extra care to work up plenty of lather, especially in all the right places. Drying her off afterwards with a towel didn't prove to be all that objectionable either. When I had dried us off, she leaned against me and put her arms around me and held onto me. I stroked her back. I could hear the ticking of my watch as we stood naked together in the stillness.

"I need to get dressed," I finally said, pulling back a little.

"Aw . . . "

I put a finger gently to her lips. "Shh . . . "

"You won't spend the night?" she asked.

I didn't feel ready for that yet. I didn't know exactly why, but I didn't. Something was holding me back, and I felt I had to let her know that.

"Maybe another time," I said.

She looked down for a moment, then back into my eyes. "Is somebody else waiting for you?"

I shook my head. "No, not really."

She kissed me again on the lips and then unhooked from me and walked to the bed. I couldn't help staring again at her bottom as she stepped away. Vowed to myself I'd find where the pulse was. And Jim Bob and Orville thought Rumpulina had the best backside on the planet. There should have been a playoff or something, I thought.

She lay on her side on the bed, still naked, and looked back at me as I got dressed. I pulled on my shirt and buttoned it, then stepped into my pants. As I did I noticed something on her dresser. A stick. I reached for it and picked it up. It was the baton she had done the spanking with. I studied it, turning it around and inspecting it. Sure enough, as I had thought, the end had been carved into the likeness of an upper torso and head. The face was a woman's, with long hair and a big nose and a jutting chin. No beauty. Below were two large boobs. The torso flowed into the rest of the baton at waist level.

"It was my grandfather's," she said, still looking at me. "He was a cop in Boston. He carved it himself and used it as a billy club. He called it his Maiden Head."

"Lovely little toy," I noted, putting it back on the dresser. "So how'd you get into all the domina stuff?"

She spoke matter-of-factly, as if she were discussing something that had happened at the office that day. "It's a long story. I found out along the way that there are certain men who like to be spanked and humiliated and even hurt. It seems crazy, but they exist. Quite a few of them, in fact, when you look under the right rocks. They'll pay for it too. Pain and pleasure somehow all get blended together for them. It even goes beyond that. It's almost like they have a *need* for it. So I developed kind of a client list over a period of time."

"They pay for that?"

"Very nicely."

"You do it a lot?"

"Not all that much. People call me from time to time. I meet someone at a club or some other place of their choosing. I try to keep it discreet. I don't let anybody come here."

"So it's not some great big turn on for you?"

She shook her head. "No, I'm just a working girl. The extra income allows me to have some things in life I wouldn't otherwise be able to afford." She seemed to be studying me for a moment, watching me closely. "Does that bother you? Do you think it's horrible?"

I thought about that. "Different, but I don't really think it bothers me. Don't know that I'd mention it to the Sunday School Class, though."

She snickered. I could see her nose wrinkle. She had continued to watch me closely.

"Would you do something for me?" she asked.

I had tucked in my shirt and was just zipping up my pants. "Sure."

Her eyes were wide and luminous. "Would you lie here beside me?"

I swallowed. "Sure."

I could feel the thudding of my heart as I stepped back to the bed and lowered myself onto the sheet beside her. Never once did she take her eyes off mine. She unbuttoned my shirt again, spread it open, and rubbed a palm across my chest.

"I like a hairy chest," she said. "Good pecs too. You have a great chest, Walt."

"Yours is not all that bad either." I stroked her hair, put a finger under her chin and raised her face to mine, got all messed up with the lasers again. Then she folded against me and we lay in each other's arms. I could hear the ticking of my watch again.

"It's scary," she whispered.

"What?"

I could hear her breathing. Still we held each other.

"What happened," she said.

"Oh."

After a few more moments in the silence, she said, "I . . . I don't want . . . I don't want you to think I'm crazy."

"Well, I don't."

"Or strange . . . or weird . . . or different . . ."

She leaned back from me and propped herself on an elbow. Her fingers stroked gently against my chest. The blueness of her eyes was a magnet.

"It's important to me," she whispered.

"Okay." I felt myself swallow again.

"I've never had an experience like that before," she said.

I didn't think I had either.

"And . . . I don't want you to think badly of me," she said.

"I don't."

I could see her eyes soften as I said that. I stroked her flank and she lay down flat on her tummy. I rubbed her back again for several minutes. Her face was toward me, her eyes closed. Her breathing got more regular, like she was drifting off to sleep. I found myself thinking of Jessica Nodman. She had been a great looking lady with a fantastic body. Just like Stan.

"Question . . ," I said. "Do you mind if I ask you about something?"

"Hmmm," she purred.

I took that for clearance. I patted her on the bottom and stood up and resumed dressing. She lay there on the bed, her eyes still closed.

"You ever feel in danger at parties like that?" I asked as I pulled on my coat.

She opened her eyes and seemed to think about it. "No, not really. Why?"

"I heard there was this girl who used to dance at the parties that got killed."

She nodded soberly and propped herself on an elbow. "Jessica. She was found beaten to death. In Austin, I think. Last summer, if I remember correctly. But I don't think that has anything to do with the club. Why do you ask?"

"Just wondering. I heard a couple of guys talking about her, that's all. I hear the people at the club used to call her Rumpulina."

She wrinkled her nose once more. "Isn't that awful? I mean, that's really insensitive. Here she is, the poor thing, she's dead now, and that's still the way they talk about her. That's very callous. I think it's terrible."

"I have a feeling the two guys I talked with haven't been through sensitivity training," I said.

"Why do you ask about her?"

"Just wondered if you ever felt in danger."

She shook her head again. "No, I really haven't."

"Be careful," I said, surprised to hear how low my voice suddenly was, almost like a whisper. "You said it yourself. The world is full of crazies. And Jessica met up with one of them. Somewhere. Maybe not at the club. But somewhere."

I knelt down by the bed and kissed her. I let the moment linger.

"You sure you have to go?" she asked.

I nodded. I still didn't feel ready to stay. Still didn't feel ready to cross that line.

She kissed me softly again. "I understand," she said.

I got up and walked to the door. As I opened it I turned back toward her. She still lay on her side on the bed, looking at me.

"Good-night, Stan," I said.

"Night, night, Walt."

DANCE YOUR HEART OUT

And then I left . . .

DANCE YOUR HEART OUT

3.

Sunday was a waste. I slept late, then did the beer and TV sports number all day. Around dinner time I called Julie’s number and listened to the message on the answering machine. Twice. I started to do it a third time but stopped myself. Then I tried to get Stan, but we hadn’t exchanged much besides names and body fluids, and I hadn’t even gotten her phone number. Just brilliant, Draeger. Oh well, minor detail. I couldn't find a Stannetta Hunter in the phone book, and Directory Assistance didn’t have her either. I found a *Stanley* Hunter listed, but I had an idea he wasn’t my type. There was also an S. Hunter, which happened to stand for Susan, I learned, but she turned out to have no interest at all in scintillating conversation. I thought about driving to Stan’s apartment at one point, but I hadn’t shaved, and the beer and the peanut butter and jelly sandwiches I had eaten for supper had left a taste in my mouth that would slay a reptile. I could have probably blow-dried Lake Superior. So I finished off a bottle of wine and went to bed polluted, right after the ten o'clock news.

Monday morning I got up, shaved, showered, and put on a coat and tie, then drove to the small frame house in Carrollton where the Fanny King lived. His car was gone. The house looked quiet. The neighborhood looked still too. I parked a block over, out of sight, then approached on foot, checking carefully to both sides. There was no answer to the doorbell. Same thing when I knocked. I looked back over my shoulder one last time. Nobody watching. I pulled on a pair of leather gloves and picked the lock in about thirty seconds. I’m very good with locks. Then I opened the door and stepped inside, as neatly as you please, and closed the door behind me.

I found myself in a very drab, very neat, middle class living room. Dull earth tones, very little color. Plain furniture. Not much decoration. Sterile. I waited in the stillness, listening. No sound, nothing to indicate somebody might be home.

Very carefully, I proceeded to check the entire house, going slowly, stepping gingerly. It was pretty basic. A fairly typical two-bedroom house. I saw a few pictures of my host here and there. In one of them he stood in what looked like a place of business, holding a lampshade, smiling pleasantly. I walked back to a desk in the living room and began to rummage through the material on top. It didn't take me long to find a small stack of business cards. Jack's Lamp Shop, they said. That seemed to fit with the picture. I started to pick up the phone on the desk to call the number listed on the card, then thought better of it. You have to figure everybody's got Caller ID these days, and I thought it might stir his curiosity to get a call from himself.

Fortunately, I had my cellphone in my coat pocket, so I used it instead. After only one ring, the phone was picked up, and I heard, "Jack's Lamp Shop."

I cleared my throat. "Yes, uh … I'm, uh, looking for … some hurricane lamps," I said, "and I was, um, just wondering if you had any of those in stock. You know, the long tall brass things with the crystal cylinders on top. Do you have any of those?"

"Indeed we do," Jack chimed. "A very fine collection. Very fine, indeed."

"Hey, great!" I said. "I've been looking for them all over town. What are your hours today?"

"I'm here from nine to five."

I moved the phone over to my other ear. "Let's see … I might be able to get by at the lunch hour. Do you close then?"

"No, no, I'll be right here," Jack said.

"Perfect. I'll try to come by at lunch. If not today, then tomorrow. I can't wait to see what you have."

"We'll be here," Jack said cheerfully.

I turned off the phone and put it back in my pocket. I had learned what I needed to know: I had time to spare. I searched the house again, this time looking in drawers and closets and under beds. It didn't take me long to find what I was looking for. A dresser drawer in the main bedroom held a collection of videotapes, all neatly arranged in rows. It was a large collection, probably about fifty tapes, all dated by month and year, all lined up in neat little rows, each one in a plastic container. The date was written on a piece of white paper on the corner of each container. Tidy.

Still wearing the gloves, I took out about a dozen or so, went back into the living room and pulled a chair up in front of the viewer. I put in the first tape, from February of a couple of years ago, and started to watch. The very first frame opened up on the party room at Jim Bob's house. Tape Time. I saw Jim Bob and Orville in the background, sitting at their card table. I could even see Jim Bob pick up his styrofoam cup, rotate it exactly ninety degrees, and set it back down. In such things is order found. I could see Orville take a deep drag on his cigarette, then start to cough. In the foreground I could see an orgy in progress like the one I had witnessed myself a couple of nights earlier. It could have been the very same orgy, in fact. There were bodies everywhere. Groping and probing. Lots of the same characters. I watched for a couple of minutes, my eye the lens of Jack's camera. His interests had persisted over time, I could tell. Backsides galore, male and female, usually up close. One here, one there. Another one. Yet another, buttocks spread this time, anus gleaming. I sighed. There's more variety in faces, I thought.

I hit the fast-forward button, then stopped for another scene. More of the same. Fast-forward. Then stop again. Ditto. And so forth. I didn't really know what I was looking for. Something. A peg to hang my hat on. I hit the fast-forward again. This time a tiny little dwarf of a guy was screwing this enormous fat lady. To say he had mounted her just doesn't paint the picture. He could have planted a flag, mountain climber style. It occurred to me he could hurt himself if he fell off. And if she rolled over on him, he was a puddle. I began to fear for his safety. Then Jack began to move around them in a circle - around and around, around and around - and I started to get motion sick, so I hit the fast-forward again.

The next stop sat me up straight in the chair. A girl danced in the center of the room. A tall girl with a striking body. Everybody stood ringed around her, clapping and stomping and cheering. The crowd seemed to swell even as I watched, like a tide surging to fill the room, as if it had a life and pulse of its own. The noise rose and broke in swells. And in the center of the throng, the girl twirled and spun in the light of the strobe on the ceiling, twirled and spun, the absolute center of attention, the colors of the strobe splintering and splashing off her body. She moved this way and that, forward and back, naked, every move made with a ballerina's grace, effortlessly, an artist at home with her talent. The crowd responded to every move she made, yelling and cheering, waving and clapping, jumping and stomping. Going wild, as Jim Bob had said. A chill ran up my back as she spun to face the camera. The lens met her eyes, caught the flash of her smile, froze her in space and time for a twinkling instant before she twirled away. I leaned forward slightly to see better, and the chill in my spine unaccountably moved farther up my back, until I could feel the hair stand up on the nape of my neck. Rumpulina. I watched, my breath caught in my throat, as she did her dance.

I hit the stop button and froze the frame, locking her in place again, and allowed myself to study her. Her body was as reported, but I found my attention drawn more to her face. She looked right at the eye of the lens again, right at me, laughing, exultant, her head thrown back, tousling her hair with one hand. I couldn't keep from looking at her. Her eyes gleamed blue; her smile sparkled white. Her lips were full, voluptuous, scarlet. I could feel her laughter. Now she was dead. Beaten to death. I remembered the accounts I had read in the newspapers, then the conversation with Sue Henderson. A shudder passed through me, involuntarily, as I leaned back in my chair again. I looked into her eyes one last time, then hit the fast-forward again and held it down hard until the scene had changed.

I gradually worked my way through the rest of the tape, then all the others. It took several hours in all. Watch. Fast-forward. Watch some more. Hit fast-forward again. Finish one tape and start another. There were lots of faces, most of them unfamiliar. I saw Hieronymous on a few occasions, always looking slightly apart from the rest of the crowd. Jim Bob and Orville appeared in every tape. But there wasn't a trace of Stan. I figured Jack probably didn't like B & D. It was late afternoon by the time I got finished. I sat slumped in the chair, limp, my mind numbed, like a gynecologist after a hard day at the office. I gathered up the last batch of tapes and carried them back to the drawer. Then I checked back through the entire collection to make sure they were all there and all in order. As I did I discovered something I had missed on the initial run-through. There was a month missing. Just one, over almost a four year span. June of last year. I checked back in the living room to make sure I hadn't left that particular tape behind. Nope. No trace of it. Gone. I wondered if that was coincidence. Rumpulina had been murdered in early July. I made a mental note to myself, then went through the house to make sure I had left no trace of my visit. I hadn't. I was careful to lock the front door behind me as I left, then made my way back to my car …

4.

I drove by Stan's apartment on the way home. I didn't see her little pickup in the parking lot but stopped and knocked anyway. There wasn't an answer, even after I waited and knocked again. Finally I got a slip of paper and wrote a note. Call me, I said. I thought for a moment. I want you to, I added. I signed it, Walt. I added my phone number and slipped it under the door. Then I drove home. When I got there I wrestled with myself for a few minutes and then tried one more time to get Julie, but I only came up with the answering machine again. I listened to the whole message, then threw the phone across the room. It bounced off the sofa and clunked onto the floor. I left it there, then spent an exhilarating evening with a six pack of Budweiser and a very long, very dull soccer game.

Next morning I got up and drove to Austin. It was about eleven a.m. when I got to the police station. Sure enough, I found Joe in his office. We had worked together for a couple of years in Houston about a decade earlier and had gotten along pretty well. Julie and Sue had been on good terms too. He seemed genuinely glad to see me when I walked in. We talked a little, exchanged a few pleasantries, reminisced some about the past. The kind of stuff you do when you meet up with somebody again after several years. I noticed he didn't ask anything about Julie and Bobby. Sue had obviously prepared him on that one.

"You still shooting?" he asked at one point.

I shrugged. "Some."

"You still the best in the department down there?"

I kind of shrugged again. "Who knows?"

I have a talent for shooting, I'll admit, but I didn't feel like discussing it. Not right then. It wasn't what I had come for.

"Sue tell you I called?" I asked, changing the subject.

I thought a frown crossed his face. I saw him nod. "Yeah, she did. Sorry I missed you. She tells me you're up in Dallas now."

"Right. Kind of a special assignment. Been there about a week now. She tell you what I asked about?"

I thought I could see a frown on his face again for a moment. He tapped his desk with a pencil. Thoughtfully.

"Yeah, she did," he said.

"You working the Jessica Nodman murder?"

He nodded. "Trying to, if you can call it that. So far it's a dry hole. What's your interest?"

I shrugged. "Oh, just something I bumped into."

He studied me again. I though his gaze seemed to narrow slightly.

"You official or unofficial?" he asked.

"Unofficial. But the department knows about it."

He considered that. I saw him tap his pencil on the desk a few more times.

"Ugly deal, buddy," he said, looking at me. "Very, very ugly."

"I read some accounts in the newspaper."

He nodded slowly. "Uh huh."

We sat in the stillness of the office. A vague sense of apprehension had started to settle in my gut.

"So … what can you tell me?" I asked.

He thought about that for a moment, then seemed to reach a decision. He leaned forward in his chair and propped his elbows on his desk. I saw him take a deep breath before he started.

"The basics are pretty simple," he said. "She was a nineteen year-old girl who was found beaten to death. Body was nude. Summertime, last year, 8th of July. Found alongside the golf course at Barton Creek. Fourteenth hole. Worker on the course was clearing brush along the fairway. Coroner said she'd been dead for about twenty-four hours. Official cause of death was a blow to the head with a blunt object, he says. That's pretty much the gist of it."

"Anything else?" I asked.

He frowned again, even more deeply this time, and shook his head. "Nothing. No connections, no tie-ins. Hadn't been seen for at least forty-eight hours, as near as we can tell. Nobody with any obvious reason to kill her. Nobody who was a known enemy. We've turned the city upside down. The whole state. Talked to everybody and his dog who'd ever had anything to do with her. And there's nothing. Nobody even smells funny."

"Was she raped?" I asked.

He shook his head. "Doesn't look like it. No semen in her vagina, mouth, or rectum. No evidence of unusual trauma to the genitals."

"Robbed?"

"No. Found her purse and her clothes in the grass beside her. Still had fifty dollars in her wallet."

Not raped, not robbed. I scratched my head, considering the other possible motives.

"The girl. What was she like?" I asked.

"Wild as hell. Worked as a stripper at topless and nude clubs in Houston and Dallas. Kind of ironic too, because she came from a good family in Dallas. Parents are real ritzy types. She was adopted, it turns out, but it sounds like she had a happy enough childhood. Went to school through the eighth grade at Hockaday in Dallas, a snotty little private school for rich girls. Did fine up until that time. Started getting into trouble in high school. Got kicked out of Hockaday. Didn't get into trouble with the law, just wild, acting out type stuff. Her mother described her as rebellious, promiscuous, staying out late, that sort of thing. She still managed to graduate from high school at Highland Park, though, about the most uptown public high school in the state. After that it got worse. She got into some prostitution, some private 'modeling' stuff. Ran with a bad crowd, but like I said, didn't really have anybody with a motive to kill her. Had cocaine in her blood when she died. HIV negative, though."

I thought of the girl I'd seen dancing on the videotape at Jack's house. I could remember her smile, the way she had laughed. I felt a hollowness in my belly.

"Anything else about the murder scene?" I asked.

"Heavy brush, like I said," Henderson went on. "She was on her side. Had rope burns on her wrists, so it looked like she was tied up at one point, but the rope was off when we found her. Never found it. No tracks or footprints we can identify. No fingerprints either. Nobody else's hair. No DNA we can trace."

"The murder weapon?"

He shrugged. "Haven't found it. Nothing at the scene, and nothing we can find that matches up with the blow to the skull. She got hit in the left temple. Blunt object, like I said, but we don't know what. Bad place to get hit, the coroner says. Bone's real thin there. Big artery there too, got a long fancy name, called the middle meningeal artery. Bleeds like hell when it gets torn, right into the brain."

"So what do you think it was?"

He shook his head. "Probably a hammer of some sort. Here, we made this model of her calvarium."

He reached into a drawer and pulled out a box. In it was a plastic model of the vault of a human skull, which he handed to me. I held it gingerly, turning it over carefully, inspecting it. The left temporal area was caved in. A deep fracture mark broke the otherwise smooth contour of the model. I traced the edges with my fingers, still going gingerly. One edge of the indentation was fairly straight and smooth; the opposite edge was jagged. I went searching for a match in my mind, but I couldn't find one.

"We've checked everywhere," Henderson added. "Hardware stores. Ski stores. Rock climbing stores. We've talked to oil field people. We've talked to carpenters, electricians, painters, cable TV people, you name it. Nobody can place it."

I ran my fingers over the edges of the wound again, then turned the calvarium over and looked at the under side. The model had been accurately reproduced. I could see jagged fragments pointing downward, into the interior of the skull. Probably some kind of hammer, I agreed. But I couldn't place it any better than the Austin police had been able to. I placed it back on his desk.

"Mind if I trace this on a piece of paper?" I asked.

Henderson shrugged. "Be my guest. Let me know if you get lucky."

He gave me a piece of paper, and I laid it on top of the calvarium, then traced the edges of the impact as precisely as I could. After that I folded up the paper and stuck it in my wallet. Henderson put the calvarium back in its box and stashed it in the drawer again. We sat there in the stillness.

"So … it's an ugly deal," I said.

He nodded. "Ugly."

I cleared my throat. "Sue seemed bothered."

"Yeah," he said.

"That kind of surprised me…I mean, you guys have been married fifteen years at least. I'm sure she's heard lots of nasty stuff before."

He nodded again. He seemed to appraise me, as if considering something. Finally he seemed to make up his mind.

"There's more," he said.

The way he said it caught my ear. The look in his eyes too. The vague sense of apprehension I had felt in my gut came back again, only harder this time. I waited.

"I'll tell you some other stuff, but you got to keep it quiet. That clear?"

I nodded.

He seemed to think about it one last time, then said,

"There were things that made it look like a ritual sacrifice of some sort. Very gory things. Things that weren't in the newspapers. Details that never got released. Stuff we kept out of the media."

"A ritual sacrifice? Why? Because her wrists had been tied?"

He shook his head. "Not just that."

There was something in his voice and something in his eyes again. The sensation in my gut had intensified. He looked at me very evenly.

"Her heart was cut out," he said.

It took me a moment to process that. I thought I hadn't heard him correctly.

"Excuse me?" I said.

He continued to look directly at me. "It was all done very neatly, by somebody who knew exactly what they were doing. Nobody knows that except me, the coroner, a few others here in the Austin PD, and now you. Don't know if that happened before or after the blow to the head. Probably after, my guess is. But only the killer knows for sure. Blow to the head is still listed as the official cause of death."

My mind went scrambling for explanations, but I couldn't come up with one.

"Heart was never found," Henderson added.

"My God," I heard myself say. My voice came out low and raspy, almost hoarse. "So … what do you think? Satanism?"

"We've wondered about that. Satanists are known to do ritual sacrifices at times. Usually just on animals, though. We went all through the community, rounded up anybody with any connection to Satanism we could find. They're a crazy bunch. Witches. Warlocks. A bunch of freaks. We never came across anybody who knew anything. We never could tie anybody into the murder in any way."

"Some other kind of cult?"

He shook his head again. “We checked out every other cult or semi-cult we could find. She’d never had any connection with any of them. They all looked clean.”

I thought about that. “Another dead end.”

“One more thing,” he said.

He had that tone in his voice and that look in his eyes again. I tried to make the knot in my belly relax.

“We’re off the record again,” he said. “I can’t allow any leaks.”

I nodded. “Off the record. You have my word.”

He was looking directly at me again. “We’ve had two other killings exactly like it.”

The feeling in my gut rose up into my chest. A chill ran down my spine.

“Exactly the same MO,” he said. “Both were young women. Both were blonde. Both were good-looking. Both were built like hell. Both were killed by a blow to the left temple with a blunt object. Fracture marks are just like this one. Both had their hearts cut out. Neither crime was ever solved. But it's sure the same guy. Or the same group. The first one was about three months before the Nodman girl got killed. The second was three months later.”

I swallowed. “So it’s a serial deal.”

Henderson nodded soberly. “There’s a real sicko out there. Somewhere. And so far we haven’t been able to lay a finger on him.”

Something else occurred to me. “You got pictures of the other two? How they looked before they got killed?”

“Sure.” He brought two folders out of a drawer and shuffled through them, then handed a pair of photos across the desk to me. “High school yearbook pictures. Both of them. Help yourself. We got plenty of copies. Let me know if you come up with anything.”

I studied the two pictures. They were fairly typical for a high school yearbook - smiling, posed, stereotyped - the kind of pictures your mother always got two dozen of to send to all the relatives. I looked at their faces. Good-looking blondes, sure enough. So young and fresh and wholesome.

"Who were they?" I asked.

Henderson motioned toward the picture in my left hand. "That one was Michelle Stanzer. She was a bank teller. Lived in San Antonio. The other one was Charlotte Raymond. Grade school teacher in Corpus Christi. Neither one of them had any connection at all to Jessica Nodman. Or each other. We never could link any of them together in any way."

So all three women had lived in different cities, but all three had been killed in Austin. Either they had come here and met up with the killer by chance . . . or somebody had brought them or lured them here. And there was a time frame.

"There's something else, isn't there?" I said.

He nodded slowly again. "You got it."

I felt myself swallow again. One girl had been killed three months before Jessica Nodman, the other three months after. An additional five months had gone by since then. The room seemed smaller, as if the walls had gotten closer together. A tightness in my chest made me aware of my breathing.

"He's overdue," I said …

DANCE YOUR HEART OUT

5.

I said good-bye to Joe and drove back to Dallas. Coming back into the city, I found myself heading to the northeast, out towards Garland. I don't remember deciding to go that way; it just seemed to happen. I wound up driving to Carter Street in far northeast Garland and pulled to a stop in front of a modest brick house. There was a boy in the front yard playing with a dog, a big, gangly, floppy-eared Yellow Lab. I opened the car door and stood up. The boy saw me and ran toward me.

"Hi, Bobby!" I said.

"Dad!" he said.

He ran to me and jumped up into my arms, locking his legs around my waist. With his arms he hugged my neck, clamping on like a vise. I held him just as tight.

"How've you been, kiddo?" I said. I patted him on the back.

"Great, Dad!"

I lowered him to the ground and stood him in front of me. I got down on one knee and put my hands on his shoulders.

"Let me just look at you," I said.

He grinned widely. The Lab he had been playing with came and nosed in between us. I stood up, and the dog raised up on its hind legs and put its front paws on my shirt. I scratched behind the dog's ears.

"Hey, Brutus, you dumb turd. How you doing?" I said.

Brutus had wet paws. He was making a muddy mess of the front of my shirt. Brutus always has wet paws. Always. There hadn't been any precipitation for at least two weeks, but it still felt like being pawed by a mop. I have wondered how he does this. Brutus could cross the Sahara and still have wet, muddy paws, I believe. It all ranks, in my mind, right up there with the bizarre Bermuda

Triangle and other great mysteries.

"He's not dumb, Dad," Bobby said. "He's smart. Brutus is really smart."

"Brutus? Smart? Did he get a brain transplant?"

"No, Dad. He's really smart. Really. I'm teaching him tricks."

"Brutus? Tricks? I'll call CNN."

"Aw, Dad . . . "

We walked up to the front door, Bobby by my side, Brutus romping around us, and went into the house. As soon as we got in the front door, Brutus rambled over to a coffee table and knocked over a vase of roses. The roses wound up in a wet sloppy mess on the floor. At just that moment, Julie walked into the living room from the opposite direction. I thought my heart missed a lub dub, but maybe that was just my imagination.

I could see the surprise on her face. Also a little uncertainty. Other than that, she looked just like the picture in my mind's eye. Short black hair. Hazel green eyes. So cute you wanted to pinch her. Trim little knockout figure. There was a moment of awkwardness. What do you do? Shake hands? I didn't know for sure.

"Hi there!" I managed.

"Well . . . hi," she said.

There was another awkward pause. Bobby watched us closely.

"Well . . . this is a surprise," she said. "I wasn't expecting you. What brings you by?"

I shrugged. "Oh, I just happened to be in the neighborhood. Thought I'd drop by and say hello."

"Well . . . great," she said.

Brutus, in the meantime, was trampling the roses. The ones he hadn't already eaten, that is. His wet muddy paws were getting even wetter and muddier from the water that had spilled. A set of tracks was accumulating on the living room rug that would have haunted an Indian scout.

"Brutus!" Julie said, coming to her senses. "Get out! Brutus, get out! Out!"

"I'll take him out, Mom," Bobby said quickly. He more or less rode Brutus across the room and out the back door into the back yard. Brutus was busily munching a rose stem as the door slammed behind them. Julie threw up her hands and bent down to start picking up the mess.

"Here, I'll help with that," I said. I bent down and started helping her pick up what was left of the roses. We had them back in the vase in no time. I went to the kitchen and got a rag, then came back and cleaned up the rug. Julie was straightening the rest of the coffee table.

"I will never, never, never, never, never, never own another Yellow Lab," she said.

"Challenging," I agreed.

Bobby came back inside. "I'm going to feed him, Mom!" he called.

"Yes, feed him, please!" Julie called back.

Bobby disappeared out the back door with a C5A sized dog dish and two cans of prime quality dog food. The door slammed shut again. Julie and I were left in the sudden quietness.

"Bobby seems okay," I said. " . . . Looks like he's put on a little weight too."

Julie was still rearranging the wreckage on the coffee table. "Yes, he's doing great. I still have my fingers crossed, but so far, so good. School's going very well. Straight A's so far."

"No trouble this year then," I said.

She smiled. "None so far. It's been real smooth. I love his teachers. So does he."

"Good. Good."

The stress, I thought. That's what messed up his grades so bad last year. He's better off now. Thank God the sixth grade's not going to be a repeat of last year. He's doing better now that you've gone, I couldn't help thinking.

I guess that's good.

Julie had finished straightening the coffee table. She sat down on the sofa and I sat down in the chair opposite her.

"So . . . how about you?" I asked. "Are things going okay there too?"

She smiled. "I'm fine. I'm really fine. We're both hanging in there."

I studied her for a moment. She did look good. So comfortable. So relaxed. I made a mental snapshot. I wanted to hold that image in my mind.

"That's great, Julie," I said.

"Uh huh. I've stayed dry three months now. Not a drop. I go to two AA meetings a week. I have lunch with my sponsor every Wednesday. I feel like I'm more in control of my life than I've been in a long, long time."

I was aware of a hollowness inside. "Super," I said. "Sounds like you're doing fantastic."

So she's better off too, I thought. They both are. Even Brutus has gotten smarter. Et tu, Brute? It's like they've all been saved from plague or something. Blow your brains out, asshole, you'll cure the whole planet.

"How are *you*?" she asked.

I shrugged. "Oh, just happy as a big sunflower."

There were a few more pleasantries. I asked about her parents. They were doing fine, she said. I told her to give them my regards. She asked if I was still on special assignment here in Dallas. Yes, I was. For how long? I didn't know. She talked about Bobby. He was playing soccer this year, she said. He seemed very interested in it. He had been wanting to tell me about it.

About that time, the back door opened and Bobby came back into the room, Brutus with him, hauling him along, straining against a choke leash.

"I need to walk him before he superdumps on the rug," Bobby said.

DANCE YOUR HEART OUT

"Please!" said Julie.

I thought that might give me a chance to talk with him about soccer. "Let's go walk him, Bobby," I said.

Brutus pretty much dragged Bobby out the front door, and I followed along after them. Walking Brutus, of course, is more like tracking a major storm than anything else. They had already made it across the front yard by the time I got out the door. Bobby finally reined him in on the sidewalk and waited for me to catch up. I fell in alongside them. As fate would have it, we had barely gone any distance at all before we encountered a lady walking her dog down the sidewalk from the opposite direction. The dog was a very well groomed little Shetland Sheep Dog. It wore a neat little black vest and a cute little red collar. Its ankles had been manicured. We're talking about a very classy look here, kind of like a Hollywood starlet on all fours. The lady, Bobby hurriedly whispered, was Ms. Randerson, a young divorcee in the neighborhood that Julie had gotten to be friendly with. Ms. Randerson wasn't all that bad, actually. She did a more than adequate job of filling out her halter-top and her short shorts. Her auburn hair complemented the Shetland's black vest and red collar, and her eyes were a nice light blue. The encounter promised to be interesting. The only problem with meeting somebody while walking dogs, of course, is that you can't predict what the dogs will proceed to do.

We stopped and spoke politely to Ms. Randerson. She was very pleasant. I even thought she maintained eye contact a little longer than necessary. She asked Bobby about school. She asked Bobby about Julie. She even asked him about soccer. She told me how pleased she was to meet me. So pleased. So very pleased. In the meantime, Brutus and the Shetland, whose name turned out to be Princess, were also getting acquainted. There was the usual sniffing of rears, the two of them fascinated by each other's orifices. I thought of the party the other night, then the video I had seen at Jack's place. I sighed. We haven't come all that far, I thought.

Ms. Randerson continued to maintain this so very satisfactory eye contact as we chatted. Smiled very warmly indeed. Seemed oh so interested in anything I might have to offer.

But what do you say to an attractive divorcee when *your* dog has his nose up *her* dog's behind? Right in front of your faces. I don't think Emily Post ever got around to covering that. It's probably not in the same league as place settings. I commented on how nice the weather had been lately. Oh yes. So nice. And wasn't it just grand that everybody kept their yards in such wonderful condition for this time of year? Yes. So nice. Then, as we chatted, Brutus proceeded to mount Princess and go to town, right there in front of God and everybody. But Princess didn't seem to be in the mood. She whined a little, then yapped back over her shoulder. Brutus wasn't bothered. He continued to grind away. Bobby reacted quickly and tried to pull him off Princess by yanking on the chain, but it wasn't going to work. Not enough strength. He tugged upward on the chain, but Brutus was too heavy for him. Brutus kept grinding. Princess yapped over her shoulder again.

"My goodness," said Ms. Randerson. "That's a bit strange. Princess can't be in heat. She's been spayed."

Brutus was still at it.

"He's not real choosy," I acknowledged.

Bobby still tugged on the chain, but he wasn't making any progress. He tried pulling up again, then pulling to the side, but Brutus, for once, was not to be distracted. It was time to intervene. So I stepped up beside Bobby, took hold of the chain with my right hand, and hoisted Brutus, wrecker style, off of Princess. For a moment I held him there by the chain, suspended on his hind legs, tottering around like a dancing bear, so Princess could make her exit. She scurried over to Ms. Randerson and hid behind her legs.

"Brutus, you're an *animal,*" I said.

Ms. Randerson kind of giggled at that. "Goodness, you're strong," she said admiringly.

I struggled to stay modest. "Aw shucks, you caught me when I'm not even wearing my Superman outfit."

Ms. Randerson giggled again. Even winked at me. I think she wanted to stick around. But Princess was definitely ready to leave the party. She still huddled behind Ms. Randerson's legs, and had begun to tug on her leash in no uncertain terms. Ms. Randerson smiled very pleasantly at me again as she said good-bye. Maintained eye contact again a little longer than needed, I thought. Even gave me a nice little wave, one of those cutesy finger twinkling deals. I saw her look back over her shoulder as they walked away. I finally lowered Brutus back to all fours when I thought they had gotten a safe distance away. He didn't seem bothered at all. Naturally. I gave the chain back to Bobby, and Brutus shook himself all over and then continued to lead us down the block again.

Along the way I had a chance to talk with Bobby. He told me about the fun he was having in soccer. I could hear the excitement in his voice. It was a little surprising to me. You see, Bobby takes after his mother's side of the family. Unlike my side, her folks are not athletic. Smart and sensitive and very beautiful, but not athletic. People on my side end up with full athletic scholarships to college. I have two uncles who were major league outfielders and a cousin who played cornerback in the NFL, along with a bunch of others who excelled at various sports in college. But on Julie's side, they either wind up in academics or rehab. And I had long ago accepted the fact that my son - this bone of my bones, this flesh of my flesh, this blending of the lines - tended to take after his mother's side. I had accepted without difficulty that he was never going to be a natural athlete. He wasn't that big. He wasn't that strong.

He wasn't that fast. His hands weren't all that great. But now, walking alongside me, he said he had gotten really interested in soccer. He wasn't very fast, he admitted. He knew that. He could deal with that. He had decided he wanted to play goalie. He didn't have to be all that fast to do that. He was willing to go for the ball, he told me. He was willing to jump flat out through the air and come crashing down to the ground. He was willing to get hurt if necessary. He could take it. He wasn't afraid of the pain. That's certainly one of life's requirements, I thought.

"Great, Bobby, go for it," I said. "Sounds like you've got the right attitude, and that counts for a lot, believe me."

We reached the end of the block and turned back. We walked along together slowly, Brutus circling around us on the chain, sniffing here and there. Afternoon had turned into twilight. An early spring breeze drifted gently around us. The neighborhood was quiet, people inside now for dinner.

"You like Dallas?" I asked.

"It's okay. Houston was better, but Dallas is okay. I'm starting to make friends."

"Your mom seems to be doing well."

"Yeah, I think she's doing real good. I really think she is, Dad. She's not drinking at all anymore. I mean, she doesn't even touch a drop. I'm not finding any pill bottles lying around or Vodka bottles or anything."

"Good. I'm glad to hear that, Bobby. I'm glad to hear she's doing better."

He nodded thoughtfully. "Yeah, I think she was just real upset all the time."

I stopped and lowered myself to one knee and put my hands on his shoulders. Brutus managed to slip away from Bobby's grip, but I let him go. I looked into Bobby's eyes.

"Bobby, I haven't ever really talked with you about

some things."

He regarded me closely.

"Your mom is a great lady, Bobby. You need to remember that. Always."

He nodded. "Sure, Dad."

I continued to look right in his eyes. "I didn't do right by your mom, Bobby. I don't know if you know that or not. I don't know how much you understand. I don't know how much kids your age realize these days. But I didn't do right by her. I had other girlfriends, Bobby. I ran around on her. I wasn't faithful to her. I don't know if you realize that or not. But it's my fault for what happened. All of it."

He looked uncomfortable, almost pained.

"I want you to understand that, Bobby. I didn't do right by her. It was my fault. That's why things didn't work out."

He looked even more uncomfortable. At one point he almost winced. I had to keep going, though.

"Always honor your mother, Bobby. She's a good person. All the trouble she had, it was all my fault. The drinking. The pills. Having to go to the hospital that time. It was all my fault, Bobby. I want you to understand that."

"Dad . . ," he said.

I kept looking right at him. The pain on his face stood out even more clearly.

"Yes, Bobby."

"Dad, you're really hurting my shoulders," he said. "I mean . . . you're squashing them."

I blinked. I looked at my right hand, then my left. They were both clamped hard on his shoulders. His shirt was all crinkled up. I let go suddenly, as if I'd gotten an electrical shock.

"Oh . . . sorry about that, Bobby," I said.

The pained look on his face dissolved away. He worked his arms around a few times. Then he massaged his shoulders with his hands.

"Yikes," he said.

I stayed on one knee. "I'm sorry, Bobby. I didn't mean to hurt you. I just . . . I was just trying to make sure you . . . "

He looked down at the ground. I saw him kick the toe of his shoe at the concrete.

"Sure, Dad. I understand. I kind of knew what was going on. I could kind of tell what was happening."

I looked hard into his eyes again. They were his mother's eyes. Hazel green. So bright. I put my arms around him and held him close to me. I felt the coolness of the breeze drifting across my face.

"I love you, Bobby," I said.

He had his arms around me too. Very tight.

"I love you too, Dad. And I miss you. I miss you real bad. I wish you'd come back. It's not the same without you."

I couldn't say anything. I just held him. I had to blink a couple of times. We stayed like that for several moments, holding each other. Scenes from the past came back to my mind.

"Uh oh . . , " I heard Bobby say over my shoulder.

"What?"

"Brutus . . ."

We hadn't been paying any attention. I turned loose of Bobby and stood up and looked back over my shoulder. Brutus was in the next yard down, frolicking, kind of like a demolition ball swinging around on the prowl, looking for something to smash. I could see a man walking up the front walk of his house towards his front door, the newspapers and the mail in his hand. Then I saw Brutus start to sniff around.

"That's Mr. Thompson," Bobby said.

Before I could comment, Brutus squatted right in the center of Mr. Thompson's nice clean walk and took a warm, steamy dump on the concrete, directly in front of Mr. Thompson's face. Bull's-eye. Six paces from the front door. That served to stop Mr. Thompson cold in his tracks. He stood on his formerly clean walk and stared down at the mess. I couldn't tell whether or not there was steam coming out of his ears too.

"Uh oh," Bobby said.

"Uh oh," I agreed.

Mr. Thompson continued to stand there on his walk, staring down, his hands on his hips. Just staring at it. He did not have the look of a pleased individual.

"We'll come back and clean it up!" I called out.

Mr. Thompson looked back over his shoulder at me. I could not see anything resembling satisfaction on his features. He sort of nodded to himself, fatalistically, then turned back toward the house, stepped carefully over the production on the pavement, and trudged dolefully inside.

Brutus, in the meantime, came running at the sound of my voice. He came to a stop in front of us, his whole body wagging, his tongue flopping out, panting happily. So pleased. So proud. So satisfied. It must be wonderful, I thought.

Bobby could only shake his head. "Brutus, you're so stupid."

I draped an arm around Bobby's shoulder. Consolingly. The other arm I put around Brutus, who had proceeded to put his front paws on my chest. They were sopping wet and muddy, of course. My shirt was getting even dirtier. Brutus thought it was all just wonderful. He panted happily in my face. He was glad to see me. He'd been gone for at least a minute, after all. He tried to lick me in the face, but I managed to hold him off. I scratched behind his ears.

"Dumb turd," I said.

"*Really,*" said Bobby.

After that we walked home. Coming back through

the living room, Brutus just had to stop and smell the roses one more time. That dumped the vase on the rug again. Preordained, I thought. I heard Julie shriek. So Brutus got consigned to outer darkness again, but not before he had managed to do some big time munching. Little bits of chewed up red rose petals lay all over the floor by the time Bobby finally managed to wrestle him out the back door. If the look on Julie's face could have killed, Brutus would already have been in the glue factory. I should have seen it coming, I thought, as I helped her clean up the mess again. I should have averted it. Then Bobby took the pooper-scooper, a paper bag, a bucket of soapy water, and a scrub brush and headed out the front door. Julie seemed to understand.

"Poop squad," I noted, as the front door banged shut behind him

"We've done it before," she said helplessly. "How he *always* hits the pavement I'll never know."

Then we were left together in the stillness. She sat down on one end of the couch. I sat on the other end, angled toward her. I propped my leg on the cushion and put my arm on the sofa back, so I could turn toward her.

"So . . . things are going well," I said.

She smiled. "Yes."

"Work is okay?"

She nodded.

"Good. Good. That's great. Bobby seems real good too, like you said. He talked some about the soccer. You guys are doing fantastic."

She looked at me very closely for a moment. "I need to tell you something, Walt."

The tone of her voice was different. I felt my heart stop, then begin to hammer. The saliva in my mouth suddenly got pasty.

"Sure . . . go ahead . . , " I said.

She took a deep breath. "I . . . I think maybe…I've

met somebody… somebody special . . . ”

My heart missed a couple of lub dubs, then started to hammer again. I started to say something, but I couldn’t get any words out.

“It’s somebody I met through one of the girls at work,” she said. “He’s . . . he’s very nice. He’s very attractive. Successful. Divorced. He’s an attorney with a firm here in Dallas.”

I was aware of listening to her, but the words weren’t really fitting together, like they were in a foreign language. She mentioned his name. Sam Wilderthorn, I heard her say. It barely registered.

“We’ve been out several times,” she said. “Bobby seems to like him too. I . . . I think I really like him, Walt.”

I looked across the room, out the window. Across the street, I could see children playing in a front yard, frolicking in the twilight. I could hear the faint tinkling of their laughter. But it all looked so far away, so unaccountably distant and remote, as if I were looking down the wrong end of a telescope.

“I . . . I thought you ought to know,” I heard her say.

I turned back toward her. The hazel green of her eyes seemed to hold an immense sadness. Her face looked so very familiar, and yet so very, very different also, as if seen from a new direction.

“I . . . I think I could be serious about him,” she said. “I’ve wondered . . . I’ve wondered whether or not to tell you. I’ve thought about it a lot. An awful lot. I . . . I finally decided it would be best to go ahead and mention it to you. To let you know.”

I felt myself nodding. “ . . . Well . . . that’s . . . that’s great, Julie . . , ” I said. “I mean . . . that’s great . . . ”

I could see wetness brimming in her eyes.

“I’ll always love you, Walt,” I heard her say, her voice a whisper. “But being around you is too painful. I can't go back to that. And I need somebody. I need a relationship. I need my life."

I couldn't possibly have said anything. I reached out for her, and she slid across the sofa toward me, into my arms. Neither of us even seemed to think about my muddy shirt. I held her as she folded against me. I could tell she was biting her lip. Then I heard the catch of her breath as she started to cry. All I could do was pat her on the back.

"You were better than anything I ever deserved," I whispered. "Much, much better."

Her breath caught again, and she started to sob.

"I'm sorry I didn't do right by you," I said. "It was all my fault."

I held her against me, patting her on the back - again and again - and stroking her hair. She leaned against me even more and I rocked her back and forth, ever so slowly. She cried for several minutes. I thought the ache inside me would burst my chest. Finally she stopped; her breathing gradually returned to normal. She pushed back from me, and we looked into each other's eyes. I brushed the wetness from her cheeks.

"I understand, Julie," I said. "I understand."

She nodded. There hardly seemed anything else to say. We held each other again for several moments.

"I probably need to be going," I said.

She leaned back from me slightly again. I could hear Bobby opening the front door.

"I worry about you, Walt," she said.

I kissed my fingers and pressed them gently to her lips.

"I'll be fine," I said. "Don't worry about me, Julie."

Bobby came into the room and I stood up. Julie stood up too. Bobby looked at us expectantly.

"I gotta scram, sport," I said.

"Aw, Dad . . . "

"Got to."

I put my arm around him and held him. Julie came to us, and I put my other arm around her and squeezed them both. I could look down over their shoulders and see the coffee table with the vase of red roses. I knew now where they had come from. I hugged them one last time. Very hard. Then I left . . .

DANCE YOUR HEART OUT

6.

I got in my car and I drove. I went up and down the freeways of Dallas, just driving. I put on a golden oldie station and listened to the music. Old songs, hymns from my youth. I hummed along with their familiar melodies. Usually just humming. Sometimes I sang with the lyrics. I never once glanced at the clock. Time slipped by me like an amorphous cloud, flowing over me but not touching me, slipping by beyond my awareness. Evening changed to night. The moon rose. I saw it come inching over the horizon. Some time later it was higher. Still I drove. Finally I happened to notice the gas gauge again. I had filled the Taurus up barely a few hours earlier. The tank was nearly empty again. I shook my head to clear out the cobwebs, then slowed and pulled off the freeway onto an access road. I took a right at the next light. Traffic moved slowly but steadily. I plodded along. Before long I was back at my apartment. I turned off the engine and sat in the stillness. More time passed. Then I got out and went inside.

I got a beer out of the refrigerator and sat down on the couch. As I did I happened to notice a copy of one of the swinger magazines I had bought not long ago. It had been lying there for days, untouched. This was the one in which I had seen the Dallas Swingers Club advertised. I picked it up and flipped through a few of the pages. It was packed with pictures and personal ads. Photographs flashed before me. Naked people, smiling and posing for the camera. Frontal views, back views, side views, bent over views. Tons of ads. People wanted.

I folded up the magazine and dropped it on the couch beside me. I sat there for awhile. I could feel the weight of my frame pressing down into the pillows of the sofa. I could feel my heaviness. You've lived a dull life, I thought.

I pushed myself up off the couch and walked into

the bathroom. I stood looking at myself in the mirror. I could see a few gray hairs starting to emerge at my temples. Little crow's feet were starting to mark the corners of my eyes. I took a deep breath and blew it out slowly.

The phone rang. Its echo resounded off the stillness of the apartment. It rang again. I told it to get screwed but it didn't listen. It rang yet again. Several times. Insistently. Finally I said to hell with it and picked it up. It could always be somebody from The Publisher's Clearing House, after all, calling to tell me I'm a millionaire.

"Hello," I said, aware of not masking my impatience very well.

"Is that . . . is that you, Walt . . ?" a female voice asked.

It actually took me a few seconds to make the connection.

"Stan . . ?" I said.

"Hi!" she said.

"Well, hi . . ."

"Thank God you're home, Walt," she said, relieved. "Thank God! Gosh, I've been trying and trying and trying to get you. I've looked everywhere for you. Everywhere! Your phone didn't answer all afternoon, and I didn't know where to find you. I was afraid you'd disappeared, or that something had happened to you. I'm so glad you came by and left me that note with your phone number. Thank God! I mean, how stupid of me! I didn't even have your address. I can't believe it!"

"Takes two to tango and get addresses," I said. "I didn't think of it either."

"I . . . I know you won't believe this, Walt, but I'm really not used to being picked up in bars. I'm really not. There's no reason for you to believe that, but it's true. And I think the whole thing just left me kind of dazed. I wasn't thinking very clearly, to tell you the truth. But I still can't believe I didn't even know where you lived."

"My responsibility, really," I said. "You know how us ex-jocks are. Take away my playbook, I can't find my way in from the rain."

She kind of laughed. "I'm . . . I'm really glad you came by and left that note. I really am."

I waited a moment. The tone of her voice - the softness - had surprised me. I didn't know what to say.

"I've missed you, Walt," she said. "I've really wanted to see you again."

I felt something inside. I couldn't identify it precisely. Not exactly a warmth. But something.

"I've wanted to see you again too, Stan," I said.

"I'm glad to hear that. I really am. I mean that. So…what have you been up to, ex-jock?"

I thought of the trip to Austin and then going by to see Julie and Bobby. I thought of hugging them good-bye beside the vase of pretty red roses. I could feel them against me. I could feel the closeness of their bodies. I could see them again in my mind's eye. I shut my eyes, but the images wouldn't disappear.

"Oh . . . I, uh . . . I've had some things I had to take care of," I finally said. " . . . Just some stuff I had to do."

I opened my eyes, looked around the apartment. The walls stared back at me. There was silence on the line for several moments. I could tell she was listening closely.

"You . . . you sound upset, Walt," she said.

I cleared my throat. Shifted my weight onto my other leg.

"No, no, I'm fine."

"You sound concerned about something. I don't know . . . you sound… very thoughtful. Like maybe you're down. I get this feeling . . . this feeling you're very, very upset about something. I'm usually pretty intuitive about those things. I don't mean to be nosy. And I don't mean to interfere. It's just that . . . you're concerning me, that's all."

I cleared my throat again and was about to try to say

something, but didn't. Couldn't find any words. I shut my eyes again, but the images still wouldn't go away.

"Do you want to talk?" she asked.

I shook my head, then realized she couldn't see that over the phone. I took a slow breath. Cleared my throat again.

"Don't think talking would do any good," I said.

"You *are* upset."

I took another breath. "Had better days."

There was a short silence again.

"Would you like to come over?" she said. "Even if you don't feel like talking, sometimes it helps to be around somebody. We could go out somewhere. We could go get a drink or a cup of coffee. Go listen to some music. Or we could just stay here. Even watch some TV if you want. It might help get your mind off whatever it is that's bothering you."

I thought about that. I looked around the apartment again. The emptiness stared back at me. I didn't really know what was happening in my life, but it didn't feel like I had any control over it. And it sounded like Julie had a new relationship. I searched in my mind for a reason not to go see Stan. Couldn't find one.

"Sounds good," I said. "Fifteen minutes?"

"Perfect," she said.

I hung up, cleaned up and put on a fresh shirt and a sport coat, then drove to her place. I hesitated for a minute at the door before knocking, like Alice on the threshold of the looking glass. Then I knocked. Seeing her open the door was a sensual jolt all over again. She was dressed in black pants again, but with a white turtleneck sweater this time. The softness around her throat seemed to accentuate the line of her jaw, the fullness of her lips, the sharp laser blue of her eyes. Just as I began to be aware of holding my breath, she moved up close to me and hugged me. She held me, and I held her in return. I didn't try to find anything to say.

"I'm glad you came by," she finally said. "You've had me worried."

"I'll be okay."

She pulled back slightly and looked up at me. The blueness of her eyes was startling all over again. Laser shock, third degree. She smiled and took my hand.

"Come on in," she said. She led me inside and shut the door. Still holding her hand, I followed her to the sofa. I sat down and she went to the kitchen, then returned with a can of beer. She popped off the top for me. It was the same brand I had been drinking in the bar. I wondered if that was chance. She sat down on the couch and regarded me closely.

"Want to talk?" she said.

I shook my head. "No, not really."

"Are you sure you're okay?"

I took a swig of beer. "I'm fine."

"Any place you want to go?"

"Not really."

The lighting in her apartment was gentle, highlighting the softness of the sweater at her neck, the creaminess of her skin, the blueness of her eyes. I couldn't keep from looking at her. I found myself getting all snarled up in the lasers again.

"You look fantastic," I said.

She smiled. "Thanks."

I couldn't think of anything else to say, so I leaned toward her and kissed her. She kissed me back, and I ran my hand along the line of her jaw and down her neck. I kissed her even harder and she responded again, eagerly. Then she pulled back from me. Our eyes met and held. She seemed to study me again.

"I . . . I promised myself we wouldn't have sex tonight," she said. "I've been thinking about it a lot, and I don't think it's wise. So I made myself that promise."

"I certainly hope you were lying to yourself."

She laughed. I pressed my mouth against hers again and felt her press back against me. I lifted up her sweater and ran my hands up inside, over her braless breasts. I could feel her nipples harden under my fingers. Then she pulled back from me once more, and I got tangled up in the lasers all over again.

"It's not that I don't *want* to," she said.

"Good. Keep thinking like that."

"It's just . . . it's just that I don't want you to get the wrong idea about me."

"What if it's an idea I like?"

I kissed her again. Massaged her breasts. Rubbed her nipple between my thumb and forefinger. I could hear her moan.

"I always try to keep my promises," she said.

"That's too bad."

We kissed again, even harder, our mouths pressing together. Between my fingers, her nipple was fully erect. The white turtleneck sweater was all the way up now. Her breasts stood out proud and bare. Seeing them emerge was like having a fifty-yardline seat at the creation of the Rockies. She kind of smiled at me.

"Then again, I could always work on creative flexibility, I guess," she said.

"There you go."

I kissed her again, even more urgently. The pace of our breathing had quickened. Our tongues intertwined.

"We could go into the bedroom," she said.

"Perfect."

I pulled her sweater off over her head, and she took me by the hand again and led me into the bedroom. We undressed ourselves more slowly this time, going gently, exploring as we went. Then she lay down on the bed and I stretched out beside her. I took her in my arms and held her. I stroked the small of her back. I kissed her again.

"Do you want to be on top this time?" she asked.

"Bottom is okay."

She leaned back from me slightly and fixed me with her eyes. "I want you to be satisfied, Walt. It's important to me. I don't want you to think I'm strange."

"Bottom is okay."

"Are you sure?" she said.

"Dammit, let's fight."

She laughed and I pulled her on top of me. She lay against me, her weight on top of me, and I held her tight. Her hair alongside my face felt soft and wispy, with a clean, fresh smell. I could feel the rhythm of her breathing. It was a combination of sensations I fancied I could get used to.

We moved together gently, slowly. She was much more restrained this time, almost subdued. I could tell she was holding back, trying not to startle me. Even so, she had several orgasms. They weren't as wild as the ones on the previous occasion, but they weren't teeny tiny either. Afterward, we lay together on the bed. She rested her head on my shoulder. We stayed like that for several minutes, our breathing gradually returning to normal. There seemed no need to talk.

"Guess what?" she finally asked.

"What?"

She looked over at me. "Can I be forward?"

"As opposed to backward?"

She smiled. "Would you be offended if I asked you out to a party?"

"I'd probably cover it up real good," I said.

She smiled again. Looked right at me. For a moment I could see a flicker of uncertainty in her eyes, like she didn't know for sure whether she should keep going.

"Sure," I said. "I'd like that."

She laid her head back on my shoulder again. I could tell she was smiling. "Good, I'm glad."

We lay that way for several minutes. Then she said, "There *is* one minor detail. I hope it won't be a problem."

"What's that?"

She raised up on an elbow and looked down at me. "It's a costume party. You wouldn't mind going to a costume party, would you?"

A costume party? I thought about that. I would probably rather die by lethal injection, I decided. A costume party had all the natural appeal of a live circumcision. I started to tell her that. I started to say no way. But I could see the expectation in her eyes. I could see the brightness there. So I swallowed real hard and managed to say, ". . . Sure . . . that's great. . . "

She smiled again, broadly. "Oh, good! Oh, that's wonderful! Thank you! Thank you! It's a special party they have every year about this time. It's a joint party put on by several of the swinger clubs in the Dallas-Ft.Worth area. I *love* to go to costume parties. I just love it! I love to get all dressed up and do charades. It's so much fun."

"Great . . , " I said.

There were a few other minor details. The party was this coming weekend. We'd have to go out and get costumes, of course. Oh, goodie! I could hardly wait. We agreed that tomorrow afternoon would be a good time to go costume hunting. She gave me her cell number so I could reach her. Don't call her at work on the office phone, she told me. Always use the cell. They got mad if the office phone was used for personal calls. Okay. Fine with me. Some time later I got up and dressed. I still wasn't ready to spend the night. She seemed to accept that. She put on a robe and showed me to the door. I found myself hugging her, and she hugged me back. We held each other tightly. Feeling her against me, I found myself thinking about Jessica Nodman again, just like I had the last time we had been together. I thought of my visit to Joe Henderson in Austin. There was still a serial killer on the loose, and he liked well-built blondes. I didn't know where he had linked up with Jessica. But somewhere their paths had crossed. I thought about telling Stan of my conversation with Henderson, but I decided not to.

"Be careful, Stan," I whispered.

I kissed her good-night. She blew me another kiss as she closed the door. Then I drove home . . .

7.

Next morning I called my attorney. When Julie decided she needed to separate from me and move to Dallas to be closer to her parents, she was advised by all her friends as well as her folks that she needed an attorney. Who doesn't these days? If you think you don't, just give it time. So she wound up going to see this lizard named Robert Mustham, who specializes in divorce cases. He has quite a reputation here in Dallas. Going to court against him, I was told, is like being sodomized with an air hammer. I think Julie actually felt kind of guilty about it, in fact. She kept insisting I needed an attorney too, since "Robert" wouldn't agree to represent both of us. I told her I didn't want an attorney, that I'd rather have genital warts instead, but she kept insisting. She kept saying she was afraid "Robert" would take advantage of me in court. How, I wondered. I told her I intended to let her have everything we had anyway, all the property and all the money, what little we had of either, custody of Bobby, who deeply needed a close relationship with his mother, the parakeet, the two turtles, all the fish, Brutus - by all means Brutus, God help us all - and anything else we might have accumulated along the way, but she was still afraid "Robert" would be tough on me. Tough on me? What were we talking about, I wondered. The air hammer? Right there in the judge's chambers? But the whole thing finally started to become a bone of contention, so I gave in and got an attorney of my own, though for what I wasn't sure. To help me sign over everything but the shirt on my back, I guess. David Jarvington was the attorney's name, and I chose him because he had a reputation for ineffectiveness.

"Walter, hello, how have you been? Tell me," I heard him say when he finally came on the line. His voice had that caring, concerned tone the truly slimy ones always manage to perfect.

DANCE YOUR HEART OUT

"Hi, David, how are you? I've been doing fine."

First names only, of course. Always friendly on the road to hell.

"What can I do for you, Walter?" he asked. "Tell me."

So I said a lady friend had asked me to get some information about an attorney. She was thinking of going out with him. Sam Wilderthorn was the name.

"Oooooh," he said.

I didn't know what that meant, but it didn't sound good, even in legalese.

"I assume we're speaking in strictest confidence," he added.

"Absolutely. This is just between you and me and the tape recorder you've got on your line."

I don't think I've ever known an attorney who didn't tape his calls. The phone recorder is as much a part of their lives as the white coat is for doctors. They probably keep it running even when they call home on Mother's Day. It must've been the case for Jarvington too, because there was an off balance pause before he spoke again.

"Well, yes, of course . . , " he said.

Pause again.

"Sam Wilderthorn?" I said.

"Yes…he's a fairly competent real estate attorney, Walter. *Fairly* competent. Not outstanding by any means. But competent. Fairly competent."

"Okay . . , " I said. "What else . . ."

"Well, there's a question of character, Walter. You see, Sam Wilderthorn is an incorrigible womanizer. He's on his fourth or fifth wife already, and he's been flagrantly unfaithful to all of them. He's a user. A taker…"

"He's still married?" I asked.

"Absolutely."

I thanked him for that information and hung up. So Sam Wilderthorn was a womanizer. And he had lied to

Julie about being divorced. I wasn't sure whether I felt bad for her sake or good for my own. I decided I'd watch very closely.

Then I went down to the courthouse. I knew the address of the property where the party had been the other night, so getting the owner's full identity wasn't a problem. Then I checked to see what else Jim Bob might own. There was a house on the south side of town in a poor neighborhood. I drove there and found a small, rundown frame structure with ratty screens on the windows. There was also a rickety front porch, complete with a spindly banister. And on that front porch sat Jim Bob and Orville, of all people, leaning back in a pair of wooden chairs, whittling. I thought they probably wore exactly the same clothes they had on the other night. I got out of the Taurus and approached the house. Jim Bob seemed to eye me rather narrowly, but he kept whittling. I stopped about ten feet short of them. Kind of grinned. Gave them a little wave.

"Hey, fellas," I said.

They kept whittling. Jim Bob sort of nodded. Maybe Orville nodded too.

I approached the porch steps. "Jim Bob, you told me the other night about that girl that got killed, the one they called Rumpulina. You guys know anything else about that?"

Jim Bob leaned forward and slurped a wad of snuff into yet another plastic styrofoam cup, which sat on a small table in front of him. Then he picked up the cup, rotated it exactly ninety degrees, and put it back down.

"Nope," he said. "Don' know nothin' about it."

"Yup, don' know nothin' about it," said Orville. As if on cue, he put his cigarette to his mouth and took another one of those toenail popping drags. I almost cringed, dreading the inevitable. Sure enough, he broke out into a fit of coughing, as wheezy and as raspy as ever, and kept on going until he almost turned blue. Sahara's not getting any easier to crack, I guess.

There was another question I needed an answer to. It had occurred to me when I had talked to Joe Henderson. There was something that didn't fit.

"Jim Bob, you said she'd been all butchered up, or words to that effect," I said. "Where'd you hear that?"

Jim Bob whittled off a sliver of wood, maybe a little more sharply than he needed to, and continued to eye me.

"You a cop?" he asked.

I nodded. "Sure am. Sorry about that."

Jim Bob whittled off another sliver. Worked his chaw from one side of his mouth to the other. Then licked along his lower lip.

"You got any ID?" he asked.

I stepped up on the porch, pulled out my badge and flipped it open for him. He studied it for a moment, then slid his chaw over to the other side of his mouth and back again.

"This ain't Houston," he said.

"True enough, but I can get the local cops out here in a hurry if I need to. You'd save yourself some trouble if you cooperate with me now."

Jim Bob whittled off another sliver of wood. He ran his tongue along his lower lip. Munched his chaw.

"So where'd you hear that she'd been butchered up?" I repeated. "Where'd you get that? Who told you?" Joe Henderson had been very clear on that point: the part about the mutilation hadn't been released to the media. That had been kept completely quiet.

Jim Bob kind of thought about it. Whittled off another sliver. Worked his chaw around.

"You want to talk to the Dallas cops, Jim Bob?" I asked.

He seemed to think about it a little more. Looked up at me for a moment. Munched that chaw.

"Heard it from Gunner," he finally said.

I felt a ripple of relief pass through me. "Gunner? Who's Gunner?"

"Guy at the club," Jim Bob said, whittling off another sliver of wood.

"That his real name, or just what they call him?"

Jim Bob licked along his lower lip. Munched some more.

"Don' know his real name," he said.

"How about you, Orville?" I asked.

Orville shook his head.

"What did you hear?" I asked Jim Bob.

"Jes' that she was all butchered up."

"Anything in particular? Any specific details?"

Jim Bob thought about it. "Nope. Jes' butchered up."

"Gunner tell you himself, or did you hear it from somebody else?"

"Jes' heard it at the club. Heard Gunner said that."

"Was Gunner there the other night?" I asked Jim Bob.

Jim Bob shook his head. "Nope. Ol' Gunner, he don' come to all the parties. Jes' some of 'em."

Timing is a matter of luck, of course. Sometimes you have it, sometimes you don't.

"How come they call him Gunner?" I asked.

Jim Bob kind of grinned at that, enough so I could see his teeth. They looked just as yellow and crooked as ever. I wondered if they'd get brushed in *this* millennium. He looked over at Orville, and they both had to chuckle.

"'Cause ol' Gunner, he can do it eight times at one party. That's how come."

"Yup, eight times at one party," Orville said.

Well, here we go again, I thought, back to calling Guinness. Two world titles, right here in the same club. Best ass, most ejaculations. What's next, I wondered. A guy with twelve balls? But I still couldn't help thinking about it. Eight times? At one party? Lord have mercy. I only hoped my prostate wouldn't roll over and die, just from the thought of it. Made me wonder why they hadn't named him Uzi instead.

Jim Bob's grin got a little wider, and he kind of chuckled again for a moment. "Ol' Gunner, he always gives it to 'em right in the ass," he said.

"Yup, right in the ass," said Orville.

That was worth another chuckle.

"Ol' Gunner, he always pulls out right before he shoots off, jes' to show ya' he really did it," Jim Bob said.

"Yup, jes' to show ya' he really did it," Orville agreed.

"You certainly have to admire that kind of integrity," I noted.

Their chuckle dwindled down. Jim Bob leaned forward and slurped another wad of snuff into his cup, set it back down on the table, then picked it up and rotated it ninety degrees before setting it back down again. Still on cue, Orville put his cigarette to his mouth and started to take another one of those drags. Don't do it, Orville, I wanted to say. Please. Just say no. But I knew it was pointless. I had to look away. Had to. Sure enough, here it came, respiratory hell, full-blown and just as dry as ever. When he finally got through, I turned back to Jim Bob.

"Anything else you heard?" I asked.

Jim Bob shook his head. "Nope. Jes' that."

So somebody named Gunner - true identity unknown - who only came to some of the parties and who would go down in history for rapid fire anal intercourse, this person named Gunner somehow, in some way, had gotten inside information. Information that had never been given to the media. Or he had known it from the outset. And, for whatever reason, he had shared it with somebody, and the word had ultimately come back to Jim Bob. One way or another. I needed to find out more.

"Who runs the club?" I asked.

"Ray and Jackie's the ones that started it," Jim Bob said.

"Ray and Jackie? You know how to reach them?"

Jim Bob shrugged. "Number's on all the ads in the magazines."

I reached in my shirt pocket and pulled out the two pictures Joe Henderson had given me.

"You ever seen either of these ladies at the club?" I asked. I held out the pictures, first for Jim Bob, then for Orville. Neither of them reacted. Jim Bob rolled his chaw around his mouth and licked his lower lip.

"Nope, never seen 'em," he said.

"Yup, never seen 'em," Orville confirmed.

I thought they were telling the truth. I hadn't seen anything in their eyes.

"One more thing, fellas," I added. "Once again, it'll be in your best interest to cooperate. I'm gonna have a sketch guy come out here from the Dallas PD and talk to you. I need to know what Gunner looks like. He'll talk with you and try to draw a face. I need you to work with him."

Neither one said anything.

"You guys have a good day," I said. I nodded politely, then got back in the Taurus and drove off. I only hoped they would cooperate enough to give me something.

I drove back across town, heading for Jack's Lamp Shop. As I did I called Joe Henderson and told him what I'd learned. I thought it would be better for him to contact the Dallas PD. He was official, after all, and I wasn't. He said he'd get right on it. I told him I'd keep him advised of anything else I might learn.

The drive was long enough to give me time to think about the man called Gunner. I had seen lots of acts of sodomy on the tapes at Jack's house. As I thought about it,

I *did* seem to remember one particular episode. A guy who pulled out and ejaculated onto the woman's back. Had there been some applause? I couldn't recall for sure. And I couldn't bring back the man's face. I thought I might need to check that tape again.

Then I got to Jack's Lamp Shop, which turned out to be in a small, single story shopping center. I parked a few spaces down from the door so the car wouldn't be visible, then walked up the pavement and stepped inside. I found myself in a small, one showroom store, very neat and clean and tidy, just like his house had been. Jack came across the floor toward me as I stepped inside and shut the door. He looked pretty much as I had remembered him. About five-six or so, slump-shouldered, pot-bellied, almost completely bald. I had estimated him to be about forty, but in this better light, he looked like he was probably closer to fifty. He smiled his pleasant businessman's smile as he approached.

"Can I help you, sir?" he asked.

I said something about hurricane lamps. I had heard he had some nice ones. Oh, yes, yes, by all means. An excellent selection. Excellent! He led me across the floor to view his collection. These here, and of course these over here. And these also. Oh, these are especially nice. We're very proud of these. Yes, we are indeed. I feigned interest, asked a few questions about vintage, inquired about prices. Yes, yes, by all means. Certainly, sir. He was very helpful. Most helpful. I wound up telling him I'd have to think about it. Certainly, sir. Certainly. He headed to a counter in the back of the store and went around behind it. I followed. There was a stack of business cards on top of the counter next to the cash register. He took one and held it out to me. Smiled pleasantly. I didn't have the heart to tell him I already had one.

"You know, you look kind of familiar to me," I added.

"Oh, really? Well, I don't know . . . "

I pretended to think about it. "I know! Didn't I see you at a party the other night? Last Saturday night? The Dallas Swingers Club. Didn't I see you there?"

A trace of wariness crossed his face for a second. I couldn't tell whether he remembered seeing me there or not.

"Wasn't that you?" I asked. "Yeah! I saw you at Tape Time. You were getting some really great close-up shots."

"Well . . ," he chuckled self-consciously.

"Yeah! That *was* you! It *was*. Hey, those must have been *great* shots. I mean, the angles and everything. And up close like that. I mean, I bet those were *super* shots."

"Well . . ." The self-conscious chuckle again, but a little looser this time, more relaxed. "Well . . . I *do* try to get some interesting close-up shots."

"Boy, I'll bet! Those must be great. Do you . . . I mean, do you ever . . . do you ever loan out any tapes? Or trade tapes? I mean, those must be great tapes. Last Saturday was my first time ever, but I'd really like to see more. Much more. I mean, if you've got tapes, I'd really be interested in seeing them."

"Well . . . of course, surely . . . "

"Do you go to lots of the parties?"

He seemed more at ease. I noticed him glance around the showroom, as if checking to make sure there wasn't anybody else in the store. He seemed satisfied. His body language changed too. He leaned forward slightly, confidentially. I could hear more lightness in his voice when he spoke.

"*All* of them," he said.

"*All* of them?"

He nodded. "For several years now. Haven't missed a one."

"And you make a tape at every party?"

He smiled. "Every one."

"Wow! What a collection! That's fantastic!"

He smiled even more broadly.

"So I guess you must have . . .gosh, thirty or forty of those tapes."

He positively beamed.

"Would you be willing to let me look at some of them?"

He winked. "I think that could be arranged."

"And you've got *all* the parties? Every month?"

His cup ranneth over. "*All* of them."

He seemed so pleased. It occurred to me he really didn't have much companionship in his life. But it had to end.

"In that case, I have just one question," I said.

"What's that?" he said, still smiling.

"Where's the tape from last June?"

It didn't register with him. I could see the confusion on his features.

"Excuse me?" he said.

"The tape from last June. Where's that one? It's missing."

The merriment was gone. He stared at me blankly. I thought I could see a vague apprehension there too, along with the uncertainty.

"I couldn't find the tape from last June when I was by your place the other day. Where is it?"

I had expected him to react to that and he did. He started to open a drawer behind the counter. It didn't take a stroke of genius to realize he was going for a gun. But he wasn't quick enough. I reached across the counter, grabbed the front of his shirt, and hauled him up onto the countertop before he could get the drawer open. He tried to struggle but he wasn't strong enough. I kept pulling, dragging him up over the counter until his knees scraped across the top. I still had hold of his shirt with both hands, suspending him between me and the countertop. His face was right up close to mine, our noses only inches apart. His eyes bugged out. I could see his lips trembling.

"I don't want to hurt you," I said tightly. "I'm not here to harm you and I'm not here to rob you. You'll be perfectly safe if you cooperate with me. Is that clear?"

His eyes still bugged out. Being held up by his shirt must have made it hard for him to breathe. I'm not sure he could have answered if he tried. But I thought he kind of nodded.

"I'm going to put you down," I said. "Do you understand?"

Another semi-nod.

"If you try anything funny, you'll regret it."

Nod.

Going gently, I stepped backward and pulled him farther forward so that his legs finally cleared the edge of the counter. I kept him from falling by holding him up by the shirt. He managed to stay upright. He stood there shakily in front of me, and I let go of his shirt.

"Are you all right?" I asked.

I think he tried to say something but couldn't get it out.

"I meant what I said. I'm not here to hurt you. Or rob you."

". . . That's good . . , " he croaked.

I told him about going by his house and looking at the tapes. And not being able to find the one from last June. Not being able to find the tape of the last party before the girl named Rumpulina had been killed.

"You said you had them all," I said.

"Yes . . ," he squeaked.

"Where is it?"

He hesitated. I could see him thinking. I took his elbow in my hand and applied pressure.

"Remember. I don't want to hurt you. But I mean to find out."

He cleared his throat. His breathing still wasn't right, and when he tried to talk, he had to clear it again.

"I . . . I gave it away," he gasped.

"Why?"

He hesitated again, and I reapplied the pressure to his elbow. He winced.

"There was . . . there was this man. He said there was something on it. Something he wanted."

"What was it?"

Jack shook his head. "I don't know. He wouldn't tell me. I don't know, so help me God, I really don't. I don't. I wasn't aware of filming anything unusual. I wasn't aware of filming anything different. I just did what I always do. But there was something he said was on the tape. That's all I know."

Jack sounded like he was telling the truth. I honestly believed he didn't know what made that particular tape special. But I needed to find it. And the man who had gotten it.

"Who was he?"

Jack looked pained. Scared. I applied pressure to his elbow again. He almost whined when he spoke.

"He . . . he said he'd hurt me if I ever told anybody. He said he'd mess me up. He was mean. Real mean. Real tough. He's lots bigger than me too."

I put an arm around him and patted him consolingly on the shoulder. I could feel the scrawny boniness of his frame, the soft flabbiness of his flesh. He barely came up to my armpit. I patted him again.

"You know what, Jack?" I said.

"What . . ?" he said fatalistically.

I patted him again on the shoulder. "*I'm* a lot bigger than you are too."

He didn't even look up at me. He kind of scuffed a

toe against the floor. His scrawny little shoulders sagged even more.

"Everybody's bigger than me," he grumbled.

I patted him again. Gently. This time he looked up at me.

"I really don't want to hurt you," I said.

He nodded and looked back down at the floor.

"But I'm not leaving here until you tell me."

I felt him take a deep breath, then slowly exhale. "I don't know his name. He comes to some of the parties. Some of them. Not all of them. I've never actually talked with him before. I've seen him at a couple of parties since, and he never said anything."

He seemed to be collecting himself, bracing himself to take the next step. I waited.

"He's pretty tall . . , " Jack finally went on. "Probably about as tall as you. Thinner, though. Not as bulked up. But real wiry. You know what I mean? Like a swimmer or a gymnast or something like that. Like he might be an athlete. He's probably about forty or forty-five, I'd say. He's got brownish hair but it's kind of gray at the temples. Looks kind of distinguished actually. And he dresses real sharp."

The images had been coming together in my mind. "And wears a red beret . . ," I said.

"Yeah, he does. You're right. Sometimes he does."

I was the one to nod this time. "Hieronymous . . ."

"What?" Jack said.

I shook my head. "Nothing. Just a name."

"You know him?" Jack asked, alarmed.

I shook my head again. "No. Not yet."

There wasn't much more to do. After a few more questions, I was satisfied that Jack really didn't know him or where to find him. I brushed Jack off, patted him on his pitiful little shoulder again. I also went behind the counter and emptied his gun, which turned out to be a 9 mm automatic, and poured the bullets in my pocket, so he couldn't drill me in the back as I left. After checking to make sure there weren't any other bullets in the drawer, I walked out of the store, stepped down the walk to the Taurus, and drove off . . .

8.

I called Stan on her cell, and we agreed to meet for a late lunch before going out to look for costumes. She told me again how much she loved costume parties. Just *loved* them. She sounded excited. I didn't feel excited at all. I still couldn't believe I was even doing it. We'd go to Clyde's Costume Castle, she said, a place she had heard of. They had some really neat costumes there. There's no such thing, I thought. Not ever, not since the dawn of time. But I kept my mouth shut.

I met her at Brandon's, a very "in" delicatessen type place that did a big lunch business. I spotted her across the room as I walked in, sitting at a table against a far wall. I had prepared myself, but it was still a jolt, even from a distance. The lasers were so very, very blue. She stood up as I walked toward her. She wore a light blue sweater, white pants, and light blue shoes. Just walking across the room, I noticed several males at other tables watching her.

"Hi, Walt," she said, smiling as I stepped up to her. She gave me an enthusiastic hug.

"Hey, Stan, you look great." I hugged her back.

And then we sat down for a nice, unhurried lunch. I had a Reuben and she had a bowl of soup. Just a bowl of soup. She was watching her figure, she said. So was just about everybody else and his dog, it seemed. Almost every male in the place was ogling her.

We chatted as we ate and found out a little more about each other, got a little farther past the names and body fluids stage. The usual sort of stuff you talk about when you're getting acquainted. She had grown up in the Dallas area, she said, on the south side, which wasn't the greatest area of the city. After high school she had gone to UT Arlington, right here in the Metroplex. Got a degree in history, but didn't want to teach, so she became a legal assistant instead. Told me the name of the firm where she worked. She also asked about me. Well, it's not all that sensational. I spent two years at the University of Houston, then joined the Houston PD. Fifteen years now in all, Homicide Division for the past eight. And so on. Still planning to finish my degree at night school, just hadn't gotten around to it yet.

Inevitably, we wound up talking about prior marriages. Always sticky stuff, but she could talk about it easily and naturally. She had been married once, to a guy who just happened to be a world class Karate Master. He ran a karate studio down in Austin these days. They were still in touch, she said. She spoke very openly. Didn't say anything bad about him. It just didn't work out. No kids. Amicable divorce. Said she was going out some now, but wasn't committed to anybody at the present time. She stressed that point, I thought. She also asked about me. I was honest with her. I told her about Julie and Bobby. Looked like it was over, but the legalities hadn't been finalized. Those barriers passed, we kept on talking. Found out more about each other. All in all, it was really quite nice. Very comfortable and relaxed. Even pleasant, I had to admit. I could tell she felt the same. It showed in her eyes and in her voice.

"Do you think we knew each other in a prior lifetime?" she asked at one point.

I shrugged. "Hard to say. I was a stone in my last incarnation. Maybe I was in your garden."

She laughed, that water over rocks sound again. It had such a lilting, easy quality. I started laughing too. It felt so natural to flow along with it.

When we had finally finished eating I picked up the tab. She objected but I did it anyway, authoritarian, chauvinistic bastard that I am. Then we left. She got the full eyeball treatment from just about every male there again as we walked out. Must be about what it's like to be

Madonna's bodyguard, I thought.

Then we got in our separate vehicles and drove to Clyde's Costume Castle. It turned out to be in a small, one story shopping center. It all looked kind of familiar, in fact. It should have, I thought, as I followed Stan into the parking lot. Clyde's Costume Castle was right next door to Jack's Lamp Shop. It bothered me that I hadn't immediately connected on that when she mentioned the name. I'm supposed to pick up on stuff like that. As I looked at Clyde's storefront, though, I realized there wasn't a sign on top, just on the front door, and it was on the other side of Jack's Lamp Shop from where I had parked. It hadn't been in my line of view. So I could partially excuse myself for not realizing where we were headed. I pulled around Stan's pickup and parked on the far side, away from Jack's front door. What a day, I thought. Here I was, about to go into a costume shop that just happened to be next door to a man who would probably like to see me dead. Jack had been rattled and afraid, and I didn't think he had gotten the license number of my car. I didn't want to let him see it now. That could always be traced. I didn't want him to recognize me, either. In particular, I didn't want to give him another chance to drill me in the back. So I got out of the car as inconspicuously as I could and stayed down low, which is not all that easy when you're six-four and two-forty, and followed Stan into the costume shop.

Clyde came out to greet us as we stepped inside. He looked to be about sixty with salt and pepper hair, a deeply lined face, and bottom teeth that looked like they had been ground down. I could see his teeth, because his mouth had fallen open when he had taken a look at Stan.

"We're here to get costumes," Stan said enthusiastically.

Clyde was able to get his mouth shut and say, "Well, you've sure come to the right place. Yessiree. See, we've got tons and tons and tons of costumes. A whole store full."

A perfect description of hell, I thought. But I kept my mouth shut.

"Did you have anything special in mind?" Clyde asked pleasantly.

Stan thought about it. She held her arms open, kind of struck a little pose. "Well, what do you think?" she said. "What do you think I should wear?"

I could read the answer in Clyde's eyes: nothing at all; not a single stitch.

But he managed to clear his throat and say, "Well, let's see what we can come up with here."

He offered a few suggestions. Indian Princess? Clown? Cowgirl? Not really, Stan indicated.

"Hey! Yeah! How about a fairy costume?" he suggested. He pulled something off a rack and held it up beside her, kind of eyeballing it for fit.

I had my doubts. Stan as Tinkerbell? The outfit looked kind of skimpy. Made me think of a butterfly with a pair of bowling balls looped over its neck.

Stan was obviously going to be very selective about this. She frowned. It had to be perfect, after all. The fairy costume was out.

He showed her some more getups. One of these, and now one of these. There was a mouse. Then a pirate. Then a godforsaken parakeet. Then something else. I didn't pay much attention. Finally she waved me away and told me to go look through the rest of the store to see what I wanted. What I wanted? Escape, I thought. But I still managed to keep my mouth shut. This was obviously going to take time.

So I wound up just kind of browsing through the store, going up and down the aisles, looking at this, looking at that. Goodie, goodie. Sure enough, they had lots of costumes. Tons and tons of them, as Clyde had said. I walked up and down the rows. It felt like strolling around through downtown Hades.

"Walt!" Stan finally called. "Come back over here. I think I've found it!"

So I trundled back over to where she and Clyde were standing, back by the changing room now, in front of the mirror. Stan was standing in front of the mirror, inspecting herself. She was wearing a kitten costume, I found out, which was basically a very tight, one piece, coal black leotard, with a long tail and with the hands and feet done up like white paws. There was a tight fitting hood that came up over her head and framed her face. There were whiskers you could glue on too, Clyde noted, along with a black nose, to make it all look even better.

"What do you think?" Stan asked.

I looked her up and down. Lordy. It was as tight as your epidermis. Got everything covered, but didn't leave a lot to the imagination. What did I think? I thought I'd have to protect her from the mobs.

"Well, it looks just super. . , " I was able to say.

Clyde obviously agreed. He was inspecting it very closely, indeed. But not for imperfections, I suspected.

"I'll do it!" she said.

So Stan was taken care of. She changed back out of the kitten costume and Clyde got it all wrapped up in a bag and then turned to me. He sized me up, looking me up and down, just like he had done with Stan, but the flavor was different, I thought. I could see him frown. I didn't know what that meant.

"Now *you're* going to be a problem," he concluded.

Good, let's call it off, I thought. But I managed once again to keep my mouth shut.

Clyde frowned again. He felt my arm, squeezed the bicep, then my shoulder. "See, you're so big. You've got such big muscles too. Gonna be hard to fit, hard to fit."

He seemed to think about it some more. "Hey! I got a Tarzan suit! Yeah! That ought to work. Not much more than a loincloth, though. Got some long hair that goes with it and a spear too. Might be a go."

"A Tarzan suit," Stan mused, a little suggestively. "Now that *would* be interesting."

But a loincloth? Give me a break. I cleared my throat and said, "I'm just a little worried about exposure here, you know, that's all. Body parts hanging out and everything. The weather too. The nights can still be pretty cool this time of the year. I don't want to freeze to death, and if I have to wear a coat, I'm afraid I'll look like a demented old flasher, what with my ankles sticking out."

Stan giggled at that. Clyde scratched his head again. The size was the problem, he noted again. The size. There were a couple of more suggestions. Captain Hook was one. Wonderful. My dreams come true.

"Hey! Yeah! I just thought of something!" he said. "I got a Superman outfit too. I just thought of that. It might be big enough to work."

What a chilling irony, I thought. I really do need to learn to watch my mouth. I'm being paid back for my transgressions.

I was going to protest, but Clyde had already gone to the back. He returned in a few moments and held it up to me. "Hey! Yeah! I bet this'll be just perfect."

I looked over at Stan, but I knew it was hopeless. There was no salvation in sight. So I took the Superman costume from Clyde and glumly stepped into the dressing room.

It was obvious from the start that I was in trouble. I put on the shirt first. It was *tight*. Very tight. It dug in at my armpits and my elbows and was almost as tight at the neck.

"Stan, it's not gonna work," I called out.

"Oh, please!" she called back. "Please! I want to see. Please!"

Okay, okay, I thought. Dammit, I'll do it.

So I finally got all the way into the stupid thing, cape and all, and stood there in the dressing room. The crotch was especially tight, even tighter than the armpits. It wasn't so much the blue leggings, it was the red trunks. Getting those on over the leggings had been a real challenge. The word again was *tight.* I could barely breathe. The back of the thing was climbing up my crotch like a bunch of iron fragments clinging to a magnet. But that wasn't the worst problem. The front was even more confining. It was really quite uncomfortable. Which brought me to a compelling question I couldn't ignore: which side do you put the equipment on? Left, I finally decided. I didn't know why. No real reason. I'm right-*handed*, actually. But I had to do something. So I lifted the trunks up in front as much as I could and pulled them over to the right, then sloshed everything else over to the left. There. At least that felt better. The blue leggings still covered everything, but they weren't nearly as tight. I could almost take a full breath. There was a mirror on the wall, and I thought about checking my Adam's apple to see how far it had risen, but I didn't think my system could stand the shock of seeing all the rest. I stood in front of the dressing room door and took another breath. Well, here I go, I thought, out into an innocent, unsuspecting world that's never before seen Superman in a thong. I've had prouder moments. But I steeled myself and opened the door and stepped out.

Clyde took one look at me and scrunched up his face and said, "Oooooh. Ouch!"

Stan also took a look. She started to giggle. She tried to control it, but she couldn't help herself. Then she started to laugh. She finally had to put her hand over her mouth. Then she doubled over.

"You don't think the people of Metropolis will be impressed?" I said.

"Oh, they'll be impressed, all right," she managed

to say.

So we decided it wasn't going to work after all.

"Hey! Yeah!" Clyde suddenly exclaimed. "I just remembered, I got this old rabbit suit in back. It's huge. Yeah! I mean *huge*. I haven't thought of that in years. It's back in storage. Lemme go get that. That'll be perfect, I bet. Perfect. You wait right here."

As if I'd leave like this.

Clyde scrambled into the back, and I stepped back into the dressing room and pulled off the Superman suit, like a snake shedding its skin. At least I could breathe again.

"Try this," Clyde said, opening the door and handing me an enormous bundle of furry pink fabric. "This'll work, I bet. This thing is huge. *Huge*. This'll be perfect."

I took it from him. It was large, sure enough. I could tell that without any trouble. It felt like holding a rug. The fabric was thick and woolly too. At least I wouldn't have to worry about getting cold. This would probably do nicely in Antarctica, I figured.

I stared at myself one last time in the mirror before trying to get into it. Now here I go again, I thought, about to try on this pink, woolly mammoth rabbit suit. Lordy. So I could go to a costume party. Stan had said something about prior lifetimes. Talk about bad karma. It made me wonder what horrible crimes and sins I must have committed. I had probably been Hitler, I decided. That might explain it.

But I managed to climb into it. The head was part of the overall suit, just like Stan's kitten, but with a big rabbit face in front instead of an opening in the hood. I had to stick my head in first, then work my way into the rest of it. It certainly was large enough. Large? It fit like a wigwam. Big Foot would probably love it, I thought. And *heavy*. There were rabbit feet and paws, and that was a problem, because with my hands in the paws, I couldn't get the zipper up in back. I called for help and Clyde was there in a flash, stepping into the dressing room and zipping me up. The legs were so long I had to pull them up to keep from tripping over the part that fell down over my ankles. When I stepped out to show Stan, she pretended to give it all a serious appraisal. She couldn't quite pull it off, though, and she started to snicker. Then she started to giggle. She finally had to put her hand over her mouth again, she was laughing so hard. She couldn't even stand up straight, she was so doubled over. But it was better than anything else I'd seen, and I didn't want to push my luck. There's only so much costume shopping a person can stand.

"We'll take it," I said.

"Excellent!" said Clyde.

Stan was still laughing.

There was a minor problem getting it off. The zipper, which ran all the way down the back from shoulder level to the seat, got stuck at the level of my upper back. Clyde tugged on it, pulling it back and forth, but he wasn't having any luck with it.

"I got some oil in the back," he said. "Be right back. We'll get it fixed right up in a jif."

So I stood there waiting while Clyde disappeared into the back again to get some oil. Stan was trying to keep a straight face, but she wasn't doing a very good job of it. She'd try to make some serious comment about how she really liked it, then she'd start to giggle. So I just waited. And waited. It was taking longer than expected.

"Good thing I don't have diarrhea," I noted.

Stan laughed again.

Then Clyde came back with a can of household oil and squirted it on the zipper. Sorry for the delay, he said, the oil hadn't been in its regular place. He'd had to search for it. He worked the zipper up and down, still tugging on it, and finally it broke free and he pulled it all the way down. I stepped back in the dressing room and took the suit off, then put my regular clothes back on and stepped out. I handed the suit back to Clyde, who was waiting at the counter.

"I'm gonna put a little more oil on this," he said. "Make sure it's working real smooth. Clean it up a little too. I think it's got some fur in the zipper track."

He took the suit and stepped into the back with it. Stan and I were alone. She put her arms around me and hugged me. I hadn't been expecting that.

"Thanks, Walt," she said softly. "I can tell you're not really wild about this. I know you're doing it for me, and I want you to know I appreciate it. I really, really do."

"Couldn't be happier," I said.

She reached up and kissed me, gently at first, then more firmly. Her arms gripped me more tightly as she pressed against me, kissing me even harder. I wondered what it would do for Clyde's day if he came back out and found us grinding our brains out on his counter.

"Here you go," I heard him say behind us. He stepped behind the counter and flopped the rabbit suit on the countertop. "I put a little more oil on it and cleaned it up a little. Should be just perfect."

Stan stopped kissing me. I pulled out my wallet and drew out a credit card and so did she. She slapped hers down on the counter like she was racing me.

"We're going dutch this time," she said, and I could tell she meant it.

Okay, okay, okay, I thought. Anything for a little peace.

So we got the costumes and headed out. She suggested going to a nearby Starbucks, and that sounded good to me. She had already told me at lunch she had a commitment that night she had to honor, but she said she had time for coffee. I followed her out of the costume shop. I stayed down low again and kept my back to Jack's as we stepped outside and got into our cars, only hoping I wouldn't experience the sound of gunfire and a sudden, thudding sensation between my shoulder blades. For once, luck seemed to smile on me.

The Starbucks was nearly empty when we got there. We wound up chatting again. Naturally, easily. But I felt the need to talk to her about something else.

"You're sure you don't ever feel in danger at those parties?" I asked.

She studied me for a moment. "No, I really haven't. I've never had any trouble."

"It never hurts to be careful."

She continued to study me. "You really think somebody at the club killed Jessica? Is that what you suspect?"

"I don't know. But I haven't ruled it out."

She seemed to think about that for a moment. "You're being serious, aren't you? You really think there's danger there, don't you?"

I thought about it. A man called Gunner apparently had inside information about the murder that had never been released. And another man I thought of only as Hieronymous had wanted a tape badly enough to threaten force to get it. Right before Jessica's murder.

"I think it's a possibility," I said.

She didn't seem to know what to say.

"Have you ever met up there with a tall guy with horn-rimmed glasses? Probably forty, forty-five, about my height. He was there the other night. Dark hair, kind of gray at the temples. He had on a red beret."

She thought about it. "No, I can't really say I've met anybody like that. But then again, I don't meet many people there. I usually just go to meet a client. Then I leave and go home. Why? Is he the one you're suspicious about?"

"I'm not sure." I didn't think I ought to tell her all

about my visit to Jack, or what Jim Bob had told me about the man called Gunner. I didn't think I should give her all those details. Not yet, at least.

"Is this what you're investigating?" she asked.

I nodded.

"I think you need to be very careful," I said. "I don't think you should take any chances. Make sure you stay with a group. Don't let yourself get isolated. And I'd be very, very careful about meeting somebody you don't know about."

"Well. . . okay . . . I mean, I'm always careful . . . "

"Good. Stay that way."

She let me get the check, and we went outside to the cars. She put her arms around me and hugged me again.

"I really wish I didn't already have this damned commitment tonight," she said. "I *really* wish I didn't."

"I'll call you," I said.

I kissed her and she got in her pickup and I got in the Taurus. I followed her out of the parking lot. She went one way, and I went the other. I got up on the freeway and headed back across town toward my apartment. I could tell Stan thought I was a little bit nuts to be worried about her safety. But I had a feeling. I would have to watch her very closely, I decided.

As I drove I started making a list in my head of other things I needed to do in the next day or so. I needed to see if any progress had been made on the composite sketch of the man called Gunner. I needed to meet with the sketch people myself, to see if I could come up with a picture of Hieronymous. I tried to remember his face as clearly as I could, tried to bring it back into focus. I thought I had a pretty good mental picture. I also had to try to find out more about the two other women who had been murdered, see if I could tie them in with Jessica Nodman in any way. And even though the Austin police hadn't been able to identify the murder weapon, I needed to see what I could come up with there as well. The phone rang as I was thinking, and I picked it up and put it to my ear and said, "Draeger."

"Hi, Walt," I heard Julie say.

I surprised myself and managed to stay in my lane. "Well, hi, Julie . . . "

"Walt, I'm really sorry to bother you, I really am, I hope this isn't a bad time for you, but I need some help with something and I was just wondering . . . "

"Sure," I said immediately, before she could even finish. I didn't feel an iota of hesitation. I would have helped her with anything.

"It's about Bobby," she added. "I need some help Friday night."

The fact that it was about Bobby only made it all the more automatic. "Sure, Julie. Anything."

"Well, one of his friends is having a birthday party, and they're having it at a bowling alley on the other side of town. It's at night, and I really don't trust Mom and Dad to drive when it's dark. Bless their hearts, they're still just sharp as tacks, but neither one of them can see worth a whit at night, and they don't do well at all on the freeways. So I was just wondering if you could possibly drive him there and pick him up. I really don't want to impose . . . "

"Sure, Julie, you're not imposing. It's no problem. I'll be happy to drive him."

"Thanks, Walt," she said.

There was silence for a few moments. I got the idea she wanted to say something more. I figured she probably had a date that night with Sam Wilderthorn, but I didn't want to make her uncomfortable, so I didn't ask her about it. It really wasn't any of my business anyway. Serves you right, Draeger, I thought.

"It . . . it was good to see you again the other night, Walt," she finally said.

That surprised me. I hadn't expected her to say

anything like that.

"It was good to see you too, Julie," I said. "Really good."

There was a pause again.

"I mean . . .we've talked on the phone a few times," she went on, "but that was the first time we've actually seen each other in so long. I mean, it's been months and months and months. . . and it just felt good to see you again. I was surprised by that."

I had slowed down the car without even thinking about it. Other cars were passing me on both sides. I heard a horn behind me. I didn't care at all.

"It didn't surprise me, Julie. I think about you all the time."

I could tell she was considering that. "Do you really, Walt?"

"I really do. All the time."

"Well . . . I think a lot about you too," she said.

There was another pause, even longer this time.

"Oh gee . . . I don't know, Walt . . . I just don't know . . . I'm all confused . . . Sam's nice, but . . . "

I waited. I could feel the drumming of my heart. More cars flew past me.

"I've missed you, Walt," she finally said. "I didn't realize how much."

I felt such a warmth inside, like a little bubble had opened up in my chest.

"God knows I've missed you, Julie. More than I can say."

There was silence again.

"Well, at any rate . . , " she said. I could hear her clear her throat. Then she took a breath. ". . . If you could help with Bobby, that would be great. I'd really appreciate it. He needs to be picked up at six-thirty. The party starts at seven. He'll have the name and the address of the bowling alley. It ends fairly early, about ten." She hesitated for a moment. "It would probably be better to bring him back to my parents' house, if you could do that. I . . . I don't know what time I'll get in. He can spend the night over there with them. That would probably be the best thing. I'll put all his stuff together to take with him when you pick him up."

I could read between the lines, but I still didn't ask for details.

"I'll be there at six-thirty on Friday," I said.

"Thanks, Walt. I do appreciate it."

There was another silence.

"Until next time," she said. The softness in her voice was surprising to me again.

"Till next time, Julie . . . "

9.

I called Joe Henderson after I got going next morning and was pleasantly surprised to learn that a composite sketch of the man called Gunner had already been done. Joe had already received a copy by fax. They were cross checking it in the Austin computer as we spoke. I decided to head down to the Dallas PD to see it for myself. I told Joe I'd keep in touch. Before I left the apartment, I found the magazine with the Dallas Swingers ad and checked for a phone number. There wasn't one, but an e-mail address was listed. I sent off a request for information about the club and gave my cellphone number. Then I drove downtown. I met with a Sergeant Atkins in the ID Division.

"Well, here's your boy," he said, slipping a sketch onto the table in front of me.

I picked it up and studied it. I found myself staring at the face of a man who appeared to be about thirty. He had dark hair, a square, blunt face with heavy features, and a thick bull neck.

"You think this is accurate?" I asked.

"Probably," Atkins answered. "We separated Jim Bob and Orville and had each one do a sketch independently. They both came up with about the same thing. Here, I'll show you."

He spread two more pictures on the table. They resembled each other closely. The final composite was a blending of the two.

"We were able to give Jim Bob a little extra motivation," Atkins added with a chuckle. "It seems Jim Bob likes to go window peeping in the neighborhood. About a year ago, the neighbors finally got fed up with it and set a trap for him. Jim Bob's currently on two years probation for illegal trespass. We were able to impress upon him that it was in his best interest to cooperate. So I think we got a pretty good likeness."

"Have you tried to run a match on this yet?" I said.

"Sure have. Already checked mug shots, ran it through the computer, the whole bit. Didn't come up with anything, though. Faxed it to the FBI too, but haven't heard back from them yet. Sent a copy down to Austin too."

"Let me know if you find anything," I said.

"Will do."

"One more thing," I said. "There's another face I need you to try to draw for me."

So I pulled up as much as I could remember about Hieronymous, and in a surprisingly short time we came up with another composite. I thought it was pretty accurate. I hadn't been able to see how he had worn his hair, so I left the red beret in place and included the horn-rimmed glasses as well. I thought it would be good enough to make an ID.

"Run this too," I said to Atkins, "and fax a copy down to Joe Henderson in Austin along with the other one, if you will. We'll see what we can find. Might not be a bad idea to show this to Jim Bob and Orville while we're at it. See if they know anything about him."

Atkins didn't seem overly thrilled, but he said he'd make sure that it all got done. I got several copies of each picture, then drove to Jack's house. On the way I called the lamp shop. I didn't think Jack would be scared enough to forsake his livelihood, but I wanted to make sure he wasn't at home.

"Jack's Lamp Shop," I heard him say after the second ring.

"Oops, sorry," I said and hung up.

So I parked on the next street over when I got there, just as I had done the first time, put on gloves, and let myself in the front door. It was almost beginning to feel like home. It took me longer than I had expected, though, to find the tape I needed. It turned out to be farther back in time than I had suspected. More than a year, in fact. When I finally found it, I studied it closely. Sure enough, the woman was on all fours and the man was on his knees behind her. Classic doggie style. Not surprisingly, Jack had shot most of the footage from the rear, but at one point he had worked his way around to the side and then to the front. I froze the tape and studied the frame more closely. I studied the man in particular. It was the same guy, sure enough. Gunner. I compared the face in the tape to the composite. It was surprisingly accurate. But the sketch had only hinted at the rest of his appearance. There had been the thick bull neck, but nothing else. Now I remembered what I'd seen before. The tape showed a powerful, heavily muscled man with bulging arms and shoulders, massive, tightly cut pectorals, and a washboard abdomen. The legs were just as developed. He had to be a body builder, I figured, probably somebody who used steroids. People just don't get that big any other way. And that told me he probably went to a gym somewhere, or to a health food store, or maybe even entered competitions. And that was at least a start. I had other places I needed to check.

I also studied the woman, especially the views Jack had shot from the front. On more than one occasion he had captured her looking directly at the camera. She was young and blonde and good-looking. I froze the frame in place again and searched Jack's desk. It didn't take long to find some white writing paper. I took a pen out of my pocket and drew a likeness of her face as well as I could. I thought it wasn't half bad, actually. I had always done pretty well in art class as a kid.

When I was satisfied I had seen enough, I put all the tapes back neatly in the drawer, leaving them just as they had been arranged, then checked the house to make sure I hadn't left a trace of my visit, and left. I drove to a Kinko's and faxed the picture of the girl to Joe Henderson. Then I waited a couple of minutes and called to make sure he had received it. He had.

"You get the picture of Hieronymous too?" I asked.

There was a slight pause. "Who?"

"Sorry. I call him Hieronymous. Just an idea that popped into my head when I saw him at the party the other night. Hieronymous Bosch was an oddball artist who lived in Europe three or four hundred years ago. He painted all kinds of weird things, demons, people who were hideously deformed, pictures of people with flowers growing out of their rear ends, stuff like that. It seemed to fit."

There was another pause. "You got some pretty strange ideas for a cop, Walt."

"Story of my life."

But he had received that picture too. They were running it along with Gunner's. They'd run the girl too. He'd call me if he found anything.

So I headed to a McDonald's for lunch. On the way my cellphone rang. It turned out to be Ray, responding to my e-mail. Ray Stammonds, to be exact, he told me. I asked him if I could meet with him. I wanted some information about the club, I said. I didn't say I was a cop, though. He seemed open and pleasant. Come by his office after lunch, he said. He'd be glad to talk to me then.

So I got a hamburger and killed some time and then showed up at the address he had given me exactly at one. It turned out to be a real estate office. I guess sex club founders have regular jobs just like everybody else. I told the secretary in front that Mr. Stammonds was expecting me, and she showed me right back to his office.

Ray was a man of medium height and weight who looked to be in his early forties or thereabouts, and he wore a very proper business suit and tie. I got the impression of prosperity. He stood up and stepped around his desk and shook my hand.

"You're the one who called about the club," he said.

"Right."

He closed the door to the office and then came back to his desk and sat down behind it. He motioned for me to sit in the chair on the other side.

"Club's perfectly legal, of course," he said with a smile, "but I try to keep it separate from my business life as much as possible. Nothing wrong with a little privacy, after all. Now, what can I do for you?"

I decided to come right to the point and showed him my badge. I also gave him my card.

"I'm investigating the death of Jessica Nodman. I'm sure you remember that. I'm trying to get some information."

I thought he seemed a little surprised, but he covered it quickly. "Well, yes, I remember Jessica, of course. Certainly. We were all deeply, deeply saddened by what happened to her. So tragic. So senseless. It was probably last summer, if I remember correctly."

"Have any ideas about the murder?"

He shook his head. "No, can't say that I do. It was a terrible, terrible surprise to all of us. So tragic. Just tragic. So brutal too. Awful."

That caught my ear. "What did you hear about brutality?"

Ray shrugged. "Oh, you know, just that it was a very gruesome killing. You know, that she was mutilated. Desecrated. That sort of thing. Just horrible. You have to wonder what kind of terrible mind would ever conceive of such a thing."

"The brutality part…did you hear any specifics about that?"

He frowned. "Well, you know, just that her body had been mutilated. The story that went around the club… God, it's horrible, but this is what I heard . . . the story was that her body had actually been opened up and internal organs had been removed. The heart, was what I heard, in particular. Hideous even to think about it, but that was the way the story went."

That settled it, as far as I was concerned. Somebody at the club *did* have inside information.

"Who did you hear that from?" I asked.

He thought about it, then shook his head again. "Nobody in particular that I can recall . . . I mean, it was all over the club . . . I think probably almost everybody heard about it at one time or another. It was common knowledge. Everybody was talking about it."

I pulled out the composite of Gunner and laid it on the desk in front of him. "You know this man?"

I thought a trace of surprise flashed across his face, but it disappeared in an instant. He studied the picture for a moment.

"Sure, that's Gunner. He comes to some of the parties. Gunner's quite an entertainer, to say the least."

"You know anything about him?"

Ray seemed to think about it. "No . . . I can't really say that I do."

"You know his real name?"

He seemed to think about it again. "No, can't say that I do."

"Where he lives? What he does?"

He thought about it, then shook his head. "No, I've never really talked to him. The club is open to the public, after all. We don't require any identification. He just shows up from time to time."

Ray paused and studied me for a moment. "Why do you ask? Do you think he's connected to Jessica's murder in any way? I mean, that's never even been suggested before, to my knowledge. Nobody's ever suggested that the club was connected to her death in any way."

"Have the police talked with you about any of this before?" I asked.

Ray shook his head. Impatiently, I thought. "Not at all. Never. As I said, nobody's ever suggested that the club was involved or related in any way. We never even got a phone call."

I wasn't surprised. I didn't think Joe Henderson and the authorities in Austin had known anything about the Dallas Swingers. I was breaking new ground.

"Which brings me to something else, officer," Ray said, leaning forward and looking at me very directly. A heavy frown creased his forehead. "This is a very clean club, officer. We've never had any trouble of any kind. And I'm a little concerned, frankly, that you seem to be pursuing your investigation along these particular lines. I don't believe there's any evidence at all of a connection between the club and Jessica's murder."

"I hope not," I said.

I put the picture of Hieronymous on his desk also, on top of Gunner's.

"How about him? You ever seen him before?"

Stammonds seemed to be losing his patience. "I couldn't say. Not for certain."

"This one?" I laid the picture of the girl I had seen on the tape with Gunner on top of the others.

"No, I don't believe so," he said tautly.

"Or either of these two?" I laid the pictures of the two other murdered women in front of him.

"No, I'm afraid not." His tone had become even tighter, more clipped. "And now, if you don't mind, Officer Draeger, I'm afraid you'll have to excuse me. I *do* have business to attend to this afternoon, and I'm afraid I've already allowed myself to get behind schedule." He stood up and walked around his desk to the door, opened it and held it open. "Perhaps some other time."

"Perhaps," I said. I didn't think he'd return a handshake, so I didn't offer one. I stepped past him without looking back. I heard the door close behind me.

I drove back to the apartment and went through the pile of swinger magazines I had bought. Most ads gave an e-mail address, just like the ad for the Dallas Swingers. A few gave a phone number. In all, I had more than a dozen listings when I was finished. I sent out e-mails, asking to be contacted and giving my cellphone number. The ones with phone numbers I called, but I didn't get anything except answering machines. I left a message each time, along with my number.

Then I got out the yellow pages and looked under gyms and health clubs. Whoever Gunner was, he worked out, I was certain of that. I thought I probably needed to check adult bookstores and other sexually oriented businesses as well. I probably needed to go looking for a possible match for the murder weapon too, but first things first. Gyms and health clubs. There were a bunch in the Metroplex area. I got a Dallas-Ft.Worth map and marked off the various locations. It was going to take time.

Then I got started. I worked each gym in the same fashion. I went in and strolled around the entire facility first, like somebody considering a membership, all the time scanning for the man I knew as Gunner. I never had any luck. Then, at each place, I asked to speak to the manager on duty. I decided it would be alarming to say I was part of a murder investigation, so I made up a little story. I said I was a private investigator, and a client of mine had hired me to find a long lost, missing relative. There had been a death in the family, and money had been bequeathed. Inheritance was owed. Here, this is his picture. Do you know him? Have you ever seen him before? And I would show them the composite sketch of Gunner. But nobody recognized him.

Along the way, as I went from one gym to the next, I got a few return calls from the clubs I had e-mailed. I used the same story, but with a slight modification. This time there were *two* long lost, missing relatives. Other family members had suggested they might be frequenting adult, sexually oriented clubs. Could I fax a couple of pictures?

See if the faces were familiar? People seemed willing to help. I stopped at another Kinko's and faxed the pictures of Gunner and Hieronymous to about half a dozen different numbers. Call me on my cell to let me know, I said. Then I went back to checking gyms, going from one to another, continuing to search.

I got several return phone calls in the first hour or so, but they were all negative. Nope, haven't seen these guys. I kept coming up dry in one gym after another too. It was frustrating. Then the phone rang again, and finally my luck changed.

"Yeah, this is Carl," a voice said as I answered the phone. "Calling from down in San Antonio. You faxed me these two pictures. These two lucky guys that got some inheritance money coming."

"Right."

"Yeah, this first one here, this is Assman. We've seen him here a number of times."

Gunner. Had to be. But in San Antonio they called him Assman. Sounded like a comic strip character. We've had my old buddy Superman, then there was Batman, then Spiderman. Now here comes Assman. I had a feeling that his adventures would be a little different from the rest. Made me wonder when the movie would be out.

"This son of a bitch is unreal," Carl went on. "I'm tellin' you, I've seen this son of a bitch do it ten times at one party, all in just a few hours."

Ten now? Lordy. I could almost feel my prostate cringing in terror.

"Always withdraws just before he ejaculates too," Carl added, "so he ain't fakin' it. It's for real. He's legit."

Gunner, for sure.

"You know how I can reach him?" I asked. "He's going to be a much richer fellow in the very near future if you can help me find him."

"No, sure don't. Sorry, but I never really met him,

you know what I mean. Don't know his name. Just seen him in action here at the parties."

"Anybody else around there who might know how to reach him?"

"Not that I know of right offhand. But I'll tell you what, we got a party coming up this Friday night. If I see him there, I'll sure tell him to call you. Can he reach you at this same number?"

"I'll be right here," I said. "By the way, what about the other guy? The one with the glasses. You ever seen him down there?"

There was a pause.

"Well, I kind of think so, maybe once or twice. Not real sure about that one, though. Seems to me there's a guy who kind of looks like this, been here maybe a time or two. Kind of keeps to himself, if you know what I mean."

"Got three ladies who're in line to get some of the inheritance too," I added. "Mind if I fax you their pictures too?"

"Send 'em on," Carl said cheerfully.

So I faxed the pictures of the two murdered women Joe Henderson had given me, along with the sketch I had made of the girl I had seen on the tape with Gunner. Carl called me back in just a couple of minutes. I noticed right away that his tone was much more somber.

"Well, I've seen one of these ladies," he said with a sigh, "but your client's not gonna like the news. Sorry to have to tell you this, but the second one of these three pictures you sent me, this lady's not with us anymore. This poor lady, she got murdered last year. Found her body over in Austin. Really good-lookin' lady. A real show-off too. Used to get plumb starkers and dance on the bar at just about every party we had. We've missed her. Sorry to have to tell you she's dead."

I knew exactly which picture he was talking about. Michelle Stanzer, the bank teller, had been from San

Antonio. And now I knew she had been at a sex club just like Jessica Nodman. And so had the men I thought of as Gunner and Hieronymous.

"Yeah, my client will be pretty upset to hear about that, sure enough," I said. "You think she knew these two guys at all?"

"Don't know. Can't say I ever saw them together, but then again, can't say I didn't. It's a pretty big club. I don't try to keep track of who goes with who, you know what I mean."

"I gotcha. Listen, if either of these guys shows up this Friday night, you have them call me, okay?"

"I'll do it," said Carl.

And that was that. It meant Michelle Stanzer had probably been in the very same room with Gunner and Hieronymous, just like Jessica. I was getting ready to call Joe Henderson when the cellphone rang again. This time it was a guy named Mike, calling from Corpus Christi.

"You asked me to call you about these two pictures you faxed me," he said.

"Right." I gave him the bit about the inheritance and the missing relatives again.

"I've seen both these guys," Mike said. "One time. At a party. Probably about nine months ago."

I was surprised by his certainty. "You're sure?"

"Yes."

"What can you tell me?" I asked.

"Don't know who they were. Never saw them before. Never seen them since. They came in together one night."

"Together?"

"Together. Stayed an hour or so and then left."

Together. At the same club, at the same time. So they knew each other. I was puzzled, though. Mike had seen them only once, almost a year ago, and only for a short period of time. But he seemed so certain about it.

"Just curious, how come you remember them so well? I'm just wondering, you know what I mean."

"They left with my ex-wife," he said.

I didn't know what to say to that.

"No big deal, we'd already been divorced for over a year. We stayed in touch a little from time to time, but we were both doing our own thing. So it wasn't like it was some great big emotional deal for me, but I can't say I didn't notice."

"Sure, I can understand that . . . "

"And so their faces, they've kind of stayed with me."

"Sure . . . your ex-wife, did you ever talk with her about it? Did she say anything about them?"

"She went with the body builder guy to a motel room. The tall guy split off somewhere. She said the body builder guy absolutely screwed her brains out. Said she'd never been screwed so many times in one night in all her life. Said he liked to put it in her rear. Said it left her sore as hell for days. She couldn't believe how many times he could do it."

Gunner.

"You think I could talk with her?" I asked. "See if she knows anything about them. See if she knows how to reach either one of them."

There was silence on the line for a moment. "You're out of luck there, pal," Mike said.

I felt a chill at the base of my spine. "Oh? How come?"

I could hear him take a deep breath. "Because she's dead."

"My God . . , " I heard myself say.

There was silence on the line again for several moments.

I steeled myself. "In that case, I need to ask you a couple of questions."

After a moment he said, “Sure. Go ahead.”

“Sounds like a crazy thing to ask, but the first question is, did she ever dance nude at the club?”

He didn’t hesitate. “Oh yeah, all the time. She was a total exhibitionist. She’d take off all her clothes and dance at the drop of a hat.”

I hadn’t faxed him the pictures of the murdered women yet, so he couldn’t give me a positive identification over the phone. That left one last question. I already *knew* the answer, but I had to ask anyway.

“What was her name?”

I heard him take another slow, deep breath. “Charlotte Raymond,” he said.

Bingo . . .

DANCE YOUR HEART OUT

10.

I was tired enough to sleep that night. I thought about calling Joe Henderson with what I had learned, but I elected not to bother him at home after hours. So I called his office first thing next morning, only to find out he had had his appendix removed during the night. He had been a typical cop about it. Hadn't said a thing to anybody all day, even though he had been hurting the whole time. But it finally got bad enough during the night so that even a cop had to do something about it, so Sue drove him to the ER at St. David's, and the next stop was surgery. His appendix had ruptured, it turned out. He was going to need to be in the hospital for several days for intravenous antibiotics. Typical cop story. I wound up calling his house and leaving a message on the answering machine, asking Sue to give me a call to let me know how he was doing. Give him my regards and all that.

So the next step was to keep checking health clubs. There were still a lot left. It was every bit as frustrating as it had been the first time. Nobody recognized Gunner's picture. If they were telling me the truth, that is, and I thought they were. Everybody seemed open and honest. I left my name and phone number wherever I went. Call me if you see him.

At one point I got a call from Stan. She still sounded excited about the party. She just couldn't wait. But she was going to have to go out of town unexpectedly today and tomorrow because of a case she was working on, so we wouldn't be able to get together again until the party Saturday night. She sounded disappointed when she said that. I could tell by the tone of her voice she wanted to say more, but she said she was at the office and couldn't talk. She hesitated but said she had to run. So we'd meet up Saturday night at her place.

I kept on going with the search. Gym to gym. At

one point I got a call from Sue Henderson too. She said Joe was doing as well as could be expected. The doctors said they expected him to make a full recovery, but he'd need to stay there several more days because he had waited so long and allowed the appendix to burst. Typical cop story. I told her I'd talk with Joe when he got well enough. So that was that.

Still I kept going, one gym after another. I called Julie at work about three, but they said she had stepped out, so I left her a message. Tell her I haven't forgotten about Bobby. Tell her I'll be there tonight at six-thirty.

Finally it was time to head back to the apartment. It was after five by the time I got there. I flopped on the sofa, tired from the frustration of it all as much as the actual process of doing the checking. I sat there and went back through it all in my mind. I had really thought I might find a connection. Gunner worked out. Somewhere. He had to. He couldn't have bulked up like that if he didn't. I just hadn't found out where. It occurred to me he could always have exercise equipment at home, but it's been my experience that the really serious guys work out at gyms. The home stuff is for the dabblers. Of course, the possibility also existed that he didn't even live in the DFW area. He came to parties thrown by the Dallas Swingers, but that didn't prove he lived in Dallas. The bodies had been found in Austin, after all. I would need to talk to Joe Henderson when he got better, to see if they had discovered anything down there. Patience, I told myself. All things come to those who wait.

I pulled out my wallet, took out the tracing I had made of the murder weapon and spread it out on the couch. As I had gone through the gyms looking for Gunner, I had also looked at equipment, with an eye to the drawing in mind. I hadn't seen anything that seemed to match up with it, though. Whatever it was, it appeared to have one fairly smooth side and another side with prongs or serrations of some sort. Looking at the drawing, there appeared to be three points along the jagged side where the contour of the skull had been battered in. The top two seemed fairly sharp. The lowest one seemed blunter. Probably a hammer of some sort, like Joe Henderson had said. But I still couldn't match it up. I decided I'd have to check sporting good stores too. God only knows how long that would take. I heard the doorbell ring, and I folded up the paper and put it back in my wallet, then walked to the door. It was a girl named Sandy, who lived in one of the adjoining apartments.

"Hi, Walt," she said. "Sorry to bother you, but do you have a hammer I could use by any chance?"

Sandy was about thirty, I figured. I had met her the first day I moved in. People had seen me carrying in boxes, and a couple of them had even pitched in and helped. Sandy had been there too. I had been invited to a little get-together that evening by the pool. Nobody went swimming at this time of the year, but the weather had been warm and pleasant, and we had all enjoyed a relaxing time. And since I was the new kid on the block, I had naturally been asked a lot of questions. Where I came from. What sort of work I did. And of course, whether or not I was married. And I had been dumb enough to say I was going through a separation and was currently unattached, and ever since then, Sandy had been coming by to borrow things. Some salt. Some sugar. The newspaper. The TV Guide. Now a hammer.

"I'm really sorry to bother you, Walt," she said. "I really am. But I need to hang a picture and I can't find my hammer anywhere. I thought I had one somewhere, but it must be lost. I was just wondering if you had one."

"Yeah, I think so, Sandy," I said. I had a little toolbox I had brought with me. You never know when you're going to need something like that. I felt pretty sure Sandy had been there when I had carried it in. So I went and fetched a hammer. “There you go,” I said as I handed it to her.

“Thanks, Walt.” She started to turn away but didn’t. “You, uh . . . you doing anything tonight? I was just wondering. I was thinking about maybe fixing some steaks. There’s plenty for two.”

Bless her heart, but Sandy has problems. She really wasn’t attractive to me. Sorry, but that’s how I felt. And I could tell she was lonely. I didn’t think guys asked her out much. So I’d walked a tightrope with her. I didn’t want to hurt her feelings, but I didn’t want to encourage her either. I was glad I could give her a truthful answer.

“Can’t tonight, Sandy. I’m taking my kid to a bowling party. Won’t be back until pretty late. Sorry.”

“Well, maybe next time . . .”

“Sure. Maybe next time.”

“Bye, bye . . .”

“Bye, bye, Sandy. See you later. Have a good evening.”

So she left and headed back down the balcony towards her apartment. I shut the door, had a quick beer, and left to pick up Bobby.

I pulled up in front of the house right on time. Then I sat in the car and waited for a few moments. I had been wondering what would happen the next time I saw Julie. I expected I’d find out. I took a deep breath, then got out of the car and walked to the front door.

But it was Bobby who answered the doorbell. He had an overnight bag slung over his shoulder, and he was set to go. I looked past him into the living room, but it was empty.

“Mom’s in the shower,” he said. “She’s running late. She said to tell you she’s sorry she missed you. She said to tell you thanks again too.”

“Well . . . okay . . .” I couldn’t see the dog either. “Where’s Brutus?”

DANCE YOUR HEART OUT

"Brutus is in big trouble, Dad," Bobby said as he closed the door and we walked to the car. "Mom's really, really mad at him. I mean, she's furious. He hit Mr. Thompson's walk again."

"Oops."

"Twice," Bobby noted.

"Double oops."

"Yeah, Mom has him locked up in the back yard. She says he may have to stay out there forever. She says she doesn't know any other way to keep him from messing up the neighborhood."

"We could always try a cork," I suggested.

Bobby made a face. "Yuck, Dad, that's gross. That's sick."

"Just trying to consider all the possibilities."

"Yuck."

So we got in the car and drove to the bowling alley. The party tonight was for one of his soccer team members, I learned. It was a club team, not a school team, so it drew from all over the city. That was the reason the party was on the other side of town. Bobby couldn't talk about anything except soccer. I listened the whole way. I enjoyed seeing his enthusiasm. I could feel it rubbing off on me too.

When we got there, Bobby left his overnight bag with me and ran off to join his teammates, who were gathered around several lanes. The party was just getting started. A beer sounded mighty good to me, but I thought that would set a bad example, so I got a Sprite and sat in the back of the viewing area. Bobby hadn't ever bowled before, and his first few efforts were gutter balls. Most of the other kids were beginners too, so they weren't exactly knocking down pins left and right. It felt good to watch, though. I had hardly seen my kid at all for months.

At one point I happened to notice a very attractive blonde lady looking over at me. I noticed several times, in fact. It wasn't real subtle. She was apparently one of the mothers, because she seemed to be helping with the party. She really wasn't bad at all. Very pretty and nicely constructed. Short blonde hair, nice outfit, good figure. It occurred to me I could probably go over and strike up a conversation. It was an appealing idea, frankly, but I shut it off. Don't, I told myself. Just cool it, Walt. You really don't need to have any more attractive women in your life. You'd be better off to have leprosy instead. So I made certain I didn't look over at her at all. Then, to make doubly sure, I got up and moved down closer to the lanes, so that my back was actually toward her. That was better, I decided. I'm not proud of it, but the plain truth is, I don't do well with temptation.

The first game finally ended, and Bobby's team got finished ahead of the team they were to swap lanes with, so he came over and sat with me. We talked a little about bowling. Then he got started on soccer again. He told me about the different players on the team and pointed them out to me. He talked about their strengths and weaknesses as players, and also about what they were like as people. The ones he especially liked. The ones he didn't like so much. That's the way it always is on a team, I said. And so on. I enjoyed just sitting with him and listening to him. It felt so right.

Then the other team got finished, and they swapped lanes and started a new game. I got up and went to get another Sprite, then came and sat at a table behind the new lane. Bobby was still rolling a lot of gutter balls, and I found myself leaning to this side or that or pushing with a foot or an arm, trying to give it the old body English and keep the ball on track. I thought he was beginning to get the hang of it a little too.

"Is this Walt?" I heard somebody say behind me.

I turned in my chair and found myself looking up at the very attractive blonde lady I had noticed earlier.

"Yes, I'm Walt," I said.

"Hi, I'm Helen Baxter," she said, smiling and extending a hand. "I'm Johnny Baxter's mother. He and Bobby are on the team together. I thought you must be his dad when I saw him over here talking to you."

"Yeah, I'm Bobby's dad."

She sat down at the table across from me. Smiled at me again. "Well, I've certainly heard Bobby talk a lot about you. You're just about his favorite topic."

"I certainly hope he hasn't told the truth."

She smiled. "He's your biggest fan. He thinks you're wonderful."

"Good, he lied, thank God."

She laughed. Goodness, but she *was* a looker. Maintained very good eye contact too. Smiled at me again. I was beginning to have visceral reactions.

"I've met Julie before," she said, still looking directly at me. The tone of her voice said as much as the words. I didn't think she was just telling me she knew Julie. I thought she was telling me she knew Julie and I were separated.

"Well, that's nice," I said. I didn't know what else to say, and I wasn't going to allow myself to respond to the hidden message. Just cool it, Walt, I told myself again.

"I'm going through a divorce too," she said. She kept her eyes fixed on mine as she said that.

I thought about everything else going on in my life, and I broke out in a cold sweat, just sitting there. My heart started pounding and my chest got tight. I suddenly felt like I couldn't even breathe. I felt a little dizzy too.

"Excuse me for a sec, I'll be right back," I said.

I got up and walked to the men's room. I was still sweating and my heart was pounding like crazy. I felt unsteady on my feet. My head was spinning. I was afraid I wouldn't make it. But finally I pushed through the door, like a runner finally crossing the finish line, and stood there with my head against the wall. I took a few deep breaths.

It seemed that my chest was opening up now. Maybe my heart was slowing down too. I was still sweating, though. Just relax, I told myself. Relax. Calm down. You're doing fine. You're just having an anxiety attack, you stupid ass.

Finally it seemed that I was better. I was breathing normally again and my heart had slowed down. Even the sweating had stopped. My hands were steady. I stood there and looked at myself in the mirror. Be careful, Walt, I told myself. Please be careful.

Standing there, I found myself thinking back to a therapist Julie and I had gone to before we actually separated. The therapist had concluded I had a problem with sex. It was all really quite clear, she said. She wasn't accusatory or condemnatory about it, just clinical and diagnostic. She said I suffered from a "sexual addiction," which meant I couldn't control my sexual impulses, just like substance abusers can't refrain from the substance of their choice. I didn't try to argue with her. God knows it sounded true enough to me. I even hoped she could help me with it. But then Julie missed a session because of a flat tire, and so the therapist - who actually wasn't all that bad - said we would use that session to focus on me. Okay with me, I said. So she asked me a lot of questions about myself, and I answered as honestly as I could. And then I asked a few questions about her. And we got to talking. And before I knew it, one thing led to another, and we wound up on her couch, doing the nasty itself and just about everything else imaginable, right there under the wall with all her diplomas and certificates. And that turned out to be the last session. Julie filed for divorce and we never went back. And my little problem didn't get solved.

Stay cool, Walt, I told myself again. Just stay cool. You can do it. I took one last deep breath and walked out of the men's room. As I did I looked at my watch and realized I had been there for at least fifteen minutes. Fortunately, Helen Baxter had apparently gotten tired of waiting and had moved. I couldn't see her anywhere, in fact. Thank God for small favors.

So I sat in a different place and started watching Bobby and his buddies again. Bobby was actually getting better, I thought. He was learning to approach the lane better, swing the ball more freely. It didn't always go in the gutter now. And then he actually got a spare! I pumped my fist and said, "Yes!" I wanted to jump up and down and yell, but I didn't want to look like some sort of fanatical Little League parent, so I stayed in the chair and controlled myself. I did pump my fist again, though. I could tell he felt good about it too. I saw him look over at me, checking to see if I had noticed. I gave him a thumbs up and he laughed. It did feel good to be there watching him.

"You disappeared on me," I heard a voice say behind me.

I knew who it was. I didn't want to turn around, but I didn't want to be rude either. So I looked back over my shoulder at Helen Baxter.

"Yeah, that's the way it is with us serpents," I said. "We'll slither away on you if you don't watch us real close. Always feels real good to get back under my rock."

She laughed and sat down. "That was a nice spare Bobby made, don't you think?"

"How about that."

"He tells me you were quite an athlete. All-District and everything."

She was maintaining eye contact again. I could feel my heart starting to pound again. My chest started to feel tight.

"Long time ago," I said.

"So . . . how do you like Dallas?" she asked. "Are you getting settled in? Finding your way around?"

"Sort of," I managed. "It's a mighty big place. Haven't really learned the city yet."

She looked directly at me. "You ought to call me some time if you ever need anything. I'd always be glad to help."

That did it. I could feel the sweat starting to break out on my forehead again. My heart was hammering even harder than before. My chest got tight as a drum. The room was spinning again.

"Excuse me, I'll be back in just a second," I said. I managed to stand up but didn't feel all that steady.

"Are you all right?" she asked, studying me with a concerned expression on her face.

I didn't even know if I could answer, but I thought I *had* to say something. "Diarrhea," I finally managed to croak. "Bad diarrhea. Very bad. All day long. Horrible. Now go little boy's room. Back soon."

Somehow I made it to the men's room again, the image of Helen Baxter's horrified expression still lingering in my mind. It took at least as long to cool down as it had the first time. I could finally understand why people with panic attacks agree to pay psychiatrists such enormous fees. That might be my next stop, I thought, just before they slam me in the asylum. This really wasn't fair. This was grossly unjust, like yanking some poor old alkie out of rehab and locking him in a bar.

I finally got myself back in one piece and went back out to the party. I sat in yet another location, and Helen Baxter didn't come by again. I think the bit about the diarrhea had finally done it. I did notice her looking over at me once, seeming a little puzzled. I don't think she was used to being avoided.

Finally it all ended, and they did the birthday party bit. Everybody had a great time. Then Bobby and I left and went to an IHOP and got pancakes. Bobby was still talking about soccer.

"Do you know much about soccer, Dad?" he asked.

"No, not much."

The truth is, soccer bores me. I mean, guys run up and down the field all day long and somebody finally scores one single goal. I think it's dull. But I couldn't tell Bobby that. "Never really played it myself. But I think it's supposed to be the most popular sport in the world."

"We got a game coming up on Tuesday," he said. He hesitated. "You doing anything then, Dad?"

"I don't think so. I'll bet I can be there."

He grinned. "Good."

We talked a little more about soccer, then about school. This year was definitely better than the last one had been. And so on. Finally I had to ask about something else.

"So how do you like Sam?" I asked.

Bobby frowned. "I guess he's okay . . . I mean, he tries to be friendly and everything . . . I don't know. . . I wish Mom wouldn't go out with him."

Me too, I thought. But I didn't say anything.

"Brutus hates him," Bobby added. "I mean, Brutus won't even let him in the house. It's been that way since the very first time he came over. Brutus growls at him and snarls back his lips and everything. Mom's scared he'll bite Sam. She has to put him in the back yard before Sam even gets there."

"You're kidding." How puzzling, I thought. I had always believed that Brutus liked everybody.

"I'm really not, Dad. Brutus hates him."

I wondered what was going on in that dull doggie brain. Did Sam have some sort of funny smell? Some sort of weird body odor? But then again, I didn't think Brutus had ever met a smell he didn't like, so that probably wasn't the explanation. I wondered if there was some primitive territorial instinct at work. Something that made him react to the presence of another male who wasn't an established member of the pack. Or was it something else? I really didn't know. But it was surprising. I had never before seen anything in him except the basic Brutus - dumb and klutzy and happy. It had never occurred to that me there might be anything more to him. It made me scratch my head.

I found Bobby watching me. "I think Mom really misses you, Dad," he said. "She wouldn't ever say that, but I can tell."

It took me a moment to respond. "I've missed both you guys. More than I could say."

Bobby nodded his head but didn't say anything. Shortly afterward we finished up and left, and I drove him to his grandparents' house. He popped open the car door, then leaned over and hugged me tightly around the neck.

"Thanks, Dad. I had a great time."

"I did too, Bobby," I said, hugging him back just as tight.

Then he was gone. I watched him head up the walk to the house and waited until the front door opened. He turned back and waved before he stepped inside. Then the door closed, and I drove back to the apartment . . .

11.

I got up Saturday and started the search all over again. I had pretty much finished up with gyms and health food stores, so I started hitting adult book establishments. But the hunt proved just as fruitless. Nobody recognized Gunner and Hieronymous. Back to square one.

I finished up by early afternoon, then hit a couple of sporting goods places. I focused primarily on stores with workout equipment. I talked with a few sales people, showed them the tracing of the murder weapon, but I came up dry again. Nobody could place it.

By then it was almost evening, time to head to Stan's place. I swung by my apartment and cleaned up a little, then went back out to the Taurus. I hauled the bunny suit out of the trunk, bundling it up in my arms, and flopped it down on the front seat. Wrestling it around that way felt like trying to mate with a tarpaulin. I still couldn't believe I was actually going to wear the damned thing.

Then I drove to Stan's apartment. I got the bunny suit out of the front seat and draped it over my shoulder and went to the door. Stan answered the doorbell quickly. She was already in the kitten costume, and she was obviously even more excited than she had been the last time we talked. She gave me a big hug and a very warm kiss, which was marred only slightly by the fake whiskers she had glued on her lip and the black rubber ball stuck on her nose.

"Isn't it just great!" she exclaimed. "I just *love* costume parties. Isn't it neat?"

She was having so much fun I couldn't bring myself to rain on the parade.

"Sure . . ," I managed to say.

She hugged me again, very hard, and pressed against me.

"I almost wish I hadn't gotten into my costume yet," she said when she finally pulled back.

DANCE YOUR HEART OUT

But the die was cast, so it was finally time to get into the bunny suit. Stan had to help me, but I finally managed to wrestle myself all the way into it, and she zipped up the back. The zipper stuck for a moment at the level of my shoulders, but she gave it a tug and it freed up. So there I was. I stood and looked at myself in the mirror. It was horrifying. But I had already agreed. There were a couple of features about the suit I hadn't noticed at Clyde's. For one thing, there was a zippered pouch in front, way down low. I was plenty glad to have it. I could at least carry something now. I put in my gun, my wallet, my badge, my cellphone, and my keys. I didn't feel quite so helpless. I couldn't work the zipper, of course, so Stan had to help me. It also had a zipper down along the crotch area, creating a kind of cloacal opening in case there was ever a need to go potty. Stan just had to try that zipper too. She worked it back and forth. That got her all tickled, and she started to giggle. She stood back and took a look at me. Then she had to put her hand over her mouth. She couldn't keep from snickering.

"Isn't this neat?" she said. "I just *love* costume parties."

"Neat . . ," I managed.

"Comfy?" she asked, looking me up and down.

"Like I was back in the womb."

She snickered again at that. Then she tried without a whole lot of success to put on a more serious face and said, "You sure you're willing to do this?"

I thought about trying one last time to get out of it, but she had that look on her face again - all the eagerness, all the excitement - so I ate my tongue and wound up saying, " I'm just so happy I'm about to puddle."

She laughed again. Then she tried to kiss me. That didn't turn out to be such a great idea. She wound up getting pink fuzz in her mouth. She giggled again as she pulled it off the end of her tongue with her fingertips.

DANCE YOUR HEART OUT

Then we were ready to leave. We decided to go in Stan's little pickup. I had decided to bring my clothes along in a bag in case I got a chance to change, and I tossed the bag on the floor in front. Then I banged my head pretty good trying to slide into the shotgun seat. Stan just had to giggle again at that. I wasn't sure I could even pull the door shut with my paw, but I managed to get it done, and Stan started the car. As she did, I noticed she had a rabbit's foot hanging on her keychain. I told myself not to take that personally. Then we were off. She let out an actual whoop, she was so excited. She was bouncing up and down on the seat like a little kid. I only hoped we didn't crash. This was not the way I wanted to die.

We drove to this private night club off Walnut Hill Avenue. A valet took the car and gave us a claim check. Stan didn't have any pockets, so she opened the zipper of my pouch and dropped the ticket down inside, then zipped it back up. That got her giggling again. Then we headed inside. Walking was just as awkward as I had figured it would be. It was hot too, unseasonably warm, and the temperature was starting to get to me. I could already feel perspiration running down my forehead.

We walked in and looked around. A sizeable crowd was already present. There were all kinds of costumes. I even spotted Superman and Captain Hook. There wasn't a Tarzan, though. Some of the outfits were pretty revealing. There were several women in costumes that revealed their breasts. One lady was wearing some sort of tight fitting outfit that I thought might be a mermaid costume, and the back had been cut away, exposing her all the way down below her bottom. I had never before wanted a suit with the rear cut away, but right then I would have gladly showed everything I had for a little fresh air.

Stan just had to stop and talk to everybody, naturally, even though we didn't really know any of the people. We finally wound up at the bar. Stan got a rum and Coke; I got a Budweiser. It was hard to drink, though. The mouth of the bunny face was stuck open in this big, stupid, idiotic smile, and it was hard to fit a can of beer through the opening. I had to pour it in, and a lot of it slopped on my face. Then some splashed down my nose and made me sputter. I almost didn't care. I would have taken it by suppository at that point. Finally I managed to get a whole can down. I stayed there and ordered another, using tokens Stan had left with the bartender, while she went exploring. I stared around glumly, trying to pour down the second brew. One couple caught my eye. They were both just enormous. They must have weighed four hundred pounds each. He was dressed as a clown, which I thought was not all that original, and she was dressed as a witch. God knows what kind of atomic broomstick it would take to get *her* off the ground. And they were here at a *sex* club party? Sex? It seemed almost unimaginable. I wondered if they had ever been captured on seismograph. Before they busted the machine, that is. I made a mental note to study up on the mating habits of tectonic plates.

There was another lady who caught my eye. She was dressed as an Indian Princess, wearing a tiny loincloth that didn't cover everything all that well, and an itsy bitsy halter top too, which also left very little to the imagination. Her hair was platinum blonde, which probably put her in a minority among Indian Princesses, I thought, and she had pulled it back tightly into a ponytail. Looking at her, I thought there was something familiar about her. It took me a moment to realize who she was. Then it clicked. This was the blonde girl who had been dancing naked on the table at the party. She had left with Hieronymous that night. I had learned some things since then, and I weighed the idea of talking to her. I thought she ought to be warned. I was about to go over to her when a group came by that she seemed to be a part of, and they headed off together. I decided to keep my eyes open for her again.

Stan was still off exploring. I'd catch sight of her from time to time, over here, over there, talking with this group, now this one, fluttering hither and yon like a turbocharged butterfly. She was having the time of her life, I could tell.

I finally got a third beer poured down. If anything, I was even hotter than before. So I made my way to the entrance, still holding up the pant legs to keep from tripping over them and still picking up my knees and flopping down the bunny feet, and stepped out onto the porch.

It was raining now. There was some wind too. Blessed relief. I pulled open the big, stupid, grinning mouth of the bunny suit as much as I could to let the breeze flow in, and it felt good on my face.

Then, as I was just standing there, a silver Buick drove up and Hieronymous got out and handed his keys to the valet, just as neat as you please. He was wearing the same red beret and the same horn-rimmed glasses he had been wearing the first time. I could have been knocked over by the proverbial feather. The car's license plate was right there on display, as big as life. I memorized it quickly, saying it back to myself as he walked inside.

I know the people in the Traffic Division down in Houston, so all I had to do was call on my cellphone, and they should be able to tell me who the car was registered to. But how to get the cellphone out of the pouch? I tried to grab the zipper with the bunny paws, but they were too big and stiff. One of the valets was standing just a few feet away. Distasteful thought, having to ask for this kind of help, but it seemed to be the best bet. I stepped up beside him and tapped him on the shoulder with my paw.

"Excuse me, but could I get you to help me with something?" I asked.

He turned back towards me. "Sure, buddy, what's happening?"

There was no other way to say it. "Could you help me with this zipper? I can't work it with my paws, and I really need to make a call with my cellphone." I motioned down towards the pouch. I pulled it up a little bit, so it didn't hang down quite so low. It wasn't exactly the same as asking him to go digging in my underwear, but the image did come to mind. I could see him hesitate, an expression of uncertainty on his face. But I was a guest at the party, after all.

"Well…sure, buddy… anything you need…"

He took hold of the zipper, going somewhat hesitantly, obviously testing new water here, breaking a little new ground, and pulled on it daintily. Finally he managed to get it open for me.

"Thanks, I appreciate it," I said.

"No problem, buddy." He turned away, looking relieved.

"Uh, one more thing," I said. "Sorry, but I can't grab the phone with my paw. Could you give me a hand again?"

He turned back toward me, looking even more reluctant than before. He eyed the pouch dubiously, like this hadn't been included in his job description.

"Sorry . . . it's an important call," I said, "and I don't know where my date went."

He still looked hesitant. "Well . . . sure, buddy . . . whatever you need. . ." He hesitated one last time, then put his hand down into the pouch. I held the suit out from my body as much as I could, but I could tell it still gave him the willies. Me too. Having somebody feeling around in my pouch like that. For one mad moment I thought about asking him if he had any plans for after the party, just to see how badly I could freak him out, but I decided to hold off. He *did* have his hand in my pouch, after all. Thank God we were both consenting adults. He finally came up with the phone and pulled it out and handed it to me.

"There you go, buddy," he said.

I knew I couldn't dial. "Got a pen or a pencil so I can punch in the number?"

"Sure . . . "

He handed me a pen, and I put it between the big, stupid, grinning bunny lips and stuck it in my teeth and managed to hit the numbers I needed. I couldn't really hold the phone, so I laid it flat on my paw, then bent my head over so that my ear was on top of it. I only hoped I could hear well enough. The phone rang a couple of times before it was answered.

"Traffic," said a female voice.

I had gotten lucky. I recognized the voice.

"Debbie, this is Walt Draeger. How're you doing tonight?"

"Great, Walt, how about you?"

"Fine, fine." Then I told her what I needed, that I wanted her to run a license for me. I gave her the number. She told me to wait for a moment, so I stood there on the porch, the phone still held flat in my paw, my head bent down to it.

"That's a rental car, Walt," she said after just a minute or two. "It's registered to the Hertz office at Love Field. There's no individual owner."

"Thanks, Debbie, I owe you one."

"Any time, Walt."

So I wouldn't be able to get the actual identity of Hieronymous from her . . . but I might be able to get it from Hertz. And that meant I might be able to track him. The fact that he was in a rental car made me suspect he came from out of town.

Then I headed back inside. I got another beer and stood by the bar, looking for Stan. I finally spotted her. There was a group that looked like they were doing charades or something, and she was right in the middle of it. Naturally. At one point, she looked over at me and waved. She looked so excited. I flopped a paw back in return. Some time later they did a line dance, and she came over and grabbed me so we could join in. We just had to, she said. Had to. She seemed to be getting a little tipsy, but I decided not to object. I only hoped I wouldn't slay myself trying to move around in the suit like that. Stan was jumping up and down like an excited kid again. So I did the line dance with her, still holding up the pants of the bunny suit, still picking my knees up high and flopping down the bunny feet, and it nearly killed me. I was sweating like a pig by the time we finished.

Then we had to go visiting again, going around the room, talking to other couples, checking out costumes. I still hadn't seen anybody who looked like Gunner. Nobody who had that kind of musculature. I kept looking, though.

I made certain to keep an eye on Hieronymous too. Mostly he kept by himself. Then I noticed him with the Indian Princess, the blonde girl who had danced naked on the table at the party, and I felt my heart speed up. She had left that first party with Hieronymous, and now she was with him again. A good-looking blonde. The thudding of my heart quickened even more. I considered again going up to her if I got a chance, giving her some sort of warning.

After awhile I broke off and got another beer from the bar, then went looking for Stan again. And when I finally spotted her, the hammering of my heart started back up again, even harder this time. She was standing across the way, talking with a group of people. And right beside her stood Hieronymous and the blonde girl in the Indian Princess outfit. I watched, a knot in my gut, as she talked with Hieronymous. Stan, a good looking blonde - just like the ones who had been killed - standing there talking to the man who had been in clubs with Jessica Nodman and Michelle Stanzer and Charlotte Raymond. I could barely draw a breath.

It seemed like an eternity. Then Hieronymous and

the Indian Princess split off, and Stan was left standing there with only a couple of others.

I made my way over toward her hurriedly, moving more rapidly than usual in the rabbit suit. She turned back toward me as I approached and waved.

"Walt, you've been missing the greatest time!" she exclaimed as I stepped up to her.

"Stan . . . what are you doing . . . who were you talking to?" The words came out sounding strained and pressured. I could see a trace of puzzlement on her features, like she had detected the unusual tone and didn't know what to make of it. "Stan, who were you talking to? The tall guy with the red beret and the glasses. Who was he?"

She studied me for a moment, then shrugged helplessly. "I don't know. . . just somebody here at the party."

"What happened? Did he come up to you?"

"Well… I don't know. . . I don't really remember." She seemed to think about it. "I mean, he was just here in the group. *They* were just here."

"Who is he? Have you ever met him before?"

I could see the confusion reappear on her face. She shrugged again.

"I don't know . . .he was just somebody here at the party…"

I put my hands on her shoulders and looked hard into her eyes. She seemed perplexed again.

"Stan, that's the guy. He's the one I asked you about at Starbucks the other day. Remember? He's the one I'm trying to find. He's the one I'm worried about."

She studied me closely again, her features still reflecting uncertainty. "Really. . . I . . . I didn't know . . ."

"He's the one, Stan. You've got to be careful."

She didn't seem to know what to say.

"What did he talk about? Did he ask anything about you? I need to know."

She thought about it, then shrugged again. "We were all . . . just talking . . ."

"Did he try to find out anything about you?"

"Well . . . no . . ."

She was still studying me closely. The others who had been standing around had drifted off, and we were alone together. I was conflicted, but I felt she needed to understand where I was coming from. So I told her some of what I had learned. The man I still knew only as Hieronymous had been at parties with two other women who were now dead, in addition to having been at Dallas Swinger parties with Jessica Nodman. And I thought there were connections. I told her about Gunner too. Not all the details about either of them. Just a sketchy glimpse. I felt I owed it to her at that point.

"All three women were well-built blondes, Stan. That's who they like. You may think all this is crazy and that I'm over the edge, but you're their type exactly. That's why it scared the hell out of me to see you talking to him. That's where I'm coming from."

She had watched me closely the entire time.

"Wow . . ," she finally said. "So you think . . ."

"Exactly." I nodded my head for emphasis. I could feel the bunny ears swaying as I did. I was looking directly at her again. "I don't want anything to happen to you, Stan. I've got to make sure it doesn't."

I could see the softness return to her eyes as I said that. "Well, thanks, Walt . . . I appreciate that . . . I really do . . ."

So that was that. We talked a little more, then worked our way back into the party scene. We chatted with a couple here, a couple there. Did another line dance. It nearly killed me again, just like the first time. Cats may have nine lives, but I didn't know the number for rabbits. Then Stan had another rum and Coke. I got another beer, but I only sipped at it, because my bladder felt ready to explode by this point, and I didn't think I could get the zipper open to relieve myself. So we kept making the rounds. The atmosphere had changed, though. Stan didn't seem as excited, not nearly as energized. A pall had been cast.

I kept my eye on Hieronymous and the Indian Princess. Stan seemed to understand what I was doing. She let me guide her here and there as I needed to, making sure Hieronymous and the girl always stayed in sight.

"I have to try to follow him when he leaves," I told her at one point.

She looked up at me, but didn't object.

"Sorry," I added.

She seemed to accept it.

I finally saw Hieronymous and the Indian Princess head for the door. Zero hour. Options closed.

"Come on, Stan. We gotta go. I have to try to follow him."

She didn't protest.

I saw Hieronymous and the girl step through the exit onto the porch. We headed over to the door and stepped through it behind them. Several other couples were also leaving, even though it wasn't all that late, and there was a line for valet service. Hieronymous and the blonde had fallen in at the back. She was wearing a raincoat now, which completely covered the Indian Princess costume, along with high heels. I didn't know how smoothly car delivery would proceed, and I didn't want to risk losing sight of them. I didn't want to stand next to him in line yet either. Not like this.

"Let's get the keys and go to the car," I said to Stan.

I hadn't closed the zipper on the pouch, and I held it open for her as she fished around inside for the claim check. She wasn't giggling this time.

We showed the claim check to one of the valets, and he gave us the keys and told us where the car was parked. It was along one side of the building, he said, and pointed in the general direction. I took another look at Hieronymous and the girl. They were still in line. I thought we had time. So I took Stan by the arm and we set out in the direction the valet had pointed. I had been concerned she might be a little on the tipsy side from the rum and Coke, but she seemed to be walking steadily on her feet.

"You doing okay?" I asked.

"Sure. I'm fine."

She didn't sound thrilled, but she was really being a trooper, I had to admit. I traipsed alongside her in the rabbit suit, holding up the pants and flopping down the feet to keep from tripping. Her pickup was so small, though, that it took us a minute or two to find it. I looked back over my shoulder a couple of times as we searched for it. The porch was still in sight. Hieronymous and the girl were still standing there, still waiting. Finally we found her truck. Stan opened the driver's door, climbed inside, and popped open the passenger door. I took one last look at the porch. Hieronymous and the girl were next in line. I slipped into the passenger seat, bumping my head again, just like the first time. No giggle from Stan, though.

"Go ahead and start it," I said. "We need to be ready."

She twisted the key, and the engine turned over easily. I looked through the back window of the cab at the porch. I had hoped there might be time for Stan to help me get out of the suit, but it wasn't going to work out that way. As I watched, the valet delivered the silver Buick, and I saw Hieronymous and the girl get into the front seat. Then they started to pull away.

"Now," I said.

Stan put the truck in reverse and backed out of the parking space, then swung around so we could follow. She really was being a trooper, I thought again. She'd been having such as a great time too. I was impressed.

"Stay a couple of cars back if you can," I said. "Close enough to see them, not close enough to be obvious."

"Got it," she said.

She seemed to be driving well enough as we swung out of the parking lot and followed the Buick down Preston Street. A one car tail is always hard, but she was doing it well. She kept at least one car between us and the Buick, but we were never in danger of being out of sight.

When the Buick got to Walnut Hill, Hieronymous turned to the right and we followed after them. Walnut Hill was a much busier street. I looked at the clock on the dash. Nine-thirty. Still early enough on a Saturday night so that there was plenty of traffic. Stan was continuing to do a good job of staying close enough, though, keeping just a couple of cars back the whole way. We came to a light and stopped, still close enough to see.

"I need to get out of this suit," I said. "Can you grab the zipper?" I turned my back to her as well as I could in the tiny cab, and she reached over for the zipper and started to pull it down. It slid down a couple of inches, but then I felt a tug at the level of my upper back, right between my shoulder blades.

"What?" I asked.

I felt another tug, then another.

"God, it's stuck," she said.

"Crap!"

She tried again to pull down, yanking even harder, but it wasn't budging. Stuck again, exactly where it had stuck at Clyde's.

"Crap," I said again.

"I'm trying."

"I know that. I'm not mad at you."

Then the light changed, and I heard a horn behind us. Give us a break, asshole. Lay off your stupid horn. Stan hit the gas and we jumped forward, but she still kept trying to pull down the zipper. Dividing her attention didn't work so well, though. The truck was weaving in and out of the lane. I heard a horn behind us again.

"Forget about it," I said. "Just follow them. We'll see what happens."

Then a car suddenly wedged into our lane a couple of vehicles up ahead, and it almost caused a wreck. Stan had to hit the brakes. We came to another stop, right in the middle of the block, a logjam up ahead of us.

"Damn!" she said.

"Just do what you can."

I looked up ahead, trying to spot the Buick, but I had lost it. We got started up again, but the light at the next intersection turned red, and I couldn't see a trace of the Buick when we came to a stop.

"Damn!" she said again. "I'm sorry, Walt!"

I was frustrated, but I didn't want her to see that. "It's not your fault. We may still be able to find them. The car is registered to the Hertz office at Love Field, so that may be where they're headed. We'll go there and see what happens."

The light changed to green, and we started up again. We proceeded on to Love Field, but not without getting snarled up in traffic again a couple of times. Neither of us talked. The pressure in my bladder felt like a tsunami by now, but I told myself to ignore it. I kept looking for the Buick along the way, but I couldn't see a trace of it. Then we got to the Hertz lot, and I saw it in an instant, parked beside the check-in building. I looked for Hieronymous and the girl, but I couldn't spot them, even when we swung by the front of the building and I looked through the glass. They had already taken the courtesy van to the terminal, I figured.

"Take me to the terminal," I told her.

She looked over at me. "Walt…are you sure? It's an airport, after all."

I had been thinking about my options. None of them were very good, but I felt I had to do something to try to save the girl.

"I *have* to, Stan," I finally said. "For two reasons. The first is that if I can find out which flight they're on, then that may tell me what city he lives in. Since he came to the airport in a rental car, it seems unlikely that he lives here in Dallas. Knowing which city he's headed to doesn't *prove* he lives there, of course, but at least it's a start. It's better than nothing."

She watched me closely as I talked but didn't say anything.

"The second reason is even more important," I said. "I really think she's in danger. I think she may be their next victim. She's just the type they like. So I *have* to try to do something. If I can find a way to get her alone, then maybe I can convince her not to go with him. I still have my badge with me. That might be enough to make her listen."

"And if you can't get her alone?" she asked.

"Then I'll just go up to the two of them and warn her right in front of his face. If he doesn't like it, then that's too damned bad. I can't just sit back and let her get killed."

She seemed to ponder that. "Then I wish you luck," she said softly.

"Thanks. I'll probably need it."

By then we had come to the main entrance.

"Pull over here and I'll hop out," I said.

We came to a stop by the curb, and I opened the door and got out. Did you say hop, I asked myself as I pushed the door shut. Watch it, Walt, this damned suit is starting to affect your mind. Then I headed for the entrance. There weren't all that many people around at ten o'clock, but the ones I passed turned to gawk at me. Then I was inside the terminal. I looked around. No sign of Hieronymous and the girl. There were Southwest ticket counters across the way, and I headed toward them. I thought about trying to find a security officer too, somebody to explain things to. I also considered trying to get out my badge, but the image of how I'd look, groping around down there in my pouch in front of God and everybody, like I was insanely digging away at my private parts, was enough to stop me.

Time was short, so I stepped right up to an agent at the ticket counter, a young woman who seemed surprised to see me. I had to barge in front of somebody to get there, but I was in a hurry.

"I need to go to the gates," I said to the agent. "I'm a police officer. I'm trying to find somebody."

She looked at me in amazement. "I'm sorry, Sir, but you can't go to the gates without a ticket."

"This is very important, Miss. There's a person in danger."

She just stared at me.

"Is there a security officer around?" I asked. I looked back over my shoulder in both directions, trying to spot somebody in a uniform, and as I did, I saw Hieronymous and the girl on a conveyor belt across the way, headed to the gate area. I checked my gut one more time. Did I really believe she was in danger? Yes, I did. I had to do something.

"Hey!" I yelled.

Several people turned around to stare, including Hieronymous and the girl.

"Hey!" I yelled again. I started toward them.

"You can't go there, Sir!" the agent called behind me.

I didn't acknowledge her. I kept moving toward the conveyor.

"Security!" I heard her yell. "Security!" A whistle blew.

I broke into a clumsy jog, moving as fast as I could in the suit. The conveyor was just ahead. Then I saw a uniformed cop off to my left, approaching on the run. I slowed down, wondering how to begin to explain, but before I even came to a stop, I was hit from behind. Somebody tackled me, and I fell forward onto the floor. The tackler's weight fell on me full force. My breath blew out, and I nearly whizzed in the bunny britches.

"Police!" I heard him say over my shoulder. "Don't move!"

"I'm a cop," I panted. "Houston homicide."

"Sure, and I'm George W. Bush. Pleased to meet you. Just don't try to move."

The other cop had come running up to us by then. He had his cuffs out. His gun was drawn. The cop who had tackled me from behind had his hands pressed down on the back of my neck, holding my head down. I knew it was pointless to resist. Up ahead I could see the conveyor belt. Hieronymous and the girl were nowhere to be seen. I had lost them…

DANCE YOUR HEART OUT

12.

Both cops were on top of me. One of them pulled my hands behind me and slapped on a set of cuffs. He had to struggle with them because the fabric of the suit was so thick and bulky. I still wasn't trying to resist. I noticed a crowd had started to gather around us. I saw a flash bulb go off.

"I really am a cop," I said.

"Sure. Anything you say. Just keep cool. Don't try to resist."

They pulled me to my feet. Not very gently. I staggered and stepped on a pant leg and nearly fell down. I saw another flash go off. Across the way somebody filmed with a video camera. Then they read me my rights and patted me down. They found all the stuff in the pouch right away, the wallet, the phone, the keys, the gun, and the badge. The officer looked up at me when he saw the Houston shield.

"I really am a cop," I said.

He shrugged. "Maybe. But we see fake ID all the time."

"This way, pal," the other cop said, moving to one side and tugging me along behind him. "Just stay cool."

They led me outside to a cop car, then shoved me down and stuffed me in the back seat. I banged my head in the process. I saw stars for a moment. Then they slammed the door. Two other cops sat in the front seat. We pulled away from the curb. I sat in the back seat, my wrists in the cuffs, the pressure in my bladder feeling like I was about to give birth. Well, I just didn't much care anymore. There are times in life when you've just had it. So I leaned back in the seat, took a deep breath, relaxed all over, and tinkled in the bunny britches. Blessed relief. It felt like a little taste of heaven. I could feel the wetness in my groin, then running down the leg of the suit. Pretty soon I could feel it down past my knee. Ecstasy. I only prayed I lived to see it rot out the fabric.

By the time I finished, though, I realized I still had another problem. I had to go poop too. Big time. Like trying to hold back a mighty avalanche. Fight it with your mind, I told myself. Just fight it. Deny it. Don't allow your mind to give it any reality. It only *feels* like you're about to pass a pineapple. Don't let your mind accept it. Hold it forever, until the end of time. Longer, if you have to. Just fight it. Use your mind, Walt. What's left of it, that is. I leaned back again and tried to relax.

The trip was a short one. We got to the station, and I was taken into a booking room. They shoved me down on a chair. I looked around as well as I could in the rabbit suit. There were three or four policemen in the room. Then two detective types came in. They didn't look friendly at all. I looked at their nametags. One said Garnett, the other said Judson. They both looked to be about forty, their faces hardened by experience.

"What's your name?" Garnett asked.

I cleared my throat. "Draeger. Walter Draeger. Houston Homicide."

Garnett looked at me suspiciously. "You want to tell us what you were doing there at the airport tonight? Dressed like that?"

So I did. I told them I was a Houston police officer with the Homicide Division and that I was working a case here in Dallas. I was following a suspect. They just stared at me as I talked, their faces blank. I could have been telling them I'd just gotten in from Mars. I didn't give them all the details, just a few brief facts. I thought, though, that their expressions softened slightly as I talked. They seemed to become a little more open and receptive, not quite so challenging and suspicious. The truth has a certain ring to it, after all. I concluded by telling them that, as one part of the pursuit, I had gone to a costume party that night.

Garnett sized up the suit. "You sure could have fooled us."

Judson snorted.

"Call Houston and check it out," I said. "My Captain there in Homicide is Robert Dickerson. You can probably contact him."

They exchanged glances. Garnett motioned to a younger officer over to the side.

"Go see what you can find out," he said.

The officer stepped out of the room.

"So how come you didn't ditch the suit when you had to go to the airport?" Garnett asked.

"It's not as easy as you might think."

Garnett shook his head and sighed helplessly, like he was tired and disgusted. Judson snorted again.

"Let's just go ahead then and get you out of all this crazy nonsense," Garnett said, still sounding put out. "We can't book you and print you in all this stupid crap."

"By all means," I agreed.

Garnett went around behind me and took hold of the zipper. He gave it a tentative try, but it didn't budge. He tugged harder. Still no luck. Then he tried giving it a series of jolting yanks. It still stayed shut.

"There's a pair of pliers in one of the desks in the other room," he said to Judson. "See if you can find them."

Judson went to find the pliers. Garnett kept working with the zipper, tugging and yanking, but it didn't yield. His breathing sounded tight.

"Son of a bitch is stuck," he mumbled.

"I noticed that myself," I said.

"Crap!" he said, after giving it yet another yank. "So this is how come you couldn't get out of the damned thing?"

"Couldn't have said it better myself."

"Here you go," said Judson, stepping back into the room and handing Garnett a pair of pliers. Garnett took them and grabbed the zipper and gave it another yank, much harder this time because of the pliers. My head snapped back, but the zipper still didn't budge.

"Stand up," said Garnett.

So I stood up.

"Turn around and bend over," he said.

I tried to maintain as much dignity as I could, staring out from behind the stupidly grinning rabbit face.

"I certainly hope you're joking when you say that," I said.

"Good Lord, Draeger, just turn around and bend over."

Judson snorted again. I heard another laugh in the background. So I turned around and bent over.

"I've never let anybody do this before," I said.

"God, Draeger," said Garnett. "Would you just shut up."

Judson laughed out loud.

"Just stay like that," Garnett added.

"You want me to grab my ankles?" I asked.

"God, Draeger, just shut up."

Judson snorted again.

Then Garnett grabbed the zipper tag with the pliers, put his foot on my behind for purchase, and pulled back as hard as he could. My head yanked back even harder. Still no luck, though.

"Damn it!" he snapped.

Judson tried not to laugh again.

Garnett tried several more times, but he never got it budged. A couple of other cops had come into the room, so there was a gathering of at least half a dozen, all watching from the side. They were trying not to laugh too.

"Get me some scissors," Garnett snapped. "We'll cut the son of a bitch off."

We waited for a few moments, and then somebody came back with a pair of scissors. Garnett elected to start on one of the pant legs. He knelt down and took it in his hand and started gnawing at it with the scissors. It occurred to me after a couple of moments that maybe that particular pant leg wasn't the very best place to start, but he was already going after it, trying to get the scissors to bite the fabric. Then he stopped.

"Hey, this is wet," he said. He held his hand out and worked his fingers, studying them. Then he put his hand to his nose. An expression of icky distaste descended over his features. "My God, Draeger, what is this? What did you do?"

"You had to be there to understand," I explained.

"Crap!" he said disgustedly, wiping his fingers on his trousers.

"Not yet," I said. "But I'm afraid it won't be long."

Garnett regarded me uncertainly, his expression somewhere between horror and revulsion. Judson snorted again. I could hear a couple of the other cops snickering.

"Do we need to get him a diaper?" Judson asked.

That was good for a satisfying laugh all around.

"Good Lord, Draeger," said Garnett.

So he grabbed the fabric of the suit at the waistline and tried to get the scissors to grab again, but they were dull desk scissors, just paper cutters, and they couldn't saw through the fabric. Finally he gave up and threw them across the room.

"Damn it!" he growled.

"Crap!" said Judson

One of the other cops in the room laughed again and then tried to shut it off.

"It's been that kind of evening," I said.

Then somebody produced a small pocketknife, but that wouldn't work either. It wouldn't cut through the zipper. Finally they got a couple of paramedics to come in from a nearby fire station, and they brought the kind of raw edge scissors they use to cut the clothes off accident victims. They could probably have dismembered the Tin Woodman, but they still couldn't get through the zipper. Finally they got somebody to come up from maintenance with an acetylene torch, and he burned a hole in the fabric of the abdomen. Then one of the paramedics was able to get the scissors into the hole and start cutting, but it was slow business. Every bite of the scissors was an effort. The paramedic had to stop and shake his hand several times before he was finally able to cut all the way around the suit. But he had done it, and finally the top half of the bunny suit came off. The room temperature air felt deliciously cool on my face. I took several deep gulps. Sweat was pouring off me. Then I stepped out of the bunny legs, and I was finally free. I looked like a drowned rat, I'm sure, standing there in just my soaking wet skivies. There was a brief round of applause.

Garnett wadded up the suit and threw it over to the side. Hard. It landed in a heap.

"Jesus, where did you get that godawful thing, Draeger?" he asked.

"Clyde's Costume Castle."

He looked over at me. "Where is that?"

"In hell, I believe."

"Christ, Draeger," he snorted.

Judson and a couple of the other cops laughed.

"Where the hell did Clyde get it?" one of the cops asked. There was more laughter.

"Probably off that space ship that crashed in Roswell," I said. "Somebody ought to send it to NASA. It might take years off the Mars Mission."

Garnett could only shake his head. Judson snorted again.

"Mind if I use the bathroom?" I asked.

"You really gotta take a dump?" Garnett asked.

I nodded. "We're talking Richter Scale. I don't even know if it's safe for the rest of you to stay in the building."

"God, Draeger," Garnett said, shaking his head again.

Judson snorted again.

So they let me use a small prisoner bathroom over to the side that only had a single stall and no other door. I washed my hands and splashed water on my face when I was finished. There *is* such a thing as a new lease on life. Then I stepped back out into the booking area. Somebody had fetched a prisoner suit, and they told me to get into it, so I did. Then they fingerprinted me and took mug shots, and I gave a formal statement.

The cop who had gone to call Bob Dickerson stepped back into the room about that time. He conferred briefly with Garnett and Judson. Dickerson wasn't on duty that night, it turned out, and he and his wife had apparently gone out to a party. They hadn't been able to reach him. They'd try again later.

"We'll keep trying to reach him," Garnett said. "In the meantime, we gotta keep you here."

So I was put in a small cell off the holding area that had a single bed in it. I stretched out, aching all over, and finally managed to drift off into a fitful sleep. Several hours later the door opened again, and Garnett and Judson stepped into the cell.

"Looks like you're cleared, Draeger," Garnett said, pulling up a chair and turning it around and sitting with his arms folded across the back. "Your ID checks out. We got you all cleared through Houston. Talked with Dickerson and everything. He'd been out to a party, it turns out. Sounded like he wasn't feeling any pain, but he confirmed what you told us. We cleared your picture and your prints too, through the main office. So it looks like you really are legit, after all."

I set up on the edge of the bed and gave my head a shake to clear the cobwebs. Bones and joints and muscles were protesting all over my body. My lower back was very sore.

"You're free to go," Garnett added. "We're making a full report, but there won't be any charges filed. Do us a favor, though, and try to keep out of trouble as long as you're here in Dallas. You got me?"

"Right," I said.

"We've got you some clothes, by the way," Garnett added.

Judson handed me a pair of raggedy pants, a tattered white T- shirt, and some jail slippers.

"We need those back," said Garnett. "That's what I always wear to the society balls."

Judson snorted at that.

"Right," I said again.

"By the way, you've made the paper too," said Garnett. "Here, take a took."

He and Judson were both trying not to laugh again as he handed me the first section of the Sunday Edition of the Dallas Morning News. The paper had been folded, and in the lower right corner of the front page I could see a small headline: MAD BUNNY TERRORIZES AIRPORT. Well, my mother always said I'd make the news.

I read through it quickly. I guess anything irregular at an airport is newsworthy these days, but somebody had obviously had a good time with it. There was a recounting of the episode, sprinkled with references to the "horrifying hare" and the "beastly bunny" and the "raging rabbit," as well as mention of the chase and the "hopping haul down." At one point there was also this mention of the "menacing marsupial." Well, rabbits aren't marsupials. I could have told them that. I knew that from biology, but I didn't think I'd be writing a letter to the editor. The entire episode had been captured on this videotape by a bystander, the report mentioned. Police were studying the tape now, trying to gather additional information. Pending more investigation, the item noted, the rabbit's identity was being withheld.

Mercifully, I thought.

So I slipped out of the prison issue and pulled on the T- shirt and the pants and the slippers. It wasn't exactly an elegant ensemble, but at least I had something to wear back to the apartment. They gave me all my stuff back too.

"Kind of sorry to see you go, Draeger," Garnett offered as he and Judson led me to the front entrance. "We were almost starting to get used to you."

They both had to laugh at that.

"My thoughts exactly," I said.

They let me use a phone to call a cab, and I went outside to wait. One arrived in just a few minutes. There was still money in my wallet, so getting back to the apartment wasn't a problem. I headed straight for the bed when I got there. I was still exhausted, and the soreness all over my body was only getting worse. I decided I needed to call Stan, though, before I tried to get some sleep, so I got the cellphone and dialed her number. It was answered on the first ring.

"Hello?" I heard her say, her voice fully awake and alert.

"Stan . . ."

"Oh my God, Walt!" she cried. "Where are you? What happened? Are you all right?"

"Yeah, I'm fine, but it's been a long night."

"Oh God, Walt, what happened? I've been so worried! I haven't been able to sleep a wink!"

So I told her.

"Oh, God, Walt! That's just awful! That's a terrible experience!"

"Don't know that I'd rank it up there with a wet dream," I agreed.

"Oh, God, I feel so bad about this. I parked the car and went inside, and they had already taken you away. I heard somebody say there had been a disturbance. I should have done something, but I was just so stunned. I guess I wasn't thinking clearly. But I should have found you. Somehow. I should have told them who you were. I should have explained everything."

"Nothing really you could have done. Believe me, their minds were pretty well made up at that point."

"But I just feel so bad that I couldn't help you. That I couldn't do something. I came back to the apartment and called the police station, but they said I couldn't talk to you. So I called one of the attorneys at the firm where I work, but lawyers don't tend to be much help in the middle of the night. He said we'd get you out in the morning. I just feel awful about it, Walt. Just awful!"

"You did all you could, Stan. And I appreciate it."

There was a pause on the line.

"Well, you're being nice . . ," she said.

"It's the truth. I mean that."

"Well . . . thanks, Walt . . . so what do you plan to do now?"

"I plan to try to get his identity from Hertz and follow him if I can. That's the only real lead I have at this point. And I've got to keep going."

She didn't say anything for several moments.

"You still there?" I asked.

"Yes . . ."

"Think I'm crazy?"

There was silence again. I waited for her to answer.

"No, I don't . . . I've thought about it, and I really don't . . . If you really think you're onto something, then I think so too. I want you to believe me when I say that, Walt, because it's the truth. And if you find out who he is and you need to go after him, then I want you to do that."

There was another silence.

". . . And I've . . . I've decided that . . . that I want to come with you. I want to help you. I mean that. I want you to let me come with you."

"Well . . . thanks, Stan . . ."

"Does that mean you'll let me?"

"I'm not sure." I hadn't thought about it until now. It was kind of a different idea.

"I want to, Walt," she said. The softness was back in her voice. "I really want to. Please let me."

"I'll think about it, Stan. I really will. I just don't want you to be in any kind of danger."

"I can take care of myself."

"Maybe. But don't forget, they like well-built blondes."

"Then maybe you could use me for bait?" she said. "Ever thought of that?"

"Lord, Stan, don't even talk like that."

"I want to help you, Walt. I really do. I don't think you're crazy at all."

"Well, okay . . ."

We talked just a little more. She told me she had to go out of town that afternoon on a case again, and that she wouldn't be back for a couple of days. I told her I had to get some rest. I'd get back with her when I got going again.

"I'll be thinking about you," she said.

I got the impression she blew me a kiss over the phone as she said that, but maybe that was just my imagination.

"Sleep tight, Walt," she said.

"Talk with you later, Stan," I said, and I hung up the phone.

Then I hit the bed. I hadn't really gotten any decent sleep at the jail, and I was gone in no time. It was three o'clock in the afternoon before I even budged. I got up and had a beer, and after giving it some thought, I called St. David's in Austin and asked for Joe Henderson's room. I figured he might be feeling well enough to talk by now, and Sue would be answering the phone if he wasn't. No Joe Henderson there, I was told. So I asked to speak to the nursing station, and I found out he had signed out against medical advice that morning. So I called his house, and Sue answered after a couple of rings.

"Well, he's being an asshole, Walt," she said. "He knows more than the dumb doctors, of course. They said he needed to stay longer and get more antibiotics, but they were just being stupid, naturally. Why would they know what to do, just because they're doctors, after all? So he signed himself out. He's still sick, though. He still hurts and he still has fever. Here, you can talk to him. I'd tell you to try to talk some sense into him if I didn't know it was impossible."

Joe came on the line in a moment and said, "Hey, Walt, how you doing?"

"How are *you*?"

"Crap, I'm fine."

"He's really not, Walt," I heard Sue call out in the background.

"Screw it, I'm doing great," Joe said.

"No, he's not, Walt," Sue called out again.

But there was obviously no arguing with him. I told him to use his head and take care of himself and call the doctor if he got worse, but I knew he'd have to get a *lot* worse before he did that.

"I need you to check something out with Hertz for me, if you can," I finally said. I told him what had happened at the party and gave him the license number of the silver Buick. I thought it would be better for *him* to contact Hertz through the Austin Police Department, rather than trying to do it myself.

"I'll see what I can find out," he said.

I felt uneasy pushing for more, but I also asked him to see if the composites had been identified. He said he'd check on that too.

"Take care of yourself, Joe," I said.

"I'm fine," he grumbled.

DANCE YOUR HEART OUT

So that was that. I watched a basketball game on television, then showered and shaved. I called a cab and went to Stan's to get the Taurus. I rang the doorbell when I got there to see if she was home, but she'd already gone. So I got in the Taurus and headed back to the apartment, but I found myself driving in a different direction instead. I didn't plan it that way. It just seemed to happen. Before long, I pulled up in front of Julie's house in Garland. I was aware of butterflies in my stomach as I rang the bell.

Bobby answered the door. "Dad! Dad! Come on in! You've got to see this! This is cool!"

He certainly seemed excited about something. I hardly knew what to expect as I stepped inside.

"Look, Dad! Look! You've got to see this! We made a tape!"

He and a friend were watching a tape on television. Bobby rewound it and started it again.

"Look, Dad! Look!"

So I looked at the tape they were playing.

"This was on the news, Dad! There was this crazy, crazy, dumb, stupid idiot at the airport last night, and he was all dressed up in this really dumb rabbit suit! Look, Dad! Look! And the cops were chasing him and he tried to run away! Look!"

So this was the video I had read about. On prime time news now. Bobby and his friend were rolling on the floor and holding their sides, they were laughing so hard. I could see why. On the screen, there was this huge, pink, clumsy looking rabbit. At first he was just standing at the ticket counter, looking stupid. Then he cried out. Twice. But coming from inside the rabbit suit, it didn't sound like a human cry. It sounded more like a roar. Then he broke away and started to run at an angle. Just great, I thought. A roaring, charging, giant pink rabbit. No wonder people freaked out. You couldn't really call what he was doing a run, though. It looked more like an accelerated stagger.

The poor dumb bastard was having to hold up his pants and take these ridiculously high, spastic steps with his knees, and then his feet would come flopping down crazily like pancakes splattering on the ground. He wasn't covering ground very fast. It was not a pretty sight.

Bobby and his friend were still rolling on the floor, positively convulsing. Bobby tried to point at the screen, but he could barely even lift his arm. Then, as I watched the tape, two cops approached. One hit the rabbit from behind, while the other advanced from the front. The rabbit went down in a clumsy pink heap and didn't put up any resistance. Then the policeman on top held him down and pulled up on his ears. Pulled up on his ears? I hadn't been aware of that at the time, but there it was on television, right in front of my face, the cop pulling up on my ears. That's brutality, I thought. Rabbits hate to have their ears pulled. Everybody knows that. I ought to file a complaint. Then it was over, and the stupid, evil, wicked rabbit was being led away. Peace and order were restored.

Bobby and his friend rewound the tape and started it all over again. They were laughing just as hard, still rolling on the floor and holding their sides.

"Isn't he crazy, Dad?" Bobby squealed. "Isn't he crazy? Isn't he?"

Looking at the tape, I really couldn't argue with him. "Sure looks like a crazed madman to me," I agreed. "What's the world coming to, for God's sake?"

I was watching it all over again when I became aware of movement over to the side. I turned and saw Julie, standing in the doorway leading from the living room to the kitchen. My heart missed a telltale lub dub just seeing her.

"Hi," I managed. "Just thought I'd come by and see how everybody was doing. Hope I'm not intruding."

She smiled, more warmly than I had expected.

"You're not," she said. "I'm glad you came."

DANCE YOUR HEART OUT

I walked over to her and took her in my arms and hugged her. She hugged me back. Warmly again. I held her for a moment, just standing there with her. It felt so good. Then she pulled back and looked up at me.

"I saw you watching that video," she said.

"Yeah . . ."

She was studying me closely. "You had a very strange expression on your face."

I shrugged. "It was a strange video."

She still looked at me closely, leaning back in my arms. "I know you too well, Walter Draeger. I can always tell when something's bothering you."

"I wish you weren't so intuitive."

I looked right in her eyes. Such a pretty hazel. The prettiest color I had ever seen. I just wanted to squeeze her. She looked over at the video playing on the screen again, then back at me. Bobby and his friend were still rolling on the floor. She looked at the video one more time and then back at me, a puzzled expression on her face.

"What's happening here, Walter Draeger? You're looking at that tape in a very strange way."

"Long story."

"I can always tell when something's eating you."

"Wish I weren't so transparent."

She looked back at the video and then at me again, still studying me closely.

"Were you at the airport last night, by any chance?" she asked.

I nodded. "I'm afraid so."

"Did you . . . did you see the rabbit?"

"All too well, I'm sorry to say."

She was watching the video again. I thought she started to laugh, but she caught herself.

"It was...such a *big* rabbit," she noted.

"Yes, it was, wasn't it."

She tried again not to giggle. "I'd have to say the

rabbit was probably…oh, about six-four at least, wouldn't you agree?"

"Yes, I think that's probably correct."

She was barely able to keep a straight face. "And it had to weigh…oh, at least two-forty, don't you think?"

"Yes, I do."

She was finally sure of the connection. She started to laugh but stopped herself. She had to put her hand over her mouth.

"Oh, dear," she said.

"My sentiments exactly."

I didn't know what else to do, so I gathered her close to me and hugged her again, even tighter, holding her close, and she hugged me back. We stood there for several moments, just holding each other. I could tell she was still trying not to laugh.

"How?" she finally said. "If you don't mind my asking."

"Like I said, it's a very long story. The bottom line is that I was undercover and I had to follow somebody. I didn't have a chance to get out of the suit."

I could feel her start to giggle, even though she tried to cut it off.

"That's undercover, all right," she said. "Nobody would ever believe you were a cop in that getup."

"They didn't. Not for a long, long time."

She was still trying not to laugh, but I could tell she was struggling with it. "Were you able to explain? Did everything get cleared up?"

"Yep. Finally. They let me go hopping right on down the old bunny trail."

She finally couldn't hold it back any longer. She gave up and started to cackle. She wound up laughing so hard she could barely breathe. It was almost like a convulsion. I just kept holding her the whole time. She laughed and laughed and laughed. Finally she pulled back from me and looked up at me, shaking her head in amazement. Then she took my hand and headed for the kitchen.

"Come help me cook hamburgers," she said, trying to collect herself. "I told Bobby I'd fix some up for them."

So she led me into the kitchen, and I leaned back against the counter as she put some patties on the stove. I could hear another outburst of laughter from the living room.

"That's Johnny Baxter," Julie said. "He and Bobby are on the soccer team together. They're becoming best buddies. They always have a great time together. They're almost inseparable."

"That's good," I said.

"I'm getting to be pretty good friends with Johnny's mother too," she added. "Her name is Helen. We have a lot of interests in common, it turns out. She's supposed to be coming over about now, in fact. We're all going to have burgers together. She said she'd be here about six, so I'm expecting her any minute."

"Shit," I said.

Julie looked back over her shoulder at me. "Excuse me? Did you say something?"

I shook my head. "Nothing. Just mumbling to myself. I do it a lot these days."

"You want to join us?" she asked, looking back at me over her shoulder again.

I thought about that. All things considered, it didn't seem like a stellar idea.

"Uh, no, I'd probably better not. Don't want to barge in."

She looked at me very directly. "You really wouldn't be, Walt. I mean that."

That gave me a very good feeling all over, kind of a generalized warm fuzzy, but I didn't feel right about being there with Helen Baxter. I didn't know how that would go, and I didn't know how to explain to Julie about what had happened in the bowling alley the other night. I decided it wouldn't be a good scene.

"Thanks, Julie, but there's something I have to do tonight. It has to do with the case I'm working on. Wish I didn't, but that's life. Thanks, though. I mean that. Can I take a rain check?"

She smiled. "Sure. I'd like that. Bobby would too."

I didn't know for sure what to say, and I happened to notice there was a full trash can by the door and a tied up garbage bag standing beside it, so I said, "I'll take out the trash for you. Looks like you've got a load here."

"Thanks."

Then something occurred to me. "Except that I don't know where the trash goes around here."

She motioned with her head over her shoulder. "The dumpster is in the alley behind the back yard. There's a lock on the gate. The key is on that chair over there by the door."

So I rounded up the trash, got the key, and headed out through the garage into the back yard. Brutus came over to greet me as soon as I stepped outside. I had to put down the trash bags and grab his forelegs to keep him from putting his paws on my shirt. I could see they were sopping wet and muddy, even though the whole back yard looked dry as a bone. He tried to lick me in the mouth too. Brutus always tries to lick me in the mouth. Always. But I have my limits. Being licked in the mouth by Brutus reminds me of kissing a pay toilet. So I held him off. I scratched behind his ears, and he panted happily in my face.

"Dumb turd," I told him.

He loved it. Then I put his legs back on the ground and finished carrying out the trash, tossing it into the dumpster in the back alley. I relocked the gate as I came back into the back yard, then walked to the house. The yard was trim and tidy, I noticed, and Julie had planted some nice shrubs along the back fence. You can't plant flowers with Brutus around, of course, because he thinks they're food. He padded along beside me the whole way, wagging his tail and thumping my leg with it. He seemed a little subdued, though. Not quite his usual animated self. I stopped at the back door to scratch behind his ears again.

"Hey, boy, is it real lonesome out here in outer darkness?" I asked him.

Judging from the expression on his face, I thought he would have told me that it was, if he'd been able to talk. He tried to get up on his hind legs to put his feet on my shirt again, but I was able to hold him off. I didn't let him lick me either. I gave him one more scratch behind the ears, then dropped him back to all fours as I opened the door to the garage.

"By the way, thanks for growling at Sam," I said. "Chew both his balls off next time, will you, if you get the chance."

Then I had to leave him there. I scratched behind his ear one last time and shut the door. Julie was standing by the counter when I came back into the kitchen, still working on the burgers. She turned back toward me as I stepped inside. I took a quick glance at my watch. It was ten after six. I figured Helen Baxter would be here any minute, and I still didn't feel I could handle that.

"Well . . . I guess I really do have to go. . . I just wanted to come by and see you guys . . . "

She came over to me and put her arms around me and laid her head against my chest, and we held each other again. I thought I could stay like that forever. Neither of us spoke. I could feel her breathing, could feel the rhythm against my body. I could hear Bobby and Johnny laughing in the living room again.

"Oh, Walt . . ," she said.

I held her even tighter. "I've missed you, Julie. Both of you. More than I could even begin to say."

"And I've missed you."

We just kept holding each other.

"Oh, Walt…I don't know. What we had was so very special…but I just don't know…there was so much pain…"

"I'm so sorry, Julie. It was all my fault. I mean that."

Still we held each other.

"See, you've got this one big problem, Walt," she finally said.

"Just one?"

I heard her sniff. "A couple of other minor little flaws here and there."

"Humbling."

"See, you're this great big guy, Walt, and you've got this fabulous body with all these totally fantastic muscles, which is really just completely disgusting, by the way, because you never work out or do anything physical at all. I mean, the only exercise I've ever seen you do is lifting beer cans."

"It's all those repetitions," I said. "It brings out the definition."

She snorted at that. "And it also just happens that you're one of the best looking males on the planet. That's totally disgusting too. I can't tell you how many women have told me along the way that they think you look better than Mel Gibson or Kevin Costner or any of those people out in Hollywood. Lois Randerson was absolutely gushing the other day. She said she wanted to jump all over you, right there on the sidewalk. So all your life, women have thrown themselves all over you like crazy, and your problem is, Walt, you've never learned to say no."

"I've been working on it," I said. "I really have. I've been practicing my no's in front of the mirror. I think I've about got it perfected."

She held me even tighter. I could feel a catch in her

breathing. Laughter drifted in from the living room again.

"I wish I could believe that, Walt. I really wish I could."

I lifted up her chin, so she was looking right up at me. The hazel green of her eyes glistened with wetness. I kissed her gently. I could feel the softness of her lips as she kissed me back. Then we pulled apart. Helen Baxter was overdue. I had to leave.

"I'll call you," I said, my voice low and suddenly husky. I kissed my fingers and pressed them to her lips. "Say good-bye to Bobby for me."

We hugged each other again, very tightly, and then I left. . .

13.

Next morning I got up and ran a few errands. It didn't take long. I was headed back to the apartment when I got a call from Joe Henderson.

"Well, we talked with Hertz," he said. "We got an ID on your boy."

I felt a chill come over me, like Pandora might have felt before she opened the box. I only hoped that we had the right person.

"Fantastic! Who is he?"

"Name's Corbin Davidson. He's forty-three years old. Lives here in Austin."

"Can't say I'm surprised. Austin seems to be ground zero. Gunner probably lives there too."

There was a pause on the line. "Gunner?"

"That's the other picture I sent you. I call him Gunner."

There was another pause. "I won't even begin to ask. Not after the Hieronymous deal."

Joe seemed to be feeling better, so I asked him how he was doing.

"Hell, I'm fine," he said. "Damn doctors were making a federal case out of it. I could probably run a marathon."

"Just take care of yourself. Don't try to overdo it."

"Sure. Sure."

"What else can you tell me about this guy, Davidson?" I asked. "Does he have a record of any kind?"

"Nope. Clean as a whistle."

"You checked out anything else about him?"

I could hear him take a deep breath. "Are you sitting down?"

"Yeah, I'm in the car. Why?"

"Get this, Walt. This guy you've managed to latch onto, it just so happens this guy turns out to be a very, very successful, very prominent physician here in Austin. Very, very uptown."

"You're kidding me."

"Nope. Wouldn't do that. Now, you want to know what kind of medicine he specializes in?"

The way he said it caught my ear. "Sure."

I heard him take another breath. "It just so happens he's a cardiovascular surgeon. A very well known one here in Austin. He does cardiac bypass operations. He also just happens to be one of the members of the most prestigious cardiovascular surgery group in town, in fact. We're talking very big league here. In addition, he also just happens to be Chairman of the actual freaking Department of Surgery at Brackenridge Hospital this year."

"My God," I said.

"You sure know how to pick 'em."

"Don't I, though?"

"Coroner's said all along that whoever took out the hearts, they knew what they were doing. Always said it was done very skillfully, right from the start. That might explain it, if he's part of the deal."

I tried to think of possibilities. "What do you make of it, Joe? You got any ideas?"

"Your guess is as good as mine."

So that was all of that. They were still gathering information on Davidson, Joe added. He'd let me know what they learned.

"I'm coming down there," I said. "I have to get packed and make a couple of calls. I'll let you know when I get there. Will you be at the office?"

He hesitated. "Not sure about that. I really think I'm okay, but I might stay out a day or two. I think I'll play it by ear, take it as it comes."

"I'll talk with you later."

I headed straight for the apartment. I called Julie on the way and got her at work.

"Hi, Walt," she said. Her tone sounded friendly and upbeat, like she was genuinely glad to hear from me.

"Did you guys have a good time at dinner last night?"

"Wonderful. It was great. I'm sorry you had to miss it."

"Me too. Just one of those things. We'll take that rain check."

"I'd like that," she said. "Bobby would too."

I could have said more, but I needed to keep moving.

"Listen, I have to go down to Austin. I'm leaving as soon as I get packed. It's about the case I'm working on. I'll stay on the cellphone so you can reach me if you need to."

"Okay, I'll stay on my cell too. That way you can reach me too."

"Right…"

We both knew that was probably a lie. You see, Julie has this little problem with her cellphone. We're all just human, after all. We all have our failings. God knows I'm the living proof of that. And with Julie, it's her cellphone. She can't remember to take it with her. I don't know how many times I've heard it ringing on the kitchen counter or on the bathroom sink, and Julie had been gone from home for an hour or more. Or I'd try to reach her on her cellphone about something, and there wouldn't be an answer, and I'd know for a fact the phone was still at home. I'd get mad, and then we'd wind up in a spat. It had actually become one of those stupid, silly things that people wind up bickering and fighting about, like whether or not the toothpaste tube gets rolled or squeezed.

"I'll try to remember to keep it with me," she added quickly. "I promise, Walt. I'll make a special effort. I know that always used to drive you crazy, and I don't want it to be a problem if you need to reach me."

"Just do what you can. By the way, tell Bobby I haven't forgotten about his soccer game. I'll be there. I want to see him play."

"That's good, Walt," she said. I could hear the softness in her voice as she spoke. "He'll love that. He's been so excited that you said you'd be there. He's talked about it nonstop ever since."

"I want to, Julie. I wouldn't miss it."

"I . . . I might need you to drive him again," she said, sounding uncertain. "Would that be possible? One of the ladies at the office is retiring after thirty years, and they're having a send-off party for her after work that evening. I feel like I ought to be there. She's such a dear, and she's been so nice to me. I hate to miss it. Any chance you could pick him up and take him to the game?"

"Sure. No problem. I'll call and check in with you about four o'clock that afternoon. How's that?"

"That's great, Walt. Thanks. I appreciate it."

Something else occurred to me. "How would you guys like to go to Six Flags this Saturday? How does that sound? It's their opening weekend, I think. We could spend the afternoon there, have some fun together."

"We'd like that," she said. "Bobby will be thrilled. It sounds good to me too."

"Then it's a done deal. Six Flags this Saturday. We'll have a blast."

"Thanks, Walt," she said.

"Talk to you later."

"Till then . . ."

So I drove to the apartment and got packed in just a few minutes, then headed out of town, south toward Austin. I thought about calling Stan. She had said she would be out of town working on a case, but she hadn't said exactly where she was going, and I didn't even know if I could reach her. I wrestled with myself for a minute or two, then dialed her cell number. I was a little bit surprised when she answered after only one ring.

"Hi, Walt!" she said. "What a coincidence! I was just thinking about you and wondering how you were doing after the other night. I was about to call you, in fact. Are you recovering?"

"Yeah, old rabbits never die. They just hop away."

She laughed. "Good. I'm glad. I've been worried about you. I still feel just awful that I didn't do something more to help you. I still can't believe I didn't try to find you outside and talk to the policemen. I still can't believe I just left and drove away."

"Not your fault, Stan. It was a hectic deal."

She paused, then said, "So . . . what are you up to now, Mr. Investigator? Any new developments?"

"In fact, there are. That's why I'm calling. I'm headed out of Dallas right now, as we speak. I think we have an ID on the guy at the party, the one with the red beret and the glasses. The one who was talking to you. I wanted to call you before I left."

"You really think you know who he is?"

"Maybe. If, in fact, he's even involved with the murders. I don't know that yet for certain, but I've sure found some suspicious connections."

"Wow!" she said. "That's getting really interesting. That's sounding very exciting."

I could tell she meant it. I could hear it in her voice. Thank God we weren't talking about another costume party.

"If I'm even on the right track," I noted.

"Remember . . ," she said. "I told you I wanted to help you. I meant that. I want to be part of it with you."

"It could be dangerous, Stan. Especially for you. We need to be very careful."

"I'm willing to take the chance."

I thought of what she had said about using herself for bait, and I pushed the thought out of my mind. I couldn't allow her to do that, I told myself. Don't even think about it. That wouldn't be fair to her. But I'd already seen Hieronymous talking to her at the party. She was exactly the type they liked, and the idea had kept coming back into my consciousness, intruding again and again, despite my efforts to keep it away.

"Where are you?" I asked, changing the subject. "You said you were going out of town on a case, but you didn't say where."

"I'm down in Austin."

It took me a moment to react. "Austin? Are you really? My God, that's where I'm headed right now. That's where all this is happening."

"Really? Here in Austin? You're kidding."

"No, I'm not. Austin is the place. Listen, I'll be there in just a couple of hours. I'll call you on your cell when I get to town. We can meet up somewhere."

"Good." She hesitated again for a moment. "I want to help you, Walt. I mean that."

"We'll talk about it."

There was another pause on the line. "I've been thinking about you," she finally said. "A lot. I mean that too."

I wasn't sure about what to say. My whole world felt upside down.

"We'll talk about that too, Stan."

"Well . . . call me when you get in, Mr. Policeman, Sir."

"I will."

And then I hung up and headed down I-35 towards Austin. The drive went quickly. I was coming into Austin in a little over two hours. I called Joe Henderson's office and found out he hadn't come to work, so I called his house and Sue gave me directions on how to get there. I told her I didn't want to come if he was still too sick. Just tell me and I'll stay away. She told me to go ahead and come by.

He'd be impossible to live with if he found out she had told me to stay away. He was champing at the bit as it was. She'd barely been able to keep him home from work today. So I followed the directions she'd given me, and I was there in short order.

Sue opened the door, looked me up and down, and said, "Walter Draeger, my goodness gracious! It's been so long! Years and years! You look just as good as you always did, you rascal!"

She stepped toward me and put her arms around me, and we hugged each other.

"Hey, Asshole!" she called back over her shoulder. "Walt's here."

"Are you really sure he feels up to seeing me? I don't want to barge in and wear him out. Just tell me, Sue, and I'll leave."

"He'll be a prick for weeks if I don't bring you in," she said, pulling me inside and closing the door. She led me across a modest living room, through a fairly standard kitchen, and into the back bedroom. Joe was in pajamas, sitting up in bed, reading the paper.

"Walt! Good to see you!" he said.

So we shook hands, and he got out of bed and put on a bathrobe. He looked pale and weak from the surgery, but he didn't seem desperately ill. He seemed able to move around easily enough as he sat in an easy chair in the corner of the room. I wound up sitting on the bed. Sue brought us each a soft drink, and we sat there in the bedroom.

"Got a little more background here for you on Davidson," he said. "Got a call about thirty minutes ago from downtown. Had them fax me some stuff. Just came in. Sue, bring me those papers, will you?"

She picked some papers off the nightstand by the bed and brought them to him. He handed a sheet to me.

"This your boy?" he asked.

I took the paper and looked at it. It was a picture. I

felt a knot in my gut as I stared into the eyes. I only had to take one glance.

"That's him," I said tightly.

"Picture was in a press release from about a year ago. Got that from the Austin American-Statesman. He was featured in an article they did at that time on the heart program at Brackenridge."

My eyes kept returning to the picture, like a moth to a flame. There was no red beret, no horn-rimmed glasses, but it was the same person. If anything, the eyes were even more direct and piercing without the glasses.

"Found out some more about him besides just the medical stuff," Joe offered. "He's truly not your average guy, Walt. Believe me."

"Tell me," I said.

"Well, first of all, there's all the academic stuff. He was an outstanding student as an undergraduate at UT. Graduated Phi Beta Kappa and Summa Cum Laude and all that sort of thing. Then he graduated number one in his class from Southwestern Medical School up in Dallas. Did all his residency training there at Parkland in Dallas, then moved down here to Austin to go into practice. Like I told you, he's at the top of the line as far as heart surgeons go around here."

I looked back down at the picture. There was such an arrogance there, something about the eyes and the expression, even in the simple picture. I could feel a coldness too.

"Hell of an athlete too," Joe went on. "He played wide receiver at UT for four years. Made All-Southwest Conference the last two years, back in the eighties when the Southwest Conference still existed. Ran track too. Held the old Southwest Conference record for the four hundred meters for a couple of years. Turns out he's a hell of a tennis player too. He's been the Austin Country Club champion about half a dozen times. Likes to go rock climbing in his spare time. Big guy. He's about your height, about six-four. Not as bulky, though. Weighs about two-ten. Not just your average guy, like I said."

He was watching me closely, studying me to see what impact the words were having.

"I think he's tied to it, Joe," I said. "No matter who he is. No matter what else he may have done along the way. No matter how outstanding he's been. I've found too much that points in his direction."

"Fill me in," he said, still regarding me closely.

So I told him all I'd learned. He listened intently.

"I think I'm onto something, Joe. I think he's part of it. Now I've got to find a way to prove it."

He nodded thoughtfully. Then he leaned forward and looked at me very directly.

"Listen to me, Walt. Listen, and listen closely. God knows I want to solve these murders as much as you do. They've haunted the hell out of me for a long time now. And I'm not about to stand in your way. But I'm telling you something, and I only hope to God you listen to what I say. You've got to be super careful with this one, pal. Super, super careful. This is a very high profile guy, to say the least. You're talking status and prestige and money and Austin society and the whole damned ball of wax. I can't be official on this yet. There's not enough data. So it's your baby at this point. You make a mess, you get out of line, you create a stir - and if you're wrong and he's not a part of it - then you're on your own. I can't be there to bail you out. I'm not willing to take the fall with you. Not like that. Am I making myself clear?"

"I hear you, Joe. I'm on my own at this point, at least until there's more evidence."

"You got the picture. I wish you luck. Keep in touch with me. You bring me any hard, solid evidence, then I'm on your side one hundred percent."

We shook hands on that. He gave me several more

sheets of paper.

"Here's some other stuff. Some more background information. Things you might find useful."

"Thanks, Joe."

Then Sue showed me to the front door and gave me a big hug.

"Take care of yourself, Walt," she said.

"I'll do it, Sue. You too."

Then I got in the car and headed downtown. I called Stan on her cell and found that she had just finished for the morning. We agreed to meet for lunch at an Outback. She was waiting for me when I got there. She came up to me as I walked in the door, gave me a hug, and held me tightly.

"Thank God you're still in one piece," she said, leaning back and looking me up and down. "I've been worried sick about you. I still can't believe I just drove away and left you there. I still feel just awful. You're sure you didn't get any serious injuries?"

"Positive. I could have probably survived a nuclear blast in that suit. They probably couldn't have hurt me, even if they'd tried."

We were seated and got our orders placed quickly. She sat across the table from me, regarding me expectantly.

"So what have you found out? You said you had gotten an ID on somebody. I've been dying to find out what you've learned."

I thought about it. "I'm really not sure how much I should tell you. It's a murder investigation, after all."

"Oh, please, Walt. Please! You can't leave me in the dark now. Not after what we've been through."

She did have a point. There was also the fact that Davidson had been talking with her at the party. She was their type exactly. I decided she needed to know what was at stake.

"Here's the guy," I said, pulling out the picture Joe had given me. "Minus the red beret and the glasses. Look familiar?" I held the paper out across the table to her, and she took it and checked it quickly. I could see her nodding.

"It's the same person I saw at the costume party, that's for sure. And you think he could be involved in Jessica's murder?"

"I think it's very possible." I proceeded to fill her in on what I'd learned. I also told her about Gunner, although I didn't tell her what he was called, and I pulled out his picture too. She checked that one as well. I also told her about the murders, even the part about the hearts. She got a revolted expression on her face when I mentioned that.

I nodded toward the pictures. "Both these guys were at Dallas Swinger Parties with Jessica Nodman," I said, "and they were at clubs in San Antonio and Corpus where two other women were killed. I think that's more than just coincidence."

She weighed that, then studied the pictures again.

"Who are they?" she asked.

"The one you were talking to at the party the other night is named Corbin Davidson. He lives here in Austin. I don't know who the other one is yet. Have you ever seen him?"

She shook her head.

"Be careful, Stan. Call me right away if you ever see either one of them. And don't let yourself get isolated."

She eyed me coolly. "Are you saying you think I can't take care of myself? Is that why you're giving me this . . . this . . . *parental* kind of talking to? This parent-child lecture. *Again,* I might add. Because you think I'm just a helpless waif who can't take care of herself. That I'm just sitting here waiting to be eaten by sharks."

"No, that's not what I'm saying at all."

"But that's what you were thinking, isn't it?"

"No, Stan, don't be silly. That's not where I'm coming from. God knows I'm not trying to get into some male-female sexist bullshit. I'm just worried about you, that's all."

She eyed me directly again. "I'm a big girl, Walt. I've seen a lot in my life. I can take care of myself."

"I know that, Stan."

"Good," she said conclusively. "So . . . since we agree on that point . . . take me with you. I want to be there when you go looking for him. I want to come with you."

I could see she meant it. "It's not a game, Stan. This isn't some costume party that's a bag of laughs."

"Take me with you. I might even be able to help you, if you really think I'm their type. I told you that before."

"It's dangerous, Stan."

"Walt!"

Her jaw was set; fire sparkled in her eyes.

"Okay, okay, okay," I said. "A little peace, please. I'll let you come with me. Just remember that I warned you."

She smiled. "Good for you, Walter Draeger. Good for you. Then we both agree, I've been warned."

We decided to go in the Taurus when we finished eating, so we left her pickup in the parking lot there at the Outback and drove to a medical office building just a block from Brackenridge Hospital. We entered an adjoining four story parking garage. I had leafed through the background information on Davidson while we were eating lunch, and I had seen what kind of car he drove - a brand new silver Mercedes, along with the license - and I found it parked in a reserved space right next to an elevator. I could see "Dr. Davidson" printed on the firewall above the Mercedes' hood.

"That's it," I said.

Stan was almost jumping up and down on the seat again. "This is exciting! I've never done anything like this before. This is neat!"

I could hear the costume party tone in her voice. I almost asked her if she wanted to go get the kitten outfit, but I held off. Instead, I drove up to the next level, found an empty space that wasn't reserved, and parked the Taurus. Then we walked inside.

"What are we going to do?" she asked eagerly.

"I don't know."

"Oh . . ."

We found the office without difficulty, on the third floor of the complex. Davidson's name was listed along with the names of three other physicians. The top cardiovascular surgery group in Austin, right there in front of us. The door was solid wood without any glass, though. I couldn't see inside, and I didn't think I was ready to enter yet.

"What now?" Stan whispered.

"I still don't know."

"Oh . . ."

So we went back out to the Taurus. I didn't know for sure how long Davidson would be in his office, but it was still early afternoon, and I suspected he'd stay there for at least a couple of hours.

"I need to learn my way around," I said to Stan. "I'm going to find out how to get to some of the other places he goes. I'm not familiar with Austin."

"I can probably help with that."

"Good."

"See, aren't you glad you brought me along?"

"More and more by the minute."

So we drove to St. David's, the other hospital where Davidson practiced, the same place where Joe Henderson had been. Then we went to the Austin Country Club, where he played tennis. Finally we drove by his house, which was an enormous mansion in Austin's very best residential section.

"The information I got on him says he's divorced,"

I noted as we drove by, scanning the opulence.

"He probably gave his wife the big house, don't you think?" Stan said. "They probably just used this as the guest place."

"You're beginning to get the feel of things, I can tell."

"Of course, I'm learning from the master."

Then we drove back to the parking lot adjoining his office building. I could feel a sense of helplessness starting to come over me. A one-person tail is just about impossible, and I realized the chance of uncovering anything was remote. I needed the sort of help Joe had said he couldn't give me - a tap on Davidson's office and home phones, a mike in his office and his bedroom and his living room, cameras, and an official tail with at least two cars. On my own, it was hopeless. And I had other things I had to do, like trying to find Gunner. I could see myself getting hopelessly bogged down just trying to follow Davidson. The frustration weighed on me as I parked the Taurus in a different parking spot, on the second floor this time, in sight of Davidson's Mercedes. I turned off the engine, and we sat there in the silence.

"What now?" Stan finally asked.

"Well, we wait for him to come out of his office and kill somebody, of course. Then we nab him. It's all very basic."

She hit me on the arm. "You goofus! No, really. I'm serious. What do we do now?"

"It beats hell out of me."

She snorted. "I can tell you've done a lot of serious planning."

"Unfortunately, I need more help." I told her about my conversation with Joe Henderson, about not having official support from the Austin Police Department at this point. "So you're right, I don't really have any great big magnificent plans on how to trap him, how to prove he's involved. I've got other things that need to be done too. Like trying to find Gunner. It's frustrating."

"Who?" she asked.

"Gunner. That's the other guy whose picture I showed you."

"His name is Gunner?"

"Don't even ask."

So we just sat there. Time passed.

"Still excited?" I asked at one point.

"It's wearing off a little."

"Funny thing about that."

Still more time passed. I saw Stan yawn. I had an idea we wouldn't be doing many stakeouts together. Cross that off the list, along with costume parties.

Then, as we sat there, the elevator doors opened and Davidson stepped out and walked directly to his Mercedes and slipped behind the wheel.

"Touchdown," I said.

"Amen," said Stan.

I started the Taurus as he pulled out of his space, then followed him out of the garage. I figured out pretty quickly where he was headed: The Austin Country Club. Why not? A busy doctor going out for a little tennis after a hard day at the office. Sure enough, that's the way it worked out. The Austin Country Club. I parked in the lot a good ways from the Mercedes and watched as he went inside the clubhouse. After a few minutes, I decided he probably wasn't coming right back out.

"Wait here," I told Stan. "Call me on the cell if you see him come out."

"Can't I come?" she complained.

"Don't like stakeouts? You're the one who wanted in on this. Remember that?"

"Rat crap," she grumbled.

So I left her there and went looking for the tennis courts. I saw Davidson as soon as I got there, playing singles with another guy. I watched from a distance. He was every bit as good as Joe Henderson had said he was. He was tall and strong and quick, and he moved with easy grace and agility over the court, hitting the ball with lashing power, an athlete all the way.

They didn't play for long. When they disappeared back into the clubhouse, I headed back to the Taurus.

"I didn't see him," Stan said.

"Well, I did."

"You did?" she asked eagerly. "What happened? I want to know."

"Oh, he killed this girl and stuffed her in a dumpster."

She hit my arm again. "No, you horse's butt! Be serious! What happened? Tell me. I want to know."

"I just watched him play tennis. He's damn good, just like Joe Henderson told me. He's been club champion here a bunch of times."

"Who's Joe Henderson?"

"Guy I know with the Austin Police Department. The one who can't give me any help right now."

"Oh . . ."

A short while later, Davidson came back out of the clubhouse and got in the Mercedes. We followed him again, this time to the neighborhood where he lived. I was concerned about being spotted if we tailed him to a residential area, so I held back and lost him, taking the risk I might miss something, and then drove by his house a few minutes later. The Mercedes was parked in the drive. I was feeling frustrated again. I needed a real tail, with spotters and at least a couple of cars. I couldn't just park the Taurus on the street in a neighborhood like this and wait for him to come back out of his house. I'd be noticed. People would call the cops. I felt very helpless.

"What now?" Stan asked.

"Don't you know any other questions?"

She laughed. "It's just that I'm so eager to see what the mastermind comes up with next."

"Well, we could always wait for him to come out and surrender."

She laughed again. "Brilliant. Just brilliant. I don't know why I didn't think of that myself."

I looked at my watch. It was almost seven.

"How about dinner?" I said.

"*Now* you've come up with an idea."

So we drove by the Outback and got her truck, then went in separate vehicles to a Chili's and had dinner. We sat there talking when we had finished. Stan had a rum and Coke and I sipped a beer. I found her studying me closely.

"You seem bothered," she said.

"Yeah, I'm frustrated. Think I'm crazy?"

She shook her head. "No, I don't. I've already told you that. If you think you're onto something, then I think so too."

"I can't do all this by myself, though. Davidson's got to be followed at all times, so we know exactly what he does, where he goes, anybody he sees. I can't do all that alone."

She was studying me again. "So . . . what now?"

"Your favorite question. Still no good answer."

So we wound up sitting there a while longer. She had another rum and Coke and I had another beer.

"Where are you staying?" she asked.

"Motel. La Quinta on I-35. And you?"

"Oh, I have friends here in Austin. I'm staying with them."

"That's convenient," I said.

She looked me very directly in the eye. "We could always go by your place."

I didn't know how I felt about that. I thought about Julie and Bobby. Everything seemed upside down.

"I don't know, Stan . . . I guess I still haven't really

recovered from my little adventure the other night . . . I'm sore all over. My stomach doesn't feel so great . . ."

She appeared to be thinking for a moment. Her eyes dropped, then came back up to meet mine.

"You're still very bonded to them, aren't you?" she finally asked.

I had told her about Julie and Bobby when we had been talking the other day, but I was still surprised she had made the connection.

"Yeah . . . I guess I am . . ."

"I'm sure they're very special to you."

I nodded. "Yeah . . ."

"Do you have any pictures of them?" she asked. "I don't mean to be forward. You don't have to show me anything if you don't want to. Tell me to bug off if it bothers you, but I'd like to see them."

"Well, sure . . ."

I had some pictures in my wallet. I pulled them out and showed them to her. She looked at them intently.

"Julie's very pretty," she said.

"She is indeed."

"And Bobby . . ." She looked from the picture to me, then back at Bobby's picture, then back at me. I could see her smile. " . . . And Bobby looks like his Daddy. I can see the resemblance there very closely. He's going to be another good-looking devil, Walt."

"Don't know. We'll see."

She handed the pictures back to me, and I put them back in my wallet. We found ourselves looking at each other again. I still felt conflicted.

"I'm tired, Stan," I said. "Beat and frustrated too. I probably ought to go back to the motel and get some rest."

I could see she was disappointed, even though she tried not to let it show.

"Sure, I understand," she said.

So we walked out to the cars. I opened the door of

her pickup for her, but instead of getting in, she stepped up close to me and put her arms around me and kissed me. Very hard. Our tongues intertwined. I could feel the pace of her breathing becoming faster. We stayed that way for almost a minute, our mouths pressed together, holding each other tight. Then she pushed herself away from me.

"I need to let you get your rest," she said. She slid in behind the wheel of the pickup and closed the door. I heard the engine turn over. The window slid down. She smiled at me, then winked. "Get your rest, Walt. There's a lot left to do. See you tomorrow."

Then she put the truck in gear and drove away. I got in the Taurus and headed back to the motel, going slowly. I sat in the car when I got there, just thinking. It was night now, and the lights of the city twinkled around me. The cellphone rang, and I answered it. It was Joe Henderson.

"Got another piece of information for you," he said. "They just called me from the station. Thought you'd like to know."

"Sure. What you got?"

"The drawing of that girl you sent me, the one you said had been at parties at that club up in Dallas."

"Yeah. I saw a tape of her with Gunner, doing it doggie style."

"They feel pretty sure they have a positive identification on her. Her name's Donna Rivers. She's from Ft. Worth."

I felt my pulse quicken. "Hey, that's great! That could be just the connection we need. Do we know how to contact her?"

It took him a moment to answer. "No, we don't . . . she's been missing since December before last. She left home that night and never returned. No trace of her has ever been found."

I felt a sudden hollowness in the pit of my gut. Missing? I didn't think so. I had seen her on the tape of the

November party of that year, just a couple of weeks before she had turned up missing. She had been with Gunner. Just like Charlotte Raymond in Corpus Christi.

"She's not just missing, Joe," I said. "You know that as well as I do. She's dead. We just haven't found her body yet."

I got the impression he ran his tongue over his lips. His voice sounded dry when he spoke.

"Yeah . . . I think you're right . . ."

"Joe, I need your help with Davidson," I went on. "He's the only connection we have right now. We can place him at clubs with all four of these women, at one time or another. He was with Gunner in Corpus Christi for sure, maybe in San Antonio too. We know Gunner was with Charlotte Raymond and now Donna Rivers. Davidson's part of it, Joe. I can feel it in my gut."

He didn't say anything. I could almost hear him thinking.

"You said you couldn't help me with Davidson, but I can't do it alone. I don't have the resources or the clout to track him to the bottom of this thing. You know that. I need your help."

He still didn't speak.

"I don't care how prominent or important this guy is, I think he's a killer. I think we need to do everything we can to nail him. We need to tap his phone. Office and home. We need an official tail, twenty-four hours a day, two cars at least, with surveillance equipment. We need a search warrant so we can search his house and his office. We won't get him any other way. You can say it's a sticky mess, politically, but four women have died, and I don't think the murders have stopped."

I waited, listening. I could hear his breathing on the other end of the line.

"Yeah . . . I think you're probably right . . ," he finally said.

"I need your help, Joe. You can do it in Austin. I can't."

I could hear the sound of his breathing again. I could feel the tightness.

"Okay . . . I'll see what I can do . . . no guarantees, but I'll make some calls in the morning. I'll talk with the Acting Chief and the DA. I'll see what I can come up with."

"Thanks, Joe. I know it's not an easy decision for you."

"I'll call you when I find out something," he said.

"I'll be here."

I went inside the motel, watched part of a basketball game, looked through the material on Davidson again, then went to bed early. I lay in bed thinking before I drifted off to sleep. Thinking of Davidson. And Gunner. And Michelle Stanzer and Charlotte Raymond. And Donna Rivers. And most of all, Jessica Nodman. Rumpulina.

The next morning I drove to Davidson's office, but his car wasn't in its assigned space. I found it in the doctor's lot behind Brackenridge Hospital. Operating again, I figured. Stymied. So I started hitting gyms again to see if anybody recognized the picture of Gunner. This was Austin, after all. Ground zero. But the hunt was just as futile as it had been in Dallas. Nobody knew him.

I decided not to call Joe Henderson, even though I was itching to find out what he would be able to come up with. No, he had said he'd call me. I'd wait to hear from him. It was hard, but that was what I had to do.

Stan called just before noon, and we agreed to meet for lunch at Bennigan's. I was already seated when she walked in. I could tell right away she seemed stressed. I hadn't seen her like that before.

"Not a good morning," she told me.

We didn't talk as much as we usually did. She wound up asking if I'd learned anything new. I told her all about Donna Rivers all and about my conversation with Joe Henderson.

"What do you plan to do this afternoon?" she asked.

I had thought about that. There was another person I needed to talk to, I had decided. Somebody who might give me a different slant on things. Davidson's ex-wife. I had seen her name and address in the material Joe had given me. I thought it might be worth a visit.

"I think I'll see if I can locate Davidson's ex-wife," I said. "It might be interesting to get her perspective on what he's like in private."

She nodded thoughtfully. "Not a bad idea. Anything else?"

"After that I have to drive back to Dallas. I'm taking Bobby to play in a soccer game tonight."

She smiled. "Well, that sounds like fun."

A couple of minutes later she excused herself and went to the ladies room. She was gone for several minutes.

"I got a call on my cell when I was in the restroom," she said when she came back and sat down. "Something unexpected has come up with the case I'm working on. I'm going to have to go back down to the courthouse. I hadn't expected that. I hate it, but I don't have a choice. I won't be able to come with you today."

We went outside, and I walked her to her pickup. She kissed me before she got inside, very hard, holding me tightly. Then she broke away and got in behind the wheel. I saw the window slide down.

"I'll call you," she said. She looked at me, held my eyes. "Take care of yourself, Walt. Be careful. Always."

Then she backed up the truck, swung it around, and drove out of the lot.

I got in the Taurus and pulled out a map of the city I had picked up at a service station. I found the street where Davidson's ex-wife lived and plotted out a route. I wasn't familiar with Austin, and I was surprised as I drove to find myself heading into a poorer part of town. I looked around and double-checked the address when I finally got there. I was in front of a very small, frame wooden house that had no garage. The yard in front was sparse and poorly tended. Other houses on the street showed a similar appearance. It wasn't a slum, but the contrast with Davidson's mansion was striking. I checked the address one last time, then got out and stepped to the door.

I had to knock several times before it finally opened. A dark-haired woman cracked it open and stared out at me past a locking chain. She had on dark glasses and a robe. Her hair looked disheveled. She wore no make-up.

"Yes?" she asked hesitantly. Her voice was weak, almost tremulous.

"Excuse me," I said. "I think I probably have the wrong address. I was looking for Angela Davidson."

"Yes?" she said.

It took me a moment to react. "You're . . . Angela Davidson?"

She seemed very hesitant again. "Yes . . . why? What do you want?"

I pulled out my badge and held it up for her. "Police. I'd like to ask you a few questions."

Her lips parted open. "Police . . ?"

"Yes, ma'am. It won't take long. It's not directly related to you. I'm just trying to get some information."

She had managed to gather her robe up about herself, protectively. She was almost huddling.

"Do I . . . do I *have* to talk to you?"

She didn't, of course, but I said, "It would be easier for you to just cooperate, ma'am. I'll have to come back with papers if you don't."

She put the back of her hand up to her mouth. I thought her lip was quivering.

"Well . . . come in then . . . it's not very clean . . ."

She undid the latch and opened the door. I stepped

inside, into darkness. There weren't any lights on, and all the windows were covered with blinds. Daylight filtered through the cracks, but my eyes still had to adjust as I looked around. She had said it wasn't clean. That was an understatement. There were empty liquor bottles lying around everywhere, along with cracker and cereal boxes and other left over debris. She stood there amidst it all, clutching her robe around her, looking at me uncertainly and waiting for me to speak.

"I don't know if I have the right Angela Davidson," I said. "Was Corbin Davidson your husband?"

She put her hand to her mouth again. I thought she was about to cry.

"Yes . . ," she said tremulously.

"I just want to ask you some questions about him."

"Why?"

"Just part of an investigation. It won't take long."

"Please don't, Officer," she begged. "Please. I don't know anything. I promise you. Please don't."

I was struck by the urgency of her plea. "You don't see him these days?"

"Please, don't tell him you were here," she said. "Please. I beg of you."

I was struck again by her desperation. "Are you afraid of him?"

"Please, don't tell him, Officer. Please. Please."

Her voice was a whisper, so low I could barely hear it. Then she broke and started to cry. She tried to suppress it, but couldn't. She held her hand closely over her mouth again, as a sob wracked her whole frame. I could smell her fear.

"Please . . ."

I looked around one more time. All I could see was wreckage. I knew I had already learned everything I was going to learn here.

"I'm sorry to have bothered you," I said. "I don't

think I'll need to come back."

"Please, don't tell him," she said, her voice still a whisper. "Please don't. He's not the person you think he is. Please."

"I won't. Don't worry about it."

I stepped back through the door and closed it behind me. Then I walked to the Taurus, got inside and drove off. I felt almost unclean for having violated her space, for having penetrated her misery. I wasn't even sure what I had learned. That something very bad had happened in her life and that she was desperately afraid of her ex-husband, that much for sure, but I had a feeling I'd never learn all the details, at least not from her.

Her words hung in my mind: he's not the person you think he is. But he *is*, I thought. He *is*.

I glanced at my watch. It was almost four. Time to head back to Dallas for Bobby's soccer game. I got back onto I-35, then headed north . . .

14.

I drove steadily, not rushing. I called Julie about four-thirty, thinking I'd reach her before they stopped answering the phones at the office, and I did.

"I'm on my way now," I told her.

"Bobby's there at the house alone," she said. "He stays there by himself every afternoon after school. I think he's big enough to do that. He says it doesn't bother him. There haven't been any problems. But I haven't ever really discussed that with you. I just kind of made that decision on my own. I hope you're okay with that."

"Sure, that's fine, Julie. I agree with you. I think he's big enough to do that. It's a safe neighborhood, after all."

There was a moment of hesitation. "Could you . . . could you possibly take him back to my parents' house after the game? I . . . I know I hadn't really asked you to do that. I'm . . . I'm sorry to just spring it on you, but . . . something else has come up, and I may be home later than I expected, and I . . . I was just wondering if you could do that?"

Serves you right, Draeger, I thought. You're getting what you deserve.

"Sure, I can do that, Julie. I'll take him there after the game."

"Thanks, Walt."

"You bet."

"Well . . . the send-off party is supposed to start in just a few minutes, and I'm supposed to help with the preparation, so I . . . I'd probably better get busy and pitch in with it."

"Sure, Julie. Have a great time."

"Thanks again, Walt."

"Sure. You bet."

DANCE YOUR HEART OUT

So that was that. Sam was obviously still very much in the picture. Serves you right, Draeger, I told myself again.

I kept heading north. Coming into Dallas, I got a call on my cellphone. It was Joe Henderson. He sounded tired. Or stressed. Or both.

"Well, we got your tail," he said. "Department gave the okay just a little while ago. Had to talk really long and hard with the new Acting Chief. Name's Ron Baker. Regular Chief got hurt in a car accident a few weeks ago. He's still in rehab. Baker got moved up to take his place in the meantime. Turns out Davidson did Baker's bypass surgery last year, and the idea of putting a tail on his heart surgeon didn't sit real well with him, but I went over all the stuff you gave me, and he finally agreed. Tail goes into effect as of now, so we got a handle on your boy, even as we speak. Got two cars, four officers, surveillance, the whole bit."

"Good. I appreciate it, Joe. I know you went out on a limb for this, but I really think Davidson's part of it. I think you'll be glad you did."

"Maybe. We'll see."

"What about the wiretaps and the search warrants? Where do we stand with those?"

"Still pending. A tail is one thing. We can do that on our own. But the wiretaps and the search warrants are a different deal. Haven't got those cleared yet. Maybe tomorrow, but there's no guarantee. It'd be easier if Davidson weren't such a high profile guy."

"Let me know what happens. I do appreciate what you're doing."

"Yeah . . ."

"How you feeling?"

"Crap, I'm fine," he grumbled. "A little sore, that's all. Still don't have all my strength back yet. Better today than yesterday, though."

"Hang in there, Joe."

"Yeah."

By then I was on the freeway coming into Dallas from the south. I checked my watch. Not even six o'clock. I was ahead of schedule. That meant I had time to swing by the apartment. A quick beer sounded mighty good. I took the appropriate exit and was at the apartment in just a few minutes. I hit the little boy's room, then went to the fridge and got a beer. I hadn't even popped the top when the doorbell rang. I went to the door and pulled it open. It was Sandy.

"Hi, Walt," she said cheerfully. "Sorry to bother you, but I was just wondering if you might have a can opener I could borrow. I have this electric one, but it's broken, and I need to get some stuff opened up."

"Sure, Sandy." So I went back to the kitchen and got a can opener and gave it to her. "There you go."

She hesitated for a moment. "Uh . . . by the way, Walt, a few of us were going to fix up some hamburgers by the pool a little later. You know, just a little get-together. Care to join us?"

Thank God for soccer games. "Can't, Sandy. Got to take my kid out again. Soccer game this time. Sorry."

"Well . . . maybe next time."

"Sure. Maybe next time."

She gave me a little finger twinkling wave. "Well, see you, Walt," she said.

"See you, Sandy."

She walked back down the balcony toward her place, and I guzzled the beer and left. I managed to pull up in front of the house in Garland right on time, six-thirty straight up. Bobby answered the door.

"I'm still getting my stuff together, Dad," he said, running back to the back bedroom. "I'll be ready in just a minute."

I looked around the living room. No sign of Brutus.

So I went through the kitchen and the garage and out into the back yard to check on him. I saw him lying over to the side, up against the back wall of the house. He got up and padded over toward me, but he didn't come running like he usually did. He walked slowly, his tail barely wagging, his head hanging down. When he got to me, he didn't even try to jump up on me and put his paws on my shirt. I knelt down and scratched behind his ear. He tried to lick me in the mouth, but I didn't let him.

"Hey, boy, are you sick?" I asked.

I felt his nose. It seemed cool enough. Then I checked one of his front paws. It was dry. Now *that* was alarming.

"You lonesome, boy?" I asked, scratching behind his ear again.

He tried to lick me again, but I saw it coming and held him off. I glanced around the yard as I stood up. Julie's shrubs along the fence were doing nicely. The rest of the yard looked neat and trim too. But I felt a heaviness.

"Hey, boy," I said as I scratched behind his ear again. "We got to get you back inside somehow. I don't think you're doing so great out here. I'll see what I can do."

He wagged his tail, but he still didn't try to jump up and put his paws on me. I stepped back through the door to the garage and shut it behind me. I found Bobby ready to leave when I got to the living room.

"Let's go, sport," I said.

So we walked out to the car, got in, and headed out.

"I know the way," Bobby said. "Mom said for me to give you directions."

"I think Brutus is depressed," I noted as we drove. "He's not acting right. He didn't try to jump up on me like he always does. And his paws are dry. Have you guys noticed anything?"

"Yeah, he really doesn't like it in the back yard,"

Bobby agreed. “I think he’s real unhappy. He’s even started to howl at night.”

“Howl? Labs aren’t supposed to howl.”

“Tell him that,” Bobby said. “Well, it’s kind of like a howl, and it’s kind of like a moan. He does it off and on all night long. One of the neighbors called and talked to Mom yesterday. Mom says she doesn’t know what to do with him. She says we have to keep him in the back yard because of Mr. Thompson down the street. Mr. Saunders too. Mr. Saunders is the landlord who owns the house. He’s a real jerk, Dad. He comes around every week and inspects the place, like we’re trying to mess it up or something. And he told Mom the other day that he found some spots on the rug, and then he said it smelled bad too. He said he’d have to keep the deposit money we gave him and even charge us extra if the house got all messed up. He’s a jerk, Dad. He really is. And so Mom says she doesn’t know what else to do. She says Brutus has to stay in the back yard. She says we may even need to give him away or something. Give him to somebody who lives out in the country, maybe. But he hates it out there, and Mom’s worried about the neighbors because of the howling. She’s pretty stressed about it.”

I thought about that. “Well then, maybe I need to have a little talk with Mr. Saunders. Maybe a little gentle persuasion might change his attitude.”

Bobby regarded me closely, not sure what to expect.

“We’ll see what happens,” I said.

Not much else was said as we drove to the soccer field. Bobby started getting into his goalie gear, and that seemed to occupy his attention. He pulled on his shoes and laced them tight. Then we were there. A considerable crowd was already present, milling around on the edge of the field. I parked in a space in a long row of cars and shut off the engine. Bobby pulled on the door latch but didn’t push the door open. He looked over at me.

DANCE YOUR HEART OUT

"I probably ought to tell you something, Dad."

"What's that?"

"Well, this team we're playing today, they're probably the best twelve and under team in the state. I mean, it's like they're just awesome, Dad. They've never been beaten. I mean, nobody's even come close so far, and they've only been scored on a couple of times. They're just awesome." He hesitated for a moment. He looked down, then back up at me. "I'm really glad you could be here today, Dad. I really am. But I thought you ought to know that."

I nodded. "Just do what you can, Bobby. That's all anybody can do."

I held out a hand, and he gave me five. Then we got out of the car and headed to the field. Bobby joined his teammates, and I wound up mingling with parents on the sideline. I was new to the scene and didn't know people. There were a couple of brief greetings, a couple of quick recognitions, just your basic courtesy and politeness, but everybody's focus was clearly on the game. There was talk of what a good team we were playing, how tough they were supposed to be. An air of tension and expectation hung over everybody's thoughts. Then I happened to spot Helen Baxter, standing about thirty feet away in a group of mothers. She was looking right at me. I gave her a nod and a little wave of my hand, and she smiled and waved back. But I didn't go over to talk with her. In fact, I turned my back and walked in the opposite direction, getting even farther away from her. I kept my back turned toward her and positioned myself alongside a couple of fathers.

Then, after a brief warm-up, the game got started. My expectations had been modest, I had to admit. These were kids, after all, just twelve and under, even if they were playing on a selective club team that drew from all over the city. And I had seen Bobby on playing fields before. I knew he wasn't a natural athlete, even though he had talked about how interested he'd become in soccer. So I had prepared myself for a lackluster performance all around. Just little kids, running up and down a field, kicking at a ball.

I was quickly surprised. These kids were good. They had been well coached too. They handled the ball well, working in formation, passing the ball off to each other adroitly as they moved down the field. It wasn't what I had prepared myself for.

Bobby surprised me the most of all. He had talked about his philosophy of being a goalie - he had said he wasn't afraid to get hurt, he wasn't afraid of the contact. He wasn't afraid to go for the ball. He could take it, whatever happened. I had heard him talking like that, but nothing could have prepared me for what I saw. My God, he played like a little madman. Like a little crazy person. He charged approaching forwards like an insane daredevil, blocked kicks full force with any part of his body, dove flat out through the air for the ball, fought for it like a tiger with kicking feet all around, flung himself crazily in front of the ball anytime it approached the goal. I was horrified. I really don't think I'm an overly protective parent, and God knows I'm no stranger to contact sports, but I still felt myself cringing like a nervous mother every time there was another full body impact, each time he blocked a stinging kick with his head or his body, each time he flew flat out through the air to block a shot and came crashing down to the ground. But every time he'd get right up and go for the ball again, or head back to the goal, covering his turf. I'd breathe a little sigh of relief, and the knot in my gut would start to unwind for a moment, and then it would start all over again.

They couldn't score on him. That's what it came down to. He guarded that goal with a ferocity that was simply amazing. Time and time and time again he blocked sure winners, diving in front of the ball, taking hits on his body and his head. He had made at least a half dozen saves by the middle of the first half. Kind of reminded me of a defensive end I knew once in high school.

"That kid of yours is one hell of a goalie!" one of the fathers called out to me at one point.

"Thanks!" I yelled back.

Then the magic happened. I had been particularly impressed by this tiny little guy on Bobby's team. He was a small wiry kid, way too small to ever play football, but he had the speed and the moves of a running back. He covered the field like a little motorized fire hydrant. He was a good ball handler too. It had taken me a couple of minutes to recognize him. This was Johnny Baxter, the kid who had been watching the videotape with Bobby. I hadn't been told that he was such a star player. And suddenly, as we watched from the sideline, he took a pass in front of the other team's goal, faked one way, dribbled the other, and then fired a low hooking ball right around their goalie, into the net.

Well, it might as well have been first blood at the Super Bowl. Parents went crazy all up and down the sideline. I didn't think some of these people had jumped off the ground in years, judging from looking at them, but they were leaping and hopping and hollering like a bunch of cheerleaders. The kids on the team went nuts too, running up and down and hugging each other and doing all kinds of crazy stuff. Here we were, the total underdog, one up on the best twelve and under bunch in the state. Looking down the line, I could see Helen Baxter jumping up and down and screaming like crazy.

"Way to go, Johnny!" she yelled. "Way to go!"

Goodness, but she looked nice. Jumping up and down like that, all the natural anatomy obeying the laws of gravity and physics. I forced myself not to stare. By dint of will, I made myself look away, back out to the field. Just cool it, Walt, I told myself. Just cool it.

"Damn, but that little Johnny Baxter is a player!" I

heard one of the fathers shout. "What a player!"

I thought about it. I'd really have to say something to his mom, as well as he was playing. It would be rude not to. But I would have to handle it very, very carefully.

Then the game got going again. We were into the nitty-gritty now, two teams battling evenly, nose to nose, trading blows. It certainly wasn't the runaway that had been expected. We hung right in there with them, matching them man for man, play for play, kick for kick. The first half neared its close.

They managed to get one by Bobby and score just before it ended. It was a squeaker, but they got it. He had blocked one shot, flying through the air, his arms outreached, then got up and blocked another, but this time the ball glanced off one of our own players, rather than flying away from the front of the goal, and one of their guys was standing there, and he hit it a good kick. Bobby had gotten up in time to throw himself through the air again, and he even managed to deflect it again, but not solidly enough this time, and the ball hit the corner post, and instead of bouncing away into the clear, it bounced into the goal.

He didn't let it get to him, though. He got up and kept going just as hard. He managed to make one more great save just before the whistle blew to end the half.

The parents all helped with drinks at half time. The kids were hot and sweaty, but exhilarated. The coach spent some time talking with them, discussing strategy, outlining a few new plays and formations. I hadn't ever paid much attention to soccer, and most of it was lost on me.

Bobby came over to me at one point, and we slapped hands.

"They're good, Dad. They're real good."

"So are you guys, Bobby. I'm impressed. I mean that."

I think his grin touched both ears. He pumped a fist

and ran back to join his teammates.

"Are you feeling better today?" I heard somebody ask at my elbow as I watched him run away.

I turned and saw Helen Baxter. Got that adrenaline rush again. Goodness, she looked nice. The excitement of everything seemed to make her look even more sparkling.

"Yeah, I'm well now, thank God."

She smiled. Kept looking at me.

"Good," she said. "I'm glad to hear that."

"Johnny's a fantastic little player," I said. "A couple more like him, and we'd be in the World Cup."

She laughed. Her smile was radiant. "Thanks. Bobby's doing great too. He's like a little barricade in front of that goal."

"Thanks," I said.

I got the impression I could have lingered there, could have stayed and talked, but I didn't think I should let myself.

"Oops," I said, reaching into my pocket and pulling out my cellphone. "Phone's vibrating. Looks like I got a call. Excuse me for a moment."

So I put the phone to my ear and turned away and said, "Yeah, this is Walt," to the empty line. I kept walking for thirty or forty feet, pretending to be listening to a conversation, until I was far enough away. I stayed there for several minutes, my back turned most of the time, sometimes walking back and forth, the phone to my ear the whole time. Finally I could see the second half starting, and I figured it would be safe to go back to the sideline.

The game quickly became a grind again, the two teams banging away at each other, but neither one able to penetrate the defense of the other and score. I watched as the ball moved up and down the field again and again. Up and down, up and down. On offense now, then on defense. Up and down.

Bobby made several more saves. He hung in there

every time they got close, charging the ball, always managing to stop it or deflect it before it got to the goal.

"God! He's a good goalie!" one of the fathers told me again.

"Right on!" I said, and I pumped my fist.

The game was grinding into the last minutes. I didn't know what provision there might be in case of a tie. One of the parents was staying in close touch with the timekeeper, so we knew where the clock stood.

With barely two minutes left, little Johnny Baxter took a pass, faked beautifully and dribbled around a defender, then outran another kid, head faked the goalie and put the ball dead in the corner of the goal. Well, this is what a heart attack feels like, I thought. God, I could barely breathe. Parents were yelling and screaming and jumping up and down and hitting each other on the back and going totally crazy all over the place, and I was right there with them. I don't think I've ever felt quite like that before, not even when we won state 5-A football championship my senior year. I had promised myself along the way that I'd never be some sort of fanatical Little League parent, but I hadn't realized how heady the intoxication could be.

"We're gonna beat these sons of bitches!" one of the fathers shouted. "We're gonna beat 'em!"

Yes, I thought! Beat 'em! Beat 'em! Beat 'em! The evil, evil, evil, nasty little twelve and under sons of bitches! Beat 'em! Beat 'em! Beat 'em!

Then it was back to the game. One more minute. We were up two to one. A brief timeout ended, and then the invaders came charging back up the field, dead set, iron determination on their faces. The ball went here, went there. They passed well, confidently. They were the best twelve and under team in the state, after all. They were invincible, and they were here to win. My heart was so far up in my throat, I couldn't have swallowed if I had wanted to. My breath was a knot in my chest.

The action converged toward our goal. A pass here, a pass there. The action going this way, then that. I saw a kid break lose toward our goal. He had a step on our guy. He took a perfect pass, cut to one side, and fired from close range.

But Bobby was there! I couldn't believe my eyes. Out of nowhere he was there, flying flat out through the air. He got a hand on the ball, deflected it. I could see it sailing toward the corner of the goal. I saw it strike the corner post. And this time it careened away from the goal, out onto the field. One of Bobby's teammates was there. He controlled the ball and started back up the field. There couldn't be more than ten seconds left.

A pass here. A pass there. Then, in horror, I saw one of their kids steal it, in their own territory now. And here they came again, back up the field, moving even faster now, more urgently, fire in their eyes. I didn't have breath enough to ask about the time. Still enough to score.

I watched, spellbound, as they advanced the ball. I could see Bobby farther down the field, standing his ground in front of the goal, watching every movement of the ball, ready to defend with everything he had. God, he looked so alone. I couldn't even call out to him.

Then, out of nowhere, little Johnny Baxter took the ball away from their very best forward - just flat out stole it, thank you - and headed back up the field with it, running like a little rocket, handling the ball perfectly all the way. He got to midfield with it, then crossed over into their territory. I felt mesmerized.

And then I heard the whistle blow, and all the action on the field died on the spot as the game ended. Players stopped running, and our guys started yelling and waving their arms and hugging each other and pounding each other on the back. The parents on the sidelines were going just as crazy. People were hugging each other and slapping palms and everything. I looked back out on the field, toward our goal. Bobby had come running up the field to join his buddies. They were all going crazy.

For some strange reason I turned around, and Helen Baxter came running up to me and jumped up into my arms. I mean, jumped right up into my arms and put her arms around my neck and her legs around my waist and hung on tight. I didn't really know what to do. It wasn't what I needed, but I still didn't want to be rude, so I kept holding her like that. Unfortunately, it felt very good. There's just something about the touch of flesh. Then, just as suddenly, she unhooked from me and stood there in front of me.

"Can you believe it!" she cried. "Can you believe it! They're the best in the state!" She laughed and hugged me. She didn't let go all that quickly. It was quite unsettling again.

"Johnny!" I suddenly heard her call. She let go of me and went running over toward her kid, who had come racing up toward us. I watched as they ran into each other's arms and hugged each other.

I did the same when Bobby came running up to me. I picked him up and held him tight. His arms locked around my neck.

"We won, Dad! We won!"

I started to say something, but there was this silly little catch in my throat that I hadn't been expecting. I had to take a deep breath.

"You sure did, Bobby! You sure did! You guys played great!"

Then he was down, and he and Johnny Baxter were slapping palms and pounding each other on the back. All the other kids were doing the same. It was really quite a scene. It took a couple of minutes to die down, and I think it finally stopped then only because somebody remembered we had to go down the line with the other team. So the guys all lined up and shook hands with the players on the other team, and our coach shook hands with theirs. The players from the other team were a somber, subdued looking bunch indeed. Both sets of parents stayed out of it altogether. Then it was over and there was talk of a party, so we wound up going to this pizza place, and it was really a very festive occasion. The thrill of victory still prevailed, and the kids had a great time. I sat and watched as Bobby and Johnny Baxter went at it on a video game across the way. I had decided not to have a beer in front of the players, so I sat there sipping a Sprite. It was one of those special rare times, when the magic of the moment was intoxication enough.

Then, as I sat there, Helen Baxter came up out of nowhere and sat down beside me. I felt myself tense all over. I only prayed I wouldn't have another anxiety attack. I really felt quite at a loss. I'd already used the diarrhea number and the cellphone as excuses, and I didn't think I could go with them again. I wasn't sure what to try next. Throw up? Pass out? A seizure? I just didn't know.

"They're having the second greatest time of their lives," she noted, nodding toward Johnny and Bobby, who were still going at it on the video game.

"Sure are," I agreed, not looking at her. I didn't think I should say any more. Didn't think I should get involved in a conversation.

I could tell she was studying me. "Have I done something to offend you?" she finally asked. "Have I said something to make you mad?"

I shook my head but still didn't look at her. "No, you haven't."

After a moment she said, "You could try to be a little friendlier, you know. I don't bite, after all."

I still didn't feel comfortable, but I didn't want to be rude either, so I turned toward her and said, "I'm sorry, Helen. I really am. I don't mean to be unpleasant or unfriendly, it's just that a lot's going on in my life right now. There's a lot on the plate. I guess I'm kind of distracted and preoccupied. I apologize if I've been rude or offended you in any way. I wouldn't want to do that."

She smiled. I could see her eyes soften.

"Thanks. I feel better hearing you say that. I was afraid I had horrified you or grossed you out or something."

"You didn't. Not by a long shot."

She smiled again. "I can't believe I actually jumped up on you like that after the game. I was just so excited. I think I came a little unglued. I'm sorry."

"Couldn't possibly have been a better ending to the game."

"Well . . . I just hope you weren't too mortified."

"I wasn't. Not at all."

She hesitated, then stood up and pushed her chair back up to the table. I think we both sensed the timing just wasn't right.

"Take care," she said, a surprising softness in her voice. "See you around."

I nodded. "See you around, Helen."

And then she walked away.

Gradually things wound down. Time passed. The excitement ebbed to a glow. Finally parents began to round up their kids and started splitting off. Bobby and I were among the last to leave. We talked a little as we drove to his grandparents' house, reliving the game. Then that faded off too, and we were both quiet.

"I guess Mom's out with Sam," I finally said.

He nodded. "Yeah. He sent her some flowers again. She always likes that." He looked down at his hands. I could tell he was frowning. "She's all mixed up, Dad. I don't think she knows what she wants."

I didn't have a response to that.

Finally we were there. Bobby gathered up his gear and popped open the passenger door. Then he hugged me tight around the neck and held onto me for several moments. I held onto him too.

"Thanks, Dad. I'm really glad you could be there. That's the best time I ever, ever, ever had," he said when he finally let go.

Then he got out of the car, walked to the door, and went inside . . .

15.

I set the alarm and got up early on Wednesday morning. I was coming into Austin before nine o'clock. I gave Joe Henderson a ring at home as I passed the city limit sign, but Sue said he'd gone to work that morning, so I called him at the office. He said he was feeling fine.

"Nothing unusual on your boy yet," he said. "Spent the night at home last night. No visitors. He's in surgery again this morning."

"How about the wiretaps and the search warrants?"

I could hear him take a slow breath. "No progress there." He hesitated again. "Look, Walt . . . I don't know what's gonna happen there. Acting Chief's really not pleased with any of this. He finally agreed to the tail, but it was like pulling teeth. I found out a little more about his heart surgery too. Turns out he was in worse shape than anybody in the department knew at the time. He damn near died, in fact. Had three cardiac arrests on the table, the whole nine yards. And Davidson saved his life, is what it basically amounts to. And Baker's doing just great now. Playing tennis again, the whole bit. He's been a tennis player all his life, so he looks up to Davidson in that area too. So you can understand how he thinks Davidson is the next thing to Jesus Christ. He's *really* not pleased with any of this, so I don't know whether we'll wind up with the taps and the warrants or not."

He hesitated again. I could hear him take another deep breath.

"And in the meantime, I'm the one on the hot seat. *I'm* the one who's gonna catch it if the whole deal goes sour. My whole career could just go up in smoke."

"I hear you, Joe. I'm sorry you're stuck in the middle. I wouldn't have asked you for help if I hadn't felt he was involved."

"Yeah . . . I know that. . ." I could hear the stress in his voice.

After a moment I said, "You say he's in surgery again this morning?"

"Yeah."

"That ought to leave one car free, shouldn't it? Doesn't take two units to track him when he's there in the hospital."

"Yeah. . ."

I didn't feel good about asking for more help just then, but I had more to do than I could manage on my own, so I said, "I got this two page list I made up of gyms and health stores and adult book places here in Austin. I'm trying to see if anybody recognizes Gunner's picture. It'll take me forever to hit all those places by myself. You think you could break free one of those units to help me?"

I could hear his breathing on the line again as he considered it. "Probably . . ," he finally said.

"Thanks, Joe. I'll fax you the list. I'll take the first page, they can take the second. Okay?"

I could hear his breathing again. "I guess . . ."

"I'll get it right to you."

I still had his fax number on a piece of paper in my wallet, so I stopped at an office supply store and faxed the list to him. Then I set out on my own, starting with the gyms on the first page. I started out hopefully, even expectantly, thinking my luck might change. This was Austin, after all. Ground Zero. But it turned out to be just as frustrating as it had been in Dallas. Nobody recognized Gunner's picture. It was surprising as well as disappointing. Gunner had to work out somewhere. Maybe he worked out at home, after all, even though I had thought that was unlikely when I had first started looking. I spent the whole morning coming up empty time and time again at every gym I checked.

Stan called just before noon, and we agreed to meet

at Hidalgo's, a Mexican food restaurant that was supposed to have "atmosphere." We met up in the parking lot, and she gave me a big hug and a kiss right there on the pavement. Typical Stan. Then we went inside and got seated on the patio in back and placed our orders. She got the standard rum and Coke, and I went with the standard Budweiser. The day was warm and pleasant, with only a hint of a breeze. We sat in the shade of a large tree, shielded from the noonday glare. I could feel myself starting to unwind.

"So . . . what happened yesterday?" she asked. "Did you find out anything new?"

I shook my head. "Not much. I talked with Davidson's ex-wife, but she didn't give me much I could use."

I proceeded to tell Stan about the visit and what I had seen. I also told her I didn't plan to try to talk to Angela Davidson again.

"Sounds like a really unhappy lady," she said. "Anything new with the heart surgeon guy himself?"

"Not so far. Tail's in place, but nothing's turned up yet. He was in surgery again this morning, presumably just doing his regular stuff."

"What was his name again?"

"Davidson."

"Yeah, that's right. Davidson." She said the name to herself a couple of times, as if testing it. "So what now, Mr. Policeman, Sir? What's the next step?"

"Your favorite question again."

"Sorry about that."

I shrugged and took another sip of beer. Then I leaned back in my chair, stretching, and glanced around the room. I found her studying me when I looked back at her. I shrugged again. I was aware of feeling tired.

"I really don't know," I said. "So far nothing's working. I guess we keep up the tail. I don't know whether we'll get a tap on his phones or not. Or whether we'll ever get search warrants. There's some real conflict in the department, it turns out, over whether or not to even keep going with it. Turns out Davidson operated last year on the guy who's now the Acting Chief. Did his heart bypass, saved his life."

"Oops," she said.

"No joke. Couldn't have been a worse coincidence. The Acting Chief's very reluctant about the whole deal. It's about the way my luck's been running lately."

"How was the soccer game?" she asked, changing the subject. "Did you make it back to Dallas on time?"

"Yeah, I sure did."

So I told her about the game. She listened intently, watching me closely. I suppose she could hear the change in my tone of voice, because I could see her smiling at me.

"You should just see yourself, Walt," she said, still smiling. "You lit up like a Christmas tree as soon as you started talking about it. I can tell how much you enjoyed it."

Well, I felt silly, being that excited about a twelve and under soccer game and being that transparent about it too. So I kind of shrugged and said, "Yeah, it was a lot of fun. I had a good time, I have to admit. I never thought I'd see my kid play like that."

She still watched me closely, still smiling. There was a tenderness in her expression.

"I know you're proud of him," she said.

"Yeah. . . I guess I am."

She looked down for a moment, then met my eyes again. "How about Julie? Did you see her?"

I shook my head. "No, I didn't. Missed her. She had another commitment she had to honor."

"I see." She was still watching me closely, studying me.

"Yeah, she went to a going away party at the office

for one of her fellow workers, and then I think she had a date after that. There's this guy she's been seeing some lately. I think she went out with him."

I didn't really know why I was telling her all that, but somehow it seemed the thing to do.

"I really don't know what's going to happen there, Stan," I added. "I really don't. I don't think she does either."

"Well, I've sure been there, done that myself," she said. "It's amazing how confusing things can get."

I certainly couldn't argue with that. I looked away from her and glanced around the room. I noticed a guy at a table across the way who seemed to be watching us. He was looking directly at us, not trying to conceal it. I had actually noticed him a couple of times earlier, but now it seemed more apparent. He seemed to be about my age with medium length blonde hair and a square face with a strong jaw line. He was neatly dressed in an open neck white shirt and a tan sport coat. I noticed that he didn't try to avoid my eyes as I looked back at him. But then again, men stared at Stan all the time. This seemed a little different, though.

"Somebody over there seems rather interested in you," I noted, turning back to face her. "He's been watching us closely for the last few minutes. He doesn't seem to be trying to keep it much of a secret either. He's at a table with two other guys over against the far wall. Blonde hair, white shirt, tan sport coat. See if it's anybody you know. Might wait a minute or two before you check it out, so we're not obvious about it."

So we chatted for a couple of minutes, and then Stan looked around in several directions, like she might have been trying to find a waiter, and when she came to the guy at the table across the room, he nodded to her, and she smiled and waved at him.

"Oh, that's Frank," she said. "He's my ex. What a

coincidence. Fancy seeing him here. I didn't even know he came to Hidalgo's. I've never seen him here before."

"That's your ex? The karate guy?"

"Yep."

She waved pleasantly at him again, then motioned for him to come over and join us. He stood up and headed in our direction.

"Are you sure this is what we want to be doing?" I asked.

"Oh, it'll be fine. You'll see. Frank and I get along great these days. Much better than we used to, in fact. And we're divorced, after all. He's not jealous or possessive at all. You'll like him."

I watched as Frank came across the room toward us. He was probably a couple of inches shorter than I am, but he was every bit as broad in the shoulders and the chest. He moved with an easy grace, suggesting athleticism. There was also a cockiness about him, something brash, a hint of a swagger in his step. I remembered that Stan had told me he was a champion karate master.

I stood up as he approached, and Stan said, "Frank, I'd like you to meet Walt Draeger. Walt, this is Frank Hunter."

I extended my hand and he took it. His grip was firm and strong, his hand lean and hard. There wasn't a trace of puffiness in it. He looked directly at me with expressionless light-blue eyes, which seemed to hold a hint of challenge. The rest of his facial expression was just as unrevealing. I found myself wondering if Stan's assessment had been completely accurate.

"Hello, Draeger," he said, continuing to shake my hand, his eyes still directly on me.

"Hi, Frank," I said.

"So what are you doing here at Hidalgo's?" Stan asked. "I haven't ever seen you here before. Used to be, you didn't like Mexican food. Have you changed?"

"Just here on some business, Babe," he said, releasing my hand and looking down at Stan. He gave her shoulder a little squeeze, then ran the back of his hand along the nape of her neck. "How about you? Business or pleasure?" He looked back at me as he said that.

"Walt's an investigator," she said. "We're working on a case together."

That wasn't exactly the way I would have described things, but under the circumstances, it seemed like the best way to put it. I saw him nod. He seemed to be sizing me up.

"You taking care of yourself, Babe?" he asked Stan. "Staying out of trouble?"

"Always," she said.

There were a few more pleasantries, then Frank said he had to get back to business. He squeezed Stan on the shoulder again.

"Take care, Babe," he said.

"See you, Frank."

"Nice to meet you, Draeger," he said evenly, looking directly at me again. Then he turned and walked back to his table. I sat back down. I still wasn't sure that Stan's assessment of things had been accurate, but I didn't say anything. Shortly thereafter we finished eating and went outside to the parking lot. I opened the door of her pickup for her.

"So what do you plan to do the rest of the day?" she asked, looking up at me and running her hand along the lapel of my jacket.

"Keep up the search. Try to find Gunner. See what happens with Davidson."

The blue of her eyes was striking as she gazed up at me. "We could always go back to your motel. That might break up the day a little."

I still didn't know how I felt about that. "Maybe later. Let me see what happens this afternoon. I really do need to find Gunner. I need to keep looking. He and Davidson are in it together, I think."

I could see a flicker of disappointment in her eyes. Then she put her arms around me and kissed me. Hard. Right there in the parking lot. I only hoped Frank wouldn't come out of nowhere and karate chop my head in two like a stack of boards.

"Call me for dinner," she said, almost huskily, pushing herself away from me and getting into the truck. "I know a great little Italian place we can go to. You'll love it."

"I'll give you a ring."

She started the car and looked up at me through the open window.

"See you then, Walt. I hope it's a good afternoon."

She winked at me, then backed out of the parking space, swung the tiny pickup around and headed out of the lot. I walked a few spaces down and got into the Taurus. I decided to call Joe Henderson before I got going again.

"Any news?" I asked.

"Nothing. Davidson was still in surgery the last I heard. Got the other car out hitting gyms, trying to get an ID on your body builder friend. Haven't heard from them in a couple of hours."

"Any way I can reach them?"

"Sure. They've both got cellphones. Here, I'll give you their numbers. I got them here somewhere."

I waited as he went searching. I could hear the rustling of papers in the background. I heard him mumble something to himself.

"Here you go," I finally heard him say. "Names are Jack Reynolds and Dave Franklin. You got a pencil and paper?"

"Shoot."

So he gave me their cell numbers, and I wrote them down, along with their names.

"Thanks, Joe," I said. "I think I'll give them a call. See where they stand. I'll let you know if we come up with anything."

"Yeah, do that. I could sure stand some good news around here."

So I hung up and called the number he had given me for Jack Reynolds and told him who I was after he answered.

"Any luck?" I asked.

"Nope," said Reynolds. "Nothing. Been to over half a dozen gyms so far, and nobody's seen this guy. You say he works out here in Austin?"

"Maybe. I'm not sure of it, but I think it's possible. Let me know if you find anything, will you."

"Sure. You bet."

So I gave him my cell number.

"Any word from the other car?" I asked.

"Nope. Davidson was still in surgery as of half an hour ago. We'll join up with them if they need help following him. Otherwise we'll keep hitting the gyms. I'll let you know if anything changes."

"Thanks. I appreciate it."

So we were still stymied. I could feel the frustration weighing down on me again. As I sat there in the Taurus, I saw Frank Hunter walk out of Hidalgo's and head across the parking lot. I saw him glance in my direction, and I was pretty sure he recognized me, but he didn't show anything. He looked away and kept walking. There was definitely a swagger there, a cockiness in his step. I stayed put in the Taurus as he got into a jet-black Corvette with a yellow lightning bolt detailed on each side and pulled out of the lot. I got a look at the license plate as he drove away. It read: K KING.

Then I cranked up the Taurus and started the hunt

all over again, one gym after another. It was just as fruitless as before. Nobody recognized Gunner's picture. By three-thirty I was even more frustrated. Irritated too. I decided to call Reynolds and Franklin again.

"Nothing new," Reynolds told me. He sounded bored. "Davidson finished up at the hospital about one-thirty. He's at his office now. The other unit's still got him. We're still checking workout places. No luck so far."

"Crap," I said.

"The old well's kinda dry, it looks like," Reynolds noted.

"No joke."

There was silence on the line for a moment.

"Chief's getting more and more pissed off with it, I hear," Reynolds said. "Says it's all a crock. Says he's not gonna put up with it much longer. It seems one of the secretaries even heard him say something about giving Davidson a call. Be kind of surprised myself if we're still at it this time tomorrow."

There were things I could have said, but I held off. "Give me a call if you come up with anything," I said.

"Sure. Will do."

So I went back to hitting gyms. Still no luck. Coming out of Fitness Master on Lamar Street, I happened to notice a nondescript gray sedan parked across the lot. I thought maybe it was a Chevrolet, but I couldn't tell for sure. Glare on the windshield from the late afternoon sun kept me from seeing the driver, but I began to get a vague sense of uneasiness. It took me a moment to connect, but I had the impression I had seen that particular car before. I thought about that some more. Yes, I thought I could recall seeing it at the last gym I had checked, or maybe the one before. The glare still kept me from seeing past the windshield, and the distance was such that I wouldn't have been able to make out any detail anyway, but I felt the hair standing all up and tingling on the back of my neck as I got into the Taurus. I was being tailed.

Just to make sure, I went to a 7-11 and pulled up at the gas pumps. I went inside while the Taurus was filling and got a candy bar and a soft drink and went to the bathroom, then came back outside. I could see the gray sedan in an adjacent parking lot, probably fifty yards away. The visor was pulled down, and I still couldn't see the driver. The tingling on the back of my neck was still there.

I pulled out of the 7-11 and headed west. Looking in the rearview mirror, I could see the gray sedan swing out onto the street, following in my direction, staying several cars back. I made a couple of turns at the next few intersections, first to the right, then to the left, then stopped at a Walgreens. I waited in the parking lot for a minute. No sign of the gray sedan. So I went inside, killed exactly five minutes by pretending to be looking for something, and went back out to the parking lot. The gray sedan was parked in the far corner, the visor still down, the driver still obscured. The crawling sensation on the back of my neck was there again. Whoever it might be, he was one hell of a good tail.

I slipped back into the Taurus and checked my watch. Almost six. I thought about trying to lose him in rush hour traffic, but I realized I didn't want to do that. I wanted to find out who he was, and why he was following me.

I decided to use myself as bait. See if I could flush him into the open. I realized as I looked around that I wasn't far from Hidalgo's, where Stan and I had eaten lunch. There was a patio there. I'd be completely out in the open. It might work. If the second serving of Mexican food in one day didn't kill me first, that is. So I headed in that direction. I called Stan on the way.

"We're not going to be able to have dinner tonight," I said.

"Really? How come?" She sounded disappointed.

"I'm being tailed. I've got to try to find out who it is. It's too risky for us to be together."

"You're what?" she asked, surprised.

"Being tailed. Somebody in a gray sedan has been following me for at least an hour or two. I'm sure of it. I did some maneuvering, and he stuck with me all the way."

"Wow! Who do you think it is?"

"No idea. But I have to handle this alone at this point, Stan. So dinner is off."

She didn't say anything right away, then asked, "Are you sure?"

"I'm sure. I'll call you later if I get a chance."

"Where are you now?"

I started to tell her, but knowing Stan, I realized she'd probably try to join up with me, so I said, "Still just driving around. Don't know exactly where I'll be heading."

"You're sure I can't come?" she asked again, still sounding disappointed.

"Positive, Stan. I'll call you later if I get a chance."

"Lunch tomorrow?"

"Call me about noon. We'll meet up somewhere."

"Well . . . okay . . ."

So that was that. We each hung up, and I headed to Hidalgo's. I parked on the street when I got there, rather than in the lot. I wanted to be able to leave in a hurry if I needed to. Then I walked across the lot to the front entrance and went inside. I sat on the patio again, just as Stan and I had done at lunch. I even had the same waiter, and he recognized me. I thought he might offer me a Maalox out of compassion, but he didn't.

"And the lady, Sir?" he asked.

"Occupied. I'm alone this time."

So I sat on display like a goldfish in a bowl and ate a slow dinner. Nobody seemed to pay me any particular attention, and I didn't see anybody acting suspiciously in any way, but the hair was still standing up on the back of my neck, and I could *feel* the eyes. Somebody was watching. And waiting. And they were good. Very good. Whoever they were.

Finally I was finished. I stopped off in the men's room, then walked out the front door. I crossed the lot, going slowly. Then I got to the street. I stood there for a moment, looking around. Then I saw it: a silver Mercedes parked down the street, between where I stood and the Taurus. Even as I stood there, I saw the driver's door open. And Davidson got out. He moved slowly, purposefully, precisely. Looking right at me, he pushed the door of the Mercedes shut. Then he started walking toward me. He still looked directly at me. I decided to start walking toward the Taurus as I had been planning to do. That seemed the most natural course of action. I couldn't very well run in the other direction, and I couldn't just stand there like a lamppost either. So I pretended to check my watch and headed down the sidewalk toward the Taurus, in his direction. I walked with my head down, not wanting to have to face him, and hoped this was just some sort of gruesome coincidence. Hoped Davidson just happened to be coming to Hidalgo's for dinner. Hoped he just happened to have parked on the street. Hoped he just happened to be getting out of his car at this particular moment, just as I was coming out of the restaurant.

I didn't get lucky. He stopped dead still on the sidewalk about fifteen feet ahead of me. I could tell that, even though I wasn't looking ahead, wasn't looking down the length of the sidewalk. All I could do was keep walking. I fished some change out of my pocket and pretended to be counting it, my head still down, but I knew it wasn't going to work. He still stood right in the center of the sidewalk, just ahead of me. He was only a few feet away now. I had no choice. So I looked up at him, trying to affect nonchalance, then angled off to my right, on a path that would take me around him, but he stepped to the side, directly into my line, and blocked me. I was up to him now, just a couple of feet away. I stopped, and our eyes met. His were even more direct and penetrating in real life than they had been in his picture. And cold. Without any hint of emotion. I felt a tingle crawl up my spine.

So there we were, face to face on the sidewalk. He wasn't budging, and I could tell from looking into those eyes that he wouldn't move aside to let me pass. Any hope this might be just a bizarre coincidence had vanished.

"Hello, Draeger," he said. His voice was flat and hard, dead even pitch, without any trace of uncertainty or hesitation. I stood there looking at him. Sure enough, he was exactly my height, and even though he wasn't as heavy, I could sense power. I could sense strength and determination and total self-confidence. The tingle along my spine had turned to ice.

"Hi there," I said.

Neither of us budged. We stood there face to face on the sidewalk, no more than two feet apart, our eyes locked together. I took a deep breath, told myself to stay calm.

"Know who I am, Draeger?" he asked, his voice still hard and flat.

I shrugged. "Punxsutawney Phil?"

I saw a tiny flicker at the corner of his mouth, a tightening of his eyes, the hint of a flare at his nostrils.

"Very funny, Draeger."

I shrugged again. "It was just a guess."

He continued to stare at me. I could see his nostrils flare again. His breathing seemed tighter, the line of his mouth harder.

"You're playing in a mighty dangerous game, Draeger," he said, his voice low and measured. "You're in way over your head. In more ways than one. You better watch yourself. Or you'll be very, very sorry that you didn't back out when you had the chance. You hear me?"

I nodded. "Very subtle, but I think I get the message."

His eyes narrowed again. I could see the flare of his nostrils one more time. The line of his mouth was a tightened slit.

"You better," he said.

Then he turned and walked back to the Mercedes and opened the door. He glared at me very directly one last time, then slid onto the seat and pulled the door shut. He started the engine, spun the wheel, and glided smoothly out of the parallel space onto the street. I watched as he drove off. And as I did, I saw something else I hadn't noticed up to that point, and the chill along my spine came back again, even stronger this time. It was a man, leaning back against the wall of a building across the street, watching me. He was wearing a blue baseball cap with "Dallas" above the brim and a blue jacket. But it wasn't just any man. No, this was somebody special. Very special. He had a massive upper body with mountainous shoulders and tremendous breadth of chest, apparent even in the jacket. His pumped iron arms were folded in front of him above a tiny, almost wasp-like waist, the enormous muscles in his legs just barely covered by spandex running shorts. Looking directly at me. Watching me.

Gunner.

I had finally found him.

The face was the same too, even though dark glasses covered his eyes, and the blue cap was pulled down low over his forehead. I could still see the squared jaws, the trunk-like bull neck.

Very slowly, showing no trace at all of hesitation or uncertainty, just like Davidson, he pointed his index finger at me and kept it trained in my direction. Then he made a hammer-like gesture with his thumb. He tipped his head ever so slightly, as if to say adios, and then he turned and walked around the corner of the building.

It took me a moment to react, but then I crossed the street and followed him. I quickened my pace as I came to the corner of the building. As I rounded it, I could see him riding away on a motorcycle. I could see "Cowboys" over the back of his jacket. I strained to see the license plate too, but the distance was too great. All I could do was watch as he rode away.

I hurried back to the Taurus, but I knew following either one of them would be impossible at that point. They had too much head start. But if one of the units was still on Davidson, and if Davidson and Gunner met up, then I might be able to get the motorcycle's plate number from them, and that might lead me to Gunner. So I slipped into the driver's seat and punched in Reynold's cellphone number.

"Where are you?" I asked urgently.

"Austin Sports Bar," he said offhandedly,"watching the Mavericks get beat on TV. Again, goddamn it. Losing money on it too, the stupid bastards."

It didn't compute. I thought I hadn't heard him correctly. A sports bar? Watching an NBA game on the tube? I could hear the sounds of conversation and laughter in the background, then a collective groan.

"Ah, shit!" I heard somebody yell.

"Goddamn it! I can't believe it," Reynolds muttered disgustedly. "Son of a bitch just hit a three pointer on us from somewhere in Louisiana. Puts us down by sixteen. I may not make the rent this month."

I suddenly felt light-headed, almost dizzy. "What about Davidson? Aren't you following him?"

I heard another collective groan in the background. Somebody said, "Ouch!"

"Didn't you hear?" Reynolds asked distractedly. Then I heard him say, "Goddamn it, the dumb bastard can't even make a simple lay-up. Wide open under the basket and the stupid son of a bitch blows it all to hell. What do these guys think they're doing? It's just the NBA, after all."

My heart was hammering and my mouth was dry. "Hear what? I haven't heard anything. What about Davidson?"

It took Reynolds a moment to answer. "That's all been called off as of five o'clock, Draeger. Order came down all the way from the top. Baker said he wasn't gonna screw around with it anymore. Guess they just haven't notified you yet. Davidson was playing tennis at the Austin Country Club when we got the word, so we left him there. Been a couple of hours now."

A ball of lead had settled in my gut. My chest felt tight. I heard another collective groan in the background.

"Sorry to have to be the one to tell you that, Draeger," Reynolds added. "Didn't look like it was going anywhere. Davidson looks clean as a whistle to me. You probably ought to be looking somewhere else."

I didn't even answer. Instead, I just shut off the cellphone. I sat there in the Taurus and thought about what I had just heard. The Acting Chief himself had called off the tail. He was convinced Davidson was innocent. He had probably called Davidson too, I suspected, just as one of the secretaries had heard him threaten to do. That was probably why Davidson knew my name. Then again, I realized I had given my name to Carl and Mike when I had faxed the pictures of Davidson and Gunner and the murdered women to the sex clubs in San Antonio and Corpus. I had given the same information at all the gyms and adult video shops I had visited too. Ray Stammonds in Dallas as well. So there were other people out there who knew who I was.

What about the gray sedan? I looked around but couldn't see it. So I started the Taurus, pulled out of my parallel space onto the street, and headed back to the motel. I kept checking the rearview mirror as I went, but the gray sedan had disappeared. I drove slowly, giving anybody who might be following a perfect opportunity to track me, but nothing materialized. I didn't know what to do next. I had lost the tail on Davidson, and even though I had finally seen Gunner in the flesh, I still didn't know anything about him except that he rode a motorcycle and that he was probably a Cowboys fan. Talk about narrowing it down.

It was dark by the time I got to the motel. I got out of the car and went to the door of my room and opened it. I turned on the light, but what I saw stopped me in my tracks. The room had been tossed. Completely. Sheets and blankets had been pulled off the beds. Drawers were pulled out and turned upside down. I drew out my gun and crossed the room, moving carefully, alert for any hint of motion. The bathroom was empty. My travel kit had been turned upside down and emptied, just like everything else. There hadn't been anything important in it, just stuff like toothpaste and deodorant and some Tylenol, so I wasn't worried about losing anything valuable, but the hollowness had come back in my gut. Still going carefully, stepping lightly, I checked in the closet and under the beds. Nothing. They had come and gone. Whoever they were. I put my gun back in the holster and stood there, looking around. Then my cellphone jingled.

"Hello," I said, aware of the tightness in my voice.

"Dad!" I heard Bobby say. "Mom's sick. I mean, she's *really* sick. She's got one of those really bad migraines, and she can't stop throwing up. We need to do something!"

I was so startled it took me a moment to respond. "What happened, Bobby? When did it start?"

"Well . . ." He hesitated. I could feel him thinking about what to say. "Well, see, Dad . . . I think she found out something about Sam this afternoon. I think . . . I think she found out he's got these other girlfriends. Like there's a whole bunch, Dad. I mean, like there's *tons* of them. And I think that got her kind of upset . . . and then she started getting one of those headaches, you know, like she sometimes used to get, and now she's real sick, Dad. She's sitting on the bathroom floor in front of the toilet and she's got her head over the bowl, and every couple of minutes she starts to dry heave. I called Ms. Randerson, but she's at some deal over in Ft.Worth, and she can't get here for like an hour or two at least, and Mom said not to call Grammer and Gramper, because they can't drive in the dark and she doesn't want them trying to come over here, and so . . . I didn't know who else to call, Dad."

I looked around the tossed motel room. I thought about Davidson. And Gunner. And Joe Henderson. And Jack Reynolds and the rest of the Austin Police. And the gyms and the adult bookstores. And Jim Bob and Orville and the sex clubs. And Rumpulina and all the other dead women. To hell with all of it, I thought. Just to hell with it.

"I'm glad you called me, Bobby. You did the right thing. I'm on my way right now. I'm coming from Austin, so it'll take me a couple of hours to get there. You stay there with your mom. I'll be on my cell. Call me right away if anything changes or gets worse. You got me?"

"I got it, Dad."

"See you in a couple of hours."

I flipped off the cell, walked out of the room and slammed the door, piled into the Taurus, and twisted the key to start the engine. Then I yanked it into gear and roared out of the lot. I-35 stood right in front of me. I pushed down hard on the pedal as I accelerated into the streaming traffic…

16.

I kept a steady, even pace all the way to Dallas. It was easy. I just kept the pedal pressed all the way down to the floor. The Taurus topped out at a little over a hundred. I was lucky I didn't get stopped.

I got an idea when I was about halfway to Dallas. One of the Medical Examiners in Houston has a keen interest in guns and marksmanship, and he and I had gotten to be on pretty good terms along the way. We'd gone out shooting together several times, and I'd worked with him on a number of homicide cases, so I decided to give him a call. I had phoned the morgue often enough in the past so that I remembered the number, and they were able to give me his listing.

"Dr. Castler, this is Walt Draeger," I said when he answered. "I'm terribly sorry to bother you at home after hours, but an emergency has come up. I was wondering if you could help."

So I told him Julie was sick with a bad migraine and didn't have anything to take for it. She had used some nasal spray called Imitrex in the past, I remembered, and I asked him if he could call some in for her. There was a Walgreens there in Garland, not far from where she lived. I had driven by it each time I had gone to her house.

"Sure, no problem, I can do that, Walt," he said. "You got the number?"

"No, I don't. But I can call Directory Assistance and get back with you on that."

"Never mind, I'll do it. You're out on the highway. You just attend to the driving. I'll get the number. The Walgreens in Garland?"

"Right. She used to have some suppositories for nausea too. She had to use suppositories because the vomiting was always so bad she couldn't keep down pills. I don't remember the name of the medication, though."

"I'll call in some Phenergan for her. That ought to help."

"Thanks, Dr. Castler. I appreciate it."

"No problem. Take care of yourself, Walt. I hope this helps."

So I made a quick stop by the Walgreens as I came into town and picked up the nasal spray and suppositories, then rushed to Julie's house. Bobby let me in.

"She's still in the bathroom, Dad," he said. "She's still real sick."

So I stepped directly to the bathroom. Julie lay on her side, curled up in a ball in front of the toilet, wearing an old flannel shirt of mine. I knelt down beside her. She looked alarmingly pale and weak. I touched her forehead with the back of my hand. It felt cool and clammy to the touch. She didn't even open her eyes.

"Bad migraine?" I asked.

She still didn't open her eyes. I could see her swallow.

"I think so," she said, her voice hoarse and weak. I saw her lick her lips. I could tell how dry they were. "Thanks for coming."

"I wouldn't be anywhere else. Are you cold? Your forehead felt cool to the touch."

I could see the tiniest of nods. "Yes, a little."

"Bobby, bring a blanket," I said.

He turned and disappeared into the bedroom, then rushed back with a blanket, and I covered her up, tucking the edges in all around her as well as I could.

"Do you want me to carry you to the bed?" I asked.

She gave a little shake of her head, barely perceptible. "Not right now. It always makes me sick when I move. I don't think I'm ready yet."

"This is a bad one, isn't it?" I said. I hadn't seen her this sick in years. It was alarming. I looked over at Bobby. I could see a worried frown on his face.

She gave another tiny nod of her head. "Yes . . . it may be more than just a migraine. I had some chicken at noon that tasted a little funny. I almost didn't eat it, but one of the sales reps had brought us lunch, and I didn't want to be rude. Now I wish I'd left it alone."

I reached in the bag I had brought from Walgreens and pulled out the nasal spray. "Here, I got some Imitrex for you. I called one of the MEs in Houston, and he called it in. Let's see if this helps."

She still didn't open her eyes, but I could see a tiny trace of a smile at the corner of her mouth.

"Thanks," she said, her voice still weak. "You're a lifesaver."

"Just call me good old lifesaver, Walt. Want me to help?"

I saw another tiny nod.

"Hold still," I said. So I put the spray in one of her nostrils and activated it. "There, I hope that helps. It used to take about twenty or thirty minutes, didn't it?"

She nodded again.

"I got some suppositories for you too. You used to need them along with the nasal spray, if I remember correctly. You want one of those?"

This time she opened her eyes and looked up at me. "Wow, you're really being Dr. Draeger here, aren't you?"

"Just being my usual helpful self. You want one?"

She frowned. "I think I might. You're right, they always helped in the past. I probably should."

"Want help with that?"

She frowned at me again. "No, I'll do that myself, thank you." Then she looked back up at me with another frown and added, "I'm afraid you'd enjoy it too much."

So I handed her one of the suppositories and stood up. "I think we should let you rest and let the medication take effect. I'll check back in about thirty minutes. How does that sound?"

She nodded.

"You want the light on or off?"

"Off, I think."

So I flipped it off.

"I'll leave the door ajar so you can call if you need us. We'll be in the living room. I'll keep an ear tuned."

"Thanks," she said.

So I left the door ajar, checked the time on my watch, and went back into the living room with Bobby. I flopped on the couch when we got there. As I did, I happened to notice a vase of red roses on the coffee table in front of me. They weren't exactly like the roses that had been there before, but the arrangement was similar. Sam, I realized. Which gave me an idea.

"Let's let Brutus in," I said to Bobby. "He's pretty tired of the back yard, I think. He'd probably enjoy some time in the house again."

So Bobby went across the kitchen and disappeared through the door to the garage. I heard the door to the back yard open. Brutus came romping in a moment later, the lights back on in his eyes, jumping all around with excitement, his tail slashing the air like a machete. He came straight to the couch and tried to put his feet up on me, but I grabbed his legs and held them away from my shirt. I looked at his paws. They still seemed dry. The recovery wasn't complete. Then he tried to lick me in the mouth like always, but I had known that was coming too and managed to avoid it. He panted happily in my face as I sat there, holding his feet away from me.

"Dumb turd," I told him.

He loved it.

"Here, take a look at the flowers," I said, motioning to the coffee table.

I really don't think he's fluent in English, but he glanced back over his shoulder in that direction, and that was all it took. He forgot about me in an instant. Life is so cruel. He pulled away, turned eagerly toward the coffee table, and put his feet up on it. Then he started to munch the roses. That knocked the vase over. It toppled over onto the table top, rolled across the surface, and flopped onto the floor.

"Aw heck," I said. "What a bad, bad dog you are, Brutus."

Bobby pumped a fist and said, "Yes! Right on! Way to go, Brutus!"

Brutus was still all over the roses. For whatever crazy reason, Brutus has always loved flowers. Any kind of flowers. And these were truly a delicacy. He munched away happily, chomping up rose petals right and left. Little red chewed up bits and fragments were accumulating on the rug. The turned over vase had left a wet spot too.

"Gosh, what a shame," I said.

Bobby laughed. "Right."

"But we probably need to clean up all the mess," I noted.

So we got some rags and cleaned up the floor, and then I threw what was left of the roses in a trash can in the garage. I felt a little conflicted about it, actually. They were pretty flowers, nature's blessing, but nothing could change the fact that they were Sam's, and I wanted them out of the house. I thought they were starting to wilt anyway.

The doorbell rang as I came back into the living room, so I went to the front door and opened it. Lois Randerson stood there with a concerned expression on her face. She looked about like I remembered her, very pretty, all neatly decked out tonight in brown pants and a long sleeved white shirt with a lacy collar. She was really quite attractive. I held the door open for her and she stepped inside.

"How is Julie?" she asked, sounding worried. "I came as fast as I could when Bobby called on my cell. I was over in Fort-Worth, helping my mother bring my father home from the hospital. He's been sick with pneumonia, and I had to help her get him squared away. I'm sorry I couldn't leave right away. Is she still sick?"

I nodded. " Bad migraine. She's had them before. I gave her some medication for it a few minutes ago. I hope it'll work in the next half hour or so."

"Bless her heart," she said sympathetically. "My sister in California has migraines. I know how bad they can be. Is there anything I can do?"

"Thanks, but I think we're probably okay for now. I do appreciate your asking, though. Thanks for coming by too."

I meant it. I was truly very appreciative indeed. The quality of the moment was marred slightly, however, by the fact that Brutus came up behind her at that point and started sniffing at her hindquarters. She brushed a hand at him, shooing him away. Brutus backed up a step or two but didn't retreat. I could see him still sniffing the air, testing it. He wasn't exactly on point, but it was close. Brutus has always been a slave, of course, to any kind of new or different aroma.

"Have you and Bobby both eaten some dinner?" she asked, recovering.

I had eaten at Hidalgo's, but I didn't know about Bobby. I hadn't even thought to ask. He stood just a few feet away, watching us, so I looked over at him. He shook his head.

"Why don't I fix you a sandwich, Bobby," she said. "I know you're probably starved."

I could tell that struck him as a good idea. He'd been so preoccupied with his mom he hadn't even had a chance to grab a bite.

"This will only take me a minute," she said. "Bless your heart, I've been here enough to know where Julie puts everything. I know you're famished."

"I'll help," I said.

"No need to," she said, smiling. "I'll have it fixed up in a jif."

So she headed into the kitchen, and I followed along behind her. Unfortunately, so did Brutus, still sniffing. I hoped he might get distracted along the way, but it wasn't going to happen. He was staying focused again. For some godforsaken reason, he had become very interested in her behind. *Fascinated* would be a better word. Enthralled. Totally captivated. She began getting some sandwich stuff out of the fridge, and he was right there behind her all the way, not being subtle about it at all, sniffing away. She brushed him away a couple of times and tried to pretend he didn't exist, but that's always a difficult trick with Brutus.

"Go away, Brutus," she said at one point, brushing him away again. But it didn't have any effect.

I didn't know for sure what the problem was. She certainly didn't look like the sort of person to have a problem with hygiene. It was puzzling. Maybe Brutus just took an odd fancy to her. God knows we're all walking delicacies, after all. Don't take my word on that. Just ask any dog that ever lived. I think it's good, in fact, that our senses aren't all that keen. It's probably supposed to be that way. Call it a blessing. There are some things you just don't want to be too aware of. It almost makes me glad I have sinus trouble.

Brutus was still at it, still following her every step she took, still sniffing, so I called Bobby and told him to come get Brutus and take him into the living room. Bobby came and dragged him away, out of the kitchen, and more or less sat on him in front of the TV.

"Brutus is such a mess," I apologized. "Julie's been keeping him outside lately, but I think it depresses him to be out in the back yard, so I let him in tonight. So it's my fault he's here. Sorry he's such a pest."

I thought that sounded better than saying I was so sorry he was all that fascinated with her ass, but it was still an uncomfortable moment.

"My encounters with Brutus have always been interesting," she noted, "to say the least."

She was getting a ham sandwich together very efficiently. I felt bad about not helping her.

"Anything I can do?" I asked.

"You just take it easy. You've got your hands full with Julie. Just leave this to me." Then she looked back at me. "Anything else you need me to do? I'm more than willing to help in any way."

I thought about that. I needed to get another car, I realized. The Taurus had been identified. It would stick out like a sore thumb wherever I went. A change of vehicle might help me avoid detection.

"There *is* one thing," I said. "I almost hate to ask. I don't want to impose."

She looked back at me and smiled. "You wouldn't be. What can I do?"

So I decided to go ahead. "Any chance you could drive me to get a rental car in the morning? My Taurus has some mechanical problems. I don't feel like taking it out on the highway, and I have to get back to Austin as soon as Julie's well."

That wasn't exactly the truth, but I thought it sounded better than saying I needed to change cars because I was being followed by these people who liked to kill blonde women and cut out their hearts.

"Sure," she said brightly. "What time?"

"I'm not sure. It depends upon what happens with Julie. Could I call you in the morning?"

"Sure, you can get me on my cell. Julie and Bobby have the number."

"Thanks," I said.

By then she had finished making the sandwich for Bobby. I put a place mat and a glass of milk on the breakfast table, and she put the sandwich on a plate and set it on the mat.

"All set, Bobby," she called.

"Coming," I heard Bobby call back.

Unfortunately, Brutus was also coming, and as luck would have it, he arrived first. I should have seen it in advance, I realized, but thinking about getting the rental car must have preoccupied me, and I was caught by surprise. A sandwich on the table is always fair game to Brutus, and the current offering was no exception. Before I even knew what was happening, he had his feet up on the breakfast table and was helping himself to Ms. Randerson's very nicely constructed ham sandwich.

"No, Brutus!" I yelled.

"No, Brutus!" I heard Bobby shout.

I heard Ms. Randerson shriek.

It was too late. The plate and the sandwich were already on the floor, and the sandwich was already half gone. Brutus was munching away happily.

"No, Brutus! Bad dog!" I yelled at him again.

But Brutus has never been much affected by guilt. He just kept chomping. So I grabbed hold of his collar and dragged him back into the living room.

"Lord, I'm sorry!" I said to Ms. Randerson as I hauled him away. "Bobby, go get his leash, will you?"

So Bobby ran to get his leash, and I tethered Brutus to the TV set there in the living room. He didn't seem bothered at all. He was still too busy munching up the rest of the sandwich. I pushed down his hindquarters and made him sit.

"Now stay there!" I scolded him.

I walked back into the kitchen. "I am really *so* sorry," I told Ms. Randerson as I came back into the kitchen. "*Please* accept our apologies. I really hadn't been expecting that."

"He's certainly a remarkable animal, I'll have to say that," she noted, collecting herself. "Here, I'll fix you a new one, Bobby."

I felt just miserable, but she still didn't want any help, and in just a couple of minutes, Bobby had another beautifully constructed ham sandwich.

"Thank you *so* much," I told her. "You can't know how much we appreciate your help. I really mean that. I do want to apologize again for the dog. We may have to put him outside again after all, depressed or not."

"He's definitely a challenge," she observed.

Then she said she really did have to go, so I showed her to the front door.

"Call me in the morning," she said. "I'll be happy to give you a ride to the rental car place. Feel free to call me during the night if you need anything. I'm only too glad to help. I mean that." She paused for a moment, then asked, "Does Bobby need any help with school in the morning?"

I hadn't even thought about it. I turned back toward the kitchen and called out to him, "Bobby, who drives you to school in the morning?"

"Mom!" he called back.

So we were probably going to need to arrange something, since Julie probably wouldn't be up to taking him. I realized I might even have to stay at home with her, as far as that was concerned. I turned back to Ms. Randerson and was about to tell her that we'd have to work out something, but as I did, I saw that Brutus had gotten up from where he was sitting by the TV - which was only a few feet away - and had come up behind her again, still sniffing. Before I could even open my mouth to warn her, I watched in horror as he stuck his nose in her crotch and nudged her. Firmly. She even had to take a step forward to keep from losing her balance. Well, that did it for her. She had had it with him.

"You . . !" she snapped, turning to face him and shaking a finger at him, ". . . are *not* my favorite dog!"

"Bad dog, Brutus!" I said. "Bad dog!"

"Bad dog, Brutus!" Bobby chimed.

Brutus thought it was all just wonderful. He panted happily and wagged his tail. I guess he was just born for outer darkness.

"Put him out in the back yard, Bobby," I said. "Now! Depressed or not. I don't care if he's suicidal."

"Brutus, you bad dog!" Bobby repeated, dragging him by the leash through the door to the garage.

"He must be a Scorpio," Ms. Randerson said shakily, trying again to collect herself. "I always have trouble with Scorpios."

"I don't think his sign's even been discovered yet," I said. "They ought to ban it forever when they finally do."

There wasn't much more to say, I didn't think. Judging by her expression, she seemed to agree.

"Well . . . call me in the morning," she said politely. "I'll drive you to pick up a rental car. I'll certainly help with getting Bobby to school too."

"Thanks again. I'll give you a ring."

Then she left, and I shut the door, feeling mortified. Bobby was coming back into the living room by then, a puzzled expression on his face.

"Yikes, Dad, what was it with Brutus and Ms. Randerson?" he said.

"I pray that I never find out," I told him. "Thank God he can't talk."

I glanced at my watch and saw that thirty minutes had gone by. It was time to check on Julie. So I headed through the bedroom to the bathroom and pushed the door open. Bobby was right behind me. I flipped on the light. Julie was still lying on the floor on her side. She looked up at me as I stepped through the door.

"Feel any better?" I asked.

She nodded. "I think so. My head doesn't hurt quite as much, and my stomach feels a little better too. I think the medicine is working."

"Good," I said, kneeling down beside her. I put my hand to her forehead. It still felt clammy to the touch. Bobby stood behind me, looking over my shoulder.

"I'm cold, though," she said. I could see her shivering, in fact, and her teeth were chattering.

"Sounds like you're having a chill," I said. "It's not very warm here on the floor either. Do you feel ready to move to the bed? It might be warmer there."

She frowned. "Okay . . . I guess . . ."

"Here, I'll carry you," I said.

She didn't protest, so I gathered her up in my arms, blanket and all, and headed back to the bed with her. She was light as a feather. It felt like carrying a child. Bobby hopped ahead of us and pulled back the sheet and the blanket. I laid her on the bed, still bundled up in the blanket I had draped over her, and pulled up the covers. I could see she was still shivering, though. She curled up into a little ball.

"I'm *freezing*," she chattered. "I can't believe I'm so cold. I think you're right. I think I'm having a chill. Maybe I have the flu."

"Here, I'll warm you up," I said. I flipped off my shoes and got in on the other side of the bed, under the covers, and worked my way up behind her. Then I put my arm around her, draping it over her side, and curled myself around her, holding her tight.

"That feels good," she said, snuggling back against me. "You're nice and warm."

I just held her, pressing her close against me. Bobby was watching us closely.

"Uh . . . I'm gonna go watch some TV in the living room," he said after a moment. "Call me if you need anything. Okay?"

He stepped out of the room and shut the door. The only light came from the bathroom. Julie still shivered all over, but I thought it might be subsiding some.

"Getting warmer?" I asked.

"I think so."

So I just kept holding her. Time passed. Nothing was said. She seemed to be shivering less, I thought.

"I heard Bobby talking to you when he called you on your cell," she finally said. "When he called to tell you I was sick."

"Yeah . . ."

She hesitated. "It's . . . it's not because of Sam that I got sick. I know that's what Bobby thought, but it really isn't. I've known about Sam for some time now. A couple of days at least. I heard some stuff at work. It's not just that he's got other girlfriends, although that's certainly the truth. He's got a *wife* too, no less. He lied about all of that. I only went out with him that one last time because I wanted to challenge him with it, and he *still* lied. So Sam's history as far as I'm concerned. Sam's a jerk."

I thought about telling her of my talk with David Jarvington, my attorney, but I didn't want to bash her over the head with it, so I just said, "Okay."

She was silent for awhile, then said, "There *was* some upsetting news today, though. The lady we gave the going away party for the other day is sick, it turns out. That's why she's leaving, in fact. She has cancer of the pancreas, I found out today. Bless her heart, she's such a dear, and cancer of the pancreas is apparently real, real bad. I heard it's all over her, and there's nothing they can do. She only has a couple of months to live. So that was upsetting. But, I don't know . . . the way I feel, these chills and everything, I almost wonder if it's not the chicken I ate, or the flu or something."

"Could be. I've seen you have some bad migraines in the past, but I've never seen you shivering like this before."

"Hmmm," she said.

So I just kept holding her. Neither of us said anything for awhile. More time passed. I thought she might be going to sleep. The medicine was probably taking more and more effect, I suspected, kicking in harder.

"Warmer now?" I finally asked.

"Hmm. Yes."

She had stopped shivering, in fact.

"Want me to go in the other room? Let you get some rest?"

She snuggled back against me. "No, this feels good. I like this."

So I just kept holding her. Before long I could tell she had drifted off to sleep. Her breathing had become deeper and more regular. Still I held her. I didn't know whether I'd be able to sleep like that myself, but I decided I'd stay there until morning if I needed to, whether I slept a wink or not. It was going to be a long night.

Lying there, I became aware of a low, moaning wail coming from the yard behind the house. It took me a moment to realize what it was. Brutus. Kind of a howl, kind of a moan, Bobby had said. He had described it well. Just what we need, I thought. Perfect. The timing couldn't have been worse.

A moment later, Bobby cracked open the door and stuck his head in tentatively. "Dad. . ," he whispered.

"Yes, Bobby," I whispered back.

"Brutus. He's howling."

"Yeah, I can hear him."

"What do we do?"

I thought about it for a moment. "Better let him in, I guess. We'll probably be on the SPCA most wanted list if we don't."

"Okay," he said. He started to back out of the door, then paused. "How's Mom?" he whispered.

"I think she's better. She's drifted off to sleep, I think."

He nodded, then backed out and closed the door. I could hear Brutus wail again. Julie seemed to be sleeping through it, though.

I lay there behind her with my arm over her side, listening to her breathing. It was still deep and regular, the breathing of sleep. I still suspected I wouldn't be getting much rest, though. I really wasn't very comfortable, but I didn't want to risk waking her up by moving. Now that she seemed to be feeling better, I found my mind returning to the events of the day, despite myself. I felt very frustrated and helpless. And angry. I tried to consider what my options might be, but none of the choices seemed to have any merit.

Bobby stuck his head in the door at that point and said in a hushed voice, "Hey, Dad . . ."

"What, Bobby?"

"I let Brutus in."

"Good. Let's hope he behaves."

Bobby still stood there, looking around the edge of the door. "Uh, Dad . . . could I come sleep in here with you and Mom? Would that be okay? I have a sleeping bag."

"Sure, Bobby."

So he disappeared, then returned in a moment with a rolled up sleeping bag, which he spread out on the floor. Brutus followed after him and went straight to the bathroom. I could hear him lapping from the toilet. Then he came back into the bedroom, his chops dripping wet, and tried to lick Bobby in the face as he was sliding into his bedroll.

"Yuck, Brutus! You're so gross!" Bobby said as he pushed him away. "Now lie down over here." He patted the floor beside the sleeping bag. "Lie down over here."

Brutus must have realized it was everybody's bedtime, including his, because he walked obediently to where Bobby was patting the floor, pawed at the rug, turned around in a circle a few times, and then just flopped down with a thoroughly satisfied grunt.

"Now stay there, Brutus," Bobby said. Then after a moment he added, "Night, Dad . . ."

"Night, Bobby," I whispered.

In just a couple of minutes, I could tell he and Brutus were both asleep too. I could hear their breathing, along with Julie's. The deep regular breathing of sleep. Deep and regular, deep and regular. Brutus was snoring, of course. Brutus always snores. Always. Brutus would snore with a Sealy Posturepedic on his face.

I lay there listening to them in the darkness. Listening to their breathing. Deep and regular. Deep and regular. Usually they were out of phase with each other, but on occasion they would come into synchrony for a period of time, then drift apart again. I could hear all three of them so clearly in the dimness of the bedroom. Julie. Bobby. Brutus. I found it comforting somehow. All the craziness and turmoil in my mind began to ease. I could feel myself finally starting to relax. Could feel the chaos and the conflict of the day finally starting to slip away. And gradually I drifted off to sleep . . .

17.

I slept all night long. The clock on the nightstand said six-thirty when I finally woke up. I looked around sleepily. It was still dark in the room, but I could see the first traces of daylight starting to come through the blinds. I still lay right behind Julie, my arm draped over her side. She hadn't moved much either. She still lay snuggled back against me, her knees pulled up, curled into a ball. I've read that people normally move around in their sleep, but it hadn't happened with us.

Going very slowly and carefully, I lifted my arm off her and worked my way away from her, back across the bed. She stirred slightly but didn't wake up. I sat on the edge of the bed for a few moments, trying to clear out the cobwebs, then got up and headed to the bathroom. Bobby and Brutus still lay at the foot of the bed. Brutus was awake enough to look up at me and wag his tail. It made a thumping sound on the floor. I nudged Bobby with my foot.

"Bobby, wake up," I whispered. "Time to get going. We have to get you to school."

Bobby has never been much of a morning person. He opened his eyes and looked around blearily. "Yikes," he managed.

"Let's move it, sport."

He sat up and shook his head, managed another, "Yikes," and then a groggy, "Okay."

I took a quick shower and put on the same clothes I had worn the night before. I used Julie's razor to shave. I wasn't exactly ready for the cover of GQ, but I thought I looked halfway presentable. I stepped out of the bathroom and headed back across the bedroom. Bobby was already in the kitchen, sitting at the breakfast table, eating a quick bowl of cereal.

"What should we do about Brutus?" he asked. "He won't go out in the back unless you drag him with a leash."

Brutus was lying by Bobby's chair. He could tell we were talking about him. Brutus can always tell this. Always. He wagged his tail, thumping it against the leg of the breakfast table, making a knocking noise against the wood. He sounded like a one dog bongo band.

"Better put him out in front for a minute or two," I decided. "We sure don't need him to make a mess here in the house, and if we do put him in the back yard, I'm afraid he may howl and keep your mom from resting."

"What about Mr. Thompson's walk?"

I thought about that. "We'll just risk it. Cross your fingers. By the way, what is Ms. Randerson's cell number? She said you and Mom have it."

"Right here." He gave me a piece of paper, called to Brutus, and headed for the front door. Brutus followed without hesitation. The lure of neighboring pavement must have been beckoning strongly.

So I called Lois Randerson on her cellphone. She sounded bright and chipper for that hour of the morning, and apparently wasn't harboring any residual trauma or displeasure from the night before. We agreed that I'd take Bobby to school, then swing by her place and drive to get a rental car. Her house was two doors down on the other side of the street, she told me. The only house on the block with a red door.

I stuck my head back in the bedroom before leaving and went over to the bed and stood beside it. Julie was still asleep. I decided not to wake her. Bobby tiptoed into the room as I stood there, Brutus following behind him, fresh from his excursion into the front yard.

"Lie down here at the end of the bed," I whispered to Brutus, and I knelt down and patted the floor. He seemed to get the picture and flopped down without further ado. "Now stay there, boy. You hear me?"

I thought it would work, so Bobby and I crept out of the bedroom and went out and got in the Taurus. I could see Bobby scanning the yard apprehensively as we stepped down the walk.

"I wonder where he put it," he said.

"I don't want to know," I told him. "I'm not even gonna let myself look."

So we got in the car and drove to school. It only took a few minutes. Neither of us spoke. Bobby turned back toward me just before he got out of the car.

"You think Mom will be okay?" he asked.

I nodded. "I think she'll be fine. You have a good day at school."

He got out of the car and shut the door, and I watched as he walked into the building. I said a private prayer that my optimism about Julie wouldn't prove to be groundless, then drove back home. Brutus still lay at the end of the bed when I walked into the bedroom. He thumped his tail on the floor as I stepped to the bed. Julie was still curled up in a ball under the covers. I knelt down beside her. I stayed like that for several moments, just looking at her. I could have stayed there longer, but I didn't let myself. I needed to keep moving. I reached out and gently jostled her shoulder.

"Hey there, wake up," I said. "It's morning."

She stirred, then opened her eyes and looked up at me. The hazel green was as clear as ever, just like I always remembered. I thought my heart missed a lub dub.

"Hi . . ," she said.

"How do you feel? Or can you even tell yet? You slept all night long."

She frowned. "I don't know. I think maybe I'm better . . . my stomach doesn't seem to feel sick. . . and my head feels better, I think . . . I don't know, though . . . I haven't tried to move around yet."

"Want me to bring you anything?"

She frowned again. "Maybe a glass of water. That sounds pretty good. My throat feels dry."

"Be right back."

I brought her a glass of water, and she sat up in the bed and sipped it. She seemed to be testing it as it went down. Then she nodded and took a couple of swallows.

"That's good," she said as she finished the glass. "I'm dry as a bone."

"I'll get you another."

So I brought her another glass of water. She was lying on her side again when I came back to the bed.

"Want me to put it here on the nightstand?" I asked.

"Yes, thanks. That would be nice."

Looking down at her, I thought she still didn't look like she felt all that great. Not as sick as last night, by any means, but certainly not back to normal yet either. I bent down and touched her forehead with the back of my hand. It was dry, not cold and clammy like it had been last night. I thought that was probably a good sign. She still looked pretty weak, though. And sleepy. I could tell the medication hadn't completely worn off yet. She seemed to be drifting off to sleep again as I stood there, in fact.

"I got Bobby to school," I said, "so you don't need to worry about that. I'll call the office and let them know you won't be coming in today."

She opened her eyes and nodded. "Thanks. I don't think I ought to try that today."

So I went into the kitchen and called her office, then dialed her parents. They said they'd be over shortly to check on her. They had a key to the house, they said, so there wasn't any need to leave the door unlocked. I felt conflicted about leaving, but the need to get back to Austin was gnawing at my insides, and I felt Julie's condition had stabilized and that her parents could take care of anything else she needed. They had also said they could pick Bobby up after school, so that was taken care of too.

I went back into the bedroom, carrying the mobile, and knelt down by the bed again. Sure enough, she had drifted off to sleep once more, and once again, I just stayed there watching her for several moments. Keep moving, I told myself. So I jostled her shoulder again, very gently, and she opened her eyes and looked up at me.

"You think you're doing better?" I asked.

She nodded. "Yes, I really am. My stomach isn't sick anymore, and the headache's gone. Mostly I'm just sleepy now. I feel like I'm still hung over from the medication."

I put the phone on the nightstand. "Here's the phone, right here by the water glass. I called your folks. They said they'd be over before long to check on you. They'll pick Bobby up at school today too, so you don't even have to get out of bed if you don't want to."

Her eyes were still closed, but I could see her smile. "Thanks, Walt. You've really been a help. A lifesaver. I really do mean that. I don't think I would have made it without you."

"I meant what I said last night, Julie. I wouldn't have been anywhere else. Not for anything in the world."

I could see her smile again.

I still felt conflicted about leaving. I just couldn't decide what to do. I don't know whether it was just coincidence or not, but before I even had a chance to say anything else, she opened her eyes again and said, "Don't you need to be down in Austin? Aren't you working on that case down there?"

It caught me by surprise. I shrugged and said, "Well, yeah . . . kind of . . ."

"Go ahead and go, Walt. Please go. I really think I'm all right. And if I need anything, I can call Mom and Dad. I'll be fine."

"Lois Randerson said you could call her too if you need anything. She came by last night to check on you. She said she'd be happy to help."

Julie smiled. "Bless her heart, Lois is such a dear.

She's always so helpful. And she's had a lot going on lately too. Her father's been sick, and then she had some sort of trouble the other day herself. It was some sort of problem with a hemorrhoid, she said. She had to have something drained, and then it got infected. I think she's still taking antibiotics. So she's still not up to par herself."

That explains it, I thought. Poor lady. Having to put up with Brutus at a time like that.

Julie must have been able to tell I was thinking, because she added, "Go ahead and go, Walt. I'll feel bad if you stay here because of me. I mean that. I really think I'll be fine. I know you need to get back to work."

That tipped the balance for me. She was right. I needed to get back to Austin. And I thought her assessment was correct. The worst was over. I thought she'd continue to improve.

"Okay, then," I said, finally deciding. I bent over and kissed her gently on the forehead. I kept my lips pressed there for a moment, then stood up. "I'm headed back to Austin. I'll be on the cell at all times. Call if you need me. I can come right back at any time."

"Have a safe trip," she said.

I stopped at the bedroom door and looked back at her. "See you later, Julie. I'm glad you're better. You had me worried there for awhile."

I could see her smile, even though she had closed her eyes again. "Thanks again, Walt. You really were a lifesaver."

I made sure all the doors were locked and called Lois Randerson as I left the house. I had decided I didn't want to leave the Taurus there at Julie's. I was certain I hadn't been followed from Austin, but the Taurus was recognizable now, and I didn't want it there in front of her house, so I asked Lois if she could follow me to my apartment so I could leave it there before we went to get the rental car. She said that would be no problem. She didn't sound irritated or put out about it at all. Julie's assessment of her was obviously correct: she was a nice person. Especially in light of what had happened the night before. She followed me to my apartment, and I dropped off the Taurus and parked it in the lot in front. Then she drove me to the Hertz office at Love field, where I had seen Davidson drop off the silver Buick just a few nights before. I didn't say anything about last night, but for good measure, I did keep the window open. And I didn't take any deep breaths. When we got there, I got a white, four door Grand Am and thanked Lois again before she drove off to work. Still nothing was said of the night before. She seemed very concerned about Julie and told me again to call her if I needed anything.

I was all ready to head back to Austin, but I found myself hesitating. There was one more thing I needed to do. I was long overdue on it already, in fact, but I had felt conflicted and uncomfortable about it, and I had found myself putting it off. Now was the time, I decided.

So I drove to a stately two-story house on Lover's Lane, right in the heart of Highland Park, one of the nicest neighborhoods in Texas. Or anywhere, for that matter. I hesitated in the car for a moment before getting out and walking to the front door. I paused again before ringing the doorbell. I read the name engraved on the doorknocker: Nodman. Then I pushed the bell. I heard it chiming deep inside the house.

Then the door opened, and I found myself staring at a middle-aged woman who appeared to be much younger than her fifty-two years. I knew that to be her age, but otherwise I would never have guessed it. There were lines in her face - across her forehead, little crow's feet at the corners of her eyes - but her skin was still clear and firm, well-toned, with very little sagging or drooping. The angle of her chin was clean and trim, the surface of her neck smooth and unlined. There were tiny little traces of gray in her hair, but the rest was deep and richly black. Her eyes were light sky blue and crystal clear. She was every bit as pretty as she had been in the pictures I had seen of her as I was growing up, I thought. Every bit as striking. And time had changed her even less than I would have expected. I could have recognized her in an instant across a crowded room, just from the pictures, even though I had no recollection of ever having seen her in person. She had left home when I was only two, after all, on the day she turned eighteen, and our paths had never crossed again since then. Until now.

I hadn't said anything to that point, and she stood there looking at me with growing uncertainty. Then she seemed to make the connection. I could see a change in her expression.

"Walter?" she asked.

"Hi, Nancy."

I could see her smile as she stepped to me without hesitation and put her arms around me and hugged me. I put my arms around her and embraced her in return. We stood there holding each other for several moments, our arms tightly around each other. I could feel her patting my back. The way a big sister might pat her kid brother. Then she pulled back and gazed up at me. A smile spread across her features.

"Let me just look at you," she said. "Goodness, goodness, goodness, Walter. Just look what you've grown up to be. I haven't seen you since you were two. Not even a picture. I had no idea what you looked like. I don't even know why I finally recognized you just now. I guess maybe . . . maybe it's your eyes. They look like Mother's, I think. Maybe that's it. Or maybe I just managed to sense it in some way."

"I recognized you right away, Nancy," I said. "I would have known you anywhere. You're still just as pretty as you were in all your pictures."

She smiled. “Well, you’re kind to say that. Those were from a long, long time ago. A different life, really. I’m an old lady now.”

“You don’t look like that to me.”

“Well, you’re being kind again . . . goodness, goodness, goodness, come on in, Walter. Please, come in. I can’t believe I’m just letting you stand here on the doorstep.”

So she held the door open for me and showed me inside. I stepped across the foyer and looked around as I made my way into the living room. It was basically a palace. Elegant and stylish in every way, without seeming overly gaudy or ostentatious. My sister’s good taste, I thought, along with the money of her corporate attorney husband. She led me to a very large, very plush sofa, and we both sat down.

“Anything I can get you?” she asked. “Something to eat or drink?”

I shook my head. “No thanks, Nancy. I just came by to see you. I only have a minute.”

She hesitated, considering. “I . . . I feel so bad, Walter,” she finally said. “I should have been in touch with you all these years. I feel just horrible that I wasn’t. Nothing that happened at home was ever your fault, after all. You were still just a baby when I left.”

“That’s okay, Nancy. I never held anything against you. We were sixteen years apart. We have different fathers. The paths we each walked just didn’t ever cross.” I paused, wondering about how I should continue. She regarded me expectantly, concern showing in her eyes.

“I heard about some of the things that happened,” I went on. “Mother told me a little from time to time as I got older, on those rare occasions when she was sober enough to think clearly and make sense. When she was sober enough to feel remorse about it all. I heard about how my father used to beat you up and abuse you. How he would beat Mother too if she tried to intervene, so finally she just gave up and stopped trying altogether, and drowned everything in the alcohol. I'm sure she didn't even begin to tell me everything, but I heard enough to realize what a horrible hell it must have been for you. I don't blame you for leaving when you got the chance and never coming back. I would have done the same."

I could see tears glistening in her eyes. "I didn't have a choice, Walter. I really didn't."

"I understand, Nancy."

She dabbed at the tears with a Kleenex. "She was always . . . so impaired . . . so drunk . . . I hated it, Walter, but I couldn't change her."

Images from the past came back to me, scenes parading before my mind's eye. Haunting pictures. I tried to drive them away, but as always, they were hard to dispel. I felt a great heaviness inside.

"Nobody could, Nancy. I think it might have been different if *your* father had still been around, but the situation with *my* father was a nightmare all the way. He was a jerk in every sense of the word. I'm sorry to have to say that about my own father, but it's the truth. He left when I was seventeen, and we never heard from him again. To this day, I still don't know where he is, or whether he's even still alive. Mother was very sick by then. Her liver was gone. She died about a year later, just after I got out of high school. The end was not pretty, believe me. Liver failure is a rotten way to die."

She closed her eyes, as if to drive away the images. "Aunt Ruth told me a little bit here and there along the way. She kept in touch from time to time." She hesitated. I could tell she was uncertain about continuing. "I . . . I feel just awful that I didn't go to Mother's funeral. It was all part of the way I felt about never going back. I just couldn't. I don't know if you can understand that."

I nodded. "I understand, Nancy."

Tears were welling up in her eyes again. We wound up just looking at each other. The silence in the room hung over us like a cloak.

"I'll always be grateful to Aunt Ruth for getting me out of that mess I managed to create by getting my girl friend pregnant when I was sixteen," I finally added. "And I'll always be grateful to you too, Nancy, for doing what you did. You don't know how much I appreciate it."

She smiled, but I could see the tears building up in her eyes again. "I wanted to, Walter. I mean that. Honestly. I don't know how much you've heard along the way, but my pregnancy with Janet had been a very difficult one. You've never met Janet, I know. She's twenty-six now, she's married, she has a child of her own, she's a Special Education teacher. I know it's neither here nor there at this point. But the pregnancy had been a complicated one. I developed a heart condition called a cardiomyopathy of pregnancy. It's quite rare. I hadn't ever heard of it myself, and to this day, I've never met anybody else who had it during a pregnancy, but I did. My heart just got weaker and weaker. Finally, I was in congestive heart failure, and they had to do an emergency C-section at the twenty-eight week point. Janet did fine, and I eventually recovered too, for the most part, but I still see my cardiologist every year, and he says my heart still isn't quite as strong as it would ordinarily be. My 'ejection fraction' is lower than normal, he says."

She paused for a moment before continuing. "At any rate, I was told never to get pregnant again, and Frank and I really wanted another child. And so, when we heard what had happened, when Aunt Ruth called us and asked if we would adopt . . . well, we were more than happy to do it, believe me. We were ecstatic, in fact. It was like an answer to prayer. It didn't feel like a burden at all. I just wish . . ."

Her voice broke; she had to stop. I waited while she

tried to collect herself.

"I just wish . . . I just wish it had all turned out so differently. I tried, Walter. I tried. I tried as hard as I could. I did everything for Jessica we had ever done for Janet. Everything. Whether you can believe it or not, we loved her every bit as much as we loved Janet. We got her the day she was born, after all. She was ours, just as much as Janet. We tried and we tried and we tried. But . . . she so was different, Walter. She was so very, very different from Janet. Then she went out of control, despite everything we tried to do. I don't know why. I don't believe I ever will. But it happened, and we couldn't stop it. We had her in to see counselors, we had her in therapy, we sent her away to a special boarding school for girls with bad behavior problems . . . but nothing ever made a difference. Nothing. She just kept getting more and more out of control. Getting into more and more trouble. I feel that I let her down somehow, but I honestly don't know what I could have done differently. I honestly don't. I feel that I've let you down too. I feel that I've failed so miserably."

I slid across the couch toward her and put my arm around her shoulder, and she collapsed against me. As she did, she started to weep.

"I tried, Walter, I tried," she sobbed. "I tried so hard."

"There, there, Nancy," I said. "There, there."

I couldn't think of anything more to do or say. I just kept holding her and patting her on the back.

"There, there."

Her face was buried against my chest. A great, heaving sob shuddered her frame. Still I held her.

"I know you did everything you could, Nancy," I said. "I don't know much about genetics, but for what it's worth, Jackie Valentine - her biological mother, the girl I got pregnant - she was easily the wildest girl I ever met. Just crazy wild. No fear, no caution, no hesitation. Drugs, sex, everything. She finally died at twenty-three of a cocaine overdose, I heard. I was almost a little surprised she hadn't died or been killed sooner, so . . . I don't know, Nancy . . . maybe that's the explanation. Maybe that's the reason. We probably won't ever know for sure, but I know you tried."

Still I held her. Finally she took a deep breath and pulled away from me.

"I should have called you as soon as it happened," she said, " . . . as soon as we knew Jessica had been murdered. I meant to . . . but I just didn't. I guess it's all part of my denial. All part of never wanting to go back to my past. But when the investigation just kept dragging on and on and on without getting anywhere, I finally couldn't stand it any more. I had heard from Aunt Ruth that you had become a homicide investigator . . . and so I finally decided to call you."

"I'm glad you did. I never actually saw Jessica, but she's still my biological daughter. I want to catch whoever killed her. I should have come by to see you as soon as I got to Dallas, but I've been so busy with the investigation I haven't gotten around to it until now. I . . . I guess maybe I've got some denial of my own too."

There didn't seem to be much else to say. I told her I would let her know as soon as I learned anything definite. She told me to keep in touch, that we shouldn't ever let ourselves drift apart again. I agreed. We hugged each other one more time, and then I was gone. She was standing in the doorway of her beautiful home as I put the rental car into gear and pulled away. I waved at her, and she waved back at me. Then I turned the corner, and she was out of sight.

A little over two and a half hours later I was coming into Austin. I called Joe Henderson at his office.

"Well, I kind of figured you'd be giving me a call..," he said. I could hear some uncertainty in his voice.

He paused for several moments before continuing.

"I'm sorry, Walt . . . I tried to do what I could. I want you to know that. I tried to talk him out of calling it off, but Baker's mind was already made up. Davidson's a little god to him, and he wouldn't let it go any farther. He's convinced that Davidson is completely innocent, of course. There just wasn't any arguing with him. There just wasn't anything I could do."

I took a breath. "Yeah, I know that, Joe. I appreciate your help."

Then I told him all about being tailed yesterday afternoon and then about meeting up with Davidson on the sidewalk in front of Hidalgo's. I gave him a brief account of what had been said.

"Good Lord, Walt . . . I don't know what to say. . . I just don't. I really didn't think Baker would do anything like that . . . God, it blows my mind . . ."

"I still think Davidson is part of it," I said. "I think he's guilty as hell. And I'm not about to give up on it. I'm gonna catch the son of a bitch. I don't know how right now - not having any help or anything - but I'm gonna do it. Somehow."

He didn't say anything.

"I'll let you know if I find out anything new," I said. "I'd appreciate it if you'd do the same for me."

I could hear him sigh. "You bet, Walt . . . anything turns up, I'll call you right away."

So that was that.

I was almost into the downtown area by then. I thought I might drive by Brackenridge Hospital and see if Davidson's car was there. But it was almost noon by then, and before I could even really head in that direction, I got a call from Stan. The timing seemed opportune. It was almost noon, after all, so we agreed to meet at the Red Dragon, a Chinese buffet place near the downtown area. I found Stan waiting in her pickup in the parking lot when I got there. I pulled up beside her, and she looked over at me. There was a moment of surprise on her face when she saw the new car. Then she got out of her truck, came around the front of the Grand Am, and kissed me on the mouth. Hard. Very hard. Typical Stan. This time, the kiss was even harder than usual as she pressed her mouth against mine. Her arms were locked around my neck.

"Stan, it's a parking lot," I said.

"I don't care."

She was kissing me even harder, pressing herself against me, her pelvis against my groin. Finally I pulled back and pushed her away.

"They have laws about what you can do in public," I said.

"The laws are dull. They ought to be changed."

I put my hand on her elbow and guided her across the parking lot toward the entrance of the restaurant. She let me lead her along.

"Where's the Taurus?" she asked.

"A lot's happened. I'll tell you about it."

So we got our food and sat down to eat.

"So tell me about it," she said. "The last I heard, you said somebody was trying to tail you."

"That's putting it mildly."

So I told her about everything that had happened since the last time I had seen her. She watched closely as I talked. I could see the surprise on her face as I gave her the details.

"My God, Walt!" she gasped when I had finally finished. "My God! Who was it? Why would anybody do that to you? Tossing your motel room?"

"I'm not sure. But I have a theory."

So I told her how I thought it had happened. Acting Chief Baker had called Davidson and told him about the tail. He had given Davidson enough information, or Davidson had managed to get it out of him somehow, and then Davidson had decided to have me followed. They had tracked me to Hidalgo's, and then we met on the street. Davidson was trying to scare me off. The tossed motel room was just the icing on the cake.

"My God!" she said again. "My God! That's just incredible. I don't know what else to say."

I didn't have anything to add to that.

"What happened then?" she asked. "Did you change motels? I think I would have wanted to move."

"Not yet. I drove back to Dallas instead."

So I told her about the call I had gotten from Bobby and about driving back to Dallas to take care of Julie. She watched me very closely again as I talked, but the expression on her face wasn't one of surprise. It was one of concerned attention. I wound up telling her about getting the rental car and then coming back to Austin. Which brought me up to the present.

"How is Julie?" she asked, her voice low, almost subdued.

"Better, I think. Her parents were coming over to stay with her today. I think she'll be fine."

"Well . . . that's good . . ."

We ate in silence for a few more minutes. Finally we finished, and I signaled the waiter for the check.

"So what do you plan to do now?" she asked as we were headed back to the parking lot.

"Always your favorite question."

"I think it's really a very reasonable one, under the circumstances."

I couldn't argue with that. "I plan to keep following Davidson," I told her. "I also plan to keep looking for Gunner. I don't know what else to do. I don't care what the people in the Austin Police feel about it, but I think I'm onto something. I have to keep going."

We had gotten to the cars. She stopped and looked up at me.

"I want to come with you," she said, looking me in the eye, that determined tone in her voice again.

"What else is new?"

"I mean it, Walt. I want to come with you. Let me. Please."

I had known that was coming, of course, and I had thought about it. "Look, Stan . . . things have changed now. They know who I am. And they also know somebody who's one hell of a good tail. I'm in a different car now, but it'll be much harder to stay hidden. That means they may be watching me. Right now. And that means they'll be watching anybody with me. Which could mean you, Stan. I've told you before that you're just their type. I'm not going to let them see you again, if I can help it. I'm not going to risk pulling you into this any farther. So . . . I'm sorry, but my mind's made up. I have to do this alone at this point."

She had looked right in my eyes the whole time as I had said that, and I could see the disappointment on her face. But she could tell I meant what I said. It was not a point I was going to be flexible on.

"And what about Julie?" she finally asked.

I had thought about that too. "I'll probably drive back up to Dallas tonight to make sure she's doing okay. She was pretty sick last night. She had me worried."

Stan looked down for a moment, then back into my eyes. She stepped toward me and put her arms around me and kissed me again. Not as hard this time. More tenderly. But she clung to me tightly, and she didn't show any sign of pulling away. Finally I pulled back. I actually had to push her away a little to get separated.

"Don't forget the laws about what you can do in public," I noted.

"They ought to be repealed," she grumbled.

She wrapped her arms around me again and laid her head against my chest and clung to me tightly. I put my arms around her and patted her on the back. I thought about Julie and Bobby as I did. I really did need to have a talk with Stan, I decided. Not now. Not here in this parking lot. But soon.

Finally I pulled back and separated myself. The blueness of her eyes glistened up at me. Then she leaned forward and kissed me on the lips again, very gently this time, and only for a moment.

"Take care of yourself, Walt," she said huskily, as she pulled away. "I know you feel you have to keep going, but stay out of harm's way if you possibly can. I . . . I care about what happens to you. Very much. I hope you know that."

I just nodded.

She gave me a little smile, then got into her pickup. I heard the engine start. She gave me a little wave as she put it in gear and pulled away. I just stood there for a moment, watching as she drove away. Then I got into the rental car and headed out of the lot.

There was nothing to do but keep looking. I drove back to Brackenridge Hospital and found Davidson's car in the parking lot. I called the Operating Room and told them I was a doctor in town who needed to talk to Dr. Davidson. They told me he had just started a quadruple bypass and wouldn't be finished for hours. I said I'd call back later. So I went to a few more adult bookstores, showing the picture of Gunner and giving the same story about the inheritance. There were only a few more places left on my list. The first few turned out to be just as dry as everything else. Finally there was only one more left. This one was on the far southwest edge of the city, on the Interstate to San Antonio. So I went inside, feeling very futile, and showed Gunner's picture to the clerk standing behind the counter. I gave him the bit about the inheritance too.

"Well, I haven't seen him *here*," the clerk said after just one glance at the drawing, "but I used to work at our sister store over in San Antonio, and he used to come in there all the time."

It took me a moment to react. I thought I hadn't heard him correctly.

"Excuse me?" I asked.

"Yeah, he used to come into the store over there all the time. Every couple of weeks or so."

I still couldn't believe what I was hearing. "You're sure?"

He studied the picture again for a moment. "Yeah, I'm sure. Big guy. Great big huge muscles, a body builder. This is him. He used to come in there all the time. He used to buy Butt-Plugs."

I thought maybe I hadn't heard him correctly again. "Excuse me?"

"Butt-Plugs. He used to buy lots of Butt-Plugs. Tons of Butt-Plugs."

I must have had a blank expression on my face.

"Butt-Plugs," he repeated. "Here, I'll show you."

He stepped around from behind the counter and walked to a display stand across the way. I could see all kinds of items on pegs. Just at a glance, I could tell that these were "specialty items." I could see dildos and whips and handcuffs and God knows what else. He pulled off one of the items and held it out to me. It was encased in a cardboard card and sealed in plastic, the kind of packaging you'd find for any of a million normal items.

"Butt-Plug," he said. "You never seen one before?"

I took it from him and stared at it. I still must have had a dumbfounded expression on my face.

"Sell 'em here all the time," he added. "They been making 'em for years."

I studied it some more. Standard packaging, sure enough. Cardboard backing covered with sealed plastic. The wording at the top said, "Butt-Plug." Nothing fancy, thank you. Just, "Butt-Plug." All I could do was stare at it.

The item itself was shaped like a standard red Christmas tree light - a rounded oval, tapered at the end like a teardrop, with a stem attached to the base. At the bottom of the stem was a square plate about two inches across. I still must have looked perplexed, because the clerk repeated, “Sell ‘em here all the time.” I continued to inspect it, turning it around, checking it from different angles. At one point I started to ask how you worked it, but I caught myself. Still I examined it. The purpose of the square plate at the base of the stem seemed obvious enough. To keep it from going all the way up inside, I realized. Certainly don’t want any unnatural penetrations, after all. I turned it over and looked at the back of the cardboard. There was an assurance of the high quality of the workmanship. Hand crafted, only the best of materials, safety assured, that sort of thing. There was even a patent number. Wow. A patent, no less. So this was an actual invention. Another crowning achievement of the human mind. The Butt-Plug. It would be interesting to talk to the patent holder, I thought.

“Supposed to heighten your sensation,” the clerk added. “Make you come better, you know what I mean. Supposed to work really great on the ladies, is what I hear.”

I think I kind of nodded, as if to say that was certainly interesting.

“Or you can just use it as a toy, you know,” the clerk added. “Just to kind of play around with.”

“Sure . . ,” I heard myself say.

“We’ve got different sizes too,” he added. “In fact, that’s the smallest one we stock. Here, this one’s bigger.” He pulled another item off the display stand and held it out to me. Sure enough, it was another Butt-Plug, exactly the same design and packaging, in lavender this time. To say it was bigger just doesn’t describe it. This would have been the biggest light on the tree at The White House. Clearly, this was designed for those with the truly spacious rectums. I shuddered just looking at it. All I could do was stare at it in wonder.

"Christ," I heard myself mumble.

"We used to get some super jumbos," the clerk went on matter-of-factly, "but they finally stopped making 'em, I think. I mean, those things were super huge. I heard they had some injuries, though."

I didn't doubt it for a moment.

The clerk gestured towards Gunner's picture, which still lay on the counter. "Yeah, this guy in the picture here, he used to come to the store in San Antonio all the time. He used to buy these things by the ton. Must've been a real butt freak."

That sounded like Gunner, sure enough. "So you're sure about it. This is the same guy?"

He nodded. "Yeah, positive. Same guy. Big muscles and everything. I mean, he'd come in every two weeks or so and buy fifteen or twenty of these things. We even had to special order sometimes to keep them in stock."

I couldn't think of anything to say to that. You see, I've always been impressed by extremes of magnitude. There are certain numbers that just leave me stunned. Speechless. Like the estimated number of stars in the Milky Way, one hundred billion. Or ten to the minus twenty-seventh power, the estimated mass of an electron in grams. Such numbers are beyond comprehension. They defy the imagination. But twenty Butt-Plugs every two weeks? I've never stood in greater awe.

"You know anything about him?" I finally managed to ask. "Where he lives? How to find him?"

The clerk shook his head. "Nope. Can't help you there. Like I say, I just used to see him in our sister store in San Antonio. Never seen him here, and I've been working here steady for the past six months. Been at least that long since I saw him."

That was still more than anything else I'd gotten. "Thanks," I said. "I appreciate it."

"You bet," the clerk said pleasantly. "Any time."

So I set out for San Antonio. The two cities are only about seventy miles apart, and it was Interstate all the way. I was coming into northeast San Antonio in less than an hour. The clerk had told me how to find the sister store, and I got the same response from the clerk there that I had gotten in Austin. He had seen the man in the picture, but he didn't know who he was or how to find him. So I stopped at a 7-11 and borrowed a phone book. I wrote down the names and addresses of several gyms. The lady behind the counter was able to give me basic instructions on how to reach several that were on that side of town. I pulled up in front of the first one in just a few minutes. I wasn't going to let my hopes get too high, not after so many dead ends, but I could feel the pounding of my heart as I stepped inside. The girl behind the reception desk didn't recognize the picture at all. Here we go again, I thought. I looked around the gym, frustrated. I saw a guy working out with a heavy bar in a far corner. He was obviously no novice. His muscles showed the kind of bulk that only comes from years of hard work. I stepped over to him when he had finished a set of heavy squats, gave him the bit about the inheritance, and showed him Gunner's picture. He took one look at it and said offhandedly, "Yeah, this is Clint Adcock. He's a pro body builder. Used to be, at least. Haven't seen him at any competitions for a couple of years or so. You say he's got some inheritance coming?"

I almost thought my heart had stopped. "Yeah, he does. You know him?"

The man shrugged. "Well, yeah, I know who he is. I've seen him at competitions. I wouldn't exactly say I know him like a buddy or anything. Haven't seen him in a year or two, at least, like I said. But that's who this is. Doesn't come to this gym here, though. Used to work out at Grant's Gym downtown. You might try to find him there."

I felt a rush to my head, almost like dizziness. "You know anything else about him? What else he does? Where he lives?"

He thought about it. "Used to be a cop, I think."

I felt like I had been slapped in the face.

"Got in some trouble along the way, I heard," the man added. "Don't know any details, but I think I heard he had to quit the force. Seems to me I can remember hearing something like that."

"Grant's Gym downtown, you say?" I asked.

"Right. If he still goes there."

"Thanks a bunch," I said. "I appreciate it."

So I got the phone number and called Grant's Gym from my cellphone when I got out to the car, my heart hammering in my throat as I dialed.

"Is Clint Adcock there?" I asked when the phone was answered.

"Lemme see," said the man on the other end of the line. There was a pause. "Clint in back?" I heard him call.

I waited, aware of the tightness of my breathing.

"Nope," the man said a moment later. "Not here now. Usually comes by in the morning. Might try again tomorrow about ten."

"Thanks. You got a phone number for him? Any way to reach him?"

"Nope. Sorry."

So I hung up, my heart still pounding, the rush back in my head. I sat there in the car trying to figure out what to do next, and then a call came in on the cell. It was Joe Henderson, and I could tell right away he was bothered.

"You better get down to the station, Walt," he said tightly.

I felt a sudden knot in my gut. "What's up?"

I heard him take a deep breath. "There's been a new murder. Same exact deal. Blonde lady. Blow to the head. Heart cut out. Everything. Found her body this morning in a wooded area near Horseshoe Bay."

The knot in my gut had turned to nausea. "I'm on my way, Joe. I'm coming from San Antonio. It'll take me an hour at least."

"San Antonio?"

"I'll tell you when I get there."

So I raced back up the Interstate to Austin. I was there in sixty minutes, despite the traffic. Joe looked up at me when I walked into his office. His face was grim.

"These are the autopsy photos," he said, handing me a set of pictures. "Just got them a few minutes ago. Autopsy's been completed about two hours. They say she probably died three or four days ago."

I thought I knew what I'd find when I finally forced myself to look down at the pictures. It only took one glance. The nausea in my gut came back in force. It was the blonde girl I had seen at the party with Davidson.

"I know who she is," I said.

Joe stared at me. "Tell me."

So I did. I told him I had seen her dancing naked at a sex club party when I first crossed paths with her. Then I had seen her at the party last Saturday night with Davidson. I had seen them leave together. I had seen them at Love Field, heading toward the boarding area. Now she was dead.

"She danced nude at a sex club," I said. "So did Jessica Nodman and Michelle Stanzer and Charlotte Raymond. I'll bet Donna Rivers did too. That was the connection. That's what got them killed too. Basically, they danced their hearts out."

Joe listened closely, his features becoming more and more grim as I went along.

"Anybody who can corroborate that this girl and Davidson were at the party together?" he asked.

I nodded. "Stan. We were there together."

"Stan? Who's he?"

"We saw them leave together and followed them. We had a date to the costume party."

A shocked look flickered across his face for a brief moment, but he covered it quickly.

"Stan's a girl," I added. " That's short for Stanetta. Stanetta Hunter."

He looked relieved. "Whew. Thank God, Walt. You scared the hell out of me there for a moment. I know a lot of crazy shit's happened in your life lately, but still . . ."

"I'll call her now," I said. So I dialed her cellphone number, but I only got a recording. "Stan, this is Walt," I said. "Get back to me as soon as you can. I'm on my cell. It's important."

Joe regarded me closely.

"Davidson's guilty as hell," I said as I turned off the phone. "I'm sure of it. There's too much coincidence."

He nodded. "If this lady can corroborate that Davidson and this girl were at that party together last Saturday night, then I'll see if we can get thc tail going again. A wiretap too. That ought to be enough evidence, even for Baker. Who'd you say the lady is?"

"Somebody I met up with in Dallas. Legal assistant. Used to live here in Austin. Her ex-husband runs a karate studio here."

Joe seemed to think about that.

"Who are we talking about? You got his name?"

His tone of voice caught my ear. "Sure. Frank Hunter. Why?"

A rueful smirk crossed his lips. "Well, what do you know. It's a small fucking world, buddy. That's all I can say. Frank Hunter. Haven't crossed paths with him for some time now."

"You know him?"

He nodded grimly. "Oh, yeah. We sure know Frank Hunter. He's a mean, dangerous son of a bitch, Walt. He also happens to be a two-time national karate champion.

Would have won more, but he decided to stop competing. The word was, he just got bored with it. Nobody could even begin to give him a match. He was just too much for them. He's fucking awesome. He's got incredibly fast hands. Like lightning. At one point I heard they even did some studies on his reaction time with these special electronic instruments, and his reaction time was half what a normal person's would be. He's a freak of nature. He's strong too. Real strong. Dangerous. And he's got an ugly disposition. Every now and then he winds up in a fight with somebody. Usually somebody who's crossed him in some way. People get very, very badly injured. Good old Frank always claims self-defense, of course, and he always manages to set it up so there aren't any witnesses, or that the witnesses just happen to be buddies of his. We've investigated him several times. Never could prove it wasn't self-defense. Always had to let him go. But we know Frank Hunter here, believe me. Stay clear of him if you can. He's a mean, mean, dangerous son of a bitch."

I wasn't all that surprised. I remembered the look in his eye, the hardness in his voice.

"It's almost five, Joe," I said. "I need to get back to Dallas. I'll keep trying to reach Stan. She can corroborate everything. We'll get a statement from her. Let me know if anything else happens."

I started to turn to leave, then thought of something else. "One more thing. See what you can find out about a guy named Clint Adcock, who used to be a cop in San Antonio. That's the other picture you got. I heard he may have gotten into some sort of trouble and had to leave the force. He's part of it too."

Then I shook Joe's hand, stepped out of his office, got in the rental car, and headed north to Dallas . . .

18.

I stopped at a Burger King on the way out of town and grabbed a quick hamburger and some fries, then tried again to call Stan on her cell. Still no answer. I left another message for her to call me. It was important, I added. Now, of all times, not to be able to reach her.

Driving north out of town, I passed the La Quinta where I'd stayed and stopped to talk to the manager. My room had been tossed, I told him. Oh, they were *very* much aware of that, he assured me. The cleaning woman had reported it that morning. They had been trying *very* hard to get me, he advised me, but the only phone number they had for me was the apartment in Dallas. They had left several messages for me to call, and they were, in fact, close to reporting me missing to the police. I assured him I would come back by tomorrow to claim my belongings and settle the account. I gave him my cell number and asked him to call me if they were able to determine who had been involved in the incident. Certainly, he assured me, although there had been no reports of anything suspicious on the property. So that was that. I got back in the Grand Am and headed north again.

Halfway to Dallas, I called Julie to see how she was doing. She felt fine, she said. It was like she hadn't even been sick. She was eating normally, and most of her strength had come back, so it must have been one of those twenty-four hour things. Thank God it was over, was all I could say. I told her I expected to be back at the house by nine-thirty or ten. She and Bobby would be waiting, she said. I tried again to get Stan as I was coming into Dallas, but I still didn't get an answer. I left another message, even more urgent this time. I was puzzled. I'd never been unable to reach her before. I felt a vague sense of uneasiness, an apprehension that fell just short of worry.

Then the cellphone rang, and I jumped like I'd been

stabbed. I pushed the button and said a tense, "Hello," hoping I would hear Stan's voice. I didn't recognize the caller's number, but Stan could have been calling from another phone, I told myself. But it wasn't meant to be. It was Clyde, the king of the costume shop, calling to see where his precious rabbit suit was. It had been due back Monday, he reminded me. That had been three days ago.

Well, I thought about complaining about the whole miserable deal, the zipper malfunction and everything, but as I thought about it, I just didn't want to get back into all that godawful, messy stuff, so I told him the suit had been damaged and that I'd reimburse him for it. He said fifty dollars would be sufficient, so I told him to bill it to my credit card, and he said that would be fine. End of rabbit suit disaster.

It was right about ten when I pulled up in front of Julie's house. She opened the door as I came up the walk and met me on the front step. Without thinking, I put my arms around her and hugged her, lifting her off her feet. We held onto each other tightly.

"Thank God you're better," I said.

"I think it was the flu."

"Nasty stuff."

So we went inside, where Bobby and Brutus were in front of the TV. Bobby had his homework spread out in front of him, but he was watching a soccer game on ESPN, and I didn't think the homework had been getting a lot of attention.

"Ten o'clock, Bobby," Julie said.

"Okay, okay, okay," he grumbled. He got up and headed towards his bedroom. Brutus got up and traipsed along slowly behind him. Bobby stopped at the door and turned back toward us. "I'll keep Brutus in my room tonight. That way we don't have to listen to him howl." He disappeared into the bedroom and shut the door, Brutus right behind him. By then Julie and I were in the kitchen.

There was an awkward silence for a moment.

"Have you eaten?" she finally asked.

"Yeah, I got something on the way out of Austin. How about you?"

She nodded. "We had some pizza delivered. There's plenty left if you want some."

We stood there together, looking at each other in the stillness. Then Julie stepped up to me, put her arms around me, and held me. I hugged her in return.

"I really do appreciate all that you did last night, Walt," she said.

"Wasn't much. I wouldn't have been anywhere else. I meant it when I said that."

She continued to hold onto me. Then she laid her head against my chest. We stood there for several moments, quietness all around us.

"It felt good to sleep with you last night," she finally said. "I'm . . . I'm so used to being in bed all alone these days."

I pulled back just a little, lifted her chin with my finger, and kissed her. She kissed me in return. I rubbed my hands over her back, then down along her sides.

"It felt good to me too," I said.

We kissed again, harder this time. Memories came flooding back to me. Memories of things I had thought I would never experience again.

"We *are* still married, you know," I said.

She smiled up at me. "My thoughts exactly."

"And Bobby's gone to bed, after all."

"How perfect."

Without saying anything else, I picked her up and carried her in my arms into the bedroom. Then I put her back on her feet. We stood there for a moment, looking at each other, but there was really no need to talk. We'd been here so many times before. Very slowly we undressed each other, then got onto the bed and made love. Very slowly, very gently. Julie was on top, as always. Because of the difference in size, she says that when she's on the bottom, it's like trying to make love to a rockslide. When we finished, she snuggled back against me like she had done the night before, curling up in a ball with her back toward me, and I draped my arm over her side and held her while she drifted off to sleep. I lay there, savoring the moment, even though I was tired. Gradually, the fatigue overtook me, and I drifted off to sleep, with Julie in my arms for the second night in a row.

The next morning was just like old times. Just like I had never been gone. I got up ahead of Julie and took a quick shower. I still had only the clothes I had been wearing, and they had become pretty rumpled by now. I should have gone by the room when I had stopped at the La Quinta, I told myself, but I had been eager to get back to Dallas, and I had wanted to avoid delay. I decided I'd run by the apartment here in Dallas on the way back to Austin and pick up a couple of fresh changes.

We all got ready on schedule, just like in the past. Julie took a quick shower too, then fixed Bobby some eggs and bacon. He had ESPN on again, watching another soccer game.

"Time to go, Bobby," Julie called. "Put Brutus out in back. He can't stay inside all day when nobody's home."

So Bobby got the leash and dragged - literally dragged - Brutus across the kitchen and out through the garage into the back. The neighborhood pavement was safe for another day. We were ready to leave. I hugged both of them, gave Julie a quick peck on the lips, told her I'd be back that evening, and then we got in our separate cars and headed out.

I drove directly to the apartment and parked in my regular assigned space behind the building. Once inside, I looked out the front window and could see the Taurus where I had left it. I also checked the answering machine.

As the manager of the La Quinta had said, they had tried several times to reach me. There were a couple of other messages, including a call from Clyde, but nothing that seemed important. In particular, there wasn't anything from Stan. I tried her cell again, feeling that same vague sense of apprehension, but I only got the answering machine again. I thought about trying to get her at the office, even though she had told me not to do that. They didn't like personal calls at the office, she had said. I was beginning to be worried, though.

Before I could even give it any more thought, the doorbell rang. I tensed all over, on guard in an instant. Who would be ringing my doorbell here at the apartment on a weekday morning? I pulled my Glock out of its shoulder holster and made my way to the window. I stood at the far edge and angled my line of sight through the slit between the blind and the edge of the window frame. I felt a sudden rush of relief. It was Sandy. Of course. Who else? I let out a sigh, put the Glock back in its holster, and opened the door.

"Hi, Walt," she said cheerfully. "I just happened to see you come in a minute ago, and I thought I'd come over and say hello. I haven't seen you around for a couple of days . . . I was beginning to be worried about you. Have you been okay?"

I fought down a twinge of irritation. "Sure, Sandy. Been fine. Had to go out of town on some business. That's all."

Well, that's good," she said. Then, after a pause, she added, "Actually, I need to ask you about something else too. That's the other reason I came by. I need to see if I can borrow your car for just a minute. I need to run to the store real quick, and mine has a dead battery. The car people said they couldn't get here until about ten, and I really do need to run this quick errand right now. I'll be right back. Would that be okay?"

Some things just don't ever change, I guess. "Sure, Sandy," I said, trying to make sure my voice didn't betray any impatience. I went to the bedroom, got the spare key, and brought it back to her. "Here's the key. I'm actually in another car today, and I'll be leaving in just a minute or two. If I'm gone when you get back, just keep the key until I see you again."

"Thanks, Walt," she said, smiling. Then before she turned away, she added, "Oh, by the way, one more thing. We were going to have a little get-together again tonight. You know, fix some steaks, that sort of thing. Come on by if you get the chance."

"Thanks, Sandy. Probably won't make it, though. I'm headed out of town again. Probably won't even come back to the apartment tonight."

She smiled again, then gave me a little wave. "Well, drive safely. And thanks again for the car."

"Sure, you bet."

So I shut the door and scratched my head. I thought again about trying to get Stan at the office, but she had been so very clear that she shouldn't be called there. I wasn't even sure that I remembered the name of the law firm she worked for, as far as that was concerned, so I decided to hold off on trying that. Keep calling on the cell. But I felt an uneasiness deep inside, something I couldn't quite put my finger on.

I told myself to keep moving. I got some spare trousers and a couple of shirts out of the closet, then some socks and underwear from the drawer. The traveling bag was still down at the La Quinta in Austin, so I headed to the kitchen to get a paper bag to put things in. Before I even got there, though, the entire building was jolted by a tremendous explosion. The floor trembled beneath my feet. Windows rattled. In the kitchen just ahead of me, a glass on the counter fell over, rolled across the counter top, and crashed on the linoleum floor. I stood there dumbfounded for a moment, then came to my senses and ran into the kitchen. I shot a quick glance out the window over the sink. The back of the apartment was clear. I stepped quickly across the living room to the front door and pulled it open. A huge flaming ball of fire, billowing enormous columns of thick black smoke, raged wildly in the parking lot no more than fifty feet away. Right where the Taurus had been parked. It took me a moment to comprehend it. I stared at it, stunned. Now there was nothing but a huge ball of fire and the towering columns of smoke. Even as I looked at it, I could still barely fathom the meaning of what had happened. I realized dimly there was nothing I could do but call 911. I grabbed up my cell, dialed quickly, and reported the blast. Units were already on the way, they said. Stay clear of the area.

The fire still raged furiously, the massive columns of thick black smoke turning higher and higher into the sky. Standing in the doorway, I suddenly felt weak, my head swimmy. I slumped to the ground, sliding down against the doorframe, and leaned back against the doorjamb. I could hear voices now, yelling and screaming and shouting. And the wail of a siren in the background, coming nearer. All I could do was lean back limply against the doorframe and watch. I hadn't realized Sandy would be in any danger. Maybe I should have.

The grisly scene played out over the next hour or so. More fire trucks arrived. Hoses were turned on. Water spewed under high pressure. Finally the flames were extinguished. Police cars with lights flashing encircled the area. A crowd had gathered around. Gradually order was restored. Still I just sat there.

Finally, there was nothing left to see except the hulk of twisted, steaming metal that had been the Taurus. I shook my head, then got up slowly and went over to a policeman standing over to the side, and identified myself as the owner of the car.

"What do you know?" he asked.

I swallowed. My throat felt dry. "A girl named Sandy wanted to borrow my car to go to the store. I gave her the keys. Then I heard the explosion."

He grimaced. "So there was a person in there?"

I felt myself nod. "I'm afraid so."

"Jesus . . ."

He proceeded to ask me if I knew why somebody would plant a bomb in my car. I told him I was a police officer involved in an investigation. The people being investigated didn't seem to be all that happy about it. That's what I thought it was about, I said.

"Jesus . . ," he muttered again.

So he got my name and my address, along with my badge number, my driver's license number, and my phone, all the elements of any police report.

"Stay in touch with us," he said.

"Sure."

I stood around for a few more minutes, still stunned, just staring at the charred hunk that had been the Taurus. Before long, the news had gotten around to the crowd. Sandy was dead. I could see a couple of her friends, tears streaming down their faces. I thought about going over to offer condolences, but I didn't have it in me. Then the Jaws Of Life equipment began to move in, preparing to break open the twisted hulk of the Taurus to retrieve Sandy's body, and I didn't have it in me to watch that either. I had to leave. There just wasn't any other option. So I walked heavily back to the apartment and got my spare clothes, then went out to the back and got in the Grand Am. I wound up just sitting there for a minute or two. A low grade nausea hung in my belly. I held out a hand and noticed a tremor in my fingers. Finally I stuck the key in the switch and turned it, then backed up, swung around, and pulled out of the lot, heading back to Austin.

I drove on instinct, not even thinking. I still felt just

completely numb. Finally I was coming into north Austin. I tried again to get Stan on her cellphone, hoping against hope, but there still wasn't an answer. I left yet another message. The vague sense of apprehension I had been experiencing rose even higher.

I drove directly to Joe Henderson's office. I found him behind his desk when I got there, studying a report. He seemed momentarily surprised and off balance as I walked into the room.

"Got some more info on that latest body," he said. "Name was Susannah Jacobson. Came from Dallas. She was a waitress. Didn't have any clear connections to any of the other victims. Parents weren't in close touch with her. Didn't know who she was dating, that sort of thing. Said they didn't know anything about a party Saturday night, or anything like that."

I nodded grimly. "I'm still trying to reach Stan. I'll get her down here as soon as I can."

I could have said more, but I decided not to. Joe sat there watching me, a sober expression on his face.

"You find out anything about Adcock?" I asked.

"Working on it. He was apparently terminated about a year or so ago, but I don't have any details yet. Said they didn't have a current address on him. I've got a call into their Internal Affairs guy, trying to find out more, but he hasn't gotten back to me yet. Adcock's not in the phone book. Haven't been able to find a cell number either."

"Let me know if you hear anything."

"Sure."

"One more thing," I added. "I need to use the range. Now."

"Well . . . okay . . ," he said.

So he led me to the basement, and I put up a target and ran it out to fifty feet. Joe was watching me closely as I did. Then I pulled out the Glock and fired off the whole magazine. I reeled the target in and checked it. Joe was still watching closely. There was only one hole, right in the center of the target, but it was bigger than I liked, and the edges were jagged, where slugs had passed through off center.

"Haven't shot in over a month," I noted.

So I reloaded, ran out another target and emptied the magazine again. Then I reeled it back in. The hole was smaller this time, more rounded.

"Don't want to get too much out of practice," I said. "Got a feeling I may need to use this before it's all over."

"Lord, Walt," Joe breathed, "you're still just as good as ever. The best I've ever seen. Never met anybody who could match you."

"Like riding a bicycle. Stays with you."

We went back up to the first floor. Joe seemed hesitant as we stood just inside the entrance.

"I, uh . . . I haven't gone back to Baker yet about Davidson, Walt," he said. "Kind of waiting to hear from this girl, Stan, you know, just to make sure I've got . . . well, independent confirmation, I guess. . . I hope you understand that."

"Sure, Joe. I'll get her down here as soon as I can."

He scratched behind his ear, then shuffled his feet. Then he extended his hand.

"I'm doing everything I can, Walt," he said. "I hope you know that."

I took his hand and shook it.

"Sure, Joe. I do."

So I left and got back in the car. It was time to go to Grant's Gym in San Antonio. Time to try to find Clint Adcock. Gunner. On the way out of Austin, I tried Stan's cell again. Still no answer. The knot in my gut got tighter. Thinking about it, I decided to try to reach Davidson. I could feel the hatred stirring inside me as I thought about it. I wanted to confront him again - if not face to face, then at least by voice. I wanted him to know he hadn't scared me off, that I was still after him. I wanted to get in his face with it. So I called the OR at Brackenridge Hospital and identified myself as "Doctor Miller" and asked to speak to Dr. Davidson. He wasn't operating today, I was told, no cases scheduled. So I called his office and tried the same thing.

"Dr. Davidson…he's not in the office right now," the receptionist told me.

"When do you expect him?"

"We're . . . we're really not all that sure . . . we're not certain," she said. There was a hint of uncertainty in her voice, as if something wasn't quite right and she was trying to hide it. I wondered what that was all about. Had Davidson given any special instructions about receiving phone calls? I didn't know.

"Would you . . . like to leave him a message?" she asked, still sounding hesitant.

I thought about it. "No, that's okay. I'll just call back later."

So it was on to San Antonio. I got to Grant's Gym in downtown San Antonio in a little over an hour. This was obviously a heavy workout kind of place, I could tell, as I walked in the door and stepped to a counter against the far wall. *Heavy* equipment, and the half dozen or so people I could see who were working out were obviously serious weight lifters. Big guys, big muscles. Iron pumpers. Not just overweight guys on treadmills. But there wasn't a sign of Adcock.

There was a man sitting behind the main counter, obviously another heavy lifter himself, who watched me impassively as I approached. His eyes stayed fixed on me, almost like a challenge. He chewed slowly on a piece of gum.

"I'm looking for Clint Adcock," I said to him as I stepped up to the counter. "Is he around today?"

The man just looked at me. Chewed away on his

gum. Adcock had probably learned of my call to the gym yesterday, I realized. And he had talked to people. And the welcome mat wasn't out.

The man sitting behind the counter shook his head, still slowly chewing his gum, his eyes still directly on me.

"Nope. He's not here. Sorry," he said, his voice deadpan.

"Any idea when he'll be back?"

Another head shake, his eyes still right on me, still chewing his gum. "Nope. Sure don't."

"You know how to reach him?"

Another head shake. "Sure don't."

"Thanks a bunch, anyway," I said. I looked around. Everybody in the place was watching me. My skin crawled. It occurred to me Adcock could be sequestered back in the shower area, so I said, "Mind if I use the men's room?"

I didn't wait for an answer. The Glock felt good under my arm as I stepped to a door at the very rear of the building. I could *feel* the eyes on me. But Adcock wasn't there. So I stepped back into the workout area, said, "Have a nice day," to the man behind the counter, and went outside and got into the Grand Am and pulled away.

I could feel the frustration rising inside me. I tried again to call Stan, but only came up with the answering machine again. Something was wrong. She'd never been out of touch like this before. I tried to get Davidson again too, but he still wasn't in his office. The receptionist sounded even more off balance this time.

"Honestly, we . . . we really don't know for sure when he'll be in . . ," she finally concluded. "I'll be happy to take a message if you'd like."

"No thanks. I'll try again later."

So I decided to go down to the Austin Courthouse to see if I could find Stan there. Or some trace of her. That wasn't the same as calling her at the office, after all. I found the Courthouse with only a little driving around and went inside. I wound up walking around, just looking. I checked in courtrooms, in offices, in conference rooms, anywhere I thought she might be, or might have been. No luck. Finally I stopped off by the snack shop, described her to the guy working behind the counter, and asked if he had seen her. Anybody who had seen Stan would have noticed her, I figured, but he said he hadn't seen anybody who fit that description. I went back out and got in the Grand Am and sat there, even more frustrated. And worried.

The phone rang, and I jumped at it, hoping again it might be Stan, but it wasn't. It was Joe Henderson. I could tell right away from his tone that something had changed.

"You sitting down?" he asked.

"Yeah. I'm in the car. Why?"

"It's about Davidson," he said.

I felt myself tense. "What's up?"

There was a pause. I could hear him take a breath.

"You're not gonna believe it, Walt," he said.

My heart had suddenly started to hammer. "How come?"

There was a silence on the line again before he spoke. "He's dead, Walt . . ."

Of all the things he might have said, nothing could have surprised me like that. It felt like the computer in my brain just completely shut down. I couldn't even begin to think of anything to say.

"He didn't show up at the office this afternoon like he was supposed to," Joe went on. "The office staff got concerned, especially when they couldn't reach him by phone. Finally somebody drove out to his house. His car was there, but nobody answered the door. So they called 911 and a unit went out there. Got in the back door. Found him dead on the living room floor."

I could still barely process the data. "My God . . ," I heard myself say.

"Just found this out a few minutes ago," Joe added.

"Body's still at the house. I don't know any more details, but I thought you'd want to know. Coroner's supposed to be headed out there now."

"Wow . . ," I managed.

"No joke."

I gave my head a shake. "I'm headed down to the station, Joe. I'll see you there in just a few minutes."

"I'll be here."

So I started up the Grand Am and headed for the Austin Police Department. I was still too stunned to think clearly. Davidson was dead? It just didn't compute. If, of course, the body turned out to be his. Natural causes? Always possible, I thought, but he was only a little past forty, and he was obviously fit and athletic and in great condition. It didn't seem likely. And with his confidence and his arrogance, he didn't seem like the kind of person who would panic and do something desperate like ending his life, even if he had been under a lot more pressure than the little I'd been able to apply. It just didn't add up.

I was almost to the station when the phone rang again. I jumped at it once more, hoping again that it might be Stan, telling me she was sorry to have been out of touch, that her cellphone had broken, or something like that. But it still wasn't her. It was Julie this time.

"Walt!" she said urgently. "Somebody tried to break into the house this afternoon when Bobby was there after school!"

It felt like my heart had stopped again. "My God, Julie! What's happened? How is he?"

"He's fine. The lady who lives next door - her name is Connie - told me she heard a commotion in the back yard. Then she saw a man jump over the fence. So she ran over to our house and got Bobby and took him to her place, and then she called me. I was almost home by then. So I picked Bobby up and drove to Mom and Dad's. We're with them now. We're both doing fine."

"Stay there, Julie," I said. "I'm on my way. I'll be coming from Austin, so it'll take me a couple of hours. Don't go back to the house under any circumstances. Is that clear?"

"We'll wait here, Walt."

Without even giving it another thought, I swung around in rush hour traffic and headed for I-35, frantically dodging cars right and left, swerving here, swerving there, going as fast as I could through downtown Austin. The puzzle about Davidson would have to wait . . .

19.

It was another fast trip back to Dallas. I kept wondering all the way: was my family in danger now? It gave me a sick feeling in my gut.

Along the way I called Joe Henderson to let him know what had happened and to explain why I hadn't showed up at his office. He still didn't have any further report on Davidson, he said. He'd let me know as soon as he learned anything.

I called Julie as I was coming into the city. She and Bobby were still at her parents' house. I told her to meet me at her place in ten minutes. Stay out front in the car with the doors locked and keep the motor running. Leave right away if anything looks suspicious.

They were already there, parked in front of the house, when I arrived and pulled up behind them. They got out of the car, and I went straight to Bobby. He looked none the worse for wear.

"You doing okay?" I asked.

"Yeah, I'm fine, Dad. I never even saw anybody. I just heard Brutus barking like crazy in the back yard. Then Connie came over and rang the doorbell and said she'd seen this guy going over the fence. So I stayed over at her place with her, and we called Mom."

"Here's Connie now," I heard Julie say.

I turned and saw a slightly heavy woman about Julie's age coming down the front walk of the house next door.

"Hi there, I'm Walt," I said, extending my hand as she stepped up to us. It didn't seem like the time for a lot of social niceties, so I got right to the point. "Can you tell me exactly what happened? I need to know anything you can remember."

She nodded. "Well, I was in the kitchen starting to get dinner ready, and then I could hear your dog, Brutus, barking in your back yard. Only it wasn't *regular* barking, if you know what I mean. It sounded more like . . . well . . . it sounded . . . vicious, I guess you'd say. Kind of like a wild animal. Like a wolf or something. It was alarming to me, so I stepped out the back door real quickly, and I saw a man going over the fence into the alley. Brutus was right behind him, and I could see Brutus try to go over the fence too, but he couldn't make it. I could still see the man's cap as he ran off down the alley. Then I came right over and rang the doorbell and brought Bobby to my house. That's when I called."

"What can you tell me about the man you saw?" I asked. "You could only see him from the back as he went over the fence?"

"Right," she said. "Well . . . he was a big man, I could tell that. Very thick and stocky. I remember having the fleeting thought that it was surprising to see such a big, heavy man going over the fence so easily."

"A *fat* man?" I asked.

She frowned. "No . . . not fat, I wouldn't say that. Just big and thick and stocky, like a football player or something."

"What was he wearing?"

She frowned again, concentrating. "I remember he had on a blue jacket and a blue cap. The jacket said 'Cowboys' across the back. But that's all I recall."

I had heard enough. There wasn't any doubt in my mind. The sick feeling came back in my gut.

Clint Adcock.

They were after my family now.

"Have you noticed anything since?" I asked.

Connie shook her head. "No, I haven't."

"I need to go check it," I said. I turned to Julie and Bobby. "Both of you get in the car and stay there. Start the motor and keep it running. If anything unusual happens, drive off right away. Call me on my cell. If I don't answer, call the police and have them come to the house. Report a felony. But don't go back inside yourselves. Drive straight to your parents' house instead. If there's any chance at all that you're being followed, drive straight to the Garland Police Station instead and go inside. Do you know where it is?"

Julie nodded. I could see the apprehension in her eyes. Bobby's too. I stepped up to Julie and hugged her, then wrapped an arm around Bobby too. Then they headed to the car. I watched as they got inside. I could hear the engine start. Julie looked out the window at me.

"Better get inside too," I said to Connie, "in case there's trouble."

She didn't argue, but without further ado, turned and walked quickly back to her front door and disappeared inside. Then I pulled out the Glock and approached the front of the house.

I checked carefully all over, under beds and in closets, every nook and cranny, but it was empty. Finally I stepped through the garage and out to the back yard. I glanced around quickly, the Glock in my hand, but all I could see was Brutus. He was lying on the grass across the way. He got up slowly as I looked at him, moving stiffly, and began to walk toward me. I could tell right away he had been injured. He kept his right front foot off the ground every second or third step, and when he did put it down, he limped on it. He looked tired and weak too. His head was down, his tongue hanging limply out the side of his mouth, and he was panting as he came toward me. After one more quick glance around the yard, I put the Glock back in its holster and scratched him behind one ear as he came up to me. He didn't try to jump up on me like he usually did. He just stood there panting. I knelt down and took his right leg off the ground and gently felt along its length. He made a slight whining noise, but he didn't try to pull it away. It seemed to be most tender at the knee.

The joint looked swollen there too. I know dogs can tear ligaments and cartilages just like humans, and I thought that was probably what had happened. I felt his other legs, then his chest and his belly, but there didn't seem to be any other sore places. He didn't put up any resistance. He just stood there panting, his head down, his tongue hanging out. I scratched behind his ear again, then got up and walked to the wooden picket fence that separated the yard from the alley. I noticed right away that a couple of the shrubs Julie had planted against the fence were trampled down. I could see bent and broken branches. Then I noticed something else. There was blood on the fence. Several splotches, running in a line, from down low almost to the top. I hadn't seen any cuts on Brutus or blood on his coat, so the blood wasn't his. It had to be Adcock's.

I stood there studying the scene. Trampled bushes. Blood on the fence. And I remembered what Connie had told me: what she had heard hadn't been the sound of normal barking. It had sounded very different. Wild and vicious. Like the sound of a wild animal. Like a wolf.

I glanced back at Brutus. He still stood where I had left him, his head down, his tongue still hanging limply out the side of his mouth, still panting. He gave his tail a couple of tired wags as I looked at him.

There had been a very real fight here, I realized. Not just some barking and growling, but a real fight. Adcock had come over the fence into the back yard, and Brutus - somehow, on some level, whether it was just because of a sense of territory, or whether it was because of something even deeper and more instinctual - Brutus had somehow recognized danger and evil, and he had defended his turf. He had defended the pack. And because of that, Bobby was alive and well now.

I walked back to him and knelt down and scratched behind his ear again. "Hey, boy," I said. "I owe you a bunch. I'm sorry if I ever even *thought* anything bad about you."

He panted happily in my face. Then he tried to lick me in the mouth, just like always. I thought about it, then let him do it this time. His tail started to wag again. He thought it was just wonderful. I thought I was probably being infected by all kinds of hideous bacteria and parasites that not even Stephen King could have imagined. I scratched him behind the ear again, then stood up and walked back to the garage. He sort of halfway followed along behind me, still limping on his right front leg. I went inside to the kitchen, wiped off my mouth with a wet cloth and rinsed it out, then called Julie on her cell.

"What have you found?" she asked. I could hear the tension in her voice.

So I told her. Empty house, signs of a very real fight in the back yard. Brutus had a hurt knee.

"My God . . ," she breathed, " . . . so Brutus . . . my God, Walt . . . he . . . he saved Bobby's life. He *really* saved Bobby's life."

"That's sure the way it looks to me."

There was silence on the line for a moment.

"What do we do now?" she finally asked.

I had been thinking about that. "Right now I'm going to leave some food and water out for him. Then I'll follow you to your parents' house. But I want you and Bobby to stay in a motel tonight. Your Mom and Dad shouldn't stay at home either, as far as that's concerned. If Adcock could find where you and Bobby live, then he can find out who your parents are and where they live too."

"Adcock?" she asked.

"That's who did this. I'll tell you more when I get a chance. Wait there for me in front until I've fed Brutus. After I get you and Bobby squared away, I'll come back here and take him to one of those emergency vet places. We can't keep him over at your parents' place, because they don't have a yard, and they have two cats. But I don't want him staying here. Adcock could come back and shoot him over the fence. I'll be back out front in a couple of minutes."

So I opened up a big can of dog food and emptied it in his dish, then made sure he had plenty of fresh water. I scratched him behind the ear again.

"If I had time, boy," I told him, "I'd fix you a nice juicy steak, and then after that, I'd take you down the street and let you shit right on Mr. Thompson's mat. I mean that."

I almost thought he understood. He panted up at me. I could see his tail start to wag again. I patted him on the head, then left him in the back yard, made sure the house was locked up, and went out to the car.

"I'll follow you," I told Julie. "I want to make sure nobody sees us. If I think we're being tailed, I'll call you on your cell. We might need to go in separate directions."

She nodded, and I got in the rental car and followed as she pulled away. It had started to rain slightly, decreasing visibility, but I watched the rearview mirror all the way as we drove to the townhouse where her parents lived, checking around on all sides too. There wasn't anybody following us.

Just as we were pulling up in front, my cellphone rang. I looked at the caller ID number and felt a huge rush of relief. Stan! Finally! Thank God!

"Stan!" I said urgently. "Where the hell have you been? I've been trying and trying to get you since yesterday. I've been worried as hell about you. Why haven't you returned my calls?"

But there wasn't an answer.

Only silence.

Then I heard something. A chuckle. Very low and deep and sinister. Even though nothing was said, I could feel *power* coming over the line. And evil. A chill crawled up my spine. I felt myself shudder.

Then a deep male voice said, "Sorry, Ace. Close, but no brass ring this time. This isn't Stan you're talking to."

My breath caught in my throat. I couldn't speak. A band of tightness spread through my chest.

"We got her, though, Ace," I heard, along with another low, deep chuckle, pulsing with malice. "Saw her with you at that restaurant yesterday. Too bad you didn't know I'd been following you. You need to be a little more careful there. Great looking lady, I got to admit. Got to hand it to you, Ace, you got really good taste. Couldn't pass up a piece as nice as her. So we kind of followed her when she left, know what I mean. Kind of took her into custody, if you get the picture. Can't wait to have some fun with her, Ace. I'm sure you know what I'm talking about."

I listened, still not able to speak, not even able to breathe. Adcock. I knew it, could sense it. He was the one who had tailed me in the gray sedan. As good as they get. I should have watched more closely.

"Goddamn you, Adcock!" I snapped. "Goddamn everything about you!"

I heard the chuckle again. "Aw now, you're gonna hurt my feelings, Ace, talking real mean and ugly to me like that. See, I'm actually a real sensitive sort of guy. I get my poor little feelings hurt real easy. You wouldn't want to do that to me, now would you?"

I didn't answer. I waited on the line, holding the phone to my ear. I could still barely breathe. Up ahead, Julie and Bobby had gotten out of her car and headed toward the front door. I saw Julie stop on the walk and turn to look at me, even though there was a light drizzle. Then Bobby turned around too. I pointed at the phone and motioned for them to go inside. I watched as they turned back toward the house and walked to the front door. Julie opened it with her key, and they stepped inside.

"Yeah, we're gonna have a real good time with your

lady friend, Ace," I heard Adcock say. "Like I said, I'm sure you know what I'm talking about."

I waited on the line again, not speaking, feeling the hatred burning in my gut. I was aware of being tense all over, all my muscles knotted up, and I willed myself to try to relax.

"Got to hand it to you, though, Ace," Adcock went on with another sinister chuckle. "Yeah, I got to hand it to you. See, you're the only one who managed to get it all figured out. The cops never even had a clue. But you did. You kept going. So I got to hand it to you."

Still I waited on the line. I saw Julie come to one of the front windows of the townhouse and look out at me, a concerned expression on her face. I pointed to the phone again, and I saw her step away, back into the interior.

"Now what that means," Adcock went on, "is that you've turned into a little problem for us. See, you're the only one who knows about us at this point, so we'd really like to have a little talk with you. We might even get two birds with one stone, in fact. See, if we can come to an agreement, we might just decide to let your lady friend go. Now wouldn't that be nice? You and she could just waltz on off somewhere and have yourselves a real good old time together, just like the good old days. Sounds nice, now doesn't it?"

I didn't believe that for an instant. They'd never let me go. They'd kill me the first chance they got. But as I thought about it, I realized that if I played my cards just right and used myself as a bargaining chip, I might be able to get them to release Stan. If they really had her, I thought.

"How do I know you're not bluffing, Adcock?" I said. "How do I know you've even got her? Having her *cellphone* is one thing. Having *her* is another."

"Aw, you don't think I'd lie to you about something as important as that, now do you, Ace? You're starting to kind of offend me again, doubting my integrity like that."

"Maybe you're full of shit, Adcock. Maybe this is all just a bluff."

I heard him chuckle again, that same low, deep, evil chuckle, and then he said, "Then listen to this, Ace."

I waited, my breath caught in my throat all over again, and then I heard a female voice ask hesitantly, "Walt. . ?"

The voice sounded low and weak and subdued, shot through with fear, and I could tell it was Stan. I felt a great heaviness come over my entire body, almost like a paralysis. I could feel the frantic pounding of my heart.

"Stan . . . are you okay? Have they done anything to hurt you?"

I could hear her take a breath. ". . . No . . . not yet..." Her voice was still very low and faint, almost a whisper.

"I'm coming to get you, Stan. Somehow. I'll find a way. I promise. I'll get you out. Just hang in there."

She didn't answer.

"Satisfied, Ace?" I heard Adcock say. "Still think we don't have her? Still think I'm bluffing?"

I managed to take a breath. Up ahead at the house, I saw Julie at the window again, looking out at me. I pointed again to the phone, and she stepped back inside.

"What do I need to do?" I asked.

"Well now, I think you're starting to get the picture a little better, Ace. Glad to hear it. Thought you'd be smart enough to come around sooner or later."

I didn't say anything. Forced myself to try to relax again.

"Where are you now?" Adcock asked.

I wasn't about to tell him the exact location, so I just said, "In Dallas."

"Well now, we need you to come back down to Austin, Ace. You need to leave right away. Now! I'll give you three hours. No more. You got me? I'll call in exactly three hours, and if you're not in Austin by that time, then we start to play our little games with the lady. You get the picture?"

"I get it," I said tightly.

I heard that chuckle coming over the line again, just as low and as deep as ever, and just as evil. My skin crawled as I listened to it, and I could feel the hatred boiling up inside me again.

"Now that's a better attitude, Ace. Glad to see you're being a little more cooperative. I can tell we're gonna be able to work together real well on this."

"Call me in three hours," I said. "I want to talk to her again when you do, to make sure you haven't done anything to her."

"Three hours," Adcock snapped.

And the line went dead.

I sat in the car for a few moments, trying to steady myself, then got out and went up the walk and into the house. Julie was in the living room, and I went straight to her. I put my hands on her shoulders and looked into her eyes.

"Julie, something's happened," I said. "Something I didn't expect."

I could see a flicker of uncertainty in her eyes, the shadow of old memories, old experiences. It tore at my heart, but I had to keep going. "The case I've been working on down in Austin . . . the one I've told you about. There's been . . . there's been another person working with me on that case. And that person is in danger now. I have to try to help that person. I don't have a choice, Julie. And that means I have to leave and go back down to Austin. Now. I wish to God I didn't, but I have to."

She had watched me closely as I had talked. Her lips parted slightly. I could see the uncertainty in her eyes again.

"I love you, Julie," I said. "I always have, ever since the first time I met you. I always will. I'll come back as soon as this is finished. I promise. I want to be with you for the rest of my life."

I could still see the uncertainty on her face, but I could also see a softening in her expression, and I pulled her to me and wrapped my arms around her. She hugged me in return.

"Oh, Walt. . ," she said.

We stood there holding each other for several moments. My heart was aching. I would have given any material possession I had not to have to leave, but I still didn't have a choice. I pulled back from her and looked into her eyes again.

"I want you and Bobby to go to a motel," I said. "Your parents should go too. I had planned to drive you myself, but they only gave me three hours to get back to Austin, so there isn't time. But you need to go to a motel, preferably on the other side of town. Make sure you're not being followed when you go."

"Walt, Dad is sick," Julie said urgently. "I haven't even had a chance to tell you that, with all that's been happening. He's been having vomiting and diarrhea all afternoon. I told Mom we should take him to the hospital, but you know how stubborn he is. I don't think he'll go. And I . . . I don't know how I feel about leaving Mom here alone to take care of him. I hear what you're saying, but..."

I squeezed her shoulders as I held her at arm's length and looked in her eyes. "Julie, it's important! Trust me! Talk to both of them. Take him to the hospital if he'll go, but if not, all of you go to a motel. Please! You have to, for your safety and for Bobby's. I mean that."

I could see the hesitation in her eyes again as she stared back up at me. Apprehension too, just short of fear. The ache in my chest was even worse, but too much time had already passed, and with wet highway waiting for me, I had to keep moving. I hugged her one last time, gave her one last kiss, very gently on the lips, and then I tore myself away and forced myself to walk out the door into the night.

The rain was coming down steadily now as I made my way back through the city toward I-35 South to Austin. I checked my watch as I pulled out on the Interstate. Thirty minutes had already gone by. It was going to be close. I tried to make myself relax, but the knot in my gut persisted.

About halfway to Austin I got a call on my cell. It was Joe Henderson.

"Finally got some information," he said.

"Let me hear it."

"First of all, it *was* Davidson. He's dead, Walt. That much is for sure."

"Jesus," I said. ". . . What else did they find?"

I heard Joe take a deep breath. "He was murdered, Walt. Looks like he was beaten to death with some sort of blunt instrument. Coroner says probably a baseball bat or a two by four, or something similar. He had a bunch of broken bones all over the place. Had broken ribs on both sides. Had a forearm fracture. Had a broken jaw. Had a skull fracture on one side. Bruises all over his back. Coroner says the final cause of death was probably a fractured larynx that crushed his windpipe. Said his voice box was completely shattered."

"Jesus . . ."

"So . . . he was beaten to death with some sort of blunt instrument by somebody very powerful. That's the way it looks right now. No other clues. No other signs of disturbance. No evidence of forced entry to the house. No official idea yet about who might have done it, no suspects. But it had to be somebody strong as hell to overpower a guy like Davidson in the first place, then beat him up like that, baseball bat or no baseball bat."

"Clint Adcock," I said. "The guy who used to be a cop in San Antonio. The one I asked you to find out about.

Adcock was a professional body builder. He's got the strength. He and Davidson have been in this together, but something must have happened. So Adcock killed him. I can't prove that yet, but that's sure the way it looks to me."

Joe didn't say anything for several moments. "Could be, Walt . . . could be . . . God, I wish the tail on Davidson hadn't been called off. We might have more of a handle on this now."

I didn't comment. I wound up telling him about the phone call I had just gotten from Adcock and about heading back down to Austin to try to find Stan. I thought again about how badly Davidson had been beaten. He was strong and athletic and tough and mean, but he had still been overpowered and killed. The thought was chilling.

"I could sure use some help with Adcock," I said.

Joe waited for several moments. "I'll see what I can do," he finally said.

So that was that. I hung up and kept heading down the road to Austin. He called back a few minutes later. I could tell right away the news wasn't good. I could hear the stress in his voice.

"I . . . I don't know how to tell you this, Walt," he said.

I felt myself swallow. "Tell me what?"

"Christ . . ," he said.

I waited on the line.

"Well . . . I'm sorry to have to be the one to tell you this, but . . . well, there's a warrant out for your arrest, Walt . . . you're considered the primary suspect at this point… After all that's happened - the tail on Davidson, all that - well, Baker thinks you're some sort of wacko crazy who's gone on this totally loco wild goose chase. That you've become totally obsessed with Davidson for some reason, and he thinks you went crazy and killed him when you couldn't prove anything on him."

I didn't say anything. But one thing was clear: I

wouldn't be getting any help with Adcock from the Austin Police. And now I was on the run myself.

"Walt . . . you there. . ?" Joe asked.

"Barely. What's left of me."

I heard Joe take a deep breath. I had told him I was driving down to Austin, so he knew I was out on the road. I found myself wondering about something.

"Have you told the Highway Patrol I'm on the road to Austin?" I asked.

"No . . . I haven't . . ."

"Are you going to?"

He hesitated for a moment. "No . . . I don't think so. . . not yet…"

I thought it sounded like the truth.

"I hope to God you know I didn't have anything to do with Davidson's death," I said.

"Oh, good Lord, Walt, I've known you too long to think you'd ever do anything like that. But Baker is convinced. Is there somebody who can vouch for where you were at the time of Davidson's death?"

"Probably not. I was alone all afternoon. I had gone looking for Adcock, but judging from the reception I got from his friends, I don't think anybody's gonna be in a great big hurry to come forward and testify on my behalf."

Joe didn't say anything.

I knew he had already done me one favor by not calling the Highway Patrol yet. Thinking about everything, something else suddenly occurred to me, an offbeat idea, coming in sideways, lurching around crazily in my brain. I remembered meeting Frank Hunter when I had been at the Mexican restaurant with Stan. I remembered the way he had looked at her, the way he had touched the back of her neck. I thought he still cared. And Frank Hunter was a mean son of a bitch who knew how to fight.

"Thanks for not calling the Highway Patrol," I said. "I appreciate it, Joe. I'd also appreciate it if you'd give me at least a few more hours."

I heard him take another deep breath. "Sure…"

"You mentioned that we've known each other for a long time. That's sure the truth, Joe. We go back a ways. I've always liked you and respected you."

He waited on the line, not saying anything.

"So I'd like to ask you to do me one more final favor. For old times sake."

He still didn't say anything.

"You said the Department was familiar with Frank Hunter. Any way you could get me a phone number or a home address on him?"

He still didn't say anything, but I could tell he was thinking. I knew he'd make the connection. Frank Hunter, the ex-husband. And I needed help.

"I'll see what I can find out," he finally said.

So we hung up again, and I focused on the road ahead. He called back just a few minutes later.

"Well, I got a phone number and an address, Walt," he said. "For old times sake. But this has got to be it. I'm sure you understand that. I'll be canned on the spot if anybody ever finds out I've talked to you like this."

"I got you, Joe."

So he gave me a phone number and an address, and I wrote them down on a piece of paper as I drove.

"Thanks, Joe. I do appreciate it."

"Take care of yourself, Walt."

"If I can."

We hung up again, and I continued on down I-35 towards Austin. The rain stopped along the way and a full moon came up, casting an eerie glow over the countryside. As I came into the northern outskirts of the city, I tried the phone number Joe had given me, but I only got an answering machine and the voice of Frank Hunter saying, "Sorry, not here. Leave a message." But I decided not to.

I checked my watch. Adcock was supposed to call

in ten minutes. The gas gauge was low, so I pulled into a Chevron station and filled up quickly. They had city maps inside, and I got one of those too. I spread out the map and found the street where Frank Hunter lived. It was in the northwest part of the city, in a residential area on Lake Travis. I plotted out the route and put the map on the shotgun seat. The phone rang as I pulled away from the pumps.

"Three hours, Ace," I heard Adcock say. "Where are you?"

"Austin. Just like I said I'd be."

I heard the chuckle again. "Good for you, Ace. Good for you. I can tell you're gonna be real easy to work with."

I could feel the hatred rising inside me again. I struggled to slow down my breathing, relax my belly.

Then Adcock said, "You're gonna have to wait a little while longer, though, Ace, before we get to meet up together. It seems I've been delayed a little bit. See, I had to stop and get some stitches in my leg. Took longer than I expected. That old dog of yours turned out to be a surprise for me, Ace. Didn't think he'd give me any trouble, but he did. The cut wouldn't stop bleeding."

"Aw, that's a shame," I said.

I could hear that low, deep, sinister chuckle again.

"Thought you'd be concerned about me."

I hadn't even thought about Brutus since I'd gotten the first call from Adcock. He was still in the back yard. Unprotected.

"I got a score to settle with that old dog of yours, Ace," Adcock went on. "I don't take real kindly to being chewed on like that, know what I mean? I should have put a bullet in him right then, but I didn't want to cause any more commotion in the neighborhood."

"Where's Stan?" I snapped. "I want to talk to her."

"Well now, of course, Ace. Of course. Don't get

all impatient now."

There was a pause, and then I heard Stan say, very faintly, ". . . Walt?"

"It's me, Stan. How are you? Has he hurt you?"

"No . . . not yet . . ." Her voice was still faint and weak, almost muffled.

"I'll get you out, Stan. I promise."

But there wasn't an answer.

Then Adcock came back on the line and said, "I'll call you back in a few hours, Ace. Be ready to move as soon as I call. Don't try anything funny in the meantime, you understand? Or we go to work on your lady friend here."

And the line went dead.

I tried Frank Hunter again, but I still only got the answering machine. So I picked up the map and began to follow the route I had traced out, heading towards his house. It took about fifteen minutes to get there. The area turned out to be a very ritzy neighborhood with huge houses, all built around Lake Travis, northwest of Austin. The karate business had to be better these days than I had realized.

I slowed as the street numbers began to come closer to the address Joe had given me. Finally I was there. The house was on the south side of the street, to my left as I headed west, and it was just as imposing as all the others, two stories with an enormous front yard. There weren't any lights on. The house stood dark and solid and massive in the moonlight. I drove by slowly. At the far end of the property, the driveway went up the side of the yard toward the garage. Looking there, I suddenly froze, my breath in my throat. Stan's pickup! Parked in the driveway! Or was it? I couldn't be sure from this distance. The moon had taken a sudden dip behind clouds, and darkness had returned. A small pickup, yes. But was it hers? I drove down a little farther and came to a stop. Then I looked around. There wasn't anybody out on the street, no sign that I had been seen. I checked to make sure the dome light was off, then pulled out the Glock, slipped out of the car, and headed back toward the driveway and the truck. I walked at an even pace. The moon did me a favor and stayed behind the clouds.

In barely a minute I was there. It didn't take me long to confirm that it *was* her truck. So she'd been here at one point. I peered through a side window, but in the darkness, I couldn't make out much inside.

Behind me was a wooden fence. I looked over it into a large back yard, which backed up on the lake. The moon had come out again, and the water lay smooth and glimmering in the moonlight. I was too visible out here on the driveway, I realized, so I hopped over the fence into the back yard and approached the rear of the house. There were still no signs of life. No lights. No activity. Just the darkness of the house in the glow of the moon.

I crossed a terrace with a huge swimming pool and approached the back door. Still no sign of life. Deserted. I got my cellphone out of my pocket and punched in Frank Hunter's number again. I could hear a phone ring deep inside. Then the answering machine came on again. With Stan's pickup in the driveway, I had to go inside.

It took me a couple of minutes to find the security system and disarm it. Then I got the lock to the back door open and stepped inside, going slowly. Darkness. I keep a little penlight on my keychain, and I pulled it out and flicked it on. The light fluttered weakly, the battery almost gone, but I could see enough to move around. I was in a large den, a giant TV against the wall to my right, plush leather armchairs and a sofa for furniture. I stepped across the room cautiously, listening. No sound. Nothing to indicate there was anybody here.

I came to the kitchen, equally large, then passed into an enormous dining room, and then into an equally gargantuan living room, all very elaborately furnished. Then I worked my way through the rest of the house, upstairs and downstairs, going carefully. But it was empty. No trace of Stan. If she had even been here recently.

I made my way back down to the kitchen and looked back across the den toward the back door. The rear wall of the house had a large plate glass window that looked out over the terrace, and through it I could see the waters of Lake Travis shimmering in the moonlight. But it was still dark inside. I flashed the fading light of the penlight on the walls, looking for a light switch, and found one near the door to the dining room. I pushed it down, and the ceiling lights in the kitchen came on. There. I could see better.

Then, as my eyes ran down the length of the main kitchen counter, I saw something that stopped me cold. The Maiden Head. Lying there beside the sink. I stepped over to it and picked it up. Yes, this was it, the same baton I had seen at Stan's that night. So she *had* been here. But what had happened?

I stood there staring down at the elaborate carving of the baton. The face was just as ugly as I remembered, with long flowing hair and a long pointed nose above a jutting chin. Below were the two big bulging boobs, just before the torso flowed into the main body of the stick. Very elaborately carved, but very ugly. I ran my finger down over the nose, then the protruding chin. I continued to stare at it. For no particular reason I turned it to the side, ninety degrees to the left. The two bulging boobs merged into one prominence when seen from that angle. I ran my finger down over the nose again, then over the pointed chin, then over the bulge of the breasts. Nose. Chin. Breasts.

Three prominences.

Something clicked distantly in the back of my brain. I put down the Maiden Head, slowly pulled out my wallet, and got out the piece of paper I had used to trace out the lines of the impact when Joe Henderson had showed me the skull in his office. I spread the paper out and laid it flat on the counter. It was just as I remembered. Two sharp indentations, with a rounded one below.

Still going slowly, I picked up the Maiden Head again, rotated it ninety degrees so that it faced to my left again, and carefully laid it down on the tracing.

The lines matched perfectly.

"Hold it right there, Draeger!" I heard a voice say behind me. "Don't move a muscle! One little twitch and you're dead!"

I froze in place, my eyes still locked on the Maiden Head. Stupid! I had let myself get too absorbed.

"Now raise your hands over your head, Draeger," the voice behind me said. "Very, very slowly. You make one fast move and I'll put a bullet in the back of your head."

I raised my hands slowly.

"Higher!"

Finally I had gotten them up as far as I could.

"Now turn around. Slowly. Very, very slowly."

I turned around. It was Frank Hunter, pointing a .357 Magnum right at my face. Raising my hands had lifted my coat up, revealing the Glock under my shoulder. His eyes locked on it. Then he motioned toward it with a tip of his head.

"Going very, very slowly, Draeger, with just your left hand, using just your thumb and your index finger, pull that out and drop it on the floor. You try anything funny, you're dead. Blowing you away wouldn't bother me at all right now."

I didn't doubt that a bit. I moved my left hand slowly to the Glock and drew it out with my thumb and forefinger and dropped it on the tile.

"Raise that arm again," Hunter snapped. "And kick

the gun over here. Slowly."

I did what he told me to. The Glock scooted across the floor, stopping just a foot or two in front of him.

"I can explain why I'm here," I said.

"I'll just bet you can."

He picked up the Glock, pulled out the magazine, and emptied all the bullets into a trash can. He kept the Magnum trained on my face the whole time.

"Now empty out your pockets. Put everything on that counter beside you."

I did what he told me to again.

"Take off your coat. Roll up your shirt sleeves and your pant legs."

I did that. I hadn't brought along anything else besides the Glock, and now he knew that.

"It's about Stan," I said. "She's in trouble. Big trouble. She's been captured by a serial killer named Clint Adcock. I can't get any assistance from the authorities in trying to find her. I'm afraid she'll be killed too if I can't get to her in time. I thought you might want to help. I tried to get you on your phone, but I only got the answering machine. That's why I came out here."

A sneering grin spread slowly across his mouth. I got a sick feeling as I heard him laugh. Things had happened so quickly I hadn't even had time to think about adding up the pieces. But Stan's pickup was here, and the Maiden Head was the murder weapon.

"I wouldn't worry too much about good old Stan if I were you, Draeger," he said.

The sick feeling only got worse.

"You see, Stan's been in it from the start, Draeger. Fact is, Stan's the one who organized it in the first place. She's the one who got it started. Too bad you didn't figure that out in time."

Too bad, sure enough.

"In fact, I was with Stan and Clint earlier today," he

added, the twisted grin still curling his lips. “We planned to meet up again later, but then I got a phone call. See, Draeger, I have contacts inside the Austin Police Department. Very reliable contacts. And I got word you had tried to get my address and phone number. It made me wonder what you were up to. So I changed my plans and came out here. Funny the way things work out sometimes, isn’t it?”

I tried to swallow, but couldn’t. “Yeah, real hilarious.”

“See, you’ve been our one big problem, Draeger. You’re the one who figured it out. You’re the one who solved the little puzzle. So dealing with you has been our top priority.”

So they had tricked me, as simple as that. They had been trying to lure me into a trap. And I had stepped right into it.

Hunter was still smirking at me. “See, Stan is a very unusual person, Draeger. Very complex. She’s got this really nice side to her, no doubt about it. She can be just as pleasant and fun to be with as anybody you’d ever meet, but she’s also got this crazy, cruel side to her too. The fact is, Stan enjoys inflicting pain. She enjoys torturing people. She especially enjoys it if it finally leads up to killing. That’s the way she is, Draeger. She *enjoys* killing. Very much. She gets a real thrill out of it. Most serial killers are male, but Stan’s the exception.”

I still had my hands up. Hunter still had the Magnum trained on my face. I couldn’t see any way out. Checkmate.

“So we formed this little group a few years ago,” Hunter went on, seeming to enjoy himself. “Clint Adcock and I grew up together, and we’re both a lot like Stan. We all have that same sadistic streak. We all enjoy causing pain. We all enjoy watching somebody die. So it was a natural fit. We even found a way to turn a nice little profit along the way. See, we make tapes, Draeger. And we get paid for them. Very nicely. There's a very lucrative black market out there for snuff films."

I shot a brief glance to both sides, looking for some kind of leverage. Some avenue out, but I couldn't see anything. Hunter noticed, and I saw him smirk again. He kept the Magnum pointed straight at my face.

"But then you came along, Draeger," he went on. "And a funny thing happened, something I'd never seen before. See, the fact is, Draeger, Stan really took a liking to you. She let herself get emotionally involved. She let herself get hooked. Call it infatuation, call it romance, call it whatever you want to. She kind of flipped out over you, Draeger. I've been worried about her, in fact. See, Stan's always been the one who's in control. Always. Until you came along."

"Lucky me," I said. I looked to both sides again, but I still couldn't see a way out. "What about Davidson? Where did he come in?"

Hunter smirked again, that same sneering grin twisting his mouth. "Davidson was my student at the Academy. I worked with him for years. Brought him all the way up to a ninth degree black belt. He was very talented. Very strong. Very quick, very athletic. Also very cruel. Very mean. Very tough. Sadistic, just like the rest of us. Not the kind of guy you'd expect a doctor to be. But he was exactly that, just the same. I realized as I got to know him that he'd fit into our little group perfectly, and with his standing in the community and his connections, he'd give us a certain immunity we otherwise wouldn't have had. So we took him in."

"He's dead now," I said. "Why?"

Hunter chuckled. "Because he started to get cold feet. I got to hand it to you, Draeger, you've really put on the pressure. And it was starting to get to Davidson. He started talking about leaving the group, getting out, going back to being just Dr. Corbin Davidson again, eminent cardiovascular surgeon. But that would have left a break in our armor. We couldn't allow that. You're either with us all the way, or you're against us all the way. There's no middle ground. So Davidson had to go."

He seemed to enjoy talking about it, and I was curious to know the details. "So you sent Clint Adcock to kill him."

The twisted grin on his face got even broader. He shook his head.

"Not Adcock," he said. "Clint's big and strong, and he's surprisingly quick too for such a big man, but you have to understand that Davidson had advanced to an exceptional level. He was the best student I ever had. He could have competed on an international level if he had wanted to. Clint couldn't have handled him."

That was a surprise to me. "So who killed him then?"

Even as I asked, I saw the look in his eyes, and I knew the answer. The arrogance showed plainly in his satisfied smile.

"I was the only one who could have done it," he said, looking even more satisfied. "There wasn't any other choice."

"So you beat him to death with a baseball bat. That was certainly heroic of you. Just what I'd expect from a genuine, champion karate instructor. Or was it a club? Or a board? Or the Maiden Head here? The autopsy report said it was some sort of blunt instrument. Said he had broken bones all over the place."

His smile got even wider and more smug and more satisfied. "Just these," he said, holding up his hands, the Magnum still in his right. "That's all I needed. It's surprising what you can do with just your hands when you know how to use them."

I could see in his eyes that he was telling the truth.

I remembered all that Joe had told me about Hunter and about Davidson's injuries. I felt a chill along my spine.

"As good as Davidson was - and he was very good indeed, I taught him well - as good as he was, he never even touched me," Hunter said smugly. "I played with him like a toy. I did whatever I wanted, hit him any way I chose to, and he couldn't even begin to stop me. And when he tried to get back at me, I turned it all around on him. He died slowly, Draeger. Very slowly and very painfully. And helplessly. One blow at a time, until I had played with him long enough to satisfy myself. And then I finished him. Like I said, I'm a lot like Stan. I *enjoy* killing."

I still held my hands up. The dryness in my mouth felt like cotton. My pulse pounded in my temples. I looked in his eyes, and I knew what was coming next.

"Which brings us to you, Draeger," he said evenly. "Like I said, you've been our one big problem. But that's about to change, now isn't it? Because it's your turn now."

The barrel of the Magnum was still trained on my face. I could still see all the arrogance in his eyes, hear it in his voice, and I knew I only had one card left to play.

"Better shoot me now then while you have the chance," I said, "because if you don't, I think I'll come get that Magnum of yours and stick it right up your ass."

I saw a flicker of something in his eyes. Almost like pleasure. The arrogant smirk reappeared and spread slowly across his face.

"Really now?" he said.

"Really. You don't scare me, Hunter. You look like a pussy, in fact. Maybe you could handle Davidson, but I'm bigger and stronger than he was. I think you're out of your league. So I think you better shoot me now, while you still can."

"Really now?" he said again. I could see the glint of anticipation in his eyes. The expectation. The satisfaction.

"Yeah, really."

"You're tempting me, Draeger. You're *really* tempting me. It's hard to pass up something this good."

"Better go ahead and shoot me, Hunter. I don't think you got the balls to do anything else."

His smirk got even broader. "That's perfect, Draeger," he said slowly, savoring the words, the satisfaction showing all over his face. "Just perfect . . ."

He knelt down and placed the Magnum on the floor, looking straight at me all the time. Then, after one last look in my eyes, one last challenge, he scooted it across the tile. It made a grating, scraping sound as it slid across the floor. Finally it came to a stop, about halfway between us.

"It'll be a lot more fun this way," he said. "A *lot* more."

The gun sat on the floor between us, calling like a siren.

"I'm surprised you're taking this kind of chance, Hunter," I said.

He shook his head as he stood back up. "I'm not taking a chance, Draeger. Not the way I see it. Not at all. There's only a handful of people in the whole world, maybe half a dozen at most, who'd have a chance against me. And you're not one of them. I'd know about you if you were."

I could tell from the tone of his voice and the look in his eye that he meant what he said. I thought again about what had happened to Davidson, and a ribbon of fear rippled down my spine. The gun still sat on the floor between us, beckoning.

"Lost your nerve?" he asked. Then he added, "Pussy…"

I stepped forward quickly, bending down and reaching for the gun, but I didn't get to it. Hunter moved too, as quickly as a cat, and as I bent down for the Magnum, he kicked me squarely in the jaw. It felt like being hit with a hammer. I heard a cracking sound and felt a searing pain along the side of my face. The force of the impact staggered me backwards. I almost fell. I stumbled back until I crashed into the back wall of the kitchen. I've taken some wicked impacts along the way, but I'd never been hit like that before. My head was spinning. I tasted blood in my mouth.

The counter separating the kitchen from the den was just a couple feet to my left. I spun and vaulted over it, landing on the hardwood floor of the den. It was a good move, but I was slightly off balance as I landed, and I stumbled to one side, fighting to keep my feet. The door to the back yard was only fifteen feet away.

But Hunter had gone over the counter too, moving with amazing quickness and agility. He landed like a cat, perfectly balanced and poised and ready, even as I fought to stay on my feet. He came toward me, moving effortlessly, and with blinding speed. I struggled to throw a right cross, aiming for his face, and I thought I had thrown a good punch, but it didn't come close to landing. I didn't even see his hand come up, but suddenly there it was, deflecting my fist. Before I could even register what had happened, I felt a series of impacts, all hard and heavy and slamming, all seeming to come at the same instant. I felt a stabbing pain in my ribs, then an impact in my abdomen, then a blow to my forehead. There hadn't been time to react. His hands had moved like lightning. I tried blindly to put up an arm to defend myself, but even as I did, I felt another impact on the other side of my ribcage. I staggered backward, dazed, the room spinning, and fell back on the sofa under the plate glass window.

Hunter had stopped a few feet away. He stood there looking down at me, his image coming in and out of focus, spinning around and around with the rest of the room. I could see the satisfied smirk on his face again. The pleasure. The enjoyment.

"Real sorry to have to tell you this, Draeger," he said, "but you're not nearly as good as Davidson was. You're not even close. That's too bad, in a way. See, it won't be nearly as much fun as he was. It's always more fun if you have a good opponent. A little challenge always spices it up some."

I shook my head, trying to clear it. The room was still spinning, though, and Hunter kept coming in and out of focus.

"Gonna be a lousy way to die, Draeger," he went on. "Just a lot of pain, leading to the end."

My breath had been knocked out, and both sides of my chest were alive with pain. I wasn't sure I could even stand, but I tried to shift my weight on the sofa so I could get my feet up under me. Every movement was torture. The furniture was still spinning around.

"See, nobody's ever been able to match me," Hunter said proudly. "And they never will. Never. And now you know that too, Draeger. Now you know how it feels to watch yourself die."

I forced myself to move. The pain as I slid forward on the couch and pushed myself to my feet took away what little breath I had left. I felt light-headed, like I might pass out. I managed to move slightly to my left, in the direction of the door to the patio in back. But Hunter moved too, blocking me, and we closed again. I tried to throw a right uppercut as we came together, but he blocked it again, his hands moving so fast I couldn't even see them, and I felt another series of staggering impacts, all seeming to come at the same time again. I could barely register them. One hit my right collarbone. I heard a cracking sound, felt another searing pain. Then my abdomen again, even though I tried to protect myself. Then my chest again, just to the side of my breastbone. I heard another cracking sound. The pain from all the separate locations seemed to merge together, forming one solid, overwhelming wave.

In the midst of all this, I began to see things. I saw Julie, dressed in white, and I realized I was seeing our wedding. I saw Bobby being born. There were other images of both of them, sometimes alone, sometimes together, from different times in our lives. The images weren't like memories. They were experiences, and I was living them again. I wanted to cry out to them, call to them, but I couldn't.

There were more impacts, one on my face, then in my gut again, then to the side of my head. I couldn't keep them from landing. They came too quickly, like electrical sparks, and they landed with the force of battering rams. I tried to bolt to one side, but Hunter stuck a leg out before I could get clear and tripped me. I staggered to the side, my legs unable to keep up with my momentum, stumbling and staggering, until I came crashing to a stop, slamming into the wall beside the door to the dining room. My legs buckled, and I slumped to the floor, leaning back against the wall, trying to breathe.

Hunter stood several feet away, coming in and out of focus, still wearing that same superior smirk of his. Blood was streaming down my face from my nose, covering my shirt. I could still taste blood in my mouth from where my jaw had been hit. Every part of my body throbbed with pain.

"Having fun, Draeger?" he asked.

I couldn't speak.

"You've disappointed me, Draeger," he added. "You really haven't been much of a challenge. I had hoped for something better from you."

I still couldn't speak. I struggled to breathe. The room was still spinning, and his image kept coming in and out of focus as he smirked at me from across the room.

"Time's up, Draeger," he said slowly, the satisfied grin spreading across his face again. "There's no point in drawing it out any longer. You haven't even come close to keeping my interest up. You've been way too easy. It's all been pretty dull, really. So you haven't earned any more time. You see, so far, I've just played with you. Just taunted you some, like you were a toy or some kind of plaything. Like I did with Davidson. But all that's over now. Because now it's time to finish."

I still didn't think I could speak. I saw images of Julie and Bobby again, experienced them as clearly as if they were right there in the room with me. A great sadness engulfed me, crushing me like an enormous weight. It was even worse than the physical pain. I'm sorry, Julie, I thought. I'm sorry, Bobby. I'm so very, very, sorry.

Then, as I sat there, slumped back against the wall, I remembered something. I remembered coming into the house and going through it by the flickering light of the penlight. Then I had come back into the kitchen, and I had found the light switch and turned it on. I thought about it some more. It seemed that the switch had been on the wall by the door to the dining room. Yes. That was correct. Which meant it was just a few feet above my head. I thought I remembered flipping it down to turn on the light. Yes. That was also correct. And that was the only switch I had flipped. That one switch had turned on the main kitchen lights. The only lights that were on. So if I could find a way to flip it back up . . .

"You think you're ready, Draeger?" Hunter smirked. "Ready to die?"

I forced myself to try to speak. It was hard. There was so little breath. I had to clear my throat.

"I want to die on my feet, Hunter," I said, "if it's all the same to you."

The smirk on his face had come clearly into focus now. The room seemed to be spinning less.

"Suit yourself, Draeger," he sneered. "It doesn't matter to me. You'll still die like the sorry, weak piece of shit that you are."

Very slowly, I gathered my legs up under me and pushed myself to my feet, leaning back against the wall and sliding against it as I rose. For a sickening moment, I thought I might have remembered incorrectly, because I didn't come in contact with anything, but then I felt my shoulder blade slide up across the switch, flipping it up, and the room went black as pitch.

"Goddamn you, Draeger!" Hunter snapped.

Not quite black as pitch after all, I realized. The glow of the full moon shining on the lake in back of the house gave barely enough light through the plate glass window so that I could see his form as he came toward me. My advantage, I realized. There wasn't any light at all behind *me*. He couldn't see me at all. I could tell that from the way he moved. As he closed the distance, I forced myself to get past the pain and stepped to my right, giving me an angle on him, an angle he couldn't see, and as we came together, I shot my left leg behind his knees and lunged forward, using every last bit of strength I had, throwing all my two hundred and forty pounds against him. He reacted instantly, like a cat, twisting and spinning. I felt a blow to my head. But I had hit him hard enough to knock him off balance. The die had been cast. We were falling, locked together, going down, even as he tried to twist and spin away. I managed to get my hand up over his face as we fell, and as we hit the floor, I slammed the back of his head down onto the tile as hard as I could.

The sound of the impact was like a rifle crack. I heard him grunt. I knew he was stunned. But he was still moving! Not like before, not with the same speed, but still moving! I could feel motion in his arms and his legs. Coming to get me. Coming to kill me. I slammed his head down again, panting for air, the last of my strength rapidly fading. I heard him grunt again. But I could still feel him moving! Arms. Legs. He still wasn't out. I felt a flash of terror. I slammed his head down again and again, and yet again, frantically, using all the last of my fading strength, until I was completely spent. And finally he was still . . .

DANCE YOUR HEART OUT

20.

I lay there on the floor for a moment, panting for air. I throbbed all over, but I managed to push myself to my feet and make it the few steps back to the light switch, moving shakily, the muscles in my legs quivering, a tremor rippling my fingers as I probed for the switch in the darkness. I found it and flipped it down, and the lights came back on. Hunter lay on his back, bloodstains already accumulating on the tile under his head. I was exhausted, still panting like crazy, but I didn't know how long he'd stay out. I had to keep moving.

I took off my belt and knelt down by his feet, watching him closely all the time. No movement. Then I used my belt to bind his ankles together. I heard him groan as I yanked it tight and got it buckled. Then I took off the belt he was wearing and got ready to tie his wrists, but I heard him groan again, and he moved one of his arms. He was beginning to come around, so I grabbed the hair of his head and slammed the back of his skull down onto the tile several more times, using all the strength I had left, and he was still again. The bloodstains on the tile were growing larger. I had blood on my hand too. I rolled him over on his belly and pulled off his coat. Then I took his right arm and pulled it up behind him as far as it would go. I willed myself to push harder, and somehow I found the extra strength. His right shoulder levered out of joint with a grating, crunching noise, like the sound of a drumstick being torn off the Christmas turkey. He groaned again and I felt him move, so I grabbed his hair again and slammed his head down on the tile a few more times, getting even more blood on my hand, and he lay still again. Then I levered his left arm up behind him until his left shoulder came out of joint too, accompanied again by the sound of tearing sinew. He groaned again, and I could feel him try to move, but his arms were helpless now, and it only took me a few more moments to tie his hands behind him with his belt. He groaned again and tried to move his legs.

I was still breathing heavily, panting for air, as I grabbed his hair again and dragged him a few feet across the tile. I propped him up against a row of drawers that ran under the kitchen counter, his back against the drawers, his feet stretched out in front of him. Then I rinsed the blood off my hands in the sink. My nose had stopped bleeding too. I could hear him groaning again, and as I looked back at him, I could see him trying to move. I got a glass out of a cupboard above the sink and filled it with water. Then I stepped back to him and splashed it in his face. He coughed, shook his head. I knelt down in front of him and slapped him across the face a couple of times. He coughed again. Then his eyes opened. They were bleary and unfocused at first, but then he came around, and they locked right on me. The rage was there in an instant.

"Surprise, Frank," I said.

"Goddamn you, Draeger," he hissed.

"Same thing you said just before you took your little nap, Frank. You really ought to work on your dialogue some. It's a bad sign when you start repeating yourself. Everybody knows that."

He tried to move, but couldn't. I saw him look down at his legs, then around at the surrounding floor. He seemed to be mystified, unable to comprehend it.

"Thought you might be more cooperative if I tied you up a little, Frank," I said. "Sorry, but I've lost my confidence in your hospitality."

"You got lucky, Draeger," he snapped.

"I'll take luck every time."

"You're still a sorry, weak piece of shit."

"Sticks and stones may break my bones . . ."

He spit at me. I moved to the side, and he missed. Then I took a step and kicked him squarely in the jaw. His head banged back against the drawers under the counter. A red stain appeared on the wood.

"Goddamn you, Draeger," he seethed.

"There you go again, Frank. Repeating yourself. We really do need to get you a dialogue coach."

I kicked him in the jaw again. His head snapped back against the drawers once more. The red stain on the wood got bigger. Blood started to trickle from the corner of his mouth.

"Fuck you, Draeger," he said.

"Well, at least that's a start. See, you can do it if you really think about it."

He sat there on the floor, his back propped up against the drawers, glaring at me. His eyes were unwavering. The muscles of his face were taut like stone. His nostrils flared with rage every time he took a breath. I knew it wasn't going to be easy getting information out of him. Not easy at all. No matter what else might be true of him, he wasn't weak.

"You said you made some tapes, Frank. Where are they?"

"Fuck you," he said. He spit at me again.

I looked around. Behind me was another counter with drawers underneath. I started opening them. One had a collection of utensils, including some rather sharp steak knives. I picked up one of them and turned back toward him. The glare in his eyes was still there, just as strong as ever.

"Ever heard of gouging, Frank?" I asked.

"Fuck you, Draeger."

"Uh oh. Getting repetitive again, Frank. Watch it now. Watch it."

"Fuck you," he said.

I kicked him in the jaw again, sending his head snapping back into the drawers behind him. Another bloodstain appeared on the wood. The trickle of blood from the corner of his mouth grew wider. He glared back at me, hatred in his eyes, his breathing tight, his nostrils flaring.

"See, Frank, gouging was this very, very nasty sport that used to exist in this country a long, long time ago, like back in the 1700s. They had these fights, kind of like modern day boxing matches, but they had a different set of rules back then. People would let their thumbnails grow real long, and then they'd file them down and sharpen them, so they were sharp as knives. See, the objective was to use your thumbnail to scoop out your opponent's eye. If you could grab him by the hair on the side of his head and sort of steady him, then dig your nail in behind his eye, you could actually flip the whole eye right out of its socket. There were all kinds of people walking around in those days with an eye gone. Some of the really big losers got completely blinded. Sounds nasty, doesn't it?"

He continued to glare at me, the rage still burning in his eyes, his nostrils still flaring with every breath.

"Of course, I don't have a nice, long, sharp thumbnail like that, now do I?"

His eyes stayed locked on mine. The muscles of his jaws stood out like tongs. Blood continued to ooze from the corner of his mouth. I made a pretense of examining the knife I had taken out of the drawer, holding it up and studying the blade.

"I wonder if this would do instead," I said.

His eyes went to the knife, then back to me. I saw a twitch at the corner of his mouth. I knelt down beside him and grabbed his hair and pinned his head against the drawers. Then I put the tip of the steak knife in the flesh just behind the corner of his right eye. I applied pressure, just enough to make it start to dig in.

"Those tapes you said you made, Frank. Where the fuck are they?"

He didn't answer. His breathing had gotten tighter. A muscle on the side of his face kept twitching. I applied more pressure.

"Where?"

He still didn't answer.

"Am I going to have to blind you, Frank?"

Still no answer. Tight breathing. Flared nostrils. A twitch in his jaw.

"See, Frank, one of the girls you killed - the one named Jessica Nodman - well, it just so happens she was my biological daughter."

He looked at me quickly, a flicker of something in his eye.

"So there really aren't any limits to what I'm willing to do to you. No limits at all."

We glared at each other, the rage still burning in his eyes. I applied slightly more pressure, digging the knife into the flesh at the corner of his eye. I heard a catch in his breathing.

"Of course, I'm sure there're all kinds of opportunities for blind people these days," I said helpfully. "I haven't made a study of it, of course, but I'm sure there're all sorts of things that blind people can do today in our modern, enlightened, progressive society."

I frowned.

"Not so sure about karate, though," I said.

I applied more pressure to the knife, digging it in further. I heard a catch in his breathing again. "We could always get you a seeing eye dog too. Now, how does that sound? You think you'd like that? We could get you something traditional like a German Shepherd or a Collie. Or then again, we could go for something cutsie, like a Chihuahua or a little miniature Poodle. Now, how does that sound?"

I dug in harder with the knife. A trickle of blood ran down from the tip. His breathing was a tightened rasp.

"Of course, a little dog like that couldn't pull you out of the way of a speeding truck or anything like that," I noted, "but it could always bark real loud if somebody tried to steal your white cane."

I dug the knife in even harder. The tip was wedged up behind the globe. His breathing had stopped.

"In three more seconds, I flip out your eye," I told him. "Then I move to the other side, and we do it all over again."

He still wasn't breathing. The muscles in his neck stood out like dock ropes.

"One . . ."

"Two . . ."

"Wait," he said.

I continued to apply pressure with the knife. "Tell me, Frank. Make it good. If you lie to me, it costs you an eye."

He was breathing again, but in short, tight gasps. "In the study," he panted, ". . . behind the bookshelves. There's a segment of the shelves that swings out. There's a wall safe behind it."

I eased off on the knife. "You'd better be telling me the truth, Frank."

"I am. I swear."

I released pressure on the knife and pulled it away from the side of his face. The tip had dug out a small hole just behind the corner of his eye. The trickle of blood had become a flowing rivulet. The tightness in his muscles eased, and his shoulders slumped. He took several deep breaths.

Without saying anything else, I turned and walked into the study, which was only about twenty feet away, across the breakfast area from where he lay slumped against the drawers under the counter. I found a light and flipped it on. I'd come through here earlier as I had searched the house, but with the light on, I could see much more detail. Sure enough, there was a bookshelf across the way, running from the floor all the way to the ceiling along the far wall. In addition to books I could see pictures of

Frank and all sorts of trophies, the winnings of a successful champion. In some of the pictures he was dressed in martial arts attire, holding up still more trophies. In some he wore blue jeans, boots, and a cowboy hat. There were also pictures of him on horseback, sometimes with cattle in the background, and in one of the pictures, I could see an arched gate behind him, with lettering at the top that said, HUNTER RANCH. Farther down on the shelf was a plaque with his name on it, and below that an inscription that read, DISTINGUISHED RANCHER AWARD, PRESENTED BY THE LLANO CHAMBER OF COMMERCE, LLANO, TEXAS. There were pictures of other people as well, including several of Stan. Some showed her wearing a martial arts robe and holding up trophies of her own. So she had been Frank's student too.

I tested the center part of the bookshelf, and it swung out easily. Sure enough, there was a wall safe behind it, about two feet square. I glanced back into the kitchen. Hunter was still where I had left him, slumped back against the drawers.

"What's the combination, Frank?"

He hesitated for a moment, then gave me a series of numbers, and I spun them in. The safe pulled open without a hitch. With one more glance back at Hunter, I started to go through all the contents. Right away I noticed six videotapes, lined up in a row and sitting in an open box. Each one was in a plastic case, and each case had a white tag on the upper left corner. Each tag had a date on it. The fourth one had the exact date of Jessica Nodman's murder. I was sure the other dates would prove to be just as exact as well. The most recent one was from just a few days earlier. That would be Susannah Jacobson. But there were six of them. The police were only aware of four murders in all, so there were two more unsolved crimes out there somewhere. I figured one of them had to be the girl I had seen on the tape with Gunner, Donna Rivers, who had just disappeared without a trace.

There was also a lot of cash in the safe, bundles of hundreds, stacked in piles. There were also stacks of papers, along with pictures. I went through them quickly. Some of the pictures were of the murdered women. Some were of their dead bodies. Then there were pictures that seemed almost normal, like they'd been taken at a party or a picnic. Pictures of Frank Hunter standing in a docked motorboat with Stan, pictures of Frank and Davidson holding beer cans, looking relaxed, then pictures of all of them together, scrapbook type pictures, showing Hunter, Davidson, Stan, along with Clint Adcock and a couple of other people I couldn't place. The other two were men. One of them looked to be about thirty, and I could tell right away he was a body builder like Adcock. Big shoulders and arms. Burly chest. He had jet-black hair and a black mustache. The other man looked to be older, probably late forties, and he was almost completely bald, with just a fringe of red hair running around his head beneath a glistening dome, along with a thick red mustache and a generous belly. I looked quickly through all the rest of the pictures, but I didn't see any pictures of anybody else. So there were six of them in all: Frank Hunter, Stan, Clint Adcock, Davidson, and two others whose identities I didn't know. I also found a series of newspaper clippings, apparently taken from the want ads. I looked at one. It said, "Film producer seeks new properties." There was a phone number listed with a 303 area code. Other clippings seemed to be replies, like one that said, "Movie director has new offering. Please contact at regular number." So it seemed they had communicated in part through the want ads.

"Who's your buyer?" I asked Hunter.

He was still slumped back against the drawers under the kitchen counter. He hesitated. I could see him take a deep breath.

"…Guy in Denver..," he finally said. "…Don't

know his exact name. . . we never actually met up with him. . ."

"Is this his phone number?"

He hesitated again, then slowly nodded. "Yeah. . ."

"He'd contact you through the want ads when he wanted to buy a film?"

He nodded again. "Yeah . . ."

I could guess most of the rest. Films got made. Money changed hands. And the killings continued. I wrote the number on a piece of paper and put it in my pocket.

I looked back at Hunter. He didn't raise his head. I thought he was probably telling the truth about not knowing the identity of the buyer. That could be discovered by the police. For now I had a phone number, and that seemed enough. I pulled out the fourth tape and held it in my hand. The date on the white tag on the upper left corner stared back at me. I double-checked it. No doubt about it. The exact date of Jessica Nodman's murder.

"Where's a video player?" I asked.

I saw Hunter take a breath. Then he said, "Under the television. There in the den."

I stepped out of the study, crossed the breakfast table area and walked to the giant screen TV against the far wall of the den. There was a video player built into the wall underneath it. For a moment I hesitated, the tape in my hand. Then I slipped it into the slot and pushed the play button.

The tape opened on a picnic scene, and I could tell it had been shot on the terrace behind the house. I could see the waters of Lake Travis in the background. It was evening, a summer twilight, laid back and relaxed. It could have been any ordinary picnic, just as normal as you please. People were standing around, talking, holding beer cans. I saw Frank Hunter and Clint Adcock right away, then the dark-haired guy who looked like a body builder, wearing a cap with APD on the brow. They were standing together, talking, laughing, occasionally sipping at their beers. I saw them wave to the camera. Then I saw Jessica, standing with Stan and Davidson. She looked so happy, vibrant, alive. She smiled and waved to the camera too. Just any normal picnic on the terrace, and she was obviously having a good time, enjoying herself thoroughly. Relaxed. Happy. Very pretty. Just an ordinary picnic. The only one missing from the scene was the overweight, bald guy with the red fringe around his dome and the red mustache. I figured he was probably on the camera. Just an ordinary summer evening picnic on the terrace. Letting the buyer see the prey. Letting him get to know her.

I hit the button to fast-forward the tape and got more of the same. Fast-forward again. The party had moved inside now. They were in the den, exactly where I was standing. Nothing had changed. The furnishings were exactly the ones that surrounded me now.

Fast-forward again.

Jessica was dancing now. I watched as she did a striptease. She was just as I remembered her from the tape I had seen at Jack's house. Laughing, exultant, alive with energy. Teasing too, as she coyly removed her clothing. I saw her throw her head back, then laugh. Her smile was radiant as she looked at the camera. Finally she was naked, doing her dance, caught up in it completely, just as I had seen her before, an artist at home with her talent.

Then Stan joined in. They danced together, and as they did, Stan began to undress too. Soon she was as naked as Jessica. They danced together that way, two fantastic looking ladies, moving and swaying together, intertwining their arms and legs around each other, then separating. From time to time the camera caught background shots, and I could see Hunter and Adcock, clapping and yelling and cheering them on, along with the other body builder, but there wasn't a sign of Davidson.

I hit the fast-forward again. Now Jessica and Stan

were on the floor together, lying together, both still naked. I could see them kissing and touching each other, exploring each other's bodies. I watched as they began to perform oral sex on each other, locked together in a classic sixty-nine position. I could hear the cheering of the men in the background.

Then Jessica and Stan were finished, and Frank Hunter was having intercourse with Jessica. The camera caught them from several angles, moving around them, shooting from all sides. Just your standard, good old-fashioned, American home video. Then Clint Adcock was taking his turn, sodomizing her, of course, doggie style, with Jessica on her hands and knees. Again, the camera captured the scene from all directions. Then the other body builder started to take his turn. Like Hunter and Adcock, he used a condom. Of course. So they wouldn't leave any DNA in the victim. That was why the coroner's report had said there was no proof she'd had sex before being killed.

I hit the fast-forward. More of the same. Fast-forward again.

Then it started to get ugly. When the black-haired guy had finished, he suddenly grabbed her by the hair and slapped her hard across the mouth several times. I could see the surprise on her face. I watched as her excitement and enthusiasm turned to confusion. Then to fear. Then Hunter was standing beside her, kicking her. He grabbed her hair and pulled her to her feet, then slapped her across the face. I saw the helplessness in her eyes. The growing terror. I heard her ask him to stop, but he passed her to Clint Adcock, who began to pinch her breasts. Hard. Painfully. She tried to push him away, but she was helpless against his strength. Then he bit her on the nipple. I heard her scream. He passed her back to Hunter. More slaps. The other body builder bit her on the other breast. I heard her scream again.

Fast-forward.

More of the same

Fast-forward.

Still more. Rougher and rougher. Hitting her. Slapping her. Biting her. Pinching her. Laughing at her helplessness.

Then Stan came back into the picture, wearing the domina outfit, which hid nothing. The Maiden Head was in her right hand. She began to beat Jessica with it, as the men stood ringed around, cheering. First there were body blows. Jessica cringed helplessly, unable to defend herself.

Fast-forward.

Still more of the same. Torturing her. Playing with her. Brutalizing her.

Then Stan raised the Maiden Head and brought it crashing down into Jessica's skull, just above the ear, in the soft vulnerable area of the temple. An extra loud cheer went out. There was another blow, this time to Jessica's face. Another cheer.

Then Davidson stepped into the picture, holding a large knife. He bent down over her body. The camera came in close. I couldn't tell whether or not Jessica was still trying to move, still trying to ward off the blows, but any efforts would have been futile. With the camera zoomed in close, I saw Davidson run the knife in an arc down the left side of her chest, following the line of her ribs, going from her breastbone in front all the way around to her spine in back. It split open the side of her chest like opening up an envelope with a letter opener. Then he had some sort of rib spreading device. He wedged it into her chest, going between two ribs, and cranked it open. The camera caught it all. Then Davidson had the knife again. Inside her chest. There were sawing movements. Then he pulled out her heart, still beating and pulsing and dripping with blood. An even louder cheer went up as he held it aloft, displaying it for the camera.

Then Stan stepped up to him, the cheers and all the

applause still reverberating in the background, and took the heart from him. I watched, spellbound, as she put the beating heart to her mouth and took a bite out of it, tearing off a chunk of the flesh with her teeth. She chewed it for the camera, blood running out of the corners of her mouth.

I suddenly found myself gagging, but my stomach was empty and nothing came up. I gagged again. A cold sweat had broken out on my forehead. Moving numbly, almost in a daze, I hit the eject button, and the tape slid out of the slot. I felt unsteady and had to sit down in one of the armchairs in front of the TV. I sat there for a minute or two until I began to feel stronger. Then I managed to stand up, get the tape, and take it back into the kitchen. Hunter was where I'd left him, propped up against the drawers, his legs outstretched in front of him, his ankles bound together, his hands still tied behind his back. He didn't look up at me.

"Nice little bedtime movie, Frank," I said.

He didn't say anything.

"One more question," I said. "Something I haven't figured out yet. Why did Davidson take the tape from the little pot-bellied bald guy? Jack was his name. He owns a lamp shop. Where did that fit in?"

He didn't answer at first, then said, "We always made a preview tape for the buyer so he could okay the girl. That particular preview tape got damaged. We needed another one that showed her."

I nodded. "Funny the way things work out, just like you said. That was the one thing that got me focused on Davidson in the first place. The fact he made Jack give him that tape. If it hadn't been for that, I'd still be completely in the dark."

He didn't say anything.

I checked the belts around his ankles and wrists to make sure they were still secure. They were. His hands were cold and blue, in fact. That had to be uncomfortable, but I wasn't about to loosen them up any. Then I picked up the Maiden Head off the counter and went into the study. I took out one of the photos from the wall safe, one that showed the whole group. I decided to leave the safe open and the bookshelves pulled out. Then I walked back into the kitchen.

"You'll have some company pretty soon, Frank," I told him.

He didn't respond.

I got all my stuff up off the counter, including my cellphone. I picked the Magnum up off the floor and stuck it in my belt. Then, carrying the tape, the Glock, the Maiden Head, and the picture, I walked out through the dining room and living area and out the front door. I left it ajar. There was a big black Harley parked on the front walk, but I didn't see any sign of the Corvette. I walked to the Grand Am and started it. I kept the lights off and drove a few houses farther down, then turned around and parked against the curb, facing back toward the house. I could see it clearly in the moonlight. Then I got out my cellphone. But I didn't punch in a number. I sat there thinking instead. I reviewed all that had happened. I had talked with Joe Henderson. He had given me Frank Hunter's address and phone number. I had come to the house. And Hunter had showed up. I had been trapped. I remembered what Hunter had said: he had some connections inside the Austin Police Department. Very reliable connections. I hadn't even asked Hunter who it was, hadn't even asked him to name the contact. That had been denial on my part, I realized. I hadn't wanted to hear the truth. Hadn't wanted to face it. But I couldn't ignore it any longer. It felt like being slapped in the face. I had to shut my eyes.

Joe Henderson?

I couldn't make it register in my mind.

But I couldn't dismiss it either.

I knew I couldn't call Joe now. Not after all that

had happened. Go all the way to the top, I decided. Talk to Acting Chief Baker himself. So I opened my eyes, took a deep breath, and dialed the main number for the Austin PD. I got a desk sergeant.

"My name is Draeger," I said. "Walter Draeger. I'm told there's a warrant out for my arrest in the murder of Dr. Corbin Davidson."

The desk sergeant didn't say anything, but I thought I had his attention.

"I have specific information regarding that murder," I went on, "along with specific information about the serial murders of several women in the Austin area over the past year. This specific information completely solves all these killings. I need to talk with Acting Chief Baker about this. Baker, and only Baker. Can you put me through to him?"

There was a pause. Then I heard, "Just a second. I'll try to patch you through."

After a few more moments, I heard a different voice say, "Baker here."

I took a deep breath again. "Chief Baker, my name is Walter Draeger. And I have some information for you."

I gave him a summary of what I had learned and what had happened. "You better send a unit out now to pick up Frank Hunter. He's tied up, but he's a strong, tough son of a bitch, and he probably won't stay that way for long."

I gave him Hunter's address.

"You'll find an open wall safe in the study," I said. "It has what you need to get convictions."

Baker hadn't said anything, but I could hear him breathing.

"One more thing, Baker," I added. "You got a leak inside your department somewhere. Hunter has an inside connection. You need to check into that."

Then I hung up.

I sat in the car and waited. In about ten minutes two cars showed up. One was a regular Austin PD squad car, lights flashing, siren off. The other was unmarked. They pulled up in front of Frank Hunter's house. I could see activity. Two figures walked to the front door. I had seen enough.

I put the Grand Am in gear and drove slowly by the house. The front door was open. I could see lights on inside. I felt a sense of closure.

In just a few more minutes I was back on I-35, headed north to Dallas. I checked the time. Almost midnight. Clint Adcock would be calling me again in just a few minutes. I thought that was going to be interesting. I punched in the phone number of Julie's parents as I drove and was relieved to get the answering machine. Good. That meant Julie had taken my advice, and they had all gone to a motel. But I didn't know which motel, so I punched in the number of her cellphone, praying she had remembered to bring it with her. It rang twice, then a woman's voice said, "Hello, Walt."

But it wasn't Julie's voice.

It was Stan's . . .

21.

I sat there stunned, the phone to my ear, still heading north on I-35.

Stan?

On Julie's cell?

I took the phone from my ear and stared down at it. I knew both their numbers. Had I dialed the wrong one by mistake? But I knew in my heart I hadn't. An icy dread engulfed me. If Stan had Julie's cell . . .

"Are you there, Walt?" I heard.

A horn blared behind me, and I looked back at the road. I had started to drift over into the next lane. I corrected and put the phone back to my ear.

"I'm here," I said.

"I've been waiting for you to call," Stan said. "I knew you would, sooner or later."

I swallowed and said, "Where are you?"

"Oh, we're still in Dallas. We got held up a little."

I felt myself try to swallow again, but my throat was too dry. "We?"

"Yeah. . ."

I waited, not even able to breathe.

"Julie and Bobby and Clint and I," she said.

The icy dread that had come down around me got colder and tighter. I licked my lips, but the dryness wouldn't go away.

"Julie and Bobby are with you?" I said.

"Yeah. . ."

I couldn't speak.

"Gee, it's such a shame, Walt," she added, almost pensively. "You know what I mean? That it has to come down to this. That it has to end this way."

I still couldn't talk. A deadly silence hung on the line.

"I really thought there was something very *special*

between us," she finally said. "I really thought we might have a future together. You know, that we could have a great relationship together. That we were meant for each other somehow. Almost like we were soul mates. I really felt that. I thought it was so sweet that you wanted to try to save me when you thought I was in danger. I mean that..."

I still couldn't talk. The lines of the road were hazy and blurred ahead of me. I felt dizzy.

"I. . . I really like you, Walt," she added. "I mean that. . ."

I shook my head to try to clear it, but the road up ahead still seemed to be spinning. The lines on the pavement kept coming in and out of focus.

"You know, we might still work something out," she said hopefully. "There might still be a chance. What do you think? It doesn't *have* to be over, you know."

I tried again to swallow. Couldn't.

She didn't respond for a moment.

Finally she said, ". . .Well then… here's Clint. . ."

There was silence again. Then I heard Adcock's malevolent chuckle on the line, pulsing with evil and power, just as I had remembered it.

"Kind of surprised you there, didn't we, Ace?" he said. "Had to get you out of Dallas so you wouldn't be in the way. Worked out pretty good too. I wasn't all that sure you'd take the bait about Stan like you did."

I finally found my voice again and said, "If you harm either one of them in any way, Adcock, I'll kill you, I swear to God, if it's the last thing I ever do."

I could hear his evil chuckle again. "Now there you go again, Ace. Getting all rude and unpleasant with me, and here I am just trying to be real cordial and polite. Now how can we work together if you're always making nasty threats like that, you know what I mean."

"I meant every goddamn word I said."

I heard him chuckling again.

Then he said, "Heard you went looking for the house where Frank Hunter lives. How'd that work out for you?"

I knew he was fishing, and I realized I couldn't tell him what had happened. He and Stan thought they needed to reel me in because they thought I was the only one who knew what had happened. They thought they needed me. And they were using Julie and Bobby to keep me on the string. Blow that cover, Julie and Bobby were dead. I thought once more about Joe Henderson and wondered all over again how he could have done this to me.

"I didn't make it there," I said.

He seemed to think about that for a moment. "Kind of wondered how that had turned out, Ace. See, we tried to call Frank on his cell a little while ago, and we didn't get an answer."

"You'd have to talk with him about that."

After a moment I heard him chuckle again. "Got to hand it to you again, Ace. You got real good taste in women. Your honey here is a real cute little lady. Real cute. Very classy. Nice little figure too. Got a nice round ass on her. Nice and round and curvy. You don't find a nice round ass like that very often on the little ones, but I got to admit, she looks real good to me."

The muscles in my belly had gotten tighter. My breath caught in my throat.

"I'm really gonna like putting it in there when the time comes," he said. "Know what I mean?"

I couldn't speak.

I heard his chuckle again, rippling with malice. "I think I may screw your kid in the ass too, before it's all over. I haven't had a kid in awhile. I like to screw a kid in the ass every now and then. They got such nice tight little assholes. I like a little variety like that."

I managed to find my voice. "You touch either one of them, and I'll kill you," I said tightly.

Adcock chuckled again. "You talk real big, Draeger, especially for somebody without any cards. Anybody ever tell you that before?"

"How do I know you even have them?" I snapped. "Maybe you're playing the same game you played before. Maybe you're bluffing."

I heard him chuckle again. Then his voice got hard and he said, "Then listen to this, asshole."

I heard sounds of movement over the line, then something that sounded like an impact. A slap. I tensed all over.

"Walt!" I heard.

It was Julie's voice.

"Walt!"

I heard scuffling sounds again, then another impact. I sat there transfixed. It seemed impossible to me that I couldn't do anything to help.

"Stop it! Stop it! You stop it! You leave her alone!" I heard Bobby scream.

There were more scuffling sounds. Then I heard Adcock laugh, and he said, "Whoa there, little man! Whoa there!"

"Bobby! Stay away from him! Stay away!" I heard Julie cry.

I heard Adcock laugh again. "Whoa there! You're a feisty little scrapper, aren't you?"

"Bobby!" Julie shrieked, her voice shot through with panic.

I listened, my muscles tensed all over, straining to hear, my heart in my throat, but there was only silence. Then Adcock came back on the line.

"Satisfied?" he said.

"You're dead, Adcock. I swear to God."

"Still talking mighty big, Draeger, for a man with no cards. But I'll tell you what, this just may be your lucky night. Now how does that sound? See, I'm feeling real,

real generous tonight, so I'm gonna cut you a little deal here. I'm gonna give you a chance to come get your wife and your kid. Sound like a winner to you?"

I didn't say anything.

"You stay right there in Austin, Draeger. We got held up a little again, so we're still running late. Had to go pick up your honey and your brat, and then we had some car trouble. So you stay right where you are until we get everything squared away up here. Then I'll call you and tell you where to go. And maybe I'll give you a chance to get your wife and your kid back. You got me?"

I knew my only option was to cooperate. "I'll be here."

"Good. Stay on your cell. You try anything funny, then *you're* the one who's dead. Along with your wife and your kid."

The line went dead.

I put the phone down on the seat and forced myself to try to think. I needed to get off I-35, then head back to Austin. And wait. I pulled off at the next exit. There was a Chevron station with a convenience store up ahead. I pulled in and sat in the car, still not able to believe what was happening.

Stay focused, I told myself. Think! First of all, I realized how weak I was. I felt shaky and trembly all over. I suspected part of it was due to the phone call, but I realized part of it was probably also due to the struggle with Frank Hunter and all that had happened. I hadn't eaten in hours. My mouth was dry and pasty, but I went into the store and got a packaged sandwich and a small carton of milk. The clerk was alarmed by my appearance and by all the blood. I'd had a nosebleed, I told him. True enough. I went back out to the car and made myself get it all down, and I thought maybe I felt a little stronger. Then I sat there, thinking. There was nothing to do but drive back to Austin. That's where Adcock had told me to be, and I didn't have any idea in the world where they might be headed.

Then something occurred to me.

Maybe I did.

I remembered the study in Frank Hunter's house. I remembered the pictures of his ranch on the bookshelf and the plaque from the Llano Chamber Of Commerce, naming him a distinguished rancher. A ranch would be isolated, secluded, protected. A perfect place to take hostages. I had a general idea of where Llano was located, in the heart of the Texas Hill Country northwest of Austin, but I needed a map to know exactly how to get there, so I went back inside the convenience store. Sure enough, they had a roadmap of Texas. I bought one, got back in the car, and opened it up. The route was simple: up I-35 a little farther, then west on Highway 28 to Llano. I started the Grand Am and pulled back onto the Interstate.

I was there in a little over an hour. I stopped as I was coming into the town limits and checked the map again. They would be coming from Dallas, down from the north. It seemed to me the most direct route would probably bring them into Llano on Highway 16, heading almost due south. I proceeded a little further and found a cutoff to 16 without difficulty, then headed north out of town. A few miles later I passed a small country store on the west side of the road, dark and shut in the middle of the night. I figured that would be as good a place as any to wait. I pulled in behind the south side of the building and turned around so that I was facing the highway. A car coming down from the north wouldn't be able to see me here, and I'd be able to pull out quickly if I needed to. I flipped off the lights and killed the engine.

Then I waited. Time seemed to stand still. My skin crawled. My gut was tightened into a knot. My fingers were trembling, but all I could do was wait. And think. It all began to come into focus more clearly. No wonder that Adcock had been able to pick me up so easily at the restaurant with Stan. She had known exactly where we were going, and we had driven there in separate cars. She'd had plenty of opportunity to call him. No wonder Davidson had found me at the restaurant when I went back there. Adcock had been tailing me. I thought about it some more. He had been tracking me in a gray sedan, but I had watched him ride away on a motorcycle. He had changed vehicles while I had been eating, sitting there on display like a goldfish in a bowl, probably because he knew a bike would be more maneuverable in downtown traffic and would give him a better chance of eluding me if I tried to follow. Good thinking. No wonder they had known I was staying at the La Quinta. No wonder, indeed. Stan had been their link. Frank Hunter had said she cared. Maybe. She had played it all so well, so perfectly. I thought about Sandy and the bomb planted in the Taurus and felt an aching sense of sadness, on top of all the rest of what I was going through. They had known where my apartment was. Because of Stan.

I had been stupid. I had been tricked and used. I should have seen, should have known. I felt utterly disgusted with myself. I had done it all wrong.

The cellphone rang, and I almost jumped out of my skin. I turned it on and put it to my ear, my heart pounding my chest out. I licked my lips and said, "Draeger here."

"Walt, where the hell are you!" I heard Joe Henderson say. "I haven't heard from you in a couple of hours at least. I've been wondering what's happened. I thought I'd give you a call and check in with you."

All I could feel was rage. Rage and hatred. He had tricked me too. My grip tightened on the cellphone. I wanted to crush it like a piece of paper.

"You there, Walt?" I heard.

"Yeah. I'm here. . ."

"Where the hell are you? What's happened?"

I didn't say anything.

"Walt?" he asked.

"I told you. I'm here."

There was silence on the line again.

"What's happening? Where are you? Fill me in. I've been worried about you."

"Have you really?"

Silence again.

"Well . . . yeah . . ."

"Really, Joe? Now is that a fact?"

More silence.

"Walt. . . what the hell is going on here? What's happened? You sound real different. Like you're not yourself. Like you're not the same old Walt. You got me worried, buddy."

I knew exactly what was happening. There was a connection inside the Austin Police Department. I had been tricked there too. And now they needed to check up on me.

"You really expect me to believe that? You really expect me to think you're worried about me?"

Silence.

"Walt, what the hell? What's going on? You're freaking me out."

I decided not to play any more games. "I called you and asked you to find out where Frank Hunter lived."

"Yeah. . ."

"And you gave me an address."

"Yeah. . ."

"And I went there."

"Okay…"

"And Hunter showed up."

Silence again.

"Jesus. . ," he said.

"He trapped me. I nearly got killed."

"Jesus Christ, Walt. . ."

"He told me somebody had tipped him off that I

was trying to find out where he lived."

Joe didn't say anything.

"He told me he had a connection inside the Department."

I could hear his breathing. It had gotten tighter and quicker.

"Christ. . ," he said. ". . .Walt. . . you don't . . . I mean, you don't think . . ."

"Who else, Joe?"

Silence again.

"My God, Walt. . . I don't see how you could think that . . . not after all we've been through. . ."

"No joke."

There was another silence.

"Look, Walt. . . after all that's happened, I don't believe you're thinking clearly. I think it's clouded your judgment . . . when you wanted the address, I called and talked with the Patrol Lieutenant. Name's Carrington. I know him well. He looked it up and called me back in just a few minutes. Then I called you and gave it to you. I'm gonna talk to him again and ask him to call you. Stay there on your cell. We gotta get this worked out."

I didn't say anything. The line went dead. I sat there in the car, waiting. And thinking. I *wanted* to believe Joe Henderson wasn't a part of it. But I couldn't let myself be tricked again.

I could see the lights of a car on the highway ahead, coming down from the north. I tensed, watching and waiting, ready to pull the Grand Am out from behind the building and follow, but it turned out to be a dilapidated pickup, rumbling by slowly and then finally disappearing from sight to the south. I didn't know for sure what kind of car they'd be in - if they even came this way - but the rattletrap pickup didn't seem a likely choice. They'd need something faster, more dependable. I slumped back down in the seat, trying to make myself stay calm.

DANCE YOUR HEART OUT

The phone rang and I jumped again. I recognized the number in the display. I had called it enough to be familiar with it. The Austin Police Department. I took the call and said, "Draeger."

"Yeah, this is Lieutenant Carrington with the Austin Police Department," I heard. "Joe Henderson just called me. Said he'd talked with you. Said there was some confusion. He asked me to give you a call."

I was aware again of *wanting* to believe Joe Henderson hadn't been part of it, but all my warning sensors were out. Carrington was calling from the Austin Police Department . . . but I already knew there was a connection inside the Department. Was he just another part of it?

"I got a call on the other line," I said. "Can I get back with you in a couple of minutes?"

"Sure. Give me a ring."

I hung up. Thought some more. I finally decided to call the Austin Police Department number and ask to speak to the Patrol Lieutenant and see what happened. I put through the call . . . and was connected to Carrington. I took a deep breath, hoping against hope. I needed help somewhere.

"This is Draeger again," I said.

"Right. Joe Henderson called. Said there was some confusion."

"Can you tell me what contact you've had with him tonight?"

"Sure," he said, matter-of-factly. "He called me a few hours ago here at the station. Asked me to get a phone number and an address on a guy named Frank Hunter. I was working on some other stuff, so I called ID and gave it to one of the guys down there. They called me back in a few minutes, gave me the number and the address, and I called Henderson back and gave it to him. That's it."

I found myself *wanting* so much to believe it, but

still . . .

"Henderson said he wanted you to call him again," Carrington added. "He asked me to give you that message."

"Thanks."

I hung up and sat there thinking again. It sounded straightforward enough. I reached way down inside myself, searching for a sense of trust, and I thought I finally connected with something. And I *needed* help. I dialed Joe's home number.

"I talked with Carrington," I said.

"And? I hope to God you're satisfied, Walt. All I did was call and try to get the phone number and the address for you. That's it. I swear to God."

I took another deep breath, got one more read from my gut. He sounded like he was telling the truth.

"Okay, Joe. . . I'll tell you what's happened."

So I gave him a rundown on all that had occurred. I even gave him the phone number of the buyer in Denver.

"Right now I'm parked behind a small country store on Highway 16, a few miles north of Llano, on the outside chance they might be coming this way."

"You're sure they have Julie and Bobby?"

"Positive. I heard them over the phone."

"Jesus, Walt . . ."

I didn't say anything. Couldn't. I knew I was way outside the Austin jurisdiction, and I knew Joe couldn't do anything until I learned something more definite about where they were heading. It would have been pointless to ask.

"There's something real, real strange here," Joe finally said, sounding perplexed. "When I talked with Carrington just a few minutes ago, he didn't say anything at all about any of this. You say you talked to Ron Baker?"

"Yes."

"Carrington would *have* to know about it if something official was happening with Patrol. He's the

Patrol Lieutenant, for Christ's sake. But he didn't say anything. I think I'll call him back. I'll get back with you after I've talked to him again."

"One more thing," I said.

"Sure, Walt."

There was something I'd been thinking about. Julie and Bobby had been with her parents. But I didn't think her parents were being held hostage. So I asked Joe if he could have the authorities in Garland check on them. I gave him their address.

"Sure, Walt. I'll get back with you when I have something. You call me if anything happens in the meantime. I'll probably go down to the station. Sue's visiting her mother in Houston, so there won't be anybody here at the house to answer the phone. Try me downtown if you miss me."

The line went dead. I went back to just sitting there. And thinking. Time was standing still again. And all I could do was wait. The full moon was farther to the west now, casting shadows, illuminating the surrounding area and the road up ahead. From time to time I saw headlights. The ones coming from the south, up from Llano, I didn't pay much attention to. But I watched very closely when a car passed by from the north. There weren't many, only one or two per hour at this time of night. The hours dragged by with maddening slowness. I looked at my watch again. It was going on five a.m.

The phone rang and I flinched. The Austin PD number was in the display.

"It's me, Walt," I heard Joe Henderson say. "I'm down at the station now."

"What have you found?"

He hesitated. "Don't know what to make of it. Nobody down here knows anything at all about Frank Hunter or where he is. Nobody's heard anything from Ron Baker either. So we sent a unit out to Frank's house. They found signs of a struggle, some blood, some turned over chairs, but Hunter wasn't there. Found a wall safe behind the bookshelf, just the way you said it was, but it was empty. Can't locate Baker either. Tried to get him at home and there's no answer. Can't reach him on his cell either. The other thing that's strange is that he never called for any support. There's no official investigation, no nothing. Nobody here at the station knows a damned thing."

"They didn't find Hunter?" I asked, stunned.

"No sign of him."

"Jesus Christ! I left him there on the kitchen floor. Tied up and everything."

"He's gone now. I talked with Carrington. We're calling Hospital ERs. If Hunter was banged up like you said, he probably needed medical treatment, especially if he's bleeding and his shoulders are out of joint. Haven't located him yet, though."

Hunter wasn't there? No official investigation? No contact from Baker? I couldn't make any sense of it.

"You said there were six people in the group in all?" Joe asked.

"To begin with. Only five, now that Davidson's dead."

"Hunter, Davidson, and Adcock are the only ones we have pictures of. Can you describe the others for me?"

So I described them as well as I could. Stan. The black-haired body builder. The overweight guy with the bald dome and the red mustache. I thought Joe was probably taking notes as I spoke.

He didn't say anything for a moment when I finished. "Describe that last one again," he finally said. I could hear a sudden tightness in his voice.

"The guy looked like he was probably in his late forties. Kind of overweight. Big belly. Red mustache. Bald, with a fringe of red hair around his head."

There was silence again.

"Jesus Christ," Joe finally said.

"What?"

"My God, Walt…you just gave a perfect description of Ron Baker."

"You're kidding me."

"I wish to God I was."

I didn't know what to say.

"We're checking ERs, like I said," Joe finally added. "I'll let you know if we find anything. And you let me know as soon as you find out where they're taking Julie and Bobby. I'll do anything I can to help, Walt, I swear it."

"I asked you to do one more thing for me," I said.

He didn't answer.

"Julie's parents. Did anybody go by to check on them?"

I heard him take a slow breath. "I . . . I was hoping you wouldn't ask me about that yet. . ."

I felt a sinking feeling in my belly. An ominous silence hung on the line.

"Ah, shit, Walt. . ," he finally said.

I waited.

"It's . . . it's not good, Walt. . . it's real goddamned bad, in fact . . . I'm sorry . . . I'm sorry to have to tell you, but…well, they're…they're both dead, Walt… both shot in the back of the head, execution style . . . their hands were tied behind them. . . I'm sorry… I wish I didn't have to tell you that. . ."

I had to shut my eyes. I wondered if Julie and Bobby had seen that. I tried to block out the images, but the pictures of what Joe had described kept crashing into my mind.

"You there, Walt?" I heard.

"Yeah . . ."

The pictures were still exploding in my mind. I couldn't drive them out. Then, in the midst of all that, the phone started to beep.

"I wish I could have told you something else, Walt..."

I took a deep breath. The pictures were still there. The phone was still beeping. But something else had occurred to me.

"Wonder if you could have the cops in Garland check on something else for me too. . . there's a dog in the back yard at Julie's house. . . his name's Brutus. . . Adcock had a score to settle with him. . . he's had plenty of time to do that by now. I have a bad feeling about it. . . could you have somebody check it out for me?"

I gave him the address.

"I'll get it done," he said grimly.

"Thanks."

Then we hung up. I took another deep breath, thought again about Brutus. He had recognized danger and evil, and he had defended his home. He had saved Bobby's life. Now I had a very bad feeling he had paid for that with his own.

The phone was still beeping. The low battery sign was showing in the display. I reached over and opened the glove compartment to get the car charger for the phone… and realized to my horror that it had been left in the Taurus. It was just part of the wreckage now, somewhere up in Dallas. But I had to have a working phone. I had to be able to take the call from Adcock. I tried to think of possibilities. Where could I get a phone charger at this hour? The only place that occurred to me would be an all-night Wal-Mart. But that meant driving back to Austin. No Wal-Mart in a town the size of Llano. I reached forward and cranked the ignition key, and the engine started up with a low rumble. I didn't turn on the headlights, though, because there were lights on the highway in front of me again, coming down from the north. I sat there watching the lights grow brighter, waiting for them to pass. Waiting for a chance to pull out and head back to Austin to find a charger… and tensed all over as a dark Corvette sped by, a lightning bolt on the side visible in the moonlight.

There were more lights behind, quickly growing brighter. I watched as a four-door sedan, probably gray by the light of the moon, raced past. So much for Wal-Mart. I put the Grand Am in gear and pulled out from behind the small country store, heading for the highway, my heart in my throat. I kept the headlights off as I pulled onto the pavement. The red taillights up ahead were receding into the distance. I stepped down hard on the gas, and the Grand Am leaped forward, picking up speed.

I kept my lights off and stayed far enough back so that I couldn't be seen. Their taillights were tiny red dots in the distance now. Soon we were coming down into Llano. Streets were nearly deserted. It was almost six a.m. now. Up ahead they crossed a bridge over the Llano River, which flowed through the town from west to east, and then beyond that I saw their lights turn to the right. I came to the place where they had turned, another small rural road, Highway 152, and turned right also, heading west, swinging past the town courthouse, the two sets of taillights glimmering faintly in the distance, far ahead of me.

I followed them out of town, still heading west, my own lights still off. The road was narrow and winding as it cut through the gently rolling land. Occasionally the lights up ahead would disappear around a curve or over a small hill, and I would speed up enough to bring them into sight again, then start to fall back, staying just close enough to keep from losing them.

I had checked the odometer as I had passed the courthouse, and now I looked down at it again. We had gone almost ten miles out of town on the winding, undulating road, driving past ranch after ranch on both sides of the highway, spaced at intervals, their entrances marked by arching gates like the one I had seen in the picture at Frank Hunter's house. I couldn't see a trace of the ranch houses, though, just trails leading away from the front gates, into the depths of the properties. Barbed wire fences, only about four feet high, bordered the properties and separated them from the highway.

Then I came over the crest of a small hill, and what I saw up ahead made me hit the brakes. The two sets of taillights had pulled off the road in the distance. They were stopped in front of a gate. I slowed and pulled to a stop, edging over onto the narrow shoulder. Then I saw the taillights start to move again, this time to the north, into one of the properties. The car in back stopped for a moment, and I thought I could see a figure moving back toward the gate. Then, after a brief pause, the figure returned to the car, and the taillights started to move forward again.

I crept forward, going slowly, watching as the taillights receded farther and farther into the depths of the countryside. Finally I got to the place where they had turned off. Sure enough, it was another gated entry, and at the top of the wrought iron arch stretching over the entrance road I could see lettering, just like it had looked in the picture: HUNTER RANCH. My hunch had been right. We were here.

The taillights had disappeared now, vanishing into a clump of trees in the distance, probably a couple of hundred yards inside the property from where I stood. I picked up the cellphone and punched in the number of the Austin PD, barely even breathing. I only hoped the battery had enough charge left. The beeping sound kept echoing in my ears as I waited, counting the rings. Finally a voice said, "Austin Police Department."

"Is Joe Henderson there? I need to speak to him. It's urgent. This is Walter Draeger."

"Lemme see. . ," I heard. "I think he's around here somewhere. . . saw him not too long ago, I think. . . lemme try to find him. . ."

I waited, my heart hammering in my chest, the

phone beeping in my ear. Time had stopped again. Each moment was an eternity. But no voice came back on the line. The phone kept beeping.

Finally I heard, "Can't seem to find him right now. You want me to leave him a . . . " But I didn't hear the rest. The phone was dead.

I turned it off and slipped it into my pocket. Then I checked the Glock. It was ready. I slipped it back in its shoulder holster. I always carry extra ammunition with me when I travel, and I filled both coat pockets. Then I stepped to the gate. I had expected to find it locked, but it wasn't. Maybe that was normal around these parts. The barbed wire fences didn't really provide much protection anyway. I pushed the gate open and drove through, then left it open behind me in case I needed to get out in a hurry. Then I started to drive up the thin gravel road that led into the property. I went slowly, my lights still off, looking ahead to the clump of trees where the taillights had disappeared and to both sides, checking the surrounding area. The full moon hung low in the western sky now, still casting its eerie glow. I was able to see a few cows here and there, most of them lying down. To the east I could see the first faint rays of dawn starting to light the horizon. I checked my watch. Quarter past six.

Finally the gravel road brought me to the clump of trees up ahead. I approached even more slowly, watching, peering into the darkness. Nothing. I crept slowly ahead, and after a short way, the gravel road took me through the clump of trees to a clearing. I stopped short of entering the clearing, though, because I could see a one-story ranch house in the distance. I could see two cars on the eastern side of the structure, and then I saw figures, moving in the distance. I strained to make out details, but the cars were in shadow, away from the light of the moon, and I couldn't tell what was happening. Then two sets of headlights and taillights came on. I could hear the faint rumble of starting engines in the distance. Then the cars began to move. One headed off to the right, and I thought I could tell that was the Corvette. The other car headed off to the left. Adcock. Because of his size and strength, he'd be more likely to have hostages, I thought. I decided to follow him first.

I thought briefly about following on foot, but I didn't know how far they might be going, and I needed the car if I found Julie and Bobby and needed to make a fast exit. *When* I found Julie and Bobby, I told myself. *When.*

I pressed gently on the accelerator, and the Grand Am crept slowly out of surrounding trees, into the clearing, heading toward the ranch house. I got there and found a fork in the gravel road and swung to the left, following the path Adcock had taken. The road was even narrower and rougher here. Trying to get out at high speed would be dangerous.

I had long since lost sight of any taillights, but I kept going forward, checking all around as I went, the moon looking back at me from directly ahead, just above the western horizon. The road approached another clump of trees. I still couldn't see anything. I kept going slowly, my heart pounding in my throat. Then I was into the trees, still creeping along, still looking around on all sides.

Another clearing emerged ahead of me, barely visible through the trees, and this time I could finally make out something else. Across the clearing, probably at least a hundred yards away, standing by another group of trees, was a car. Adcock's car. I came to a stop, staying far enough back so the trees would hide me. Then I killed the engine and stepped out, going carefully. I left the door ajar to save time if I needed to leave in a hurry. Then I pulled the Glock from its shoulder holster and looked across the clearing again.

There wasn't any sign of movement around the car. No figures. No sign of Adcock, Julie, or Bobby. I licked at my lips. They felt like sandpaper. Moving slowly, I worked my way through the trees to the edge of the clearing and stopped behind the thickest one I could find. There was beginning to be more light now, more early morning rays of the sun lighting up the sky in the east, bringing the dawn, as I surveyed the area. The trees continued in an arc to my right, ringing the clearing on the eastern side, extending in a curve all the way over to the northern side where Adcock's car was parked. To my left, toward the west, the land was clear and open. So the choice was made. I would have to work my way through the trees to my right, along the eastern edge of the clearing, trying to get closer and closer to where the car was parked, in the hope that I could surprise Adcock. And get to Julie and Bobby. I got ready to move, but my thoughts were suddenly interrupted.

"Welcome to the party, Ace," I heard.

I stopped dead still, stunned. The voice sounded like it had come from a distance, and it had a harsh, almost technical tone to me. It was surprisingly loud too. It took me a moment to put the pieces together. Adcock had a bullhorn, the kind police use when addressing a crowd.

But how did he know I was here? My mind scrambled frantically for an explanation. How!!! I had stayed out of sight the whole way.

"Been waiting for you, Ace," I heard over the bullhorn. "Surprised it took you so long."

I was still too amazed to comprehend it. Waiting for me? I looked quickly around on all sides, all my senses on fire, the skin crawling all over my body. Where was he? Where!!! I couldn't see a trace of him. The sound of his voice over the bullhorn had seemed to come from a distance, probably from across the clearing, but it had also seemed so startlingly close, bouncing off the trees all around me.

"Saw you when you pulled out from behind that little store and started following us," I heard.

Impossible, I thought. Impossible! I had stayed too

far back. It had been too dark. I crouched down low against the tree, my back against the bark, my skin tingling all over, still looking around to all sides. But there was nothing.

"Thought you were being real smart about it, didn't you, Ace? All you did was save me the trouble of having to call you and tell you where to go. I was just about to dial your number when I saw you."

Then I could hear something else: the sound of his chuckle, coming over the megaphone, filtering through the air, just as arrogant and just as evil as ever.

"Guess you weren't quite good enough, were you?" I heard.

Impossible, I thought again. Impossible! I backed up tighter against the tree, the Glock in my hand, my head spinning. I could *feel* his eyes on me.

"See, I'm the best in the world, Ace. Nothing ever gets by me. Nothing. You're learning that the hard way. But I got to hand it to you again. You're hanging in there real tough, just like from the start. You're hard to shake. See, you surprised me when I saw you following us. Still don't know how you figured out where we'd be heading. Gotta hand it to you."

I still leaned back against the tree, panting for breath, my heart ringing like a rail. I had gotten past my shock enough to listen more closely this time. I was pretty sure the sound of the bullhorn was coming from across the clearing, near where his car was parked. I scanned to the east again, looking at the line of trees that ringed the clearing on that side. The light on the eastern horizon was growing even brighter now, heralding the sunrise. I'd be more and more visible as daylight approached. It was time to move.

"Didn't you think it was funny I left the gate open for you?" I heard. "You should've picked up on that, Ace. You should've been more careful."

I was about to move when something occurred to me. I didn't even know if he had Julie or Bobby. I hadn't been able to see anybody at all. What if this was just another trap? What if Julie and Bobby were both with Stan in the Corvette? And Adcock had only lured me here to kill me.

"Cat got your tongue?" I heard.

I knew what he was doing. He needed to spot me. And hearing my voice would help. I looked quickly around the tree again, plotting a course, scanning the trees to the east, estimating distances. It was at least a hundred yards across the clearing, I estimated. I can hit silhouettes from a hundred yards all day long, but this was different. I didn't exactly expect Adcock to stand still for me, and if he *did* have Julie or Bobby, then I'd have to wait for a sure shot. I had to get closer. I would have to work my way along the eastern edge of the clearing, taking it one tree at a time, trying to get in better range. Trying to find out if he had Julie and Bobby.

"Maybe your kid can get you to talk," I heard.

I had been all set to move, but I froze in place, still pressed back against the bark.

"Dad!" I heard over the megaphone.

Then there was silence. I strained to hear.

"Ow! Stop it!" I heard. "Dad! Dad!" Bobby's voice was shot through with pain and fear, even over the bullhorn.

"Ow! Stop!"

Pain. Fear. Not just an exclamation. A scream. Echoing off the tress, ringing through the air. Piercing right through me. I pressed back flat against the tree, struggling to breathe against the tightness in my throat.

"Draeger!" I heard. "You want to come try to save your kid? You got the guts? Or do you just want to hide in the trees while I rough him up?"

"Ow!" I heard. "Stop it! Stop it!"

I took one last breath and bolted for the nearest tree, which was about fifteen feet away. I had barely gotten halfway there when a shot rang out, then another. I felt something fly by my head, then felt a sting in my arm. But I had made it to shelter again. I leaned back against the trunk, breathing heavily. I shot a quick glance at my arm. The clothing was torn over my right shoulder. I could see a trace of red. I touched the area with my left hand, and my fingers came away stained with blood. I stared in disbelief. He had hit me! Impossible! Hit a moving target at that distance? In poor light? Impossible! But he had done it!

"You still there, Draeger?" I heard.

I pressed back tighter against the tree, still panting. I tested the arm. It seemed to move well enough. The pain wasn't all that bad either. Just a flesh wound, I figured. But I still couldn't believe it. A horrible thought flashed into my mind: I didn't think I could have done that.

"You there?"

I stayed pressed back against the tree.

"Answer me, asshole! Or I hurt your kid again!"

"I'm here!" I called out.

"Now that's better, Draeger. Much better. You're lucky you're still alive, asshole. See, you got yourself a real problem here, Draeger. Real bad problem. The problem you got is, I'm the best shooter there ever was. I hit everything I aim at, every last time. So you got yourself a real bad problem, asshole."

I waited behind the tree, still breathing hard, trying to figure out my next step. I had no choice. I had to keep going. I bolted for the next tree, moving in a crouch. I heard another shot, felt something fly by, just above the top of my head. But I had made it to the next tree. I leaned back against the trunk, then looked quickly around one side, searching for some sign of Adcock, but all I could see was the empty clearing, with his car and the trees on the other side. I pulled back and looked around the other side of the tree, and this time I saw something. Movement. His head appeared from behind one of the trees in the distance. I saw a gun in his hand. I pulled back instantly. I heard the sound of a shot as sparks splintered off the trunk beside me, exactly where my head had been barely an instant before. Incredible! To fire that quickly from that far away and to come that close! I had always had such confidence in my own marksmanship, but now I felt an icy fear. I had that same horrible thought again: I didn't think I could have done that.

But at least I had seen him. I knew where he was. And now I needed to move again. I braced myself, got ready to bolt for the next tree. It would be better to fire at him as I moved, I decided, trying to keep him behind a tree, trying to keep him from firing back. Then, just before I started, something occurred to me, very strongly. *Don't let him know you can shoot.*

With that in mind, I pushed off and jumped from behind the tree, heading for the next one, and as I did, I fired off two shots, aiming way high and to the right of where I had seen him. I got a glimpse of him as he started to look around the tree he was behind, but I saw him pull back as the shots rang out, and I made it safely to shelter. I leaned back against the trunk, my heart pounding out my ribs, my breath a razor in my throat.

"You don't shoot very good, asshole," I heard him say over the bullhorn.

Good. Let him think that.

I braced again, then bolted for the next tree, ripping off three shots this time as I ran. I aimed high again, but this time put two to the left and one to the right. It worked again. He didn't return fire. I pressed back against the next trunk.

I could hear him laughing over the horn. "You're pitiful, asshole. I know blind people who can shoot better than that."

I did the same thing again, then again, and yet again, working my way from one tree to the next, always aiming high and wide when I shot. I stopped behind another trunk and quickly reloaded the Glock. My fingers were trembling. Bad sign. That had never been a problem before. I jammed the magazine back into place and shot a quick glance around the tree. I was still at least seventy to eighty yards away. Then I saw Adcock, walking from one tree to another in the distance, with Bobby slung over his shoulder. He was getting bolder, less careful. Good. Bobby's head was in back, his feet hanging over the front of Adcock's shoulder, and I got the impression Bobby's hands and feet were tied together. I fired quickly, aiming way to the side again.

"You're pitiful, asshole!" Adcock yelled over the bullhorn as he got behind another tree. "Pitiful!"

I braced and darted for the next tree. But this time when I shot, he didn't stay hidden. He stepped out from behind the cover of the tree, Bobby still slung over his shoulder, and brought up his gun. I could see fire at the muzzle. Then I felt a searing sting, this time in my left shoulder, just above the collarbone. I had been hit again. Amazing! I made it to the next tree and leaned back against the bark. I slipped the Glock into my left hand and with my right hand felt for the wound. It was in the left trapezius muscle, just at the base of my neck. In the flesh again. But one inch closer to the midline, and the course of the bullet would have been lethal.

"Come on out, asshole! Come on out! Or I'll hurt your kid again!"

I waited behind the tree, panting.

"You want me to hurt him again, asshole? You want me to make him squeal like a little girl again? You want that?"

I looked quickly around the tree. I saw Adcock standing in the open, a foot or two clear of the tree next to him, Bobby still slung over his shoulder.

"Come on out! Come on out, if you got the guts! Come on out! Or I start to work on your kid again, and this time I'm gonna play rough!"

I shot another quick look. Adcock could see me. He twisted abruptly, and the motion slammed Bobby's head into the trunk of the tree. He was baiting me. I steeled myself and stepped out into the open. As I did, I brought up the Glock, both my hands cupped on the grip. I allowed myself the tiniest fraction of a second, just enough to bring the sight to bear on Adcock's chest. I squeezed the trigger. The Glock bucked my hand. Across the way I could see Adcock bring up his gun at the same time. I saw a spark of fire at the muzzle. The sound of the two shots merged into one. I dove hard to my right the instant I fired, going for the cover of the tree again, but I had barely even begun to move when I felt an impact. This one was harder than the others. Much harder, much more direct. The force of it ripped into my left shoulder and knocked me backwards. I tried to stay on my feet, but the hit was too strong. I stumbled and fell, landing flat on my back, sprawled out from the impact, my left shoulder and my chest on fire with pain. I was dazed, but I forced myself to roll over and start to crawl, staying low, the pain taking my breath away. I managed to drag myself to the cover of the tree and leaned back against the trunk. My whole left side was on fire, throbbing with agony. I looked at my left shoulder. I could see blood oozing from the wound there. I tried to move the arm, and it screamed in protest. I felt grinding. Heard it too. Bone had been broken. The arm was almost useless. But he still had Bobby. I had to keep going. I managed to push myself to my feet, bracing my back against the tree. Every breath was a gasp. I felt light-headed, but I shot a quick look around the tree. Nothing. Then I looked to the other side. Still nothing.

I took as deep a breath as I could and bolted to the

next tree, firing the Glock with my right hand as I ran, my left arm throbbing at my side. There wasn't an answering shot, and I made it to cover again. I waited a moment, then bolted again. I did that several more times, firing the Glock each time, working my way closer, one tree at a time.

I had to pause to reload at one point. My shoulder hurt, but I did it. Then an idea popped into my mind. He's waiting for you to get closer. He's waiting for a sure shot. Waiting to take you out. But there still wasn't a choice.

Finally I'd worked my way to within about thirty yards of where he had last been, standing by the tree with Bobby over his shoulder. Then I thought I saw something. The grass in that area was high, probably almost a foot tall, but I thought there was something on the ground. I tensed, the Glock poised, watching for movement, but nothing changed. I worked my way quickly to the next tree and checked again. I could see more clearly, and I realized it was Bobby, lying on the ground at the base of the tree. Motionless. But there was no sign of Adcock. It would be a perfect trap, I realized. Try to save Bobby, leave myself open. Still no choice. I shot to the next tree, looked again. The angle was different now, and I could see something else. Another body. Lying flat. Partially obscured by the tall grass. I watched for motion. Nothing. I started to creep forward, crouched down, the Glock in my hand, aimed at the body in the grass. I crept closer. And closer. Finally I could see. Adcock was lying on his back, spread out, his arms out to his sides. He was wearing a white T-shirt with a star on the front. He had on blue workout pants with a white stripe up the side. The same blue baseball cap with "Dallas" over the brim had come off his head and was lying beside him. I kept waiting for him to move. Still nothing. I kept advancing, the Glock trained on his torso. Finally I was there.

I stood over him. A single bullet hole, stained red, stared back at me from the upper part of his chest, just below the base of his neck, right in the midline. Above the heart, but dead in the area where the great vessels run. A mortal wound. I looked over at Bobby. I could tell he was breathing. I was about to check on him when I saw something more. A flicker of motion around Adcock's eyes. Then they opened. I saw him take the faintest of breaths, heard barely a groan. His eyes moved slowly toward me. Focused. Then went out of focus and came back again. His mouth was hanging open. I saw him try to breathe, his lips slowly opening and closing like the gaping of a fish. A trickle of blood ran down one side of his chin. Then he began to move his right arm. Slowly. His gun, another Glock, lay on the ground a few inches from his right hand. I stepped quickly over his body and kicked it away. Then I stared down at him.

"Surprise, asshole," I said. "Looks like you're not the best in the world, after all."

His eyes were barely focused on me. I thought his brow furrowed slightly, the barest essence of a frown. A look almost like confusion crossed his features. Like he knew what had happened, but couldn't understand it, couldn't believe it. His mouth opened again. I thought he tried to speak, but he was too near to death.

I started to put a bullet in the center of his forehead, but I realized that wasn't good enough. I thought of something else. I slipped my foot under his flank, then levered him over onto his belly. I heard the weakest of groans as I rolled him over. Then I knelt down beside him and yanked down his workout pants. I stuck the Glock in his crotch and jammed it up into his rectum. I heard him groan again. I could see his mouth gaping open and closed, like he was trying to talk. Good. He was still alive. He still knew what was happening.

"Here, have one in *your* ass this time, Clint old buddy," I said.

Then I pulled the trigger.

Three times.

The hollow-point shells exploded inside him like depth charges. Each one jolted his entire frame. Then he lay still.

I pulled out the Glock and rolled him onto his back again. His eyes stared straight ahead, half open, unseeing, dull, glazed with death. I didn't feel finished, though. I jammed the Glock into his mouth as far as I could. I heard the breaking of teeth, but there was no trace of a reaction. His eyes stayed fixed, staring straight ahead.

Then I pulled the trigger again.

Three more times.

His head flopped violently with each blast, like a tattered rag in a high wind. Finally I felt finished. I pulled the Glock out of his mouth and pushed his face to the side. There was nothing but open air where the back of his skull had been.

Then I stood up and stepped over to Bobby. He was lying on his side, his hands tied behind him, his feet tied together too. I could see blood on the side of his head from where Adcock had slammed him against the tree. I put down the Glock and knelt beside him. Then I jostled his shoulder. He groaned. There was duct tape over his eyes and his mouth. The tape over his mouth was loose on one end, where Adcock had pulled it off long enough for him to call to me, then pressed it back in place. I pulled off both pieces of tape, going slowly and gently. He groaned again and stirred.

"Bobby!" I said.

I heard him groan again.

I untied his hands and his feet and rolled him onto his back. Then I jostled his shoulder again.

"Bobby!"

To my immense relief, I saw him open his eyes. He looked dazed and confused, and he was having trouble focusing.

"Dad," he said.

"I'm here."

He lifted his head up slightly and looked to both sides.

"What happened?" he asked.

"He's dead. I shot him."

He looked to the side again, in the direction of where Adcock lay. He seemed to comprehend it.

"That lady took Mom in the Corvette."

"I know. We have to find them. Do you know where they were going?"

He shook his head. "No."

"Here, let me wrap something around your head."

I looked at the area where the blood was. I could see a cut there, probably about two inches long.

"Dad. . . they killed Grammer and Gramper…"

So he had seen that. He knew.

"I know, Bobby. I heard that."

His face twisted in pain. "They made them kneel down . . . and then they shot them. . . in cold blood, Dad… Grammer and Gramper weren't trying to get away or anything. . . they just killed them . . . the lady shot Grammer and the man shot Gramper."

His voice was cracking as he spoke. The look of pain was still there, distorting his features. He sat up and I hugged him tight. I couldn't think of anything else to do or say.

"They just shot them," he said, beginning to sob. "They just shot them."

I held him tight. He hadn't wept for long before he gagged and threw up. They must have fed him, because his stomach wasn't empty. His vomit wound up on the front of my shirt. Still I held him.

"I'm sorry I made a mess, Dad. I'm sorry."

"That's okay, Bobby. That's okay."

I just kept holding him and rubbing his back,

rocking him back and forth. After a couple of minutes, he seemed to collect himself.

"We gotta find Mom," he said.

"Right."

I let go of him and stood up and stepped over to Adcock. I always carry a small pocketknife, and I used it to cut his shirt off. I wrapped the shirt around Bobby's head and tied it in place. Then I stepped back over to Adcock. I picked up his gun and stuck it in my belt. I found ammunition in a pocket of his workout pants, and I put that in my coat pockets. There were keys too. Then I found something else. A cellphone. I turned it on and got a signal. Then I dialed the number of the Austin PD.

"Is Joe Henderson there? It's urgent."

"Lemme see. . . don't know where he is for sure. . . haven't seen him for half an hour at least. I think he said he'd be on his cell. . . you wanna leave a message?"

I tried to remember Joe's cell number, but with all that had happened, I wasn't able to think clearly. For the life of me, I couldn't bring up the number, if I had ever even known it, and Sue Henderson wasn't at the house to give it to me if I called there.

"Can you give me that number?" I asked.

"Not supposed to do that."

"Then I need you to contact him and tell him Walter Draeger called. I'm on a ranch called the Hunter Ranch, about ten miles west of Llano on Highway 152. I need help. It's urgent! I need you to contact him right away!"

"I'll sure see what I can do," the voice drawled.

So I hung up and put the phone in my pocket. It was time to move. I wasn't sure when help would arrive, if it came at all. I picked up my Glock, wiped the barrel on the grass, and put it in the shoulder holster.

"Can you stand up?" I asked Bobby.

"Sure."

He pushed himself to his feet, but his legs weren't

steady. He had to lean against the tree. He looked dizzy. Then he had to sit back down. I didn't think he'd be able to walk.

"Climb up on my back," I told him, and I turned my back to him and squatted down.

He pushed himself up again and got behind me and looped his arms around my neck. The pressure on my shoulder as I stood up with him sent a jolt of pain down my arm. I heard myself gasp.

"I'm sorry, Dad. I'm sorry."

"You're fine, Bobby. You're fine."

Then I started walking back in the direction of the Grand Am, carrying Bobby piggyback. I'd only gone a few steps, though, when I thought of something. I was weaker than I had realized, and carrying Bobby all that distance was going to be difficult. Adcock's car was parked just a few feet away. I had the keys. I turned and headed toward it. When I got there, Bobby slid off my back, and we got inside. I turned the key and the engine started. Then we drove back across the clearing, into the clump of trees where I'd left the Grand Am. I drove slowly, looking on all sides, checking. Stan was still out there somewhere.

We came to the Grand Am, and I was about to drive past it, when I noticed something. The door to the driver's side was shut. I specifically remembered leaving it open, so I could get in the car and leave as quickly as possible if I needed to. But now it was shut. I stopped and got out of Adcock's car. I opened the driver's door of the Grand Am and looked inside. The front seat was empty. The tape I had left there was gone. So was the Maiden Head. The picture too. Stan! She had gotten the evidence! Everything!

There was nothing to do but keep going. I got back into Adcock's car and retraced the route back to the ranch house. I didn't think Stan would leave the property - and if she *had* left, she was long gone now anyway - so I took the road I had seen her take earlier, off to the right. We started heading away from the ranch house in that direction. I drove carefully, slowly, looking in all directions, searching for some sign of the Corvette. Bobby was watching too. But there was nothing to see.

The road started to meander up a hill, sometimes running through open areas and then through areas that were heavily wooded. The sun was up now, climbing clear of the horizon, casting sharp, steep, morning shadows. Then I saw it up ahead. The black Corvette, parked at the edge of another clump of trees, directly ahead. I came to a stop and watched, straining to see. So did Bobby.

"I can't see anybody, Dad," he said.

"I can't either."

I decided to approach in the car. The sight of Adcock's car probably wouldn't be alarming to Stan. I told Bobby to get down on the floor, and then I flipped down the visor, trying to cover myself as well as I could, so Stan wouldn't be able to tell from a distance that Adcock wasn't the driver. The trees up ahead would be perfect cover for her, and I knew she had a gun.

Finally we were there. I pulled up beside the Corvette, the Glock drawn and ready. Still no sign of anybody. I looked up ahead. The land continued to rise, going uphill, and it was covered with trees. The Llano River wouldn't be much farther on.

"You wait here, Bobby," I said.

"Dad! It's Mom! I *have* to come too!"

I could hear the determination in his voice and see it in his eyes.

"Okay, but stay behind me at all times, and if I tell you to take cover, you do it in a hurry."

He nodded.

I was about to pop open the door and get out when the phone rang. It took me a moment to realize it wasn't my phone, but the one I had taken off Adcock. I pulled it out of my pocket and looked at the display. I recognized the number immediately. Stan's. I pushed the button and put the phone to my ear.

"Clint, where are you?" I heard.

I lowered my voice and held the phone away from my mouth. ". . . Can't hear. . . breaking up . . . where. . ."

"I'm at the observation point on the river. I went back to his car. He had one of the tapes. He also had the Maiden Head and a picture we took at the lake. All that was at Frank's, so he must have gone by there. I got it all. Have you heard from Frank? I tried to get him on his cell, but he didn't answer."

". . .Can't hear . . ."

"I heard some shots, then three in a row, then three more, but I couldn't really see anything," she said. "I decided I ought to let you handle it, so I left and came back here."

So she had heard Adcock die. I still didn't say anything.

"Clint?" she asked, a trace of uncertainty in her voice.

I didn't answer.

"Clint. . . is that you?"

Still no answer.

"Clint!!!"

I ended the call.

"You ready?" I asked Bobby.

He nodded grimly.

We got out and shut the doors, moving carefully, watching closely. I looked over at Bobby. He seemed to be more steady on his feet now. There was a trail leading up the hill, but I thought we'd be too visible there, so we headed directly into the trees, working our way from one tree to the next, staying out of sight as well as we could. The land continued to rise, and we were both weak, but we kept going. Then I got a glimpse of an open area up ahead. Beyond it was clear blue sky. I took a few more steps, looked around another tree from yet another angle . . . and saw Stan and Julie together. They were standing in front of a stone wall that came to about waist level. Stan was behind Julie, backed up against the wall, holding Julie in front of her. Stan had her left arm around Julie's neck, holding Julie's head directly in front of hers as a shield. Julie had duct tape over her eyes and her mouth, and her hands were behind her. Stan had a pistol in her right hand, pointing straight ahead. She had been expecting us. She must have seen something because she called out, "Clint. . . is that you?"

I motioned for Bobby to stay behind the tree. Then I yelled, "Sorry, Stan. . . it's not Clint this time!"

There was silence.

Then she called, "Where's Clint?"

I thought of Adcock, lying on the grass with the back of his head blown away. "Clint's having a bad hair day!" I yelled.

As I called out I stepped from behind the tree and headed for the next one. She saw me and fired. The bullet hit bark not far from my head. She fired again, and another shot ripped into the tree I had slipped behind. She could shoot. I jumped again for another tree. Two more shots. One hit bark, the other flew by. I was only about thirty yards from her now. Another sprint, another tree. Two more shots. Misses. She could shoot, but not like Adcock. I didn't know how many shells there were in her magazine, and her head was partially hidden by Julie's, so I couldn't return fire. I jumped again and made it to another tree. Two more shots. Eight in all.

I jumped to another tree, heard one more shot. Only one this time. Then I thought I could hear a click. I looked quickly around the trunk and saw her shaking the gun. She looked at it in disbelief. She was empty. I stepped around the tree and into the clear, the Glock poised. Stan saw me. She threw down the gun and pulled something from her belt. The Maiden Head. She still held Julie in front of her.

"Put your gun down, Walt!" she shouted. "Or I'll throw her over the edge! It's sixty feet straight down, and the shore there is solid rock! It'll kill her! Put your gun down!"

There was only a sliver of her face, just one eye, visible behind Julie's head. Stan's body was shielded too, and I didn't know how steady my hand was.

"Put it down, Walt! Now! Or I'll throw her over! You can kill me then, but she'll be dead too!"

I kept the Glock framed on the tiny part of her face that I could see. It would be very, very tight.

Then Julie started to struggle, trying to twist away. Stan's arm was still around her neck, and Julie's hands were tied behind her, but she tried to twist and break free.

"Damn you!" Stan shouted.

Julie was still twisting and turning, trying to get away, Stan's arm still around her neck.

"Damn you!" Stan shouted again.

Then, as I watched, Stan swung the Maiden Head. It caught Julie flush on the side of her head, and Julie's body went limp. Stan kept trying to hold her up as a shield, but Julie had dropped so quickly that Stan's upper torso was left exposed. I brought the Glock to bear. In that instant, Stan looked right at me. Our eyes met. The look in hers contained multitudes. I could see so much there. A tenderness. Almost a yearning. The promise of all that might have been. I could see something else as well: I could see she didn't really think I'd shoot her.

But she was wrong.

I squeezed off a single shot, and the bullet tore into the center of her chest. The impact punched her backwards. She crashed back against the wall, then flipped over it, her feet up in the air. Then she was gone. Over the edge. And there was only silence.

I ran straight to Julie and knelt down beside her. I

jostled her shoulder. She didn't move at all. There was no sound.

"Julie!" I pleaded.

There was still no response. I could see blood on the side of her head. It looked like there was an indention there too, like the bone had been caved in by the Maiden Head. I gathered her in my arms and leaned back against the wall, cradling her, rocking her. I pulled the duct tape off her eyes and then off her mouth, my hands trembling uncontrollably. But her eyes remained closed. She didn't move, didn't even groan.

"Julie!"

Bobby came running towards us. "Mom!" he cried.

"She's not responding, Bobby."

I looked again at the wound on her temple. That was where the wound had been on Jessica Nodman and the other murdered women. I remembered what Joe Henderson had said that day in his office when he had showed me the model of the skull. There was a big artery there, and it bled very badly when it was cut. We didn't have much time.

I laid her down as gently as I could and slipped off my coat and wrapped it around her head, my hands still shaking. I'd have to carry her down the hill to the car, then try to find the nearest hospital. But a town the size of Llano wouldn't have the kind of treatment she needed. There would have to be a transfer. All that would take time. Time we didn't have.

"Dad! Look!" I heard Bobby say.

I looked in the direction he was pointing, to the east. In the distance, above the river, I could see a helicopter, moving slowly, off to our right. It was moving very slowly, indeed, almost hovering, heading down to the southeast, as if they were looking for something.

I fumbled frantically in my pocket and pulled out Adcock's cellphone and dialed the number of the Austin PD. This time they found Joe Henderson quickly.

"Walt, where are you?" he asked urgently.

"The ranch west of Llano. I left a message for you."

"We've got people out looking for you right now!"

"There's a helicopter over the river about half a mile east of us. Would they be part of it?"

"You got it!"

"If you can contact them, tell them we're about half a mile back up the river, west of where they are now, right on the shore, on a bluff that looks out over the water."

"You got it, Walt!"

"Julie is badly hurt. We need to get her to a hospital as soon as we can. A hospital with a neurosurgeon. She has a bad head injury."

"I'll start working on it!"

I hung up and waited. But nothing happened. The chopper continued moving away from us, going farther and farther down river, still flying slowly, still off to the southeast. My heart sank. Then, miraculously, I saw it turn and start heading in our direction. As it got closer, Bobby and I started waving our arms. With surprising quickness, they were right above us. It was a fair sized helicopter, not a giant military transport, but not a little two-seater either. I could see lettering on the side. It read: TEXAS DPS.

A man came down on a rope, wearing a DPS uniform and cap. "Let's get you guys out of here!" he said.

He had come down with a kind of hammock, and we placed Julie in it and hoisted her up, the trooper going up with her to keep the sling steady. Then he came down for Bobby. As they were going back up, two more DPS troopers came sprinting up the hill. They ran up to me.

"Sorry we didn't get here earlier," one of them panted. "We were looking in the wrong area."

"One's down there," I said, motioning over the wall. Only then did I look myself. Stan was sprawled on the rocks below, flattened out. Motionless. Like a bug splattered on a windshield. Dead.

The trooper came to the wall and looked over too.

"Jesus Christ," he said.

"The other one's back that way," I said, nodding back to the west.

"We already found that one," the trooper said. "What was left of him, that is. That's the direction we went in when we first got here."

Then I got lifted up too. I was hauled up inside the chopper. Julie was strapped on a stretcher against the far wall, an oxygen mask over her face. Bobby was already strapped into a seat. I sat down next to him and locked the seatbelt. The trooper who had lifted us up shouted, "Let's go!" We swung to the east.

"Where are we headed?" I yelled above the sound of the rotor.

"Brackenridge Hospital down in Austin. There's supposed to be a neurosurgeon there to meet us."

I leaned back and closed my eyes and prayed we would make it in time. All I could think about was Julie. I dimly realized I had killed two people and that all the evidence proving they were murderers themselves had disappeared. I didn't even know where the Maiden Head was. I had been so focused on Julie that I hadn't even gone looking for it. Had it gone over the edge with Stan? I didn't know. And I hadn't thought to check the Corvette when we had pulled up beside it to see if the tape and the picture had been left there. Same story. I had been thinking only of Julie. Now I had no proof of anything, and there were two dead bodies on my hands. I closed my eyes again and said another prayer.

The trip went quickly, barely twenty minutes. We landed at the hospital and Julie was lifted out of the helicopter and put on a stretcher, then taken straight for a CT scan. Everybody was rushing. I kept up with the stretcher all the way, Bobby right on my heels. She still wasn't responding. I jostled her a couple of times and cried, “Julie!” But there was no answer. No movement, no stirring. No nothing. When we got to the CT scanner, they told us we couldn’t go in with her because of the radiation. I started to protest, but I realized I’d just be in the way. I’d be interfering with her treatment. It would be better to do what they told me to do, rather than cause a disturbance. So we stayed outside in the hallway. Then somebody came and took Bobby to another scanner down the hall. I knew we were getting special attention. All I could do was hope. Then I met the neurosurgeon who had been called to the hospital, a Dr. Harmen. He was clearly in command, calling the shots. He knew Joe Henderson, it turned out. They were pretty good friends, in fact. Joe had called him in person. Harmen said he’d let me know what the CTs showed as soon as they were done. He also noticed the blood on my shirt and told me I ought to get myself looked at too. But I told him I’d wait on that.

Joe Henderson got there while Julie and Bobby were still in CT. “How are they?” he asked.

“Julie’s still unresponsive.”

He grimaced. “I’ve been saying my prayers, Walt.”

“Thanks,” I said weakly.

“And Bobby?”

“I think he’s okay. He’s in CT too.”

Another man stepped up to us as we were talking.

“This is Lieutenant Carrington,” Joe said. “You talked with him earlier.”

Carrington extended his hand and I shook it.

“I know you’re focused on Julie and Bobby now,” Joe said, “. . .but for what it’s worth, Walt, the guy you described - the overweight bald guy with the red mustache - that *was* Ron Baker. He was part of it. The Acting Chief of the Austin Police Department, for God’s sake. No wonder he didn’t like the idea of putting a tail on Davidson. When you called him, he went and picked up Frank Hunter at his house. They cleaned out the safe, and then he took

Hunter to an emergency room in Round Rock. We found out Hunter was there when we started making calls. We sent four units to the hospital. When the arresting officers came into the room, Baker drew his gun and blew his own brains out. Guess he knew he was going down. We found all the tapes and the pictures in the trunk of his car. . . so it's a done deal, Walt. It's all wrapped up down here. The authorities up in Denver have tracked the phone number up there too. Turns out that it's some high profile criminal attorney. They're supposed to be rounding him up now."

It *would* be a lawyer, I thought. But I was too numb to really react. The news was good, but all I could think about was Julie.

"The sixth member of their group," Carrington interjected, "the young guy with the big muscles and the black hair and the black mustache, it turns out he's with the Department too. His name is Doug Patterson. He works in ID. He was the one I talked to when I went looking for Hunter's address and phone number. He gave me the info, but he also called Hunter. That's why you got ambushed. That's where the connection came in. Patterson left the station a couple of hours later. Said he was sick. Trying to put it all together, we think he probably went with Ron Baker out to Hunter's house. At any rate, Patterson's been taken into custody. We're interrogating him now."

All I could say was, "Okay."

"Hunter is still in the hospital in Round Rock," Joe added. "They wanted to keep him for observation. He'll probably be transferred to the jail later today."

Carrington extended his hand again. "Thanks, Draeger. We owe you a bunch."

"Sure."

Then Carrington left, and Joe and I waited in the Radiology waiting area. Dr. Harmen came out a few minutes later.

"The boy's fine," he said. "The CT is clear. Just a

concussion. I'd still like to keep him for twenty-four hours for observation, though, but I think he'll do well."

"What about Julie?" I asked.

He frowned. Hesitated. Chose his words carefully when he spoke.

"She has what's called an epidural hematoma, a collection of blood under the skull, pressing on the brain. I need to take her to surgery right away. We'll evacuate the hematoma and make sure the bleeding has stopped."

"And then?"

He shrugged. "Then we cross our fingers and hope. Right now it's impossible to say how much underlying brain damage there may be. It's possible the damage could be relatively mild. That can happen with an epidural hematoma. Then again. . ."

So they took her to surgery. Bobby came out of CT, a real bandage around his head now instead of the shirt, and wanted to stay with me, rather than go to a room. So we waited together. Joe Henderson waited with us. Then Joe got a call and said he had to leave and go back down to the station. He said he'd be back in an hour or two.

"By the way, Walt," he said as he was getting ready to leave. "One more thing. I almost forgot. The dog's fine. Garland PD sent a unit out to check on him. Said he looked healthy and perky. I'll make sure he gets fed and watered until all this is over."

I was still too numb to really react. "You might check with the lady who lives next door to the west," I said, surprised I was even able to think. "Her name is Connie. She might be able to help with that."

He nodded. "I'll get it all taken care of. Don't even give it a second thought. I'll see you again in a couple of hours."

Joe left, and Bobby and I were alone. Dr. Harmen came out some time later.

"It went very well," he said. "We got the hematoma evacuated and the bleeding stopped."

I had to ask, "Any estimates?"

He frowned. "The brain itself didn't look all that badly injured, but you can't be certain. . . I'd say I'm cautiously optimistic at this point, but I can't give you any guarantees. As a general rule of thumb, the sooner somebody wakes up after a head injury - and the more intact they are - the better the outlook."

I had to ask again, "And if they don't wake up?"

He frowned again, more deeply this time. "Then you have a nightmare on your hands."

Harmen said he'd be back to check on her in a couple of hours. She was still in Recovery. They'd be transferring her to a bed in the ICU shortly.

Bobby and I kept waiting. Finally they brought her out of Recovery. I had told myself to be prepared, but it was still a shocking sight when they wheeled her out. Her head was all bandaged up, and a tube had been stuck down her throat into her windpipe. A nurse was squeezing a black bag attached to the end of the tube, breathing for her. We followed as they wheeled her to the ICU and transferred her to a bed there. They said we could stay with her. I looked over at Bobby as we sat down again beside her bed. His eyes were red and bloodshot. Tears were running down his cheeks.

Time passed. We waited. Nothing happened. We didn't talk. There was nothing to say. An hour went by. Then one more. Julie's nurse came in every few minutes to check on her. I could tell she was concerned, but she tried to be encouraging.

"Maybe the anesthetic hasn't worn off yet," she said at one point.

I kind of nodded. "Sure…maybe…"

But there was still no change. Julie still wasn't responding. The nurse was nice. She told me I really ought to change into a clean shirt. Blood is dangerous, she pointed out. So she brought me a fresh green scrub shirt, and I took off my bloody one. When I did, she saw the wounds. I could see her frown.

"You really ought to have those looked at," she said.

I glanced over at Julie, still unconscious on the bed. "Not right now," I said.

She frowned again. "At least we can put on some dressings." Not waiting for a response, she turned and stepped out of the cubicle, returning in just a few moments with bandage material and a tube of antibiotic ointment. I started to protest, but she really was being very nice and caring, so I kept my mouth shut. The bandages were on in just a couple of minutes, and then she helped me get into the green scrub shirt.

"I probably shouldn't be doing all this, because we don't even have a chart on you," she noted, "but I can't just let you sit here bleeding. Here, I want to check your pulse and your blood pressure too, just to make sure they're stable."

I started to protest all over again, but I decided to keep quiet.

"Your vital signs are okay," she said when she was through, "so you probably haven't lost a dangerous amount of blood…but you really do need to have those looked at."

I glanced over at Julie again. "Sure. I will. Just not right now."

Then she was gone again, and Bobby and I were alone. I sat there and watched the methodical, pulsing rhythm of the ventilator as it filled Julie's lungs with air, then allowed her to exhale. Breathe in, breathe out. Breathe in, breathe out. Over and over again. It was mesmerizing. But she still lay there motionless. Helpless. Inert. I knew she'd never want to stay like that. No way. We had discussed such things. I finally got up and stood by the bed, looking down at her. I held her hand. Squeezed it. But there was no response. I tried again, squeezing harder, as hard as I dared, but there still wasn't anything. No response at all. I felt an incredible heaviness deep inside. An incredible sorrow. I looked over at the ventilator, watching as it maintained its ominous cycle. I watched it as it breathed in, breathed out for her. Keeping her alive. I could see where the cord plugged into the wall. I stared at it. Wondering. Mesmerized again. It was only a couple of steps away. I could reach it so easily. An answer to everything. It beckoned to me like a siren.

"Dad?" I heard Bobby say behind me, uncertainly.

"I'm here, Bobby."

Then I bent over the bed and kissed her gently on her forehead. So very, very gently. As gently as I could. Barely even touching her. I kept my lips pressed against her. So gently. I thought I could stay like that forever, without even moving. No questions asked, just stay like that forever. The entire area was covered by bandages, so I didn't actually touch her skin, but it still felt like a connection. I'm not very sentimental, but I almost felt that I could sense a current flowing between us, from my heart to hers. From one soul to another. I stayed like that, my lips on her forehead, letting myself absorb the moment, my heart breaking apart inside me. I couldn't let her stay like this. I just couldn't.

Well, I've never felt like Prince Charming, but to my surprise and to my tremendous relief, as I pulled away, Julie opened her eyes and looked up at me. They were Julie's eyes - the most perfect hazel green in the world - and they focused right on me. I knew in an instant that the lights were on.

"Julie!" I said.

"Mom!" Bobby yelped.

He hopped out of his chair and jumped to the other side of the bed. She was pointing at the tube down her throat. Emphatically.

"Bobby, get the nurse!" I squawked.

He bolted out of the cubicle and was back in a flash with the nurse. Julie kept pointing at the tube going down her throat.

"We'll pull it out," the nurse said. And she did.

Julie coughed and sputtered as it came out. The nurse held up fingers in front of Julie's face.

"How many?" she asked.

"Three," Julie said hoarsely. Which happened to be correct.

"What day is it?"

Julie told her.

"What month?"

Julie told her.

"What year?"

Julie told her.

"What's your phone number?"

Julie told her.

The nurse smiled broadly. "You're doing great! I'm going to call Dr. Harmen."

She turned and left. I was standing on the right side of Julie's bed and Bobby was on the left. She looked up at me, and I could see the pain in her eyes.

"Oh, Walt. . .they… they killed . . ."

"I know, Julie. I know."

It was all I could think of to say. I bent over and held her, my head against hers. I could feel her start to weep.

"The people who killed them are both dead now," I said, knowing that wouldn't really ease her pain. Still she wept.

Bobby climbed up on the bed and lay beside her, snuggling up close, trying to comfort her, even in the midst of his own pain. I looked at the bed and thought I could fit too, so I squeezed in on the other side of her. It was tight, but I made it. Lying on my shoulder hurt like hell, but I didn't even care. I put my other arm around them.

"I love you, Julie," I said, my voice barely a whisper. "I always have and I always will. More than I could ever even begin to say."

"I love you too, Mom," Bobby said, snuggling up even closer.

Through her tears Julie said, "And I love both of you. So very, very much."

We lay there together there on the bed, the three of us, huddled together. I knew the road ahead would be long and hard. It would take time for all of us to recover, both physically and emotionally. So much time. Julie and Bobby had been through a living hell, and they had seen things no person should ever have to see. But I knew they would make it. Julie had shown great strength in beating her demons once, and I knew she could come through again. And Bobby had turned out to be a much tougher kid than I had ever imagined. I knew they would come through this and emerge on the other side. I didn't just *believe* it. I *knew* it. And I knew I would be there for both of them, every step of the way. I knew I would stand beside them. I knew I would do whatever needed to be done. I knew I had come home to stay. . .